Port City

black and white

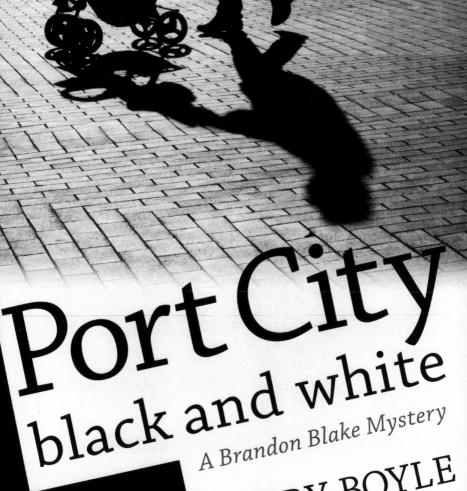

Port City
black and white

A Brandon Blake Mystery

GERRY BOYLE

Down East

Designed by Lynda Chilton

ISBN: 978-0-89272-957-9

5   4   3   2   1

BOOKS·MAGAZINE·ONLINE
www.downeast.com

Distributed to the trade by National Book Network

Library of Congress Cataloging-in-Publication Data

Boyle, Gerry, 1956-
   Port City black & white : a Brandon Blake novel / by Gerry Boyle.
      p. cm.
   ISBN 978-0-89272-957-9 (trade hardcover : alk. paper)
1. Police--Maine--Fiction. 2. Missing children--Investigation--Fiction.
3. Portland (Me.)--Fiction. I. Title.
   PS3552.O925P65 2011
   813'.54--dc22

                              2011016862

Dedicated to the memory of my brother,
James Daniel Boyle, 1942–2004.
A good man.

> *"Not to punish evil
> is equivalent to authorizing it."*
> —**Leonardo Da Vinci**

ONE

The caller didn't leave a name—no surprise, seeing as it was 3:55 a.m. in the scuffed-up neighborhood just up from the Oaks. Somebody there said they wanted the lady at 317 Granite, third floor, to turn down the freakin' television.

"Three-seventeen," Kat said.

"That's Chantelle's," Brandon said, turning off Congress.

"Lance just got out of Cumberland County," Kat said.

"Cuddle up on the couch with her sweetie."

"Watch a movie."

"And smoke some crack," Brandon said.

"Ah, romance," Kat said. She smiled. Brandon hit the gas.

It had been a quiet Thursday night in Parkside, drug dealers and buyers scared away by a sweep that bagged four people for trying to score crack and three for trying to sell it to them. Average night, but the blue lights and undercover cops had the junkies and dealers spooked, at least for a day or two. Now Granite Street, with its triple-deckers and scruffy maples, looked almost as it had been intended when the city was laid out, Brandon thought. A quiet residential avenue overlooking a tranquil city park.

Brandon grabbed the mic, said, "We'll be off."

He double-parked and they got out, looked up. From the sidewalk they heard shouting, tires screeching, gunshots. The third-floor windows showed the lightning flicker of a television playing in the dark.

"Guess Lance wouldn't go for the chick flick," Kat said.

Brandon frowned.

"Doesn't she have a baby?" he said.

They hustled up, Kat the triathloner taking the stairs two at a time, her equipment creaking. At the fourth-floor landing they paused. There were beer cans piled in the corner, a torn white T-shirt on the floor, a red brassiere beside it, like the person inside the clothes had been vaporized. Kat listened for a moment at the door, heard angry voices. "De Niro," she said, and knocked.

The movie blared. Nobody answered. Kat pushed and the door swung open with a long, languid creak. The sour smell of cigarettes and alcohol billowed out, tinged with a faint whiff of burnt crack cocaine. They stepped in.

"Chantelle," Brandon said. "Portland PD."

Somewhere inside the apartment a beer can clanged. "Chantelle," Kat called.

They walked into the front room, dimly lit by the blue glow. There was trash on the floor and it crunched underfoot. A torn easy chair overturned against the wall, stumpy legs turned out. Table smashed, splintered wood scattered. Lamp on its side, the shade crushed flat.

"A good time was had," Brandon said.

"Oh, yeah," Kat said.

They walked into the next room, saw the back side of the television. It was five feet across, thick as a coffin, the kind they had twenty years ago in sports bars, everybody cheering Larry Bird and Magic.

A woman cried out but it was the movie. Kat went around one side of the television, Brandon around the other. Chantelle was slumped on a broken couch that listed to one side. She was nested in a dirty blanket, holding a potato-chip bag. Sour cream and onion. Her feet, in white footie socks, were up on the edge of the cushion. She was wearing gray cotton sweatpants, a black tank top. The two cops stood in front of her but to the side, not blocking her view.

"Hey," Kat said.

Chantelle continued to stare at the screen. Brandon looked at her: strawberry blonde, drug-haggard but still faintly pretty, a looker in high school. Her peak.

She looked up at Kat, surprised to see her standing there.

"Hey," Chantelle said, like they'd awakened her from a dream. "This flick, it's called *Hide and Seek*—like the game, you know? This girl, she has this wicked scary friend who's, like, invisible."

She looked back at the screen. Brandon grabbed the remote from beside her, turned down the volume.

"When was the party?" Kat said.

Chantelle looked up blankly.

"Oh, you mean Lance? That was, um, last night? But a lot of people hung out after. What's today?"

"Friday. They all gone now?" Kat said.

Chantelle looked around, then back at the television.

"I guess."

Kat slipped a flashlight off her belt, leaned close, and shined it into Chantelle's eyes. The pupils were black pinpoints.

"You're high, honey," Kat said.

"No, I'm clean, Kat," Chantelle said. "I swear to God."

"We look around here, we gonna find drugs?" Brandon said.

"You find anything, it ain't mine. All these people here, Lance's friends. I didn't know half of 'em. He makes friends easy in jail, why he's always going back. I told him, I said—"

"Chantelle," Brandon said. "Where's the baby?"

She looked up at him.

"Lincoln?"

"You have another baby?" Brandon said.

"No."

"Then where is he?"

Chantelle shrugged. Her breasts moved, meager under her tank top, her ribs showing under a thin layer of tautly stretched skin.

"Sleeping," she said.

"Where?" Brandon said.

"In his room. Back there."

There was a door that led to the kitchen, liquor bottles on the counter reflecting the television light. Brandon walked back, saw another door on the far side. It was ajar, the room dark. He stepped over trash, kicked a baby bottle, rolling it across the floor. At the threshold he flicked his flashlight on. Pushed the door open.

Brandon stepped in, swept the room with the light.

A bare mattress. A box of Pampers, torn open. Tiny socks and T-shirts strewn on top of a broken bureau, the drawers hanging open like the place had been ransacked.

No baby.

He walked back to Chantelle and Kat, looked at his partner, shook his head.

He picked up the remote, turned off the movie.

"What are you doing, Blake?" Chantelle said. "It's not over."

"Chantelle," Brandon said. "There's no baby in there."

She looked at him, peering through a haze.

"Sure there is. He's sleeping."

"He's not. He's not there. Where would he be? Did Lance take him?"

"Lance? Who never changed a freakin' diaper in his life? No way. Besides, it's not his kid. It's Toby's kid. So Lance, he acts like Lincoln doesn't fucking exist. I say to him, 'He's a freakin' baby. Don't take it out on him. Besides, I didn't even know you when me and Toby hooked up.' "

"Get up," Brandon said. "Get off your lazy, drugged-out ass and show me the baby."

Chantelle stared at him, muttered as she started to get herself up.

"Don't have to get all wound up, Blake. Not my fault if—"

"It is your fault," Brandon said. "You're his mother. Your responsibility."

"You think I invited those guys here? That buncha crack-heads? Lance, he wanted to party. I'm like, 'Why can't we just get Chinese, chill out?' "

"The baby, Chantelle," Kat said. "This is about the baby."

Chantelle glared at Kat, too, heaved herself off the couch, wavered for a moment, then walked unsteadily toward the bedroom.

She reached inside the door, flicked the light switch. The light didn't go on. She walked in anyway, Brandon and Kat following. They turned their flashlights on the mattress, the rubble. Chantelle stared.

"What is he?" Brandon said. "Six months old?"

"Yeah."

"Does he crawl?" Kat said.

"Rolls over," Chantelle said.

"I don't think he rolled out the door, down the street," Brandon said.

"Who would have taken him?" Kat said. "Was your mom here?"

"I don't think so," Chantelle said. "I don't remember."

"Well, let's call her," Brandon said. "You can tell her you lost your kid."

They stepped back into the kitchen light and Brandon held out his cell phone. Chantelle took it, stared at it for a moment, then pressed the numbers. They waited.

"She ain't picking up," Chantelle said.

"Let it ring," Brandon said.

They stood and waited. A fly buzzed inside a beer bottle. The refrigerator hummed and rattled. The kitchen smelled of rotting food.

"When did you put him to bed?" Kat said.

"Jesus, I don't know. Before Leno?" Chantelle said.

"And you were on the couch ever since?" Kat said.

"Yeah," Chantelle said.

"Didn't get up to pee?" Brandon said.

"No," Chantelle said, and then, "Ma. Ma, it's me. You got Lincoln? . . . Lincoln. Do you have him there? . . . Ma, will you friggin' listen? Do you have Lincoln in your house?"

Brandon and Kat watched her expression shift from impatience to puzzlement to panic.

"Oh, my God," Chantelle said, not to the phone, not to the cops, but to herself. "Somebody took my baby."

TWO

It was four thirty-five, the sky turning from black to deep blue, east to west. The team leader, Sergeant Perry, called Lieutenant Searles, asked if they should put out an Amber Alert. Searles said, no, not yet—not with a druggie mom who could have pawned the kid for a dime bag and a forty. Perry turned to the assembled team, supplemented by Detective Sergeant O'Farrell and Christiansen and his German shepherd.

"Boyfriend, the dad, the grandmother, whatever," Perry said. "I want to go through their houses, make sure this isn't some domestic thing, just getting the kid out of there for a night. And all the neighbors, starting with this building, fanning out. I'd like to know who called in the noise complaint."

The sergeant, who played senior league baseball, did his dugout thing, extending his fist: "Ready? Let's go."

The dog went first, clattering up the stairs, the cop following at the end of the leash. They waited in the driveway, then heard claws on the stairs. The dog lunged out of the door, down the driveway. He circled, nose down. Circled some more and doubled back.

"Car," Christiansen said. "Whoever it was got in."

Perry said, "Let's go."

Brandon and Kat led O'Farrell up the stairs to the third floor. On the way, O'Farrell asked for background on Chantelle Anthony, which they gave: not a bad person, when she wasn't using. Kat got her for Hydrocodone, forging prescriptions. Brandon had busted her for OxyContin, another time possession of crack, an eighty she'd gotten as a present from Lance on their two-month anniversary. Cleaned herself up a little when she was pregnant, the father of the baby, a hard-drinking lobsterman named Toby Koski, a good influence. But they'd split up right after the kid was born, and the new guy, Lance McCabe, a total dirtbag, was dragging Chantelle back down.

"And the kid's name is Lincoln?" O'Farrell asked, as they approached the apartment door. "What, for the president?"

"No. Supposedly the baby was conceived in the back of a Town Car," Brandon said.

"Of course," O'Farrell said.

Chantelle was back on the couch, a big bleached blonde and tanned woman on one side, a smaller bleached blonde and tanned woman on the other. A potbellied guy in his thirties, NASCAR shirt, baseball cap backwards, sunglasses on the hat, leaned against the wall. The television was on, an infomercial for a diet supplement.

"This is my ma," Chantelle said. "Stacy."

"I'm Ronnie, Chantelle's sister," the smaller woman said, making it sound like an accusation. "This is our brother Jason."

The police introduced themselves. Jason glowered. "This the guy?" he said, looking at Brandon.

"Blake," the mother said, and she and the sister scowled as though this predicament were somehow the cops' fault. O'Farrell found an unbroken kitchen chair, dragged it up in front of the couch, and sat. Took out a notebook. "Yesterday, ladies," he said. "I want to hear all about it."

They started to gabble and O'Farrell held up his pen hand. "One at a time," he said.

Brandon and Kat went back out and down the stairs, the idea that one would ask questions while the other looked around. At the second-floor apartment, Kat knocked. Brandon sniffed, smelled spices. Curry?

Kat knocked again.

"Police officers," she called. "We need to speak with you."

There was a rustling sound from inside, the door rattled, and there was the rustle again. Then whispering. Not English. *Yel-la. Obreeza.*

"Sudanese. They're saying, 'Hurry—it's the police,' " Kat said.

"Hurry up and open the door, or hurry up and hide?" Brandon said.

The rustling and whispering continued. Brandon knocked once more, rapping the door hard with his flashlight. Kat reached out and grabbed his arm. "Easy," she said. "They're getting the man of the house."

After five minutes, the door finally opened a foot and he stared out, a black man in his forties. Before dawn, and he was already fully dressed, in khaki slacks, a striped sport shirt, black polished shoes. "Yes," he said.

"Portland Police, sir," Brandon said. "We need to speak to you."

The man opened the door wider and stepped out, closed the door behind him. "My name is Ali Otto," he said.

The police introduced themselves. Kat asked Otto if he knew Chantelle.

"Miss Anthony," Otto said. "I know her."

"How long have you lived here?" Kat said.

"Two years, almost. Four years since Sudan. I work at the chicken factory. Chicken fingers."

"And who lives here with you, sir?" Brandon said.

"My wife, my two sons, and my daughter. Altogether that's five."

"How well do you know Chantelle?" Kat said.

"She's our neighbor. We help her."

"Help her how?" Brandon said.

There was a rustle behind the door, someone listening.

"The baby," Otto said. "My daughter takes care of him."

"She babysits?" Kat said.

"Yes, that's what you call it."

"Is she babysitting Chantelle's baby now?"

Otto hesitated. There was a flicker of a frown.

"No."

"He's not in your apartment now, sir?" Brandon said.

"No, he's not."

"The baby may be missing from this building. May we check for ourselves?" Brandon asked. Kat gave him a look. *Go easy.*

"Is something bothering you about the baby, Mr. Otto?" she said, and smiled.

Otto looked away.

"This is just between us, sir," Kat said. "You can talk to us."

Otto frowned, pursed his lips. There were deep creases running across his forehead. Brandon thought of the saying, *a furrowed brow.* Furrows. Brandon figured he'd been a farmer in Sudan, before the chicken fingers. Been through the refugee mill.

"Sir," Kat said. "Please. This is important."

"Miss Anthony," Otto began. "Her friends—"

He paused.

"Her friends what?" Brandon said.

The go-easy look from Kat again. The smile.

"Have her friends bothered your family?" she said.

A longer hesitation. Otto licked his lips.

"My daughter, she takes the baby some of the times, when Miss Anthony and her friends, they want to have the big party." He said it awkwardly.

"And they had a big party yesterday, didn't they?" Kat said.

"Yes, the friends, the boyfriend, they partying hard," Otto said.

"Did you call the police to complain about the noise?" Brandon said.

Otto shook his head. "No. I never complain."

Lying on that one, Brandon thought.

"And Chantelle didn't bring the baby to you?"

"No."

The frown again, in the eyes more than the mouth.

"Did something happen with the friends?" Brandon said. "Something bad?"

"No," Otto said. "Everything's good."

"Are you sure, sir?" Kat said.

"I don't believe you, Mr. Otto," Brandon said. "Tell us the truth."

There was a long pause, Otto staring away. Someone whispered behind the door.

"You can tell us," Brandon said.

"Maybe we can help you," Kat said.

"Okay," Otto said. "So. It's like this. These guys, they called us some bad things, yeah."

"Who?" Brandon said.

"The men going to Miss Chantelle's party. Yeah, it's so. They called my daughter a bad name."

"In the hallway?" Brandon said.

"Out front. My daughter was with her brothers. My sons, they want to fight them. My wife, she hears them. I am at the chicken fingers, yeah. She goes down, tells the boys to come inside. But then they walk right past our door, these tough guys. My boys hear them calling out. 'Come fight.' My wife stopped the boys, but next time, they get their—"

He paused.

"—friends."

Gangbangers, Brandon thought.

"So the baby wasn't with you?" Kat said.

"My daughter, she loves the baby Lincoln. But this time, I hear this guy, he's yelling at Miss Anthony. That she can't bring the baby down here. But her place, you see, it's not good for a baby. The dirt. The party."

"What were they yelling at Chantelle?" Brandon said. "The friends."

Otto didn't answer.

"You can tell us," Kat said.

Otto took a deep breath. "The big man, the bald head. He say, 'You not bringing that baby to no—"

He hesitated.

"You don't have to tell me," Brandon said.

"Most people here, they're good people," Otto said.

"This guy with the bald head—" Kat said.

"He was gone for a long time," Otto said. "I thought he won't come back. But he did."

"If he ever bothers you again," Brandon said, "call me."

He handed Otto his card. Otto looked at it. Nodded. The look from Kat.

"And now, Mr. Otto," Brandon said. "May we look inside your apartment?"

THREE

Two young guys—tall and thin, late teens—leaned in the kitchen, arms folded on their chests. They wore basketball shorts, NBA jerseys: The younger one, New Jersey Nets, glared at the cops. The older one, Denver Nuggets, stared impassively.

Otto's wife and daughter—long robes, head scarves—sat side by side on the couch in the living room, the room so neat it looked like it had been sanded. Above them was a painting, a landscape of desert and mountains.

"Who's the artist?" Brandon said.

The mother looked at the daughter.

"Very nice," Brandon said.

Fatima, pretty under her red head scarf, looked away.

They checked the apartment, Kat doing the room where Fatima slept, maybe with her mother. Brandon did the guys' room, posters of Tupac, Jay-Z, LeBron. Basketball shoes lined up in a row.

No baby.

In the living room, the sons standing there now, still with arms crossed. Kat said, "Do you know of anyone else who might have taken the baby? Just to take care of it?"

The family stared, silent. Finally, the dad shook his head.

"No. We talk to Miss Anthony but we don't know her outside of this place."

"Was it all men at the party?" Kat said.

Otto said something to his wife in Arabic.

"Two girls," Otto said.

"Hoochie mamas," the younger of the guys said. "Crack whores."

"Shush," Otto snapped.

"What's your name?" Brandon said.

"This is Samir," Otto said. "His brother is Edgard."

Samir was older, bigger, his hair combed out. Edgard was wiry, broader face, hair in tight braids like Tupac on the poster. The brothers stared.

"Samir is studying at the community college. He is in studies to be a nurse."

The father beamed. Samir looked at the cops, said nothing.

"Edgard," Otto said, "he is in the high school."

No beam this time, in the face or the voice. Edgard glared at the cops.

Kat handed her card to the father, said, "Please call if you think of anything." Brandon held his card out to Edgard and Samir. Samir took it, folded it in half. Otto put Kat's card in his shirt pocket. Brandon and Kat moved to the door. Kat was outside in the hall when Brandon turned back, looked at the two brothers.

"Yo, like we're gonna be hitting up Five-Oh," Edgard said. "Fuck that."

"Shut up, bro," Samir said, smacking his brother on the shoulder. Edgard shoved him back. The door swung shut.

There were work boots outside the door to the first-floor flat, rear. Brown leather spattered with white paint. Kat knocked. They waited.

"They're gonna go at it with Lance's crew, you know," Kat said.

"The guys insulted their sister," Brandon said.

"So somebody will end up stabbed or shot," Kat said. "So stupid."

"I don't know," Brandon said. "You have to stand up for something."

A pause.

"As your field training officer, I'm going to pretend I didn't hear that," Kat said.

There was the thump of someone big crossing the room inside the apartment. Then the footsteps stopped.

"Police," Kat said.

They heard deadbolts sliding, a chain coming off. The door opened. A man stood there in plaid boxers. He was an inch or two over six feet, muscled, long, tanned face. Hair in a ponytail, a tattoo of a smiling skull on his shoulder. Underneath it: BLADES MC.

The stripped-down Harley in the driveway.

"Yeah," he said.

Kat took the lead, explained the situation. The guy cut her off.

"Ain't seen no baby," he said, started to close the door. Brandon put his hand out, stopped it.

"If we could have just a couple minutes."

"I gotta work, dude. Gotta be up in an hour."

"We'll make it fast."

The biker let the door fall open and they stepped inside.

It was neat, in an industrial sort of way. A couch under a poster of a vintage Harley, a topless woman astride the bike. Cases of empty Budweiser longnecks, stacked. A recliner in front of a small TV on an overturned wooden crate. A cell phone next to the TV.

They stood. Brandon asked the guy's name.

"Cawley," he said.

"First name?"

"Awful lot of questions."

"Almost done. First name?"

"Tony. You sure you're old enough to be a cop?"

"I'm sure. You live here alone?"

"Sometimes my girlfriend stays."

"What's her name?"

"Way too many questions."

"Name?"

"Tiffany. Tiffany Rox."

"R-O-X?"

"Yeah. She's a dancer."

"Cool," Kat said, breaking in. "Did you call in a noise complaint?"

"You bet your ass. I get up at six. Fuckin' welfare scum, up all night."

"You ask them to be quiet before you called?" Kat said.

"I go all the way up there, somebody's gonna get his head busted, and it ain't gonna be me."

"So you never saw them. Or the baby."

"No."

"But they'd all left when you called."

"TV was still friggin' blaring."

"Do you know Chantelle Anthony?" Brandon said, his turn.

"Sure, I know that crackhead."

Brandon held up a hand. "Easy."

"What she is," Cawley said.

"She doesn't take care of the child?" Kat said.

"I see the scum goin' up there. Don't take a rocket scientist to know they ain't singin' it a fuckin' lullaby every night. 'Scuse my French."

"But you didn't report it, then maybe get the baby out of there?" Brandon said.

"What?"

"What I said."

"Hell no. Mind my own business. But you ask me, I'll give it to you straight."

"The guys up there, they bother you, say anything?" Kat said.

"You kiddin'? Those punks know, they screw with me, they're gonna have shit come down on them like they never seen."

"The club?"

"Stick one of us, we all bleed," Cawley said. He tapped the tattoo. "Like cops. You understand."

They did. Brandon got out his card, handed it over.

"You think of anything, hear anything," he said.

"Sure," Cawley said. "But I'm tellin' you, best thing for that kid is, you take it away now, give it to somebody who'll take care of it, you know what I'm sayin'?"

They did.

"It was a dog, somebody'd call the SPCA."

They knew that, too.

FOUR

They were in the driveway when Chantelle came down with O'Farrell and her mother, sister, and glowering brother. Chantelle was shrieking, saying "I want my baby!" over and over. The two women were consoling her, like the baby was already dead.

O'Farrell sidled up on the way by. "No way she sold it," he said.

"Baby snatcher?" Brandon said.

Chantelle wailed. O'Farrell opened the car door, held it for Chantelle and her entourage. She turned back, saw Brandon. "You guys gotta find my baby," she shouted, and dissolved into sobs and tears. They got in and O'Farrell closed the door and drove away.

"Trying," Brandon said.

The first-floor front apartment had its own entrance at the front of the house, an ornate wooden door with a long glass window, a lacy curtain hung over it on the inside. The mailbox said M. and A. Young. Kat pressed the bell. They waited to see if it worked.

Four minutes later—Brandon was clocking it—an inner door rattled open. A woman appeared behind the gauze, peered out. Kat held up her hand and smiled.

"Police, ma'am," she said. "Just need to ask you a couple of questions."

More rattles, then the window door swung open. The woman stepped back and they stepped in. She was in her forties, red-faced and slightly pear-shaped, a thick hank of auburn hair tied back. She was wearing a white flower-print bathrobe and white slippers. A matching flannel nightgown peeked out from her neck. She wrapped her arms around herself like she was naked.

"Mrs. Young?" Kat said.

"Miss Young," the woman said, scolding.

"Right," Kat said.

Kat gave the spiel about the baby. Brandon looked around the entrance: a pair of low rain shoes, the kind you get at Wal-Mart, placed neatly on a plastic tray. A wheeled wire cart, a stack of reusable grocery bags inside. A yellow slicker on a peg.

"Do you know Chantelle? The woman on the third floor?" Kat said.

Miss Young wrinkled her nose like the milk had soured.

"We keep to ourselves," she said.

"We?" Brandon said.

"Mother and I," Miss Young said.

"You live here with your mom?" he said.

"That's what I just said."

Brandon felt himself bristle, choked it back.

"What is your first name, Miss Young?" he said.

"I don't see that that's any of your business," she said.

"Investigation of a missing child," Brandon said. "It *is* our business."

Miss Young pursed her lips, irritated.

"Annie," she said.

"Your mother?" Brandon said.

"Marguerite."

"Just the two of you?" he said.

"Yes. Since my dad passed away."

"I'm sorry to hear that," Kat said.

"When was that?" Brandon said.

"Twelve years ago. He was killed in an industrial accident, if you want to know. On the waterfront."

"Very sad," Kat said.

"Your mother up?" Brandon said.

"No. I figured it wasn't necessary for both of us to be disturbed at this hour."

"We'd like to talk to her," Brandon said.

Kat glanced at him, knowing he was putting the screws to the woman.

"I can tell you anything she would," Annie Young said.

"Better to hear it directly from her," Brandon said.

"I'll see if I can wake her," Annie Young said.

"Mind if we step in?" Brandon said.

"Does it matter if I do?" the woman said.

"No," Brandon said. "As a matter of fact, it doesn't."

She opened the inner door, another big wooden thing with a window, grand in its day. The door opened to a parlor sort-of room, a lamp lit beside a big couch, the back of the couch draped with more lacy things.

Annie Young shuffled off. Kat and Brandon looked around.

There was a television in the corner, a big wooden console, a picture of JFK hanging above it. A dark glass-fronted armoire filled with fancy dishes. A big stuffed chair, worn into the shape of someone. Magazines stacked on a table beside the chair. Brandon stepped over.

Ladies' Home Journal. From the nineties.

"Nice museum," Kat said.

"Can see why they wouldn't have Chantelle in for tea," Brandon said.

"You're pushing Miss Young pretty hard."

"She didn't seem to care that a baby is missing. It bugs me."

"Because you're suspicious, or because you're pissed off by the whole situation?" Kat said.

"Makes biker boy look like a bleeding heart."

"Gotta watch that, Brandon. Letting your emotions control your decisions."

"Gotcha. But she's still a snob."

There was the sound of approaching voices from deeper inside the apartment, then the shuffle of slippers. Annie Young appeared, guiding an older woman by the shoulder. The woman was in her bathrobe and nightgown, too, gray hair sticking out. Mom looked just like the daughter, aged twenty-five years.

They both scowled. Bookends.

"You sit in your chair, Mama," Annie Young said.

"Whose baby?" the older woman said, as she was led across the room. "That trollop upstairs? Ought to sterilize those people before they can reproduce."

"Mama, shush," the daughter said.

"Well, the apple doesn't fall far from the tree," the mother said.

She turned and fell back into the chair, revealing mottled ankles, gray-blue veins showing on the tops of her feet. She looked at the police like she was the queen and they'd been granted an audience. Annie Young crouched by the chair, the lady in waiting.

"Mrs. Young," Kat said.

"Do you know what time it is, young lady?" Mrs. Young said. "Respectable people are in bed."

"We're sorry to disturb you, Mrs. Young," Kat said. "But this is an emergency. A baby is missing."

"The girl upstairs? You know there's no father."

"Well, I'm sure there is one," Kat said.

"Druggies and Africans. I'm glad my husband isn't alive to see what's happened to this city."

"Do the Ottos bother you?" Brandon said.

"Parents keep their place well enough," Mrs. Young said. "But those boys, the younger one, he's headed for trouble, mark my words. I imagine the girl will just get pregnant and end up on welfare. It's what they come here for, you know. The welfare."

"Mother," Annie Young said. "The police have questions."

"You didn't see anyone leaving with a baby?" Brandon said.

"No," Mrs. Young said.

"Hear anything unusual?"

"Other than the usual hooliganism?" Mrs. Young said. "Foul language? Disrespect?"

"Yes," Brandon said.

"No," Mrs. Young said. "How old is the child now?"

"Six months," Kat said.

"You sure she didn't trade it for drugs or something?"

"We're still in the initial stages of the investigation," Kat said.

"Well, if she lost the baby someplace, I hope there are consequences," Mrs. Young said. "Worst thing is, the children grow up just like the parents. Give that baby fifteen years, she'll be knocked up, too."

"It's a he," Kat said.

"So he'll be a daddy. A deadbeat one. It's all these people know. Drugs and booze and sex and not a lick of work. When I think how hard my husband worked to put food on the table, to make sure we had a roof over—"

"You're getting yourself upset," Annie Young said, patting her mother's Einstein hair.

"Well, it's upsetting."

"That a baby is missing?" Brandon said.

"The way these people reproduce," Mrs. Young said. "Like rabbits."

There was a pause. Mrs. Young started to cough. Her daughter patted her back.

"What do you do for work, Miss Young?" Brandon said.

"Hanniman," she said. "The bakery department. And I take care of my mother."

"My husband was killed, you know," Mrs. Young said. "Fixing a conveyor. Someone didn't hit the kill switch. Started up and Harry was caught up in it."

"I'm sorry," Brandon said.

"Lucky for us he had insurance. A pension. Still providing for us to this very day."

"That was smart of him," Kat said.

"Not like these animals. Drinking and drugging and fornicating, not a thought for anyone or anything. Children having to see it. Crying shame, what we've come to."

There was no hint of tears.

"Yes," Brandon said. "Sometimes it is."

They left cards again, went outside. Perry was in his SUV. He said the dog had followed another track to the basement that ended at the washing machines. Chantelle had done laundry before the party, jeans and her favorite top. "Hit the neighborhood," Perry said, and pulled away. Kat and Brandon got in the cruiser and headed up the street.

There were two black men at the bus stop on the corner, lunch pails held in front of them. They said they hadn't seen any baby, just their own, back at home, sleeping. The men smiled. The cops turned away.

"There goes the neighborhood," Kat said.

"What they said when the Irish arrived," Brandon said.

Across State Street they saw Big Liz, one of Portland's homeless. She was pushing a cart, a bag of empty cans loaded on top. Brandon pulled up and he and Kat got out.

"You got electricity comin' out of your eyeballs, Blake," Big Liz said. "Everybody does."

"Right, Lizzie," Kat said. "Everybody does. You seen a baby?"

"A baby what?" Big Liz said.

"A baby baby, Lizzie," Brandon said. "You know, a human."

"Ain't seen no humans," the woman said. "Ain't seen no real humans in a long time."

"You walking all night?" Kat said.

"Yeah. The electricity, it gets you, you stop movin'. Right through the feet. Why you gotta dance." .

She shuffled her feet in unlaced Nike high-tops.

"Didn't see anything on the street?" Brandon said. "Down there, near that green house?"

"Nah. Ain't seen nothin'. Got fuckin' gum, Blake?"

"I got gum, Lizzie." He reached into his shirt pocket, took out a pack. Held it out and the old woman snatched it away, stuffed it somewhere under her layers. Sweatshirt, sweaters, greasy parka.

"You think of something you forgot, you give a shout, honey," Kat said.

"I had a baby," Lizzie said. "Gestapo took it."

"Sorry," Brandon said.

"Had the devil in her," the old woman said. "You gotta drive a stake in 'em. You gotta drive a stake through their little hearts."

She smiled, not quite toothless. They looked at her uneasily, got back in the cruiser.

"There's a birth mother you don't want to go searching for," Brandon said.

"I guess," Kat said.

"So where do you think it is?"

"The baby?"

"Yeah."

"I don't know," Kat said.

"Maybe she killed him, by accident," Brandon said. "Got rid of the body. Or maybe one of the crackheads killed him, took the body with him when he left, tossed it in the trunk."

"Jeez, Blake," Kat said. "Glass half empty or what?"

FIVE

It was 7:30, an hour and a half after the shift ended. Brandon was on a laptop in the duty room, writing the report. He was down to the daughter and her mother, the bitter old woman. He wondered what they did for fun, the two of them. Watch TV? Play cards? Go on and on about the way the neighborhood had gone down—

His phone buzzed. He flipped it open.

"Hey," Brandon said.

"Hi there. You coming home?"

"Just about out of here. Had a missing kid, right at the end of the shift. Reports to do."

"What, the kid wander off?" Mia said.

"No. It's a little baby."

"That's weird."

"Very."

"One of those custody things?" Mia said.

"I don't know. I don't know if anyone else wanted him."

"Sad."

"Yes."

Brandon typed.

"I had a thought," Mia said.

"Yeah?"

He heard gulls, the slosh of a wake, the floats rattling.

"I just thought maybe when you got home, we could rock the boat a little," Mia said.

"That would be nice," Brandon said, picturing her sitting on the foredeck, wrapped in a blanket, cup of coffee in two hands.

"But now it's too late. I have to go to work."

"I'm sorry," Brandon said. "I tried to get out of here."

"It's okay," Mia said. "I understand. A baby."

Kat walked into the room, caught his eye. Brandon got up from the table.

"Be right there," he called. Then to the phone, "Sorry, I just have to catch her."

"It's okay," Mia said.

"Home in twenty minutes."

"Right," she said, and she flipped off the phone, put it down on the deck. Gulls swooped low, checking to see if maybe there was a muffin with that coffee. Mia wrapped the blanket tighter around her. There was a big sailboat motoring out from the marina next door, a pretty wooden yawl, forty-five feet of gleaming varnish. She sipped, wished Brandon were here to see it. Wished Brandon were just here.

Kat was waiting in the garage, where the cruisers were lined up.

"Let's take a walk," Kat said.

They crossed the garage, the German shepherd in the K-9 car pitching a fit as they walked by. On the far side Kat stopped, waited for the dog to settle down.

"Today," she said.

"What about it?" Brandon said.

"You lost it a little."

"With Chantelle? She needed to hear it."

"Right then? From you?"

"It's true. She's an irresponsible mother."

"Yeah, but there's a time and place."

"We needed her to focus. That got her attention," Brandon said. Kat waited.

"Okay. My turn then. You've got issues, Brandon."

"I don't think—"

"We all do. Something. But you can't bring 'em to the job."

"But she lost her baby."

"And you came on too strong."

"What was I supposed to say? 'It's only a baby. Let's do some more drugs.' "

"Brandon."

She grabbed him by the shoulder, turned him toward her.

"I'm trying to help you. I like you. I want you to succeed."

He didn't answer.

"Your mom."

"It was twenty years ago. I'm over it."

"I don't think so."

"You a shrink or you my partner?" Brandon said.

"I'm your field training officer. Training, as in teaching. I teach, you learn."

Brandon looked away.

"Being a parent isn't a game," he said.

"Like your mom treated it?"

He swallowed.

"Yeah, maybe. If she'd stayed home with her kid, she'd be alive right now. Instead she goes off on her South Sea pot-smuggling adventure."

"I understand that," Kat said. "But here's what worries me: What if I hadn't been there today? What if you went to that call alone? Would you have chewed that girl out? Worse?"

"She needed to hear it."

"She needed help. The baby needs our help."

Brandon didn't answer.

"Okay, here's another thing that worries me, and this isn't your FTO talking. This is somebody who's trying to be your friend. Why do you find it so hard to let people in?"

Brandon shrugged. "How I roll."

"Don't let anybody close, you don't get burned, right?"

"Jeez, Kat. You really oughta apply for the shrink's job at the academy. Big raise, nobody shoots at you."

"Because it's true. The keeping people out."

"I've got Mia. I'm not keeping people out."

"She slipped in and the door slammed shut behind her," Kat said.

"I thought we were talking about a crackhead on Granite Street."

"We are. And about how your personal experience affects the way you do your job as a police officer."

They both paused. A detective walked past the dog and it started up again. The detective nodded, kept walking.

"So what's yours?" Brandon said.

"My what?" Kat said.

"Your issue. The one you carry around. You said everybody has one."

"You really want to know?"

"Sure."

Kat looked away, scowled.

"Okay. Fair enough. My brother . . . he's three years older."

"The rich guy."

"Right."

"I thought you liked him."

"He's fine. We don't have a lot in common or anything. I mean, he thinks I'm nuts, doing this job."

"Maybe you are."

"Well, anyway, growing up, he was smarter than me, better looking, more popular. Harvard on a scholarship, Wall Street; wife is pretty, MBA from Duke. They've got two gorgeous little kids. Two-million-dollar house in Connecticut."

"But can he do a leg hold?"

"Me, I've got a one-bedroom apartment, an ex with a gambling addiction who still comes by and cadges money. My cat has three legs and diabetes, meds cost two-fifty a month. And I'm gay."

"I don't see how those things are in the same category."

"They are for my parents," Kat said. "They've written me off as a total loser."

"Who can run triathlons, wrestle with crackheads, rescue babies from burning houses, and break down a Glock. And your partner is a college professor."

"Literature. Another waste of time to them."

"But you're a good person."

"Doesn't matter."

"Why's that?"

"Because they don't love me," Kat said.

A pause.

"Huh," Brandon said. "Why's that? Because you're a lesbian?"

"No. They didn't love me before. Me being gay, that's just a good excuse."

"Whoa," Brandon said.

She was looking away, staring at nothing. Her eyes were moist and she blinked, wiped them with a finger. Wiped the finger on her uniform trousers.

She mustered a grin. "How's that for baggage, Blake?"

He smiled back. "Not bad."

"Go home to your honey," she said.

"I'm trying. I got waylaid."

"I got waylaid, but it's been a while," Kat said.

Brandon looked at her. She smacked his arm.

"It's a joke, Blake," Kat said. "Lighten up."

SIX

Brandon drove through the gate at 8:10, parked his pickup in the reserved slot, that privilege and the free slip his only perks as very part-time marina manager. He hopped out of the cab, reached back for his briefcase. It was sunny but cool, dry northwest wind, a little chop on the harbor. Boat owners were standing on the floats, chatting, coffee mugs held belly high. They waved to him but didn't approach, something about the uniform, like he was still working. Brandon walked down the first float to his slip, No. 2, second on the right. He climbed the stairs, stepped over the transom and down. *Bay Witch* rocked almost imperceptibly. He went through the salon to the helm, heard Mia below. Brandon bent and moved down the steps to the cabin.

"Hey, baby," he said.

"Hi, honey," she said. She slipped a tank top over her head, yanked it down, reached for a sweater.

"You leaving?"

"Gotta be there for nine."

He moved toward her, put his case, his gun belt, on the berth. "Shoot. I thought—"

"That was almost three hours ago, Brand. Where've you been?"

"Reports. The baby."

"They find it?"

Brandon shook his head, hugged her, lifted her blonde hair and nuzzled her neck.

"Nope. Not yet."

"Maybe one of her friends took it home for safekeeping. She's a drug addict, right?"

"Yeah, but not totally gone. In and out of it."

He nuzzled her some more.

"You sure you have to go?"

"Only if I want to get paid."

"Let 'em check out their own books."

"They wouldn't. They'd steal them, and I'd have to call you to arrest them."

"My pleasure," Brandon said. "We can make love now. I'll arrest them all later."

Mia squirmed away, reached for her sandals with her foot, fished them toward her with her toe.

"Must've been long reports," she said. "I would've thought my offer would've had you out of there on the run."

"Well, then there was Kat. She wanted to talk."

"What was it this time?" Mia said, alert.

"Nothing too bad," Brandon said, starting to unbutton his uniform shirt.

"How bad?"

"Oh, she thought I came down too hard on the mom."

"Did you?"

"She's cracked out, has no idea the baby's gone. Six months old, for God's sake."

"What'd you tell her?"

"The truth. That the baby was her responsibility. Hers, nobody else's."

"You gotta go easy, Brandon. You're still on probation."

"Doesn't mean I have to coddle these people. This Chantelle, she's sitting on the couch, zoned out in front of the tube. Place is a total pigsty, unbelievable pit. Kid's bed is a dirty bare mattress on the floor."

"Call the State?"

"Detectives will, I'm sure."

"They're watching you. They told you they would be. After everything from before."

"I know that."

"Then let somebody else be the bad cop."

"I'm not a bad cop," Brandon said.

"You know what I mean. Just bite your tongue sometimes. For your own sake."

Brandon did. Tossed his uniform shirt on the berth, his T-shirt. Mia was leaning into a tiny mirror, inspecting her face.

"How'd the writing go?"

"Good. Most of a chapter. I like it."

"Great. You're rolling. Is this the part about the handsome rookie cop?"

Mia hesitated. "That's another story. But I gotta run. I'm so late. We're going to dinner, remember. Drinks on the deck first. We have to be there at six."

"Who is it?"

"Lily and Winston."

"Oh, yeah. Where's he from again?"

"Barbados."

"Huh."

"She's been with him a couple of years. Before it was this preppie jock stockbroker, played lacrosse at Amherst."

"From lax bro to West Indian chef. Broadening her horizons."

"And Winston is way more exciting. Just opened his own place on Exchange Street."

"Right. You told me the name."

"Rendezvous."

"He's got money, right?"

"I guess. Lily said he sold a restaurant in Barbados."

"Long way from home," Brandon said. "Why Portland, Maine?"

Mia shrugged. Put the mirror back on the built-in shelf.

"I don't know. Change of scenery?"

"Witness protection program?"

"Brandon," Mia said. "You're off duty." She gave him a quick hug, a longer kiss. "Relax."

And she was up the three steps, pretty legs under her denim skirt, and headed for the stern. He felt the slightest lift of the boat when she stepped off the stern, heard her sandals slapping on the wooden slats of the float. And then Mia was gone.

He kicked off his boots, picked them up and put them in the cabinet. Peeled off his uniform pants, put on shorts, a T-shirt, flip-flops. He took his phone, went through to the salon and grabbed a beer, then went around to the foredeck. Mia had left the chair up there and Brandon sat down, opened the beer and sipped. He looked out on the marina, saw Johnny C. easing his big Grady-White up to the fuel dock, twin 150s ready to suck up some gas. Sylvie and Sarge LaFrance polishing brass on their vintage Hinckley sloop. A new couple, scrubbing an old Pearson 32, good entry-level boat, little blond kids playing behind the rail netting. Beyond the marina was the harbor: a tug nosing an oil barge upriver, a scallop dragger approaching the fish pier under a cloud of gulls, the ferry terminal empty, the *Casco Princess* in Nova Scotia.

And then the waterfront. Houses rising up the hill, the downtown skyline, and just out of sight, Granite Street. Brandon took a long swallow of Shipyard, picked up his phone, punched a number.

"Choo-Choo, it's me, Brandon. . . . Anything new on that baby? . . . Listen, will you run the mom for me? Right. Chantelle Anthony. Warrants, probation conditions, like no drugs or alcohol —anything you can find. Also, the boyfriend. Lance something. Lance McCabe, I think. Should be under Chantelle's known associates. Anything in there about kids, sex offenses, assaults on children. . . . I owe you one, Chooch. Mocha latte, extra grande, coming your way. Me? No, I'm off, back Sunday. Just doing a little homework."

He hung up. Stared out at the water. A wake approached and the boat rocked. Brandon picked up the phone.

"Chooch, me again. Listen, this thing with Anthony. Between us, okay?"

SEVEN

Chantelle had noticed it, had told her mother when she brought the baby over there to let her mother have some Grammie time. "He's starting to roll over, Ma," she said. "You watch."

Lincoln had been on the rug, in the living room of the little house in South Portland, out past the interstate. Chantelle's mother had just come in from the porch, a cigarette break. She sat down on the floor next to the baby. Like a dog, Lincoln rolled over on cue.

"He'll be walking soon enough," Chantelle's mother said. "Then he'll keep your ass running."

Chantelle had stuck a cigarette in her mouth, hunted for her lighter in the couch cushions. She got up and bent over, her T-shirt riding up, showing the bones in her spine, the tattoo of a moon and stars.

"Look at the little pissant," her mother had said. "There he goes again.

Now Lincoln could string together five or six rolls, all to the right, his heavier head and shoulders serving as a sort of anchor, his feet and legs moving ahead. The result was that he moved in a sort of semicircle. When his legs hit the wall, he'd start to cry in frustration so you had to get up quick, pull his legs past the wall, let him complete the circle.

That worked pretty well, but you had to pay attention, just like at night. You had to get right over to him with the bottle, the pacifier, as soon as you heard that little whimper. If you waited, he'd turn up the volume and that would not be good.

So it was tiring, this baby thing. Hard to get anything else done, not if you wanted to do it right. Lincoln ate every two or three hours, chugging that bottle right down, Chantelle figuring the breastfeeding wouldn't be good, with her still using. He liked a little rice cereal, too. Sometimes you could let him sort of gnaw on the spoon, the one coated with rubber, which seemed to make him happy. He had a tooth coming through on the top. Have to get one of those teething rings, the kind filled with water or something, let him chew on that.

Hopefully, he wouldn't start to really fuss about the teething, the way the magazines said some babies did. The magazines were usually right. It was their idea to get the gurgling-water CD, which worked like a charm. He'd lay there on his back, sort of gurgling himself, and before you knew it, he'd be asleep.

And quiet. For now, quiet was the most important thing.

EIGHT

Brandon slept for six hours or so, woke up at three p.m. He lay in the berth for a while, the fan humming, the cries of the gulls wafting through the bow hatch. He could hear the faint rumble of passing boats and ships and could gauge the approach of the wake. Counting down from twenty, he'd say, "three, two, one," and then feel the boat start to rock.

That one was the tug, headed for the outer harbor. It was out of sight when Brandon came up to the galley. A quick glance showed a few boats out, three couples hauling coolers up float No. 2 in dock carts.

Nothing pressing, nobody waiting for him, not like launching time, early in the season, when he barely slept, getting floats and boats in, messing with the rickety boat lift, cleaning up and heading off to the overnight shift at the PD.

They told you to get rest, that your judgment was off when you were tired and stressed. He'd survived it. He and Mia had, too. One thing about writers—they liked time alone, and she had plenty.

Brandon went to the refrigerator, took out sliced turkey, Swiss cheese, spicy mustard. He made a sandwich on fresh pumpernickel from Mia's favorite bakery in the Old Port, poured a glass of milk. He ate it at the table, listening to the weather radio. It was clouding up, scudding from the south. The radio said low pressure moving in, rain by midnight, winds out of the southeast, 10 to 15, increasing to 20 knots late. Seas building, 4 to 8 by daybreak. They'd have to close up the boat before they left for dinner.

He finished his lunch, washed the dishes in the galley sink, dried them and put them away. Then he went below and showered, put on shorts and a Red Sox jersey, Jason Varitek. Tek was his kind of player: serious, hardworking, no melodrama. Thinking about Tek led him to Kat and her talk, him not letting people in. He soured, said aloud, "If she doesn't like it, screw her," but then regretted saying it, even to himself.

Back in the salon, he checked his phone. A call from City of Portland, aka Choo-Choo, the dispatcher. He called back, heard voices, radio chatter, reached over and turned up his scanner. A car accident, Forest Avenue, Johnny Fiola signing off there. Brandon waited.

"Okay, Brandon," Choo-Choo said. "Chantelle Anthony, no warrants. Misdemeanor drug possession, one in '09, three in 2008. DWI, 2007. Operating after suspension, same year. Lance McCabe, just out, as you know, did six months for possession of methamphetamine, burglar tools, assault. Record longer than both our arms and legs. Probation conditions: no drugs or alcohol, random checks of person and premises."

"Address?" Brandon said.

"Last known, 233 Quebec Street, number 2."

"Thanks. Can you e-mail me his face?"

"Thought you were off," Choo-Choo said.

"I am."

"Just a wild and crazy guy, huh?"

"That's me," Brandon said. "Hey, is O'Farrell on?"

"Until eighteen hundred," Choo-Choo said, and rang off. Three-thirty; Mia would be home from the library by five. He had time.

Brandon put on running shoes, a black baseball cap. He went back below, unlocked the cabinet in the cabin, and took out his radio and off-duty carry gun, a Glock 26, downsized from his department issue 19. He snapped a clip in, slipped on his waistband holster, covered it with his shirt, and was on his way.

Quebec Street was on the west side of Congress on Munjoy Hill. The east side was swarming with Volvos and people like Mia: young, good-looking, had money themselves or rich parents for backup. The west side of the hill was a couple of blocks and a world away: beat-up tenements, scruffy people, streets where you had to watch your step after midnight or you'd get rolled.

Brandon crossed the bridge, looked out at the bay, white sails flecking the waters between the islands. Boats were headed in after a good cruise, a few million dollars' worth of toys that soon would be tucked in for the night. He drove his pickup through the Old Port, the early birds flocking to the bars. A group of guys, already staggering, stepped in front of the truck on Middle Street. Brandon braked, waited, resting his head on his hand. One of the guys stopped and looked at him, shouted, "Red Sox suck!" and flipped him off.

Brandon took a deep breath. Fun for the night shift.

He drove across Cumberland, down North, took a right. Lance's address was a big white apartment block, cars parked helter-skelter in the lot out front. There were six guys, a young woman, leaning on a Tahoe pulled up to the curb. They eyed Brandon when he went by. He circled the block, came back to the corner, and parked by the scrubby park on the edge of the projects.

He sat. Opened his e-mail on his iPhone, clicked through to Lance McCabe's mug shot. Shaved head. Goatee. Tough, stoic Irish face, like somebody out of Southie, which he might have been. All kinds of dirtbags working their way north from Lawrence, Boston. In the photo, Lance looked bored, maybe a little irritated. The kind of guy where getting arrested was a hassle, not a disaster.

Brandon looked over at the apartment house. The guys and the girl were still there. One of the guys had put his arm around her, staking his claim. She was drinking from a soda bottle. Green. Mountain Dew. Another guy was on the phone.

They moved to the street, the guy and girl sitting on the curb. The guys stood on the sidewalk, looked up and down. They stepped into the road, one shoving the other as a car passed. He yelled something, shoved the other guy back.

At that moment, a guy came out of the side door of the apartment house, headed for the little square of backyard, an old van rotting there, tires flat. The guy disappeared from view and Brandon sat, waited. The group in the street had crossed to the opposite side. They started up the sidewalk, moving away. The guy from the side door popped out onto North Street a block up, crossed the street, started down the sidewalk toward Kennedy Park.

Brandon started the truck, followed.

He passed him, pulled over and stopped. In the side mirror, Lance was headed his way.

Lance walked past, smoking a cigarette, flicking it to the ground just ahead of the truck. He was wearing basketball shoes, baggy shorts hanging down, a tank top showing tattoos, prison blue. Brandon watched as a car passed, a low-cut Honda, throbbing exhaust. It pulled alongside Lance. He came around, got in.

Brandon put the truck in gear.

They cut over to Franklin Street, Brandon three cars back, then drove under the interstate, a quarter-mile out to the supermarket. The car pulled in, double-parked out front. Lance and a smaller guy went inside. They didn't stop to get a cart.

Brandon pulled into a parking slot and waited.

Ten minutes later, the pair came back out. Lance had a thirty-pack of Bud. The smaller guy had a box of Pampers.

"Yes," Brandon said.

The Honda circled the lot, leaving the way it had come in. Brandon followed, along the mudflats of Back Cove, the tide out. They drove back up Franklin, into the white-walled, graffiti-scrawled project, out the back side.

Brandon had the phone out, scrolled down the list. Called O'Farrell.

"Blake, what's up?" O'Farrell answered.

"Tailing Chantelle's boyfriend."

"Talked to him this morning. Said he'd rather have hemorrhoids than a baby."

"Him and some buddies just picked up beer. And a box of Pampers."

"Where are you?"

"East on Fox."

"Didn't know you were working."

"It's not work," Brandon said.

There was a pause.

"I'm on Washington. Come up behind you. You in your truck?"

"Roger that."

The Honda cut across Washington, buzzed up Walnut, headed back toward Lance's neighborhood. On Montreal Street it sped up, turned right. He gambled, drove to the end of the block, pulled into a driveway. Waited. The Honda reappeared, passed him coming the other way, pulled into the driveway of another big apartment block. Brandon watched in the rearview; they all got out, Lance carrying the diapers, the other guy the thirty-rack.

Brandon backed out, slalomed down the street, into the driveway, blocking the car. The last guy was headed back to the car. He saw Brandon get out of the truck, stopped in his tracks, turned and ran.

"Police," Brandon shouted. "Stop right there."

The kid hit the stairs, pounded up, Brandon ten steps back. He heard a door slam above him, had his gun out, held low. The door was closed. He heard shouting. Men's voices. A baby started to cry.

"Portland PD!" Brandon shouted. "Open the door."

Murmuring now, somebody saying, "Fucking Five-Oh," the baby crying, somebody saying "Shut that kid up or I will." Brandon took a step back, put his shoulder to the door. It shuddered open and he lunged in, saw the driver going out the window onto the fire escape. "Freeze," Brandon shouted, but the guy kept going. Another door to the left, voices behind it. Brandon turned the knob, slammed it open. Lance, two other guys, just shadows, the room dark.

"On the floor," Brandon screamed, gun out in front. "Show me your hands."

"Fucking A," Lance said, dropping to the floor. The other guys were behind him, one with his hands up. The third, smaller, started for the window and Brandon cut him off, put him on the floor.

"On the ground!" Brandon screamed at the guy still standing, and he dropped to his knees, then to his belly.

The baby was crying from somewhere deeper in the apartment. Brandon eased upright, stepped over the guys, Lance saying, "Fucking crazy cop." There was a door across the room. Brandon went to it. The baby took a breath, let out a scream. Brandon opened the door, peered in.

Dim light, but a crib showed against the wall. A chair. A woman sitting in it, the baby on her shoulder. "Don't hurt my baby," she said. "Don't you hurt him."

She was young, a teenager. Black, hair braided neatly. The baby was black, too.

Brandon lowered his gun. Scanned the room.

"You live here?"

"Hell, yes."

"What are these guys doing here?"

"Mario, he lives upstairs with Lisa. They were going to get beer. They got me some diapers. You break that door? 'Cause I can't stay here if the door won't lock, not in this neighborhood. Landlord's gonna be pissed, but I'm telling him, Don't complain to me. Cops did it. Smashing in here. Fucking crazy-ass cops."

Brandon stepped out into the other room just as O'Farrell stepped in, the driver cuffed in front of him.

"Why'd you run?" Brandon said.

He looked at Brandon with cold hatred.

"Probation," O'Farrell said. "No alcohol, no drugs."

He looked around.

"There's a baby?"

"Yeah," Brandon said. "It's in there."

O'Farrell cuffed the driver to a chair, stepped through the door, stepped back out.

"I don't think that's him," he said.

"Nope," Brandon said.

"Let's search these guys. See if we can salvage something outta this cluster."

NINE

The driver had a couple of joints and the probation hold. The second kid had pot, too, maybe an eighth of an ounce. Misdemeanors, but better than if they'd been Boy Scouts on their way to help out at a nursing home. Lance had nothing. "You got a house?" he said to Brandon, standing by the cruisers in the driveway. " 'Cause I'm gonna own it. My lawyer, he's gonna be on the phone with the mayor Monday morning. Dude, you are messing with the wrong guy."

He moved closer. Brandon, leaning against O'Farrell's car, ignored him.

"This is harassment, dude. I got a right to walk down the street. I got a right to go about my business. You listening to me, junior cop? You listening to me?"

Brandon turned to him, got in his face.

"Where do you think the baby is?" he said.

"What? I ain't talking about no baby."

"I figured you were running your mouth anyway, maybe something useful would come out."

"Don't you get lippy with me."

"How 'bout we take you in, have you piss in a cup," Brandon said. "No drugs on your probation, right?"

"You can't do that."

"Search at will, right. And now you're fraternizing with known drug users."

"They aren't known."

"They are now."

"Go to hell."

"The baby."

"I don't have her kid. I told the other cops, I'd rather have—"

"I heard. But somebody has it."

"So you say."

"She owe anybody money?"

"Like I'd tell you?"

"So what do you think happened to the baby?"

"I don't know. Who'd take a kid? I mean, what are you gonna do with it? Change its shitty diapers?"

"Some people like having a kid," Brandon said. "Pay a lot of money to get one."

"Not me. So you can lay off."

"What about Toby?"

"Lobster boy? Who knows? We don't hang out."

"Oh?"

"Last time wasn't pretty. Cold-cocked me, the pussy. I got up, knocked out two of his freakin' teeth."

"Blake."

It was O'Farrell, headed for the car, a brown Ford, scraped and dented. He beckoned, one finger. Brandon followed. They got in the front seat. O'Farrell started the motor, hit the AC. They sat, windows rolled up, the chief detective staring forward.

Brandon waited. Lance walked by the front of the car, grinned and saluted. O'Farrell gave him a hard stare and Lance kept walking.

"Old-timers would've taken him for a ride for that," the detective said.

"That was before there were lawyers," Brandon said.

"He know who you are?"

"Why? Maybe he'd think twice?"

"I don't know. Probably doesn't think much."

Brandon didn't answer.

"I'm gonna cut right to it, Blake."

"Yes, sir."

"I went out on a limb to get you on the job," O'Farrell said. "A lot of people here thought you had too much baggage."

"Shoot a guy about to murder your girlfriend? I'm not sure I'd call that baggage. All due respect."

The radio crackled. O'Farrell turned it down.

"There's that, but the rest of it, too. Not going to the police with Fuller when you had a chance. Having it out with that foreign guy."

"You can say it," Brandon said. "They blamed me for Griffin. Blamed me for getting a cop killed."

"Not *blamed* you."

"Then what?"

"Associated you."

"Like I'm a Jonah? The guy the sailors don't want on the ship?"

O'Farrell didn't answer. He shifted, adjusted his holster.

"You're a hard-ass, Blake. Especially for a young guy just starting out."

"I'm not good at feelings."

"Community policing. It's about more than nailing bad guys. You heard it all at the academy."

"I figured it was good for the community, taking the dirtbags out of it. I thought that's what we did, catch the—"

"You know what I mean, Brandon," O'Farrell said, irritated now. "I talked to Kat."

"The thing with Chantelle."

"Not the first time."

"Crackhead lost her baby. She's not the victim here."

"I know. And this isn't gonna sound like much, but it's not always what you do—it's the way you do it. It's like you're on a mission. A vendetta."

"That would mean revenge. Who would I be getting revenge on?"

O'Farrell turned to him, hard, sharp-edged face, temples reddened.

"You tell me, Brandon. Who is it?"

Brandon stared forward. Kids walked by the car, peered at

him. Vargas, the hockey-dad patrolman, started to walk toward them, saw their expressions and turned around. O'Farrell waited.

"It's everybody who breaks the law," Brandon said. "Who won't follow the rules. People who are soft and lazy and weak and let other people take the fall for it. People who are predators, who make a mockery of the ones who try to do the right thing."

O'Farrell looked at him, turned away.

"You're gonna flame out, Brandon. What are you, twenty-three?"

"Twenty-four in a month."

"You gotta pace yourself. You're like a dog chasing rabbits who catches one, then another one runs by so he goes after that. One after another until he drops."

"I think it's more like I'm chasing rats. Rabbits are harmless."

"It's a job, not a crusade."

"I'm not crusading."

"You're off-duty. On duty you can't even ride alone yet. You're out here staking out the 'hood when you should be with your girlfriend or whatever."

"It's a missing baby. I'll donate my time."

"I got a girl in there says you traumatized her, busted in, put a gun in her face."

"I didn't know who was in there. A baby crying. Could've been the kidnapper."

"Just telling you what she said."

"That's bullshit. I didn't know who was behind that door. Perps ran from me when I identified myself as a police officer. Somebody saying to shut the kid up."

O'Farrell held up his hands, crossed them. Time out.

"Take the rest of the weekend off, Blake."

"The baby—you need the help."

"You're not the only cop in the city."

"But I'm a good one," Brandon said.

"Could be," O'Farrell said. "You're not yet."

Brandon was silent for a moment. The mother with the baby came out of the doorway, was met by a skinny white guy, glasses, a shock of blond hair. Pale face, concerned expression. They shook hands. The guy started writing in a notebook.

"Shit," O'Farrell said. "Press. You got no comment."

"Toby," Brandon said. "When did his boat go out?"

"This morning at four."

"So he was in port last night?"

"Blake," O'Farrell said.

Brandon held his tongue.

TEN

"You all right?" Mia said.

"I'm fine," Brandon said.

"You don't seem it."

"Just tired."

They were coming to the end of Congress, the bay spread out in front of them, dark blue water against the lighter blue summer sky, the texture of the chop making it look like an oil painting. Boats on their moorings, sails off to the east by the islands, powerboats scudding between them.

Pick one, Brandon thought. I'd rather be on it.

Mia turned left onto the Eastern Promenade, looked up. There were people on the roof deck of a big Victorian. They were holding drinks.

"Party's started," she said. "Sorry."

"It's okay."

But she wheeled the Saab hard into the drive, squeezed it in between a new Land Rover and a Subaru wagon, kayaks on the roof of the Subaru, a racing bike on the Rover. Both cars had school stickers on the back window: BOWDOIN and CHOATE, DARTMOUTH and HOTCHKISS. Mia's Saab said COLBY—Fit right in, Brandon thought. "I'm gonna get a sticker for the Criminal Justice Academy," he said. "Put it on the truck."

"Do they make them?" Mia said.

He slipped the holster and gun from his waistband, put them in the glove box, and locked it. They got out, heard the prattle of voices from high above. Mia locked the car and they started for the door.

"Pretty fancy place," Brandon said.

"Her parents bought the condo as an investment," Mia said. "She lives in it."

"Huh."

"Please don't judge them, Brandon. She's very nice."

"And the chef?"

"I haven't met him, but everybody says he's a good guy. Very good for her. She has this way of sliding down, getting discouraged."

"About what? Being rich and idle?"

"Brandon, please."

"Sorry."

"I guess he's very upbeat, keeps her spirits up."

They were headed up the stairs, the treads sanded and varnished, stained-glass windows and a built-in seat at the landing. Brandon thought of the other stairs he'd climbed that day: the smell of urine, the dirty underwear.

At the third floor there was a piece of paper taped to the door. It had a picture of the hosts: Lily, sharp-featured and pretty with short dark hair; Winston, dark and handsome, head shaved, gleaming even in the printout photo. The note said, "Follow the stickies to the deck."

They pushed the door open. There were lime-green sticky notes on the floor. They led through a big kitchen, with stainless appliances, a granite-topped island.

"Oh, isn't this beautiful," Mia said.

"I think you're beautiful," Brandon said. He was trying. Positive energy.

Mia turned, smiled. Brandon meant it: blonde hair flowing, a black tank top and swirly print skirt. And the eyes.

"I think you're beautiful, too," Mia said, and she kissed him gently, took his hand and led the way.

The notes led to an outside stairway, like a fire escape. They climbed, popped out on the roof. There were maybe twenty people, nobody over thirty. A bar was set up away from the water, liquor and mixers, wine and beer. Lily turned from a couple in madras shorts and polos, saw them and hurried over.

"Mia," she said. "I'm so glad you could come."

They touched both cheeks, fake-kissing like Europeans. Lily turned to Brandon, said, "Brandon, it's so good to finally meet you. Mia's told me so much about you."

Brandon took her hand but she leaned in, gave him the Euro kisses, too. Her dangling earring tapped him on the neck, and she turned, still holding his hand, and guided him away.

"I want to introduce you. Especially to the other people in the book club. Mia talks about you a lot, you know. And now we finally get to see the famous Brandon Blake in person."

She paused. A big red-haired guy had just opened a Heineken with an opener on his keys. Lily snatched it away, said, "Sorry. We have a VIP."

Lily handed Brandon the beer. The guy looked at Brandon, smiled and bowed. They moved across the deck to the water side, three women and another guy talking. Lily squeezed in, Brandon in tow. "Guys, I want you to meet someone. This is Brandon, Mia's Brandon."

They turned and looked at him curiously. An Asian woman in a short red sundress said, "Well, finally," and shook his hand. "You live on a boat, right?" she said. "I think that's so cool."

The guy—tall and lanky, blond dreads, khaki shorts, and beat-up Birkenstocks—said, "Welcome aboard, dude." He held out his beer bottle and Brandon tapped his against it.

"Thanks. Nice to meet you."

A small woman with a mane of dark hair, a gold stud in her nose, reached her bottle in, too. She clanked hard and spilled, beer spattered their feet. "You're shut off," Birkenstocks said.

"Shouldn't have pre-partied," the dark-haired woman said, then clapped a hand over her mouth, took it away. "Whoops," she said loudly. "Gotta be careful, talking to a cop."

There was a moment of stop-action, the movie paused. Birkenstocks started it up again, said, "No shit. You mean, like a real policeman?"

Brandon could feel others listening, a lull in their conversations.

"Yeah, I guess you could say that."

"Right here? Portland PD?" Birkenstocks said.

"Yup."

"Wow. Very cool. I've never met a cop before. I mean, except when I was getting a ticket."

"Is it true some women go gaga for a man in uniform?" the dark-haired woman said.

"Sarah," Lily said. "Please."

"I read about it in *Cosmo* once. They put a cop uniform on this model guy. He was really hot, but you're pretty hot, too."

"Sarah."

"Well, it's true. This guy, he walked around Manhattan in his police uniform and you wouldn't believe the women who hit on him. Not just waitresses, either. These rich East Side ladies and everything."

"Must be a New York thing," Brandon said.

Sarah took a swallow of beer, went on. "They'd say things like, 'Officer, you can handcuff me anytime.' "

They laughed.

"Definitely a New York thing," Brandon said.

"So, dude," Birkenstocks said. "Do you, like, carry a gun?"

"Lily," Sarah said, raising her voice, "does this mean we can't smoke pot?"

They laughed again, Sarah saying, "But I'm serious." Lily took Brandon by the arm and guided him away.

"I'm sorry. Sarah's really a sweetheart, but get a couple of drinks into her, she starts to do standup."

"It's okay," Brandon said.

"I think it's so exciting what you do," Lily said, pulling him closer. "I mean, it's dangerous, right? There are really bad people out there."

They crossed the deck. Brandon saw Mia over by the bar, a serious-looking guy, gold-rimmed glasses, talking to her, Mia nodding. Then it was another cluster of people along the rail. Lily said, "Sorry to interrupt. I just want you to meet Brandon. He's here with Mia—from our book group."

More smiles, bottles and wineglasses clinking. Winston held out his hand.

"Brandon, this is Winston. And Laura and Rod and Kikki and Bill."

"Welcome, Brandon," Winston said, a deep voice, West Indies accent. Brandon felt Mia slide up to his side.

"Thanks for having us," Brandon said. "This is a great spot." He motioned toward the bay.

"Brandon and Mia live on a boat," Lily said.

"Oh, really," Winston said. "I did the live-aboard thing for a year or two."

"Probably a little easier in the Caribbean," Brandon said.

"You don't stay on the boat in the winter, do you?" Lily said.

"Oh, yeah. You cover it up, hunker down."

"How big a boat?" Winston said.

"Thirty-two. An old Chris-Craft."

"It has this great name," Lily said. "What is it?"

"*Bay Witch,*" Mia said.

"Sweet," Winston said. "I love it. When I had the restaurant in Bridgetown, I lived on my partner's sailboat. Fifty-seven feet."

"So you were on the west side of the island," Brandon said.

"Yes," Winston said.

"No real deep harbors on the island, even in, what is it, Carlisle Bay?"

"No, but we get by."

"West side is sheltered, but in the fall, I'd be worried if the winds shifted, came out of the west. In a big blow, nowhere to hide," Brandon said.

"You've been to Barbados?"

"No," Brandon said.

"Brandon reads a lot," Mia said.

Winston grinned, gave Brandon a slap on the shoulder.

Brandon felt the strength of him, a solid, muscled guy. "Oh, you absolutely must come down. When Lily and I go next winter, we'll take you. It's a beautiful place."

"You have family there?" Mia said.

"No, they're all scattered. That's the thing about the Indies— very beautiful, but limited opportunities. Many young people, if they can do it, they go. UK, Canada."

"But you came to the U.S.," Mia said.

"Oh, yeah. I figured I'd come to the land of opportunity. I love the States. You hustle here, you work hard, the sky's the limit."

Lily had moved toward him.

"And of course, there are also the most beautiful women." He gave her a hug and she smiled.

"He thinks he's such a charmer."

"What do you mean, he *thinks?*" Winston said.

Dinner was served buffet-style in the dining room, salads and bread and soup set out on the table. There was a mound of lobster salad, grape and chicken salad with curry, a plate of curry goat, plates of things that looked like turnovers.

Everyone moved around the table, filling their plates.

"Oh, lobster salad to die for," Sarah said.

"You gotta try the curry goat," Winston said. "Very West Indies. Very delicious."

Brandon was next to the serious guy who had been talking to Mia. Brandon introduced himself.

"Crane," the guy said. "Like the big tall bird."

He was wiry and lithe, like a rock climber. He turned to Winston. "Does everything have meat? Because I'm a vegetarian."

Brandon saw Winston give the guy an annoyed look, then slap the smile back on. He looked up and down the table. "The wine," he said. "The wine is vegetarian."

Crane scowled, served himself salad, poured a glass of Chardonnay to the brim. He turned away, leaned against a bureau, and started to eat. Brandon and Mia found chairs, ate with their plates on their laps. Winston and Lily sat at a side table. Some people drifted back to the deck.

"The goat is great," Brandon said.

"I'm glad. I knew you'd love it."

"Winston's running a restaurant here," Lily said.

"All food from the Indies," Winston said.

"Rendezvous is high-end," Lily said. "Not just a barbecue place. Organic goat meat. All local vegetables and fish."

"You think when you kill the goat, it cares if it's organic?"

It was Crane, off to the side. Brandon saw that the wineglass was almost empty. Crane reached the bottle from the table, poured again.

"The goat, he leads a happy life," Winston said.

"It's not like they know what's coming," Brandon said. "And then it's the end. Boom."

"Well, you would think so," Crane said. "You kill people for a living."

The room went quiet. A chair scraped.

"What's that supposed to mean?" Mia said.

"It's what cops do," Crane said. "In this country, they're executioners."

"Oh, Crane," Lily said. "Spare us."

"No, it's true. Police have the right to kill you whenever they feel it's justified. They're the judge, the jury, the executioner."

"But then they have the investigation," Winston said.

"And they investigate themselves. Remember that Sudanese guy? Cops killed him, right there on Congress Street. Nothing happened to them."

"He was pointing a loaded gun at them," Brandon said.

"He was mentally ill," Crane said.

"Doesn't matter whether he was crazy," Brandon said. "If he'd pulled the trigger, they would've been just as dead."

"So you'd have taken him out."

Brandon hesitated, then plunged in. "If I had no other choice."

"So all cops are killers when it comes down to it," Crane said.

"They're protecting people," Mia said.

"People like you," Lily said.

"Let's be honest: Cops just get off on power. The power to take a life. It gives these guys a hard-on."

"Oh, my God," Lily said. "Crane, why don't you—"

"Brandon knows," Crane said. "I mean, he's done it."

"Just shut up," Mia said.

He drank, swallowed, smiled.

"Oh, sorry. The elephant in the room, right? That the regular guy standing right there took somebody out. I mean, I guess he was a bad guy, so we're told, but still."

He turned toward Winston, stone-faced across the room.

"Just before you got here, Winston. It was in all the papers, on TV. Brandon was this big hero. Lily told you, right? How this psycho grabbed Mia, was threatening to kill her—at least, that's what they said in the paper. Brandon, he wasn't even a cop then, he got a gun and shot the guy right in the—"

"Enough," Brandon said.

"I'm surprised the police took you on," Crane said. "How many brand-new cops have already whacked somebody? Or maybe that was a good thing. Proved you could do it."

Brandon put his plate on the floor and stood. Mia was up, too, holding his arm.

"No, Brandon. It isn't worth it."

"See, violence is always the first option with you people," Crane said.

Brandon started for him, dragging Mia, but Winston was quicker, already across the room. Crane raised his hand and Winston caught the wrist, clamped it, twisted the glass from Crane's grip. Crane flailed as Winston put the glass on the table, then turned back. He slapped Crane across the face, forehand and backhand, four times, the blows coming rapid-fire, the force knocking Crane sideways, first one way then the other. Blood spurted from his nose and mouth and he put his hands up. Winston turned him around, jammed his arm up his back.

"You motherfucker," Crane gasped. "Let go of me."

"You're disrespecting me," Winston said. "You're disrespecting this house."

"This is assault," Crane shouted. "You've got no right to touch me."

"You're lucky," Winston muttered. "In some places, you'd already be dead."

He hustled Crane out of the room and they heard the door slam, footsteps down the stairs. There was a long silence and then Brandon said, "I hope he's not driving."

"He rode his bike," Lily said. "He doesn't believe in cars."

She turned to Mia, who was ashen, eyes welling with tears.

"It's all because you wouldn't date him," Lily said. She turned to Brandon. "He has this obsession thing with Mia."

"Understandable," Brandon said.

"I didn't think he'd do this," Mia said.

"It's the alcohol," Lily said. "He's one of those people—"

"There are a lot of those people," Brandon said.

"I'm sure you see it all the time, with your job," Lily said. "But you should be able to go to dinner and not have to listen to that."

"Yeah, well," Brandon said. "We should go."

"Yeah," Mia said. "Don't want to put any more of a damper on the party."

Winston came into the kitchen, went to the sink and washed blood from his hands. He turned to them and grinned. "There," he said. "How 'bout coffee and dessert?"

Lily mustered a smile.

"Stay, guys," she said. "Winston made plantain tarts."

ELEVEN

They skipped the tarts, drove back to the boat in silence. When they'd parked in the dirt lot at the marina it was almost dark, lights glowing on the floats, the city skyline emerging across the harbor.

"I'm sorry," Mia said.

"Goes with the turf," Brandon said. "I'm sorry for you."

"You ought to be able to go out like a normal person," she said.

He smiled.

"Cops aren't normal people. And I'm not even a normal cop—or so people keep telling me."

"Maybe we should move," Mia said. "Someplace where nobody knows."

"We have a life here. You've got your writing, your job. I've got the marina, the boat."

"How 'bout Portsmouth, New Hampshire? It's a nice city, has a harbor. We could move the boat down, get an apartment."

"I'm not letting people like that drive us out," Brandon said. "Besides, I've got work to do here."

"The baby?"

"Yeah. And everything else."

They walked to *Bay Witch*, didn't meet anybody on the way. On board they went below. Mia went into the cabin to change into warmer clothes. Brandon stood in the stern and called Choo-Choo, doing a twelve-hour shift. He put the phone away as Mia, in jeans and a sweater, came up from below.

"Anything?" she said.

Brandon shook his head. "No."

"Want to sit?" she said.

"Sure," he said.

They took two blankets from the locker and went around the side deck and up to the bow. There were two chairs on the foredeck and they sat facing the harbor, wrapped in blankets.

"Look at us," Mia said, smiling. "Couple of old duffers."

Brandon smiled, squeezed her hand.

"Sorry to ruin your party," he said.

"That's just Crane. He's basically an ass when he's drinking."

"I know, but still. You were looking forward to it."

"It was okay other than that. Well, maybe Sarah . . . but people would get over that after a while, right? Start to treat you like a regular person."

"Maybe," Brandon said.

He paused.

"This Crane guy. What does he do?"

"Oh, gee. Works in a coffee shop in the Old Port. Writes angsty, self-absorbed stuff about how screwed up the world is and how he's always a victim."

"He's obsessed with you?"

"It was when I first moved to Portland. Before I met you. He was in my fiction workshop, until he quit because we dared to criticize his stuff."

"I thought that was what they did at workshops."

"You think?"

"And he had the hots for you?"

"I guess. A crush or something."

"Infatuated," Brandon said.

"But now he really dislikes me. And that means he dislikes you."

"Of course. Dangerous?"

"I didn't think so," Mia said. "Just a bad drunk."

They were quiet as darkness fell and the sky turned from blue to black. Above them stars emerged, east to west. On the water, navigation lights floated, the ships and boats behind them showing as vague shadows.

"Winston," Brandon said.

"Yeah?"

"Tell me his story again."

Mia tucked her feet under her blanket, reached over and took his hand. They squeezed.

"Well, he came here from Barbados. Owned a restaurant there. I think maybe he sold it, or his share in it or whatever. Has Rendezvous now, on Exchange Street. Lily says he has this idea that he could open a restaurant back home again, maybe go back and forth. Things are pretty dead in the Caribbean in the summer, so it would work out."

"Why Portland, Maine?"

"I think he'd been here once before—I don't remember why. But I guess he liked it. And then there was that story in the *Times* about the Portland restaurant scene, how hot it was."

"He saw that?"

"Lily said he carried it around with him when he first got here. Went to all of the restaurants in the story, to see how he could fit in."

"So he's got some cash?"

"From the sale."

"Maybe he hit up her family," Brandon said.

"I got the impression he wouldn't have to, but I don't know."

They were quiet again. A woman on one of the boats broke into laughter. It echoed across the water like a loon's call on a lake.

"When Winston went at it with your friend there . . ."

"He's not my friend. I hope I never see him again."

"Okay, but when he hit him—it wasn't the first time."

"That Winston hit Crane?" Mia said.

"No, that he hit somebody."

"Really? He didn't even punch him."

"I know, but that was somebody who can fight. Somebody in control. Bang, bang, bang, like a blur. He was totally calm.

Didn't lose his temper, just took three steps, slapped the guy's face, whipped him around, and marched him out. And this Crane guy looked pretty strong."

"Maybe he was a bouncer or something. In Barbados."

"Maybe," Brandon said.

They sat, Mia kneading his hand in hers.

"I like him," she said. "He's really good for Lily."

"I didn't like the stockbroker."

"No," Mia said. "You didn't."

She looked out on the water, sparkling like a sea of black diamonds. The wail of a siren wafted across the harbor, a glimmer of blue lights.

"Early for the bar fights," Brandon said.

Mia felt her contentment slipping away. She took a deep breath, said, "Is this the way it's always going to be?"

Brandon turned to her.

"What?"

"You always working."

"We were talking," Brandon said.

"Part of you was talking; the other part was someplace else." She nodded toward the lights across the water.

"Over there."

"I'm sorry," he said. "Hard day."

She looked at him.

"It's okay, baby," Mia said. "I'm just trying to figure out what I signed up for." Another siren rose from the city, weaving with the first like jazz. Brandon glanced over, caught himself, looked back at Mia.

"Sorry. It's the baby," he said. "I mean, he's out there somewhere."

Mia squeezed his hand.

In the morning, they got up, brushed their teeth, slipped back into the berth. Their lovemaking was slow and steady and relentless, no rush and no turning back, the two of them oblivious to the rain drumming on the deck above. Mia held him tightly, held him down, then clenched him close to her, pressing herself tightly against him so he couldn't slip a hand in between, could only return her embrace. When they were finished, she continued to hold him, gathering him against her, as if to keep him from slipping away.

The boat rocked gently. The rain continued to drum on the deck.

"I'm not going anywhere," Brandon said.

"I know," Mia said.

"Are you worried?"

"A little. I don't want to lose you. Cops, they're always splitting up."

"Not all of them."

"Some of them."

"Not this one, Mia," Brandon said, and he kissed her forehead. "I'll bet they all think that," Mia said, "before it happens."

"You don't have to worry."

She kissed him on the cheekbone and rolled off. They intertwined arms, clasped hands. And Brandon's phone rang. Three rings. A pause. One ring.

"It's Sarge," he said, and Mia let his hand go. He slipped out from under the comforter and, naked, got the phone off the folding table. Mia looked at him, his strong back, his butt. She still wanted him but she knew he was gone.

"Blake," Brandon said. "Yeah, Sarge. . . . Sure. . . . Gimme forty-five."

He rang off, climbed back under. Mia lay there, the two of them naked but apart. "OT today. Powers that be want all out on the baby."

"So is there anything new?"

"Gonna round up everybody that was at Chantelle's party. Let the detectives have at 'em. Squeeze 'em, see what pops out."

"Bunch of druggies?" Mia said. "Think they'll even remember anything?"

"Won't know until we ask. And Toby's coming back."

"The dad?"

"Boat turned around. They want to meet him as he steps onto the dock."

"In case he knows something?" Mia said.

"Or in case he doesn't and wants to go kill somebody."

"Like the ex or her boyfriend?"

"Or both," Brandon said.

Mia was quiet for a moment.

"Maybe you should go," she said.

TWELVE

The *Marie G* had left port at six on Thursday night, twelve hours before the police had converged on Granite Street. A day later it came down the harbor fast, the seventy-foot trawler looming out of the rain, throwing up a big, rolling wake. Brandon and Kat stood on the pier by the cruiser, watched as the boat approached. They could see somebody in the wheelhouse, another guy in yellow oilskins on deck, on the starboard side.

The boat was a hundred yards off when a battered, jacked-up pickup rolled in behind the cruiser and stopped. A big barrel-chested guy got out of the passenger side, reached back in the bed for a tattered brown duffel. There was a woman behind the wheel, a child in a car seat in the middle, a gun rack behind the kid. The woman was smoking, blowing the smoke out the open driver's window in big puffs like she was sending smoke signals. The kid was gnawing on a pacifier.

It was a girl, brunette hair, pink hat. Brandon and Kat both checked.

The guy leaned in the truck window, said something to the woman, reached out and bumped the child's fist. The kid grinned and reached to do it again but the guy had stood, looked out at the approaching boat. The woman put the truck in reverse, backed down the pier. The guy came over and stood. He nodded.

"You Toby's replacement?" Brandon said.

"Bad for him," the guy said, staring out at the trawler. "Good for me. Serious cash, lobstering offshore."

"I'm Brandon. This is Kat."

"Booker," the guy said.

"You heard about the baby, Booker?" Kat said.

"Oh, yeah. On the news. Sucks."

"What do you think happened?" Brandon said.

"Shit if I know," the guy said.

He reached into the front pocket of his flannel shirt, dug out a cigarette. He lit it with a lighter from his jeans, sucked a long drag. They waited.

"Crowd Chantelle runs with, anything's possible," the guy said.

"Not Toby's crowd?"

"You kidding?"

"Never met him," Brandon said.

"Toby, he'll have a few beers, we get off the boat. Maybe get in a ruckus, you know what I'm saying? I mean, he was in friggin' Afghanistan. You can't just stop fighting."

"No?" Kat said.

"Gotta ease off'n it."

"That's right," Brandon said.

"Toby ain't like them, those wasted fucks."

He looked at Kat.

"Sorry."

"It's okay," she said.

"Crackheads," he said.

"Then why'd he hook up with Chantelle?" Kat said.

"You can ask him, but I know for a fact that she was a lot better-looking two, three years ago. The drugs, man—just eat you up." Booker shook his head.

The boat was close, rusted patches showing like scabs on the black-painted hull. There were orange buoys stacked in the stern like missiles, big wire traps.

"Musta killed him to leave his baby with somebody like that," Brandon said.

"Guys always get the shaft," Booker said. "You can bet on it."

They could see the skipper now, standing at the wheel. Above him the roof of the wheelhouse bristled with antennas and radar dishes. Exhaust fumes pumped into the air, mingling with the odor of cigarettes and fish.

Booker picked up his duffel, walked to the top of a ladder at the edge of the wharf. He flipped his cigarette into the space over the water.

"Serious business," he said, not looking at either of them. "Messin' with a guy's kid."

And then Toby appeared at the top of the ladder, tossed his duffel on the pavement, and pulled himself over. He was tall and broad, dark and bearded like the Taliban. He and the big guy clenched fists. "Dude," the big guy said. "I get back. Anything you need. Anything."

Their eyes locked. Toby nodded. The guy went down the ladder as Toby started for the cruiser. Kat opened the back door and he tossed his duffel across, slid onto the seat. Brandon and Kat got in, and Brandon put the cruiser in gear.

"Well?" Toby said.

"No," Kat said. "Not yet."

"He's gotta be fucking somewhere."

"Yes," Kat said.

"I mean, a kid doesn't just disappear into thin air."

"No," Brandon said. "Not usually."

Brandon drove up Commercial Street, went slow. They passed sailmakers, paint shops, a sushi place leading the way for the other restaurants to follow. A young couple coming from the yacht harbor, shoulders wrapped in sweaters, started to cross and Brandon stopped. They waved. He waved back. Sarge had said go slow with the guy, see what pops out, before we get him at a table.

Now Toby was staring straight ahead, lips jammed together hard. They could smell him, diesel and salt.

"You were in Afghanistan, right?" Brandon said, turning toward him.

"Eight months," Toby said.

"And you've been back—"

"Two."

"So Lincoln was born—"

"While I was in Helmand Province. I'm chasing Afghans

around mud huts. She's barely popped him out, starts screwing around, the coke, the Oxy."

Brandon eased along, like they were out for a cruise. Kat turned and looked sympathetic.

"So how'd she get custody?" she said. "A veteran, you'd think—"

"I'd get a fair fucking shake? Fat chance. Send you over there to get shot at, you get home, you get shit on. I mean, there sure as hell weren't no parade."

"But the baby?"

"Went to court. Chantelle can act, I'll give her that. Did all the plays in high school, up there on the stage, strutting around."

"So she said what?" Brandon said.

He turned onto Milk Street, waited for three old drunks, headed out to cadge beers from tourists at the bar up the block.

"Said I was violent. Had PTSD. She's all afraid for her son's safety. She even cried."

"And they bought it?" Kat said.

"Hey, my head wasn't screwed on tight when I got back. You try it. You shoot somebody, what do you get? As a cop, I mean?"

Kat glanced at Brandon.

"Administrative leave," she said. "Time with the shrink. Don't go back until they sign you off, FFD. Fit for duty."

"Okay, you try shooting people every day, them shooting back at you. You're cutting them in half with a freakin' fifty on a Humvee. Their bombs are blowing your buddy's legs off, maybe his arms, too. He's a fucking stump with a head, and the head is screaming."

"And the next day you do it again," Brandon said.

"If you're lucky. If you aren't, you're in a box. Or you're a quad. Or you're fucking blind. Or both."

"Huh," Kat said.

"So the judge there, maybe he shouldn't've been so surprised, I punch some guy's lights out in the Port. You shitting me? Some douche bag starts shoving *me* around? Those first few days, I didn't care if you was ten feet tall—I was gonna cut you down."

They pulled into the lot behind the PD. Brandon parked, let the motor run.

"So she got custody?" Kat said.

"I got supervised only. My own son. Fought in a fucking war, gotta have my mommy with me I want to hold my kid." He paused, his eyes starting to water. "I want to hold my boy again," Toby said.

Kat and Brandon looked at each other.

"Well, that's the idea," Brandon said, and they got out, let Toby out, too.

They left him inside with O'Farrell, him an Iraq vet, the two of them talking units and regiments and battalions. Brandon and Kat were on their way down the hall on the second floor when Perry stopped them.

"What do you think?" he said.

"If he took his own kid, he's a damn good actor," Kat said.

"Coulda grabbed him, handed him off to a relative, got him squirreled away someplace," Perry said. "Deeking us."

She looked at Brandon.

"What do you think, Blake?"

"I think he lets you look all the way inside his head," Brandon said.

"What you see?" Perry said.

"Is what you get," Brandon said.

"Or maybe that's what he wants us to think," Kat said.

"My gut says no," Brandon said.

"And if you're wrong?"

Kat and Perry looked at him, eyebrows flickering. Perry headed for the interview room. The patrol cops didn't.

THIRTEEN

They had a list of everybody Chantelle and Lance thought had been
at the party. Detective division didn't have the manpower, so patrol
was dividing it up. The list had eight full names; fourteen, nicknames only; a half-dozen people designated only by description:
guy from Lewiston, one eye doesn't move. Asian woman from Riverton Park, tattoo on her neck of a dragonfly. Or a butterfly. Some
bug.

Brandon and Kat had one of each, all locals, including the
woman with the bug tattoo. Back in the cruiser, Brandon looked at
the list, handed it to Kat in the passenger seat. He started to type
in the first name on the laptop, but Kat reached over and took his
arm.

"Just a sec," she said.

He looked at her.

"Back there," she said, looking away.

"What?"

"You can't take sides," Kat said.

"I know."

"Nope. You think this baby's better off with the dad."

"Than with the crackhead mom or the totally whacked-out,
violent, crackhead boyfriend?" Brandon said.

"Not our job, Blake," Kat said. "Our job is to find the kid,
figure out who grabbed him. Let the courts decide where he ends
up."

"I know that."

"You gotta be cool," Kat said. "Professional, not emotional.
Remember at the apartment, getting on Chantelle's case?"

"High as a kite. She has responsibilities," Brandon said.

"Brandon," Kat said.

"Okay," he said.

"Okay," Kat said.

He put the cruiser in gear, drove out of the lot. They were turning onto Congress when Kat said, "Somebody oughta be talking to Toby's mother."

They started with the Asian woman first, figuring Riverton Park Housing Project was small enough, somebody would know about the dragonfly tattoo. This was an Asian woman who hung out with Lance's crew, so probably she'd done time, most likely for drugs. How many could there be?

Riverton was out past the interstate off Forest Avenue. Two-story units surrounded central parking lots like walled cities, summer-nights kids hanging out on the sidewalks, crowding the basketball court like the game was over and they'd spilled out of the stands.

It was morning so only old people and little kids were up, anybody between fifteen and fifty still in bed, listening to the rain. They pulled alongside a Cambodian woman, fortyish, slim in skinny jeans and a green slicker, pushing a stroller, an umbrella over the baby. Kat got out, went up to the stroller and crouched. Brandon stood by the cruiser.

"Oh, your daughter's beautiful," Kat said.

"Grandchild," the woman said. "This is my daughter's child."

"You must be so proud," Brandon said.

The woman smiled. Kat bore in.

"We're looking for a young woman. We need to talk to her, see if she can help us. It's about a lost baby, a little older than yours."

The woman frowned.

"They lose baby?"

"Yes. It just sort of disappeared."

"*Neak ta,*" the woman said. "Spirits. They will take a baby."

"Could be. But we need to find one of the mother's friends. We don't know her name, but she has a tattoo of a dragonfly on her neck. The right side."

Brandon touched his neck.

"Here."

Suddenly the woman looked afraid, then nothing at all, a pale mask.

"I don't know this girl," she said. She clenched the handle of the stroller. Kat reached for the baby, let it grab her finger, pinning the stroller in place.

"She's not in trouble," Brandon said. "We just need to know who was there, give us a clue. The mother was asleep."

"They not asleep, they on the dope," the woman said.

She pulled the stroller back, started to turn it. Brandon reached out, stopped the stroller.

"This is about a missing child, ma'am," he said. The woman looked away, pulled at the stroller. Brandon held on.

"How many people living in your apartment?" he said. The woman looked at him, suddenly aware of every word.

"What's your limit with Portland Housing? Four? I hear they kick people out if they're over the limit. Go back on the Section Eight list, right at the bottom."

Kat looked at him, the lady, too.

"We make a trade," Brandon said. "You give me her name—which building—and I keep our little secret."

"The building number four," the woman whispered. "Sasha."

"Thanks," Brandon said. He let go of the stroller. The woman wrenched it away, turned and wheeled down the sidewalk. Kat looked at him.

"Playing it a little close to the edge, aren't you, Blake?"

"It's a missing kid," he said.

"That doesn't mean you can strong-arm witnesses."

"Doesn't mean you can't," Brandon said.

FOURTEEN

Number four was just like numbers three and five. Two stories, brick on the first floor, siding above, nobody answering the door when the cops came knocking.

Brandon and Kat walked back to the cruiser, parked in the street out front. Brandon pulled into the driveway, blocking in a beat-up Civic, a Penthouse Pet air freshener dangling from the mirror. They got out, and Brandon leaned against the cruiser while Kat looked the car over. She checked the inspection sticker, saw that it had expired.

"Want to run these plates?" she said, and Brandon went around, got in, typed the registration into the laptop. The number came back to a Chevy pickup, 1991. He got out.

"Swapped off a truck," Brandon said. Kat bent down, yanked the plate off the back bumper. She was on her way to the front when the door of number four rattled open and a kid came storming out.

"Hey, what you think you're doing?"

They both stared at him for a moment, then another. He was a good-looking Asian guy: Cambodian, hair gelled up, same outfit as the Sudanese guys: big shorts, high-tops, an NBA jersey. Carmelo.

"This your car?" Kat said.

"Yeah. You can't just start pulling things off, come in here like—"

"Like I'm about to write you for illegal attachment, expired inspection, no registration. You got a license?"

"Yeah, I got a license."

Kat held her hand out.

"Produce it."

"It's in the house."

She looked at him.

"Sasha in there, too?"

"Don't know nobody with that name."

"You go in there, come back out with either Sasha or the license. You bring Sasha, we leave the car. You don't, we get the hook."

The kid looked at her, then at Brandon, then back at Kat.

"What is this?" he said.

"A hell of a deal," Brandon said. "I'd take it."

The kid shook his head, saved face by spitting on the ground. Then he turned, walked back inside.

"We're even," Kat said.

"You're learning," Brandon said.

A minute later, the door opened and a young woman appeared. She closed the door behind her, walked up and stopped.

"I'm Sasha," she said.

"I'm Kat. This is Brandon."

"We old friends already?" Sasha said. "First-name basis?"

They looked at her. Pretty, big hoop earrings, black hair tied back. Bike shorts and a peasant blouse. Bare feet with red nails. A dragonfly tattoo on the right side of her neck.

"You were at Chantelle's?"

"I don't know who that is," Sasha said.

"I thought we were friends," Brandon said. "Thought you were gonna help us out, save us the time, driving you downtown to see the detectives. Pain in the butt, have to wait around all day, waiting for them to spring you loose."

Her eyes narrowed. They could see the telltale redness around the nose, hint of wrinkles, cracks feathering out from her eyes.

"Maybe I know her," Sasha said.

"The one who's missing the baby," Kat said.

"Oh, yeah."

"You there Friday morning? End of the party?"

Sasha thought for a minute, deciding whether to lie.

"Yeah. Me and this friend of mine. But we didn't take the baby, if that's what you're thinking."

"Not thinking anything," Brandon said. "Just trying to figure out who saw the baby and when. When did you leave?"

"I don't know. One? It was dead."

For a moment Brandon thought she meant the baby.

"The party?" Kat said.

"Yeah, like boring. People sitting around this big honking television. All blurry. I think it was really old."

"Was the baby there?"

"Yeah. I mean, it wasn't in the room. She had it out for a while, giving it a bottle on the couch, you know? People, like, took turns holding it."

"It's a him," Brandon said.

"Right. Holding him. He's drinking the milk or whatever."

"And then what?"

"Then the bottle runs out and he starts screaming and whoever it was holding him, they give him back to Chantelle. She's, like, trying to make him happy, but she's—"

"Pretty messed up," Brandon said.

Sasha shrugged.

"Then people were wanting to roll, you know. The baby crying and everything."

"So then what?" Kat said.

Sasha thought about it, how much she wanted to say.

"She put the baby back in the bed."

"Did he stop crying?" Brandon said.

Sasha thought.

"I don't know. I don't remember."

"And then?" Kat said.

"We hung out for a while and then people left. And then I left, me and this other girl."

"Who was there when you left?" Brandon said.

"Nobody. Just Chantelle and the baby. And they were both asleep."

"So that was it?" Kat said.

"Yeah. I mean, it wasn't any big deal. Just a few people, this guy, he—"

"We know," Brandon said. "He just got out of jail. It was a party for him."

"So you leave, they're both zonked," Kat said. "Nothing else?"

Brandon smiled. "There has to be one more thing. Just one."

"Nope."

"Come on. You can think of one."

"What?" Kat said.

"Or we haul your boyfriend's ride," Brandon said.

She looked back at the house, then down the street.

"We're sitting there. The movie's on, some cop thing. And somebody knocks at the door. So I get up to answer it."

"Yeah?" Brandon said.

"And nobody's there. So I go back, watch the movie. It's boring, you know. And it happens again."

"The knock," Kat said.

"Right."

"So you get up."

"And there's nobody there. It was creeping me out."

"*Neak ta?*" Brandon said.

Sasha stared at him, this white guy speaking Khmer.

"No," she said. "Not a ghost. More like there was an ax murderer out there."

"But there was nobody there?" Kat said. "And when you left, still nobody?"

"No. I went back, I shook Chantelle. I'm like, 'Honey, there's Freddy Krueger out there or something.' "

"What did she say?"

"Not much. She was—"

"High," Brandon said.

Sasha didn't answer.

"It doesn't matter. What did she say?"

"She said that one time she felt like there was somebody in the apartment. When she was sleeping, I mean."

"She didn't say who?" Kat said.

"No, just that she woke up, felt like somebody had been there, you know? The smell of them. Then she figured it was a dream."

"Can you dream a smell?" Brandon said.

"We're leaving, she's already nodding out. I tell her—" Sasha hesitated.

"It's okay," Kat said. "We're here about the baby."

"I tell her, you lay off the shit. Don't want to be wasted, somebody's creeping around."

"So after that?" Brandon said.

"Hell if I know," Sasha said. "Me and my girlfriend, we bounced."

They looked at each other. Brandon glanced at the house, saw the curtains move. Sasha started to turn away but Brandon called to her. "You talked to her since then?" he said.

"Yeah. She called. I didn't call her. I mean, what am I gonna say—'Sorry your freakin' baby's gone'?"

"What did she say when she called?"

"She was pretty messed up. She said she could hear the baby. At night, her sister came and stayed with her, but even then, she said she'd wake up, thinking she could hear him crying."

She looked at Brandon.

"There's your fucking ghost," she said.

Sasha went back to the house, padded inside, closed the door behind her. They walked to the cruiser and got in, sat for a moment.

"Somebody knocking, still somewhere around there after Sasha and her friend leave the apartment," Brandon said.

"Who knows what Chantelle remembers?" Kat said.

"Worth somebody talking to her."

He started the motor, tapped the laptop. He started back through the project, feeling that there were people watching them from every window. *What did Sasha tell the cops? Who did Sasha rat out?*

They were passing the basketball court when Kat's cell rang. She yanked it out.

"Yeah."

Kat didn't say anything else. Still didn't. Brandon looked over at her, saw something bad. She put the phone down.

"Head for the bridge," Kat said. "A floater. They want us to come down, see about an ID."

"Why us?"

"Because we just saw her. At the apartment. Chantelle."

FIFTEEN

The water was blue-black, flecked with floating trash. Plastic bottles, chunks of broken brown foam, clumps of knotted yellow rope. A blue-and-yellow spray can. WD-40. Brandon thought of a story he'd read about an expanse of ocean north of Hawaii that the circling currents had filled with garbage. He looked away, then back.

This was at the municipal wharf, cruisers and an ambulance parked above, the Coast Guard inflatable tied up below. On the float by the boat they gathered in a tight circle over the body, a bare foot and ankle sticking out from under the tarp. The foot was blue-white. The nails were pink. There was a tattoo around the ankle, a Celtic-looking design. Blue on blue.

"That's Chantelle," Brandon said, and the senior cops looked at him. "I remember the tattoo, the nails."

"Nail polish matches. I guess we can go home now."

Brandon looked up. Jimmy Dever, a second-year patrolman, grinned at him and snorted.

"Uncover the face," growled one of the day detectives, a weathered guy named Pelletier. Kat did, and there she was. Lips barely darker than her cheeks, eyes open wide, like there had been a moment of shock: *My, that water is cold.*

"That her?" Pelletier said.

"Yeah," Kat said. "Chantelle Anthony."

"So that's what happens when you lose your own kid, huh?" Dever said. "You take a swan dive."

"We don't know that she lost him," Brandon said. "We just know he's gone."

"What's the difference?" Dever said. "She was a fuckup . . . just another fuckup."

Brandon looked at him, felt the anger rising up. Handsome, tanned, Oakleys on his head even though it was raining. Kind of cop who liked to chat up the uniform chasers, the college girls coming out of the bars on Exchange Street. And Dever was last one in at a bar fight, nobody you could count on to save your ass.

"*Lost* implies it was her fault," Brandon said, thinking back to the hard time he gave Chantelle, now just a carcass on an oil-stained float.

"So what do you think happened, Sherlock Holmes?" Dever said, smirking.

Brandon expected Pelletier to cut it off, but he didn't, just looked at Brandon, like he wanted them to duke it out.

"I think somebody grabbed the kid, somebody she knew," Brandon said.

"Why?"

"To trade him for something. Maybe one of her dealers, leverage to shut her up."

"Well, it worked," Dever said. The same smirk. One of those cops who showed off their bravado, everything a joke.

"You think this is funny," Brandon said, "this frigging mess?" Kat reached over, touched Brandon's arm.

"Enough, children," Pelletier said. "Feel like I'm at home."

They turned away, Dever still smirking, Kat's grip tight on Brandon's arm.

"Easy there," she said. "He isn't worth blowing your career over."

"He's a chickenshit," Brandon said.

"And you take a swing at him, you're an ex-cop."

They parted, got into the cruiser. Brandon took a deep breath.

"You know who I'm really pissed at?" he said.

"Yourself," Kat said. "For getting up in her face at the apartment."

"It's just that, you know, the parenting thing—"

"But you know you treated her a little like Dever did. Like she was beneath you."

Brandon put the cruiser in gear. Kat told Dispatch they were back in the car.

"Saw a little bit of yourself in him and you didn't like it," she said.

Brandon turned onto Commercial, hit the gas, headed away from downtown. "Sometimes I think you know me better than I know myself," he said.

"None of us really know ourselves," Kat said. "Always a step behind."

They were headed west, Brandon figuring they'd drive up to Cumberland Street, ask around among the junkies for the Lewiston guy with the frozen eye.

Brandon looked left as they turned off Commercial, saw the blue lights on the bridge, the Portland side. He slowed. Blue lights and orange ones. A wrecker.

"Her car?" Kat said.

Brandon put the lights on, took a left. They swung out onto the bridge and he shut the lights off. As they rolled up, the wrecker driver was on his back on the pavement, hooking a chain onto an old beater Buick, white with a light blue driver's door.

They stopped, got out. A couple of day-shift cops were standing by their cruisers watching, older guys, lots of seniority. One was halfheartedly directing traffic.

"The jumper?" Kat said.

"Parked it and went over the rail," the cop said.

He looked at Brandon. "Seen you around," he said.

"Blake," Brandon said.

"Six weeks in," Kat said.

"Zachary," the cop said. "Sixteen years."

"Long time," Brandon said.

"Just a job," Zachary said. "You probably think you're gonna save the world."

Brandon didn't answer.

"Well, you ain't gonna save this one. Eighty feet to the water."

"We saw her," Kat said.

"Left it running?" Brandon said.

"What, the car?"

"Yeah."

"Running when we got here," the cop said.

"Wonder how long a car can idle on a tank of gas," Brandon said.

"Detectives talked to the bridge operator. Nobody saw her go over. Got light, they noticed the car, called it in."

The car scraped the pavement as it was drawn onto the ramp truck. Brandon looked beyond it, the tanker docks, the Fore River snaking its way into the tidal flats. At one time, the British had loaded masts up there, cut from Maine forests, shipped back to England.

"You know who she is, right?" Zachary said. "The one with the missing kid?"

"Yeah."

"Gonna be a cluster, with the press," Zachary said.

"Speak of the devil," Kat said.

SIXTEEN

"So you were the officers who responded to the scene, when the baby went missing," the reporter said. It was the skinny guy who'd talked to the woman on Quebec Street, after Brandon had pulled his weapon. He beamed like this made them old friends, reunited after twenty years.

"Matt Estusa," he said. "I know Kat there, but I don't think we've met."

He nodded toward Kat, helping move traffic, slowed by gawkers. He looked at Brandon's name tag.

"Officer Blake," Estusa said. He held out his hand, gave Brandon the smile again. Brandon shook the guy's hand, felt like the guy held on a little too long. They disengaged.

"First jumper?" Estusa said.

"Yeah."

"Must be hard when you know the victim," he said.

"Not hard. Just sad," Brandon said.

"Yeah, from what I hear, this Chantelle had kind of a hard life. Drug problems, father of the child away in the war. Then this with the baby."

Estusa had his arms folded, a notebook stuffed in the back pocket of his jeans. Topsiders, an expensive-looking runner's jacket, a runner's watch. Brandon wondered if Mia knew him. Or Lily and Winston.

"I was just talking to the detectives," Estusa said. "They said she was pretty freaked out."

"Who wouldn't be?" Brandon said. "Her baby."

"Yeah, but the drugs. Not like she was the perfect mother."

"Doesn't mean she wouldn't be upset."

"So she kills herself. Kinda too bad. I mean, now the kid's got nobody. The dad, I guess he's a combat vet, got PTSD, she had to go to court to get custody. Now the guy's at sea, didn't even come back when his baby went missing. You'd think that a father would—"

"He's back. Boat turned around soon as they heard."

"Oh, well. My apologies to him. Toby something."

"Koski," Brandon said. "I'm sure it's in the reports."

"Oh, yeah."

They stood as the wrecker driver checked the hooks. There was a Wellesley College sticker on the back window.

"Must be a previous owner," Estusa said, nodding toward it.

"I don't know," Brandon said.

"I mean, she doesn't seem like Wellesley material. Maybe community college, on a welfare program." Estusa grinned.

"What do you know about her?" Brandon said.

"Just what I heard."

"Shouldn't believe everything you hear. Or read."

Estusa's eyebrows twitched. He kept up the smug grin as the wrecker pulled away.

"You ID her?" he said, like he was commenting on the weather. Rain letting up.

"Some of us knew her," Brandon said.

"Is that hard for you?"

Brandon turned and looked at him. "What?"

"The violent death stuff, I mean. After, you know . . . what happened with you."

"Thought you said you didn't know me."

"No," Estusa said. "What I said was that I hadn't met you. I read the stories from back then. Everybody did. Would have written them but I was on City Hall."

Brandon didn't answer.

"You still with her? The woman you saved?"

Again, no answer.

"Mia, right? I always thought that was a cool name. So some

of us, we were surprised when we heard you'd joined up with Portland PD. Or any PD, for that matter. I mean, when you've already had that experience, the fatal shooting and all, to put yourself in the position of maybe having to do it again."

Brandon turned to him and smiled. "Geez, Matt, I thought you'd want to cover today's story. Chantelle Anthony and the missing baby. Not my story."

"In a way, it's all connected," Estusa said, easing his notebook out of his back pocket, a pen from the other side, like a dove from a hat. "All of the death, the trail of tragedy, you know."

Brandon didn't answer.

"So," Estusa said, "maybe we could get a coffee, when you get off your shift. Talk a little."

"About what?" Brandon said.

"About how you're doing. I know this may be difficult for you to dig back up, but it's very unusual for anyone to have done what you did. Had to do. How many police officers begin their careers with that experience? And recent, too. It's not like it was ten years ago."

Estusa smiled, his eyes crinkling. His sympathetic face, Brandon thought. The guy was good.

"I'd love to talk to Mia," he said. "About her recovery, the two of you coping with the past, and now the present. Does she worry about you? Does she fear that you both dodged a bullet and another one might be coming?"

Brandon looked away. Flashed back to Fuller, the black blood spatter on the white wall. His cry as the life drained out of him. Mia's dry sobs as Brandon led her away. He turned to Estusa, his smile still in place.

"There's nothing to say," Brandon said.

"Oh, I know how you feel. But it really is of interest to anyone who read those stories. I mean, Sergeant Griffin's murder—it shook the community to its core. They'll want to know how you're doing, what it's like to move forward with this. As a young guy. As a young police officer."

"I don't think so," Brandon said. "It's over. Done."

"But you must think about it. I mean, when you hear a gunshot? When you see Griffin's friends? When you and Mia are alone? I mean, it has to be there."

"Sounds like you've got the story written. Don't need me."

Estusa grinned. "Oh, that's just the writer in me. I don't know what the actual story would say."

"No, I'm really not interested."

"Well, just think about it," Estusa said. "We can touch base tomorrow, the next day."

"I did think about it. No, thanks."

Estusa's expression changed, smile in place but harder, like concrete had dried.

"You know I can write it without you," he said.

"How will you know what I think when I hear a gunshot?"

"I can talk to your fellow officers. I can talk to experts."

"Sounds pretty dull to me."

Estusa sidled closer.

"Brandon, I'm gonna be straight with you: This is a good story. It's a very good story. An important story. And no offense, but I'm not gonna drop it just because you don't want to take part. What kind of reporter would I be?"

"A reporter who cops'll talk to."

"Hey, don't pull that one on me. I have plenty of sources. More than enough. In a year I'll be out of here anyway."

"Headed for the big time?" Brandon said.

"Bigger," Estusa said.

"*National Enquirer* hiring?"

Brandon paused.

"Okay, you know what I want to say?" Brandon said. He moved close, took Estusa by his thin, bony arm. Light rain spattered the notebook page but the pen was poised. Brandon leaned over, close to Estusa's ear.

"Go to hell," Brandon said.

SEVENTEEN

Whatever Toby told the detectives, it convinced them he didn't have the kid stashed in the hold of the boat. The chief, Edmundo Garcia, direct from Pittsburgh PD, called a press conference. Estusa was there, along with two local TV crews, with woman reporters all made up, and a blogger, a bearded guy in a khaki suit and black sneakers.

Estusa made eye contact with Brandon from across the room. Garcia, in full uniform complete with gold braids and hat, said investigators were turning to the public, as the leads they'd been tracking since the baby went missing hadn't panned out. He held up an eight-by-ten of Lincoln Anthony Koski, let the TV cameras zoom in. The baby was smiling, didn't know what was coming.

"We are asking that if you have seen this child, or have seen suspicious activity that might be related to his disappearance, please call 911," Garcia said, staring into the cameras. "We need your help."

And then he asked for questions, the cops staring at the press like bodyguards.

One TV reporter, blonde, made up like a movie star, sunglasses pushed back on her head, asked if the police had any theories. Garcia said they could speculate but needed more information to know in which direction to move.

The other TV reporter, not to be upstaged, asked if police thought the child had been abducted by a stranger. "And if so, should parents in the community be more protective at this time?"

Garcia said he had no idea who had taken the baby—that's why he was asking for help.

And Estusa, moving up in front of the cameras like the TV reporters were his warm-up act, asked if an Amber Alert had been issued. "And if not, why not?"

The chief said no. At the time the disappearance was reported, there was the possibility that it was a misunderstanding, that a family member had the child.

"Because the mother was under the influence of drugs?" Estusa said.

"We're not commenting on the details of the investigation," Garcia said.

"Who first discovered the baby missing?"

"Two patrol officers responding to a noise complaint."

"The mother didn't call to report that the child was gone?"

Somebody had been talking, Brandon thought.

"No," Garcia said. "That's not my understanding. Not initially."

"Had she been cooperating with the investigation?"

"Yes, fully. She was very upset, as you can imagine."

"Had she been investigated for child neglect prior to this?"

"I don't know that there was a formal investigation, no," Garcia said.

"But there were complaints?"

"Again, those are details we aren't ready to discuss at this time."

"When will you be ready?" Estusa said.

"You'll be the first to know, Matt," Garcia said.

He started to move away, press conference over. But Estusa called out, still holding his notebook. "Who were the patrol officers who responded to the mom's apartment?"

Garcia stopped, looked at him, over at Lieutenant Searles.

"I don't know, offhand. But we can get that information for you."

"I'm told one of them was Officer Brandon Blake," Estusa said.

Garcia glanced at the lieutenant. The lieutenant nodded.

"Yes, I believe that's true. Officer Blake and his partner were the first responders."

He looked at Estusa. Waited. Estusa looked at Brandon and smiled. He closed his notebook. "That's good for now, Chief," he said.

"He's a weasel," Brandon said.

"Screw him," Kat said.

"You're not on probation."

"No," Kat said. "I'm not."

They were in Kennedy Park, after bouncing around Parkside looking for the guy with the bad eye, everybody offering up somebody but not the guy they wanted.

"It's like Iraq," Brandon said. "Turning in your enemies for the American bounty. You want a terrorist? I'll give you a terrorist."

The head scarves were like Iraq, too, but the little girls were from Sudan and Somalia, all covered up as they pedaled pink Wal-Mart bicycles. Brandon and Kat got out of the car, approached an older African man who was shouting at a line of teenagers, leaning against a graffiti-sprayed block wall.

"They spit," the man said. He pointed down at the leg of his black trousers, the white glob of mucus. "That is assault. They commit assault on me. I want them arrested, taken to the jail."

One of the teenagers laughed. Someone said, "Stupid old fuck."

Kat turned to them, smiled, and strode to one end of the lineup. Brandon took the other. Kat said, "I smell weed. That's probable cause. Empty your pockets."

A tall white guy, sallow and sweaty, chains around his neck, said, "Yeah, right, bitch."

Kat smiled, moved slowly to him, until their chins almost touched. "Go ahead," she said.

"What?"

"I thought you were a tough guy."

He didn't answer.

"Guess you're not. All talk, can't get it up. That's what your girlfriend said anyway."

The rest of the group laughed. Kat smiled, turned to them.

"Who spat on this gentleman?" she said.

The faces turned to stone.

"Okay, the pockets," she said. "The pockets or the spitter. Your choice."

She looked at the sallow guy. "You the spitter, Ace?"

The sallow guy stared at her, silently loathing.

"I'm gonna count to five. And then I'm gonna smell weed and I'm gonna think I saw crack tossed. This is an area known for drug transactions."

They stared, unblinking. Brandon waited.

"One," Kat said. "Two. Three. Four."

"I did it," the sallow man said.

Kat turned to him, smiled broadly. "Don't you feel better now, telling the truth?"

He didn't answer.

"Turn around," Kat said. He hesitated. She touched the top of her Taser. He turned. The cuffs came out, snapped on, first one wrist, then the other. She took his wallet out of the back pocket of his shorts, flipped it open, closed it.

"Pleased to meet you, Byron," she said.

She patted him down, front and back and inside his legs, fished inside his basketball shoes, big and unlaced. From the right shoe she pulled a box cutter.

"Don't tell me. You work at the Piggly Wiggly."

Kat turned him, led him to the cruiser. She took the back of his head, guided it under the doorjamb. He jerked his head away, turned and spat in her face, saliva spattering her forehead.

She leaned close, wiped her forehead on his back. Brandon took the guy by the shoulder, jammed him into the cruiser, slammed the door. "You just got yourself six months, chump," she said.

"Friggin' dyke," he said. "Why don't you go find that fuckin' baby instead of jerkin' us around."

"This is bullshit," one of the guys said.

Kat nodded toward the old man, standing off by himself, arms folded, waiting. "Take his statement, Blake," she said. To the line of guys she said, "You got somewhere to go, boys? Or you wanna go for a ride, too?"

EIGHTEEN

It was 5:30. They'd arrested a kid for assault, for punching his girl-friend in the face in the parking lot of the Back Bay supermarket. Called MEDCU for a guy who was on the sidewalk at Longfellow Square, depressed and threatening to slash the arteries in his ankles. Different.

They cited a homeless guy for pissing on a fire hydrant on Forest Avenue. ("Dogs do it.") Arrested a rich lady from the sub-urbs—khaki skirt, lime-green sweater, pearls—on Congress for drunk driving and refusing to submit to arrest (slapping Brandon's hand away). Standing by her Lexus SUV, Miss Pearls claimed she'd had one Grey Goose martini, but then she blew a 0.28, three times the legal limit. At the station, she said Brandon had groped her breast as he put her in the police car. Kat said in writing that noth-ing of the kind had occurred.

"Like cops don't always stick together," the woman sputtered as they rolled her fingers in ink. "I want my lawyer right now, you hear me? I'm gonna own you, you limp-dick loser."

Underneath they're all the same, Brandon thought. He said nothing.

At 6:05 he pulled into the marina lot, took his kit bag from the truck, locked it. He glanced over, saw a silver Mercedes SUV, a sticker on the back window: a blue flag with a yellow trident. Like Poseidon, Brandon thought, as he buzzed through the gate and walked across the yard, down the float. From a distance he could see people in the helm area of *Bay Witch*. Then he could hear reggae music, laughter. Mia's voice, another woman, then a man, a big hearty laugh.

Lily and Winston.

"Damn," Brandon said.

He sighed, then took a deep breath, tried to gear up. Stepping aboard, he crossed the aft deck, started to move forward to the stateroom. Mia called: "Brandon, come on up. Lily and Winston are here."

He put his bag down, climbed the ladder to the helm, tried to get a smile on, stepped into the lounge.

"Hey, baby," Mia said, coming out of the captain's chair. She gave him a hug, a wine-flavored kiss. Lily and Winston smiled from the L-shaped settee, in shorts and flip-flops, half-full wineglasses in hand.

"Hello there, Brandon," Lily said.

"Love the boat," Winston said. "We're ready to move in."

"Spend a winter aboard," Brandon said. "That'll cure you."

"Oh, she's just lovely," Lily said. "Boats are female, right?"

"And the name, *Bay Witch*," Winston said.

"Boat names are so lame most of the time," Mia said. "There's one here, *Boys 'n' Gulls*."

"This is just spot-on," Winston said.

"I told Lily and Winston we'd take them out on the bay soon, Brand. Brunch on Great Diamond?"

"Sure," Brandon said.

"Oh, you'd love it," Mia said, a burble in her voice that told Brandon this was her second glass. "Mimosas on the back deck."

"Aft," Brandon said.

"He's always correcting me. Why don't they just say front and back? You know what I mean."

"Heave to there and shiver the forelock, matey," Lily said. "You are the first mate, aren't you, Mia?"

"I'm not the first but I'm the best," Mia said, then clapped her hand over her mouth. "Did I say that?"

They all laughed and Brandon smiled, figured maybe they were three glasses in. He must have looked weary because Lily said, "Hard day at the office?"

"Oh, the usual nonsense," Brandon said.

"I don't know how you can stand it," Lily said. She crossed her long, tanned legs and smiled. "I mean, some of the people you must have to deal with."

"Somebody has to do it," Winston said. "Brandon stands between us and anarchy."

"Or at least a crime wave," Mia said.

"You've been in the Old Port on a Friday night," Winston said. "Man, it's craziness."

"Where's your gun, Brandon?" Lily said. "Your billy-club thing and handcuffs?"

"I left them below. After a whole day lugging that stuff, you're ready to get rid of it."

"Sometimes in the morning I know it's Brandon coming down the dock because I can hear all his stuff creaking," Mia said. "You want a beer, babe?"

"I think a shower first."

"Lily and Winston asked us to come to the restaurant tonight for dinner."

"Our treat," Winston said. "After what happened at the house."

"Oh, don't worry about it," Brandon said.

"No, we absolutely insist," Lily said. "And Winston is trying out a new assistant chef, so he may actually be able to sit with us."

"Eight o'clock, honey," Mia said. "That gives you time to wind down."

She turned in the captain's chair toward Lily and Winston.

"Sometimes Brandon needs a little transition time," Mia said. "To go from criminals and all of that to regular people."

"I'm sure," Lily said. She sipped her wine, eyed Brandon. "Hey, I heard about the mother of that baby, the one that disappeared?"

Brandon looked at her.

"What about her?" Mia said.

"It was on the radio," Lily said.

"I've been writing," Mia said.

"She jumped off the bridge," Lily said.

"Oh, my God," Mia said.

"Man, that's just too sad," Winston said.

"What happened, Brandon?" Mia said.

They looked at him. He told them. Hundred words or less.

"Oh, my God, the poor thing," Lily said. "She probably blamed herself."

"And the baby was maybe the one good thing in her life," Mia said. "Guys come and go, her family totally dysfunctional. Drugs and alcohol."

"But she created this baby," Lily said. "They couldn't take that away from her."

"The one thing she had accomplished," Mia said. "And then she messes that up, too."

"And it's too much for her to take," Lily said. "The last in a long string of disappointments."

"You know we're with a writer," Winston said.

"So where is the baby, Brandon?" Mia said. "Do they have any idea?"

"I think *they* is Brandon," Lily said. She smiled at him, switched legs, a little flirty now. The wine, Brandon thought.

"Just tracking down leads," he said.

"I just figured it was one of those custody things, you know?" Mia said. "The dad decided he'd grab the kid and take off. Is that what they think?"

"Still checking things out," Brandon said. "The chief had a press conference, looking for tips from the public."

"So they don't know anything," Winston said.

Brandon looked at him, didn't answer.

"Oh, I know," Lily said. "You can't talk because it's a—what do they call it? An ongoing investigation."

"Very good," Brandon said.

He said, "Great seeing you," and headed for the ladder. When he turned to go down, he glanced back, saw Lily watching him over her glass. He heard Mia saying, "Is that the saddest thing you've ever heard? The baby disappears and she jumps off the bridge. What if they find the baby tomorrow?"

"And then he has no mom," Lily said. "How could she do that?"

Good question, Brandon thought as he started down the ladder. He pictured Chantelle, the look of utter devastation on her cracked-out face when it had sunk in that the baby was gone. He stopped, his head above the deck. He heard Lily, a little drunk and loud, say, "I've got it. She knew the baby was dead. And she couldn't keep up the lie."

Then Mia, "I'll bet it's tiring to live a lie like that."

And Winston, "I'm sure it would be. Just you and your secret, all alone."

They all drank and chatted, like it was a TV show they were discussing, Brandon thought. He continued down the ladder, down, down, down.

NINETEEN

Rendezvous was on Exchange Street, just up from the Regency. The walls were brick, the lighting muted, the dozen tables black lacquer. Paintings on the wall were seascapes, but almost abstract, vivid blues and greens.

"The artist, he's from Bridgetown," Winston was saying, his dark eyes glittering in the candlelight. "We grew up together. When we were decorating, I called him. I said, 'Man, I need a touch of the island. Send me what you got.' Barko, he sends me these paintings, crates of them. We've sold five already. I just keep putting up new ones."

They were on coffee, dark and strong. Dinner had been Bajan Barbadian, Winston disappearing into the kitchen. He was gone for forty-five minutes, Mia sipping wine, Lily a rum punch, Brandon, a carry gun in his waistband, a sparkling water.

Winston returned to the table followed by a waitress who handed around the plates: fried flying fish on cutter, a Barbadian salt bread. Rice and peas in a spicy mix, sweet potato cou-cou—everything flavored with chives and pepper and garlic.

"Delicious," Brandon said.

"Simple," Winston said. "That is the secret of Barbadian cuisine, just as it is Barbadian life. Simple but with the spice of life."

"It really is," Lily said. "It's like a different time there. Not like the other islands. It's peaceful and kind of quaint. Like where Winston grew up."

"Rendezvous," Winston said. "Like the name of the restaurant. Little place about four kilometers outside of Bridgetown. Wildlife sanctuary there—that place is like paradise. Adam and Eve could live there."

"Then why did you leave?" Mia said.

"Oh, us island people, we like to wander, you know. And you're living on the big wide ocean. It—what is the word?"

"Beckons?" Brandon said.

"Yes, perfect," Winston said. "Beckons. Hey, you know there's a place north of Bridgetown, it's called Brandon's Beach."

"Oh, Brandon," Mia said, leaning over and putting her arm around him. "We have to go. You can tell us where to stay, Winston. Or maybe we could all go."

Lily looked at Winston, touched his hand.

"That would be fun," she said, "But you know my favorite is Barbuda, off of Antigua? It's just so undeveloped. I mean, there are resorts and golf and all that, but once you get away from—"

"Mr. Kelley?"

They looked up. A woman had gotten up from a table across the room and was coming toward them. "Mr. Kelley, so nice to see you again."

Winston smiled. "I don't think we've—"

"Oh, you look wonderful. I like the shaved-head thing—but what happened to those beautiful dreadlocks?"

Winston smiled, shot a glance at Lily.

"I'm sorry, ma'am. I'm afraid I'm not the person you're thinking I am."

"This is Winston Clarke," Lily said.

The woman—in her seventies, carefully made up, white hair swept back under a tortoiseshell headband—looked puzzled. She glanced back at her husband, silver-haired, studying the wine list. "Oh, I'm so sorry. You look just like a fellow we knew. You even sound like him. We met on a cruise. You're not Alston Kelley? With an E? Who worked on the *Ocean Princess?*"

"No, ma'am. I'd like to go on a cruise, but I have to stay here, run the restaurant."

"You own this?"

"Well, yes. But sometimes I think it owns me."

Winston grinned. The woman smiled, relieved that he was being so gracious.

"Oh, I'm so sorry to have bothered you. You really could be Mr. Kelley's twin. He's from Jamaica."

"Winston is from Barbados," Lily said.

"Oh, the accent, I was sure—"

"Oh, now I am truly insulted, if you say I have a Jamaican accent."

The woman looked chagrined again but Winston reached out, touched her arm. "Just joking," he said. "But actually, Jamaican is a very different sound. We speak Bajan patois; it is West African and English, all blended up."

"And Jamaican is more Irish- or Scottish-based," Brandon said.

"Oh, really," Lily said. "How do you know that?"

"Brandon reads a lot," Mia said. "You never know what he's going to come out with."

"Your husband, he's going to order wine?" Winston said to the woman. "You tell him I'll have something special sent over. Because I disappointed you that I was not your friend."

"Oh, that's not necessary," the woman said.

"Oh, but my dear," Winston said, "I insist." He got up and put his big arm on her back, guiding her back toward her table. "It is Barbadian hospitality. You see? You didn't find your old friend, but you made a new one."

There was dessert, cou-cou flavored with peppers and chocolate. Then a rum liqueur from Martinique, Winston asking if they could taste the Creole spices. They could. Brandon abstained.

A long good-bye followed, full of promises to get together soon, to go for a boat excursion on *Bay Witch* (Mia talking), Lily launching into a story about people she knew who, once they were offshore, always sailed naked. The three of them laughed. Brandon smiled.

"Is *Bay Witch* clothing-optional?" Lily said, looking to Brandon.

"Suit yourself," Brandon said. "I tend to bring an extra fleece. Cold out there."

"Party pooper," Lily said, giving him the flirty look again. He took Mia's arm, started to steer her toward the door. They passed the older couple, who looked to Winston and raised their glasses. "Thank you," the woman said, her gaze lingering. "It's very, very nice."

Outside it was cool, damp, smelled of the harbor. Brandon took Mia's arm and she snuggled close to him. The rum?

"Well, that was fun," she said. "I really like them."

Brandon hesitated for a minute.

"Yes," he said. "It was a nice time."

"You didn't mind not drinking? I hope we weren't too silly for you. You looked so serious sometimes."

"Just a little tired."

"I know you've got a lot on your mind," Mia said as they walked down the hill toward Commercial Street and the car. "But baby, you've got to be able to shut it out. Otherwise, this job's going to eat you up."

She was right, Brandon thought, but how did you leave the baby behind? Chantelle?

"I know," he said. "But this one, it's just—"

They were overtaking another couple, the guy big and barrel-chested, the woman in a tight skirt, high heels. She wobbled on the cobblestones like someone on stilts crossing a rocky streambed. Mia and Brandon slowed.

"Oh, I was so embarrassed for that poor woman, thought she knew Winston," Mia said. "You know, the whole *They all look the same* thing. But Winston handled it so well. He's really very charming, don't you think?"

Brandon, listening to the couple in front of them, didn't answer.

"You were all over him," the guy was saying.

"I never touched him. Tommy, what are you talking about?"

"I could see the looks. Why didn't you just jump on his fucking lap?"

"I don't know what your goddamn problem is. I hadn't seen the guy since high school, for God's sake."

"Musta been in the backseat of a car."

"You're paranoid. Maybe you ought to get some help."

They'd turned the corner onto Commercial. The guy yanked the woman into a doorway, out of view.

"I'll give you some help," he muttered.

"Let go of me," the woman said.

Then a slap, followed by another and another. The woman cried out, started to whimper. When Brandon and Mia came to the doorway she was hunched against the wall, hands over her face. The guy had his arm cocked, fist clenched.

"Hey," Brandon said. "Stop it."

"Keep walking, asshole," the guy said, glancing at Brandon. Even in the dark he was red-faced, drunk.

"Nope," Brandon said. He moved Mia away to the curb, turned as the woman tried to squirm loose. The guy punched her in the back of the head and she yelped, stumbled, fell to her knees. As she started to sob, he lifted her by the shoulder, raised his arm again.

"Police officer," Brandon said. "That's enough."

"And I'm the fucking SWAT team, dickhead," the guy said. "Get lost."

Brandon moved between them, yanked the guy's arm off the woman's wrist. She tottered away. The guy jerked his arm back, said, "You are so dead."

He was big but heavy and drunk and slow. The punch was a big roundhouse right and Brandon stepped inside it, grabbed the wrist with both hands, and twisted. He spun the guy out onto the sidewalk, kicked a leg out from under him, and put him down on the pavement on his belly with a thud and a grunt. The guy tried to writhe away, but Brandon jammed the guy's right arm up until he felt the tendons start to stretch. He put his knee between the guy's legs and pinned him to the sidewalk with a forearm to the back of his neck.

"You're breaking my arm!" the guy bellowed. "Get off me!"

At the academy they'd done it a thousand times—the other cadets fighting back, in better shape than this chump.

"Call 9-1-1," Brandon told Mia, and she grabbed her phone from her bag.

The guy bellowed again, said, "My arm's broke. My fucking arm."

"Don't resist," Brandon barked, and he kept him pinned, his cheek pressed to the cobblestones, blood running from his nose, bumped when he hit the ground. Another couple approached, four college guys behind them.

"Get off him, dude," one kid said.

"I'm a police officer," Brandon barked. "Stay back."

"You're hurting the guy, man," another kid said.

The big guy beneath him bellowed again, said, "I'm not resisting. I'm not fucking resisting."

"Let him go," a woman shrieked. "What do you think you're doing?"

"Hey, he's got a gun," her boyfriend said.

"What's this, some undercover cop thing?" a college kid said.

"Oh, my God," the guy's girlfriend said, moving closer, her slapped face pink in the streetlight. "Stop it. Just stop it."

They all started to move closer. "Back off," Brandon shouted.

"If you're a cop, this is police brutality," one of the college guys said, holding up his phone and filming.

"They're coming," Mia said.

A cruiser swung onto Commercial from Franklin Street, blue lights flashing. Another came around the corner, roared up, and swung in. The crowd turned.

"Everybody back," a cop said over the PA. And then they were there, four of them, patrolman Vargas moving in, snapping cuffs on the big guy.

"This son of a bitch assaulted me," the big guy said. "I want to press charges."

"Domestic violence assault," Brandon said, on his feet, pulling his shirt down over his gun.

"Forget it," the woman said. "Let him go. I just want to go home."

"Not the way the law works, ma'am," Vargas said. "Once there's evidence of domestic violence assault, the perpetrator is arrested."

"You're arresting him? Now? He's gotta work in the morning, for Christ's sake."

"Maybe somebody can post his bail."

"Bail? Oh, my God."

She reached into her bag, took out a phone, flipped it open. In the phone light, Brandon could see the hand marks on her cheeks.

"Three slaps, one punch to the back of the head."

"You'll do the paperwork?" Vargas said.

"Yup."

The other patrolmen gathered around, the onlookers melting away as soon as the big guy was shut in the cruiser. Zachary was there; Dever; a woman officer named Shelley something, just back from having a baby.

"Jeez, Blake," Dever said, glancing at Mia. "Sure know how to show your lady here a good time."

He turned to Mia, grinned. "Honey, next week he's gonna take you to serve some warrants."

"The guy was beating that woman," Mia snapped. "What did you expect him to do?"

"Whoa," Dever said. "Easy there, sweetcakes."

"Who you calling sweetcakes?" Mia said.

"Just kidding around. Hey, Blake, your girl's a real pit bull. Nobody gonna bother you with her around."

"Let's go," Zachary said, touching Dever on the shoulder. "Before you wear out your welcome."

To Brandon he said, "You coming in now, fill out the paperwork?"

Brandon looked at Mia, her eyes flashing in the blue strobes, her lips a thin line. "Give me twenty minutes," he said.

TWENTY

They drove in silence, up the hill, onto the bridge, past the spot where Chantelle had gone over the railing. Mia was looking out the window, her hands folded on her lap.

"Sorry," Brandon said.

"It's okay," Mia said. "It's not like you had a choice."

"But still—you were having fun. It was a nice night."

"I thought we'd go back to the boat and make love," Mia said.

"I won't be long," Brandon said. "Quick report and out of there."

He looked over at her as they came off the bridge. Her face was pale, frozen in place. Brandon stopped at the light.

"Brandon," Mia said finally, staring straight ahead. "Is this the way it's going to be?"

He glanced at her, frowned. "No," he said. "I mean, it's not like you can't walk down the street around here without seeing an assault in progress. Most times, we would have just come home. Like—"

"Like normal people?" Mia said.

Brandon didn't answer. The light changed, and they were silent again as Brandon drove into the parking lot of the marina. He stopped the car, shut off the motor. It was quiet, but for the rustle of the water. Across the harbor lights twinkled on the skyline, slipped across the water. Brandon waited.

"My dad says being married to a cop is worse than being one," Mia began. "You're always worried and there's nothing you can do about it. Cops see all this awful stuff that they can't leave at the office. And they have more in common with other cops than regular people so they end up having affairs and getting divorced. He says they end up with PTSD, even if they don't know it."

"So what makes your dad an expert?"

"He's a lawyer."

"Right. A corporate lawyer. Mergers and acquisitions."

"When he was in law school they had to do criminal work," Mia said.

"So two weeks twenty years ago makes him an authority?" Brandon said, and caught himself.

"He's just worried about me, Brandon."

"No, he's worried about me. Doesn't want his daughter with her Colby College degree hooked up with some street cop."

"Brandon."

"Driving around busting crackheads, touching smelly homeless people."

"He respects what you do," Mia said.

"He just doesn't want you to have anything to do with it."

"That's not—" She hesitated.

"Not what?" Brandon said. "Not true?"

Mia didn't answer.

"It is true. He didn't raise you to end up with somebody like me."

"It doesn't matter what he thinks," Mia said.

"Then why'd you bring him up?"

"I don't know. It's just—" She sighed. A tear rolled down her right cheek, stopped just above her chin. The trail glistened in the parking lot light. Brandon waited.

"It's just that I worry," Mia said.

"About what?"

"I worry that I've lost you already. That your job will always come first. That . . . I don't know . . ." She swallowed, wiped at the streak on her cheek. "That you'll always be thinking about this baby, this woman on drugs, this guy you arrested, this drug dealer you got information on, this prostitute, this gang member, the crazy homeless people."

Another swallow, another wipe.

"I worry that compared to all that, I'm just boring. Working in a library, writing my stories, a novel that probably will never be published."

"Sure it will. You're a great writer. I love your stories," Brandon said. "And you're not boring. You're wonderful."

"Okay, then, maybe it's not that I'm boring. Maybe it's more that you'll be bored and you'll leave, find somebody with a life more like yours. This Kat you're always talking about. You like her."

"Kat's a lesbian."

"Okay, then some other Kat who's straight. Women find you very attractive. I'm sure there are woman cops who—"

"I'm not going anywhere."

Mia turned to him. Another tear spilled down her cheek, like a raindrop running down a window.

"Even if you don't, Brandon. Our friends, my friends—because they're more mine than yours—it's like you're watching them, always standing back. It's like you're not there."

"It's hard when I can't drink," Brandon said. "I mean, out in public."

"Oh, I know, but like tonight. It was fun—the food, the company. They were nice and interesting. And it was like you were, I don't know, bemused or something."

"I was tired."

"I know," Mia said. "But—"

"And it's hard to just shut everything out. I mean, Chantelle lying there dead, her eyes open. I mean, I was just talking to her. And the baby gone—"

"I know, Brand, but then tonight it all turns into this big fight on the street, and now you're going back to work. I mean, what are we going to do, honey? What are we going to do?"

She reached over and took his hand. The tears were coming faster now, silver streaks on her cheeks. "How are we going to make this work, baby? Tell me, because I need to know."

"So you can decide whether to stay or go?" Brandon said.

Mia paused.

"I love you," she said.

"And I love you," Brandon said.

"But I can't love you and only get this little piece of you back."

"I know."

He squeezed her hand. With his other hand he adjusted his gun.

TWENTY-ONE

The big guy made the cops take him to the ER, claimed his arm was broken. They took him to Mercy Hospital because Dever, freshly divorced, had his eye on this PA who worked the night shift there. She told them the guy's arm wasn't broken, just strained—that he should take ibuprofen and ice it, he'd be fine. The big guy said he'd go to a real doctor, not some stupid fake doctor bitch.

Dever told him to watch his mouth, gave the PA a nice smile, which she returned, and then they hauled the big guy to the PD to process.

A successful visit all around.

Brandon filled out his statement, what he'd seen and when, the precise amount of force needed to subdue and restrain the combative suspect. Depending on if he had any money to burn, the big guy might sue, and, as Zachary put it, "You want all your ducks in a row."

It was after 1 a.m. when Brandon pulled out of the PD lot. Down Middle Street, he weighed whether Mia would be up, whether she'd worry. He continued down Spring Street, headed for the bridge, stopped at the light and watched three guys—middle-aged conference types—stagger across the street, headed for the Holiday Inn.

Brandon glanced at his phone. 1:23. The wine and drinks—Mia was probably out cold. He hesitated, slowed down. Took a right.

Up the hill, left on Congress. People were out: knots of drunk kids walking home from the Old Port, a couple of Goths from the art school, alcoholics and mentally ill people standing in front of the Landmark Hotel. Nobody noticed him in the old truck, and

Brandon liked that, sliding along unnoticed, invisible. Kat said detectives had a boring job, never in on the action, always showing up when everything was over. But Brandon thought he'd like going undercover, nobody knowing he was a cop until he slapped on the cuffs.

He went through the square, saw a cruiser pulled up by the porn shop, probably cops rousting somebody for soliciting. And then he took a right, saw the moon low over the rooftops to the west.

It was a new moon, a sliver on the bottom, the palest shade of green. It would be pretty over the water. Soon.

Granite Street was quiet, dark and leafy and still. He drove past 317, saw lights on in the Ottos' apartment. Immigrants had a different clock, up all hours, kids, too. Brandon continued down the block, past a gaggle of kids on bikes. A woman walked past them— tight jean shorts, white high heels. They called to her in Arabic and she flipped them off, kept walking. Brandon circled the block.

On the second approach he saw the glow of a cigarette in the driveway. He pulled over. Got out. The glow moved like a firefly, then sailed, landing in a brief shower of sparks. Brandon walked up the driveway, saw Mr. Otto. He was sitting on a plastic fish crate. Brandon walked up, said, "Mr. Otto. It's me. Officer Blake."

"The policeman," Otto said. "Now you a detective, like on TV?"

"I'm off. Headed home."

"Where you live?"

"South Portland. On a boat."

Otto looked away. Smiled. "Must be nice. Peaceful."

"Yes, it is. Unless there's a storm."

"Oh, yeah," Otto said. "A storm. The wind blow."

He was wearing blue Dickies like an old Mainer. Shaking the pack, he took out another cigarette and held it out to Brandon.

"No. But thank you, though," Brandon said.

Otto lit up, drew deeply, the glow illuminating his face, his eyes.

"The mother of the little boy—she's dead, right?" he said.

"Yes. They found her in the water under the bridge."

"When was that?"

"They found her this morning. Went in the water sometime last night."

"I knew that. I knew that ahead of you."

"You did?"

"Yes. I know last night."

"How is that, sir?" Brandon said.

He waited as Otto smoked, looked away, seemed to be considering how to say something.

"*Shabah.* The spirit."

"Spirit? Spirit of what?"

"The child. The girl's child. The baby's spirit come back. He's looking for his mother and don't find her because she lost, also."

"Huh," Brandon said. "You saw the spirit?"

"Fatima. She can see these things."

"More than you?"

"Yeah. Men, they have the less power."

"So Fatima saw the spirit? Lincoln's spirit."

Otto dropped his cigarette to the driveway, stepped on it with his work boot and stood. "You wait here, okay? I have her come tell you."

Otto turned and walked to the door. It slammed behind him and Brandon heard his boots clomping up the stairs. He stood and waited, wondered if the appearance of the spirit would help fix the time of death.

And then there was more clomping, the door rattling open, Otto and Fatima there, Fatima behind her father, Samir and Edgard behind Fatima. They crossed the driveway to Brandon, circled him.

"Yo, Five-Oh," Edgard said. He smiled but his eyes were hard. Samir, his Sixers cap sideways, said, "Why you keep coming around, Mr. Policeman?"

Otto looked at them, said, "Go." The brothers looked at their father, sauntered down the driveway and across the street to the kids on bikes. The older man turned to Fatima, in cotton sweatpants and flip-flops, black *jilbab* hanging to her knees, arms folded protectively across her chest. Her eyes were on the ground.

"You tell the Portland Police," Otto said.

"Tell him what?"

"About the *shabah*," Otto said. Fatima looked away. She was very pretty, Brandon thought. He stared at her mahogany skin, luminous dark eyes.

"You'll make fun of me," she said.

"No," Brandon said. "I won't."

She wouldn't meet his gaze, looked at the street, her brothers, standing on the far sidewalk talking on the phone.

"Yeah, well. It's just that they don't let me sleep."

"The spirits."

"Right. I fall asleep, right away they wake me up."

"More than one of them?"

"Yes. They call me." She glanced at him. "Now don't you laugh."

"I won't. I'm not. But then what happens?"

Fatima fidgeted, wiggled her toes. Her toenails were painted pink, showing even in the dark against her brown-skinned feet.

"Tell him," Otto said.

"Then they make me listen," Fatima said.

"To what?"

"To the baby's spirit."

"What does it sound like?"

"It cries for its mother. It cries for what it can never have."

"You know Chantelle is dead?"

Fatima nodded. "She jumped, right?" she said. "That's what somebody said."

"That's what they think."

"So her soul will roam the earth forever."

"I suppose so," Brandon said.

"And the baby's soul is trying to find her," Fatima said.

"Is that what you think?"

"That's what I hear," she said.

"You can tell from what? The crying?"

"They're two spirits—*shabah,* the baby and the mother—but they can never, ever meet again," Fatima said.

"She knows these things," Otto said.

Fatima didn't deny it.

"They're apart forever. The baby cries for his mother."

"But the spirit comes here?" Brandon said. "The *shabah?*"

"It's where they were together."

"The baby and the mom."

"Yeah."

Brandon paused. The three of them stood for a minute, Otto looking at his daughter sadly, like this power to hear ghosts was an incurable illness.

"You don't believe me, do you?" Fatima said.

"Yes," Brandon said. "I do."

"You'll go back to the other police and tell them and laugh. This big joke, crazy girl," she said.

"No," Brandon said. "I won't."

They stood. Fatima folded her arms tighter. Her father looked at Brandon, as though waiting for some sort of instruction.

"What time did you first hear the spirits, the crying?" Brandon said.

"It was almost one o'clock," Fatima said. "At night."

"It woke you up?"

"Yes. At first I think it was a dream."

"Where were you?"

"In my bed."

"How long did it cry?"

"Every little while. Like, a few minutes."

"And then it stopped?" He didn't wait for the answer. "Have you heard it tonight?"

"I'm too scared to go to sleep. Sleeping is when it comes." She looked at her father.

"This is a bad thing," Otto said. "Can make you sick. Even make you die. We maybe have to move."

"I'm sure she'll be okay," Brandon said.

Fatima finally looked at Brandon. "How do you know?" she said. "You're just a policeman."

He ignored that, said, "Fatima—if the baby's alive, but he's just lost or kidnapped or something, can he still have a *shabah?*"

"No," Fatima said.

"For *shabah,*" Otto said, "it gotta be dead."

MOTHER OF MISSING BABY FOUND DEAD, the headline said. CHANTELLE ANTHONY, 24, OF PORTLAND, DIES IN BRIDGE LEAP.

Estusa's story was first on the *Portland Tribune*'s local news list. Brandon read it on his laptop, seated at the helm, bent over the glowing screen. The story had Chantelle's death—her body in the harbor, car on the bridge—tacked on top of the story about Lincoln going missing.

> *The sequence of events that ended with Ms. Anthony's death began when police were called to her 317 Granite Street apartment to investigate a noise complaint, said Sergeant Joseph Perry. Officers Kat Malone and Brandon Blake questioned Ms. Anthony and discovered that the baby, Lincoln Anthony, six months old, was missing from his bed, Perry said.*
>
> *Ms. Anthony is estranged from the child's father, Toby Koski, of Portland. Asked if the incident could stem from a custody dispute, Perry said the case was still under investigation.*
>
> *According to court records, Ms. Anthony has a history of drug offenses. Perry said he could not confirm reports that the young mother was under the influence of drugs when police entered the apartment. Toxicology results that would show the presence of drugs in her body at the time of her death were not available Saturday night.*
>
> *Meanwhile, the dead woman's mother and sister and brother, Stacy, Ronnie, and Jason Anthony, all of Portland, said Chantelle Anthony felt police blamed her for the child going missing. "Instead of pointing their fingers they should have been looking for Lincoln," Stacy Anthony, the dead woman's mother,*

said Saturday. "Chantelle had some personal issues, but she was a good mom, and she never would have done anything to hurt her baby. She loved him very much."

Ronnie Anthony said Chantelle told her that police were "accusatory" at the apartment, and later at police headquarters, where she was questioned again. "Just because she had substance abuse problems don't mean you treat her like dirt," the sister said.

Asked if harsh treatment by police may have contributed to her sister's death, Ronnie Anthony said, "It was unfair. First, she has her baby gone, and then on top of that they say it's her fault. I'm sure this was too much to put on her shoulders."

Added Jason Anthony, "Those cops, Blake especially. He killed her just like he'd put a gun to her head and pulled the trigger. He's gotta pay for that. In this life or the next, you know what I'm sayin'. What goes around comes around."

Toby Koski, contacted Saturday, said he had been on a fishing trip aboard Marie G, *a Portland-based lobster boat, when the boat received a report that the baby had gone missing. The* Marie G *returned to port, where Koski was questioned by Portland detectives, he said.*

"I just want my son back," Koski said, before Chantelle Anthony's body was found. "That's all I want."

Like he'd pulled the trigger. Brandon felt himself sinking. And there was more. The guy who spotted the body. The car on the bridge. Neighbors, "who asked that their names not be used," saying there had been a big party at the Granite Street apartment the night the baby disappeared.

"She was quiet when they weren't partying," one resident of the building said. "She was a nice girl, very nice to the little boy."

"When she wasn't high as a kite and forgetting she even had a kid," Brandon said. "Give me a break."

TWENTY-TWO

Mia was asleep, clothes tossed on the deck between the berths. Brandon slid in beside her, felt her naked body next to his. So she hadn't given up on him. She'd been waiting. He'd let her down twice in one night. Maybe her father was right.

Brandon tried to sleep but couldn't. Mia. The guy on the street. Chantelle's eyes. Fatima and her ghosts.

He lay on his back and listened. He could hear Mia's breathing, soft and shallow. A wake rolled in and the boat rocked, fenders creaking, the float knocking on the pilings. There was a horn somewhere, someone leaning on it. And then a siren, the blip of a Portland PD cruiser. Another.

And then quiet. Brandon started to drift off. The boat rocked so imperceptibly that it might have been imagined. And then he was asleep, dreaming that *Bay Witch* had come loose from the dock and was drifting and—he heard it.

Crying. He came to slowly, fighting his way to the surface. He listened. Heard Mia breathing. The berth creak. And then the cry, faint and faraway, but somehow close. A haunting cry, high-pitched but falling away. And then another. Closer.

Brandon tensed. Waited.

He heard it again. The sighing cry . . . that turned into a gull's chattering laugh.

In the darkness, Brandon sighed and closed his eyes. And slept until he heard crying again. Opened his eyes to see Mia, leaning on one elbow, talking on the phone, the crying coming from it. She was saying, "Lily. Lily. Calm down. Please calm down. Who's dead? Who is it?"

TWENTY-THREE

Brandon sped over the bridge, Mia beside him. It was a little after six, a Sunday morning, no traffic. He hit seventy, the harbor flashing by, Mia holding onto the seat. On the Portland side of the bridge, he slowed, ran the light on Fore Street, blasted through the sleeping Old Port, flashed up Fore Street and onto the Eastern Prom.

They saw the blue lights, an ambulance coming off Congress. Brandon slid the truck to a stop and Mia jumped out and they trotted toward the house. O'Farrell was in the driveway, talking to a detective Brandon didn't know. In the unmarked cruiser behind him Lily sat alone, a tissue pressed to her face.

The detective walked back toward the house. Brandon and Mia approached O'Farrell, who said, "So I hear you know these folks." He looked at his notebook. "Lily Lawrence and Winston Clarke. With an E."

"Lily's a good friend of mine," Mia said. "Is she okay?"

"Physically okay," O'Farrell said.

"You talk to her?" Brandon said.

"Tried. She's pretty shook."

He looked at Mia. "You want to see if you can get her calmed down so we can get a better idea of what happened?"

He walked with Mia to the cruiser, opened the far door. She got in and Brandon saw her embrace Lily, Lily bury her face in Mia's shoulder. O'Farrell came back.

"Hope it helps," Brandon said.

"Your girlfriend was her first call," O'Farrell said. "They go way back?"

"I don't know about that. Book club. They hit it off."

"Well, they've got something in common now."

Brandon looked at him.

"Shootings, I mean," O'Farrell said. "How many people have—" He saw Brandon darken, dropped it. Took out a notebook, flipped the pages.

"Renford Gayle. Black guy. New York."

"He's the dead guy?"

"On the kitchen floor as we speak. Nine millimeter right through the heart. Boom."

"Who shot him?"

"She says she did. Your friend."

"My God. I just thought it would have been—"

"The boyfriend. I know. But he said this Gayle guy broke in, had a gun, demanded money, then the boyfriend—"

"Winston."

"Right. The dead guy, not dead yet, he orders Winston to give him all the money."

"From what? The restaurant?"

"I guess Mr. Winston—"

"That's his first name, actually," Brandon said.

"Right. I guess he sometimes took the receipts from the restaurant home with him. Looks like preliminarily the perp followed him home a little after three, waited until everybody was asleep. Breaks in. Door was pried open. They look up, he's standing by the bed, pointing a three fifty-seven."

"Jesus."

"So your friend Lily there, all she's said is that she couldn't let him die. Her boyfriend."

"So she got the gun away from him?" Brandon said.

O'Farrell looked away as the crime-scene guys arrived. "Third floor. Can't miss him."

They trudged past, boxes in hand.

"Had her own gun—or they did. Way I picture it, the intruder gets the drop on the guy, orders him out of the bedroom to get the money. Doesn't realize there's a gun in the bedroom. The girlfriend, she gets the gun, follows them out, and pow. All she wrote."

"One shot?"

"Hers. Down he goes."

"But if he's brandishing a weapon, making threats."

"Self-defense, way they tell it."

"Where's Winston?"

"They're taking his statement out back."

"He upset?"

"Not as much as the lady. Then again, he maybe just got his life saved. What do you know of him?"

"Just met him a couple of times. Seemed like a nice guy. Likes to tell stories, buy people drinks at Rendezvous—named after his hometown on Barbados."

"I knew he was from somewhere like that," O'Farrell said.

"He and the girlfriend pretty tight?"

"Oh, yeah. I mean, very. Kind of the cool Portland couple."

"What's she do?"

"Hangs out. Socializes. I don't know what else."

"Not hurting for income, looks of things."

"I think her family has some serious cash," Brandon said.

"Trust-funder," O'Farrell said, like it explained a lot.

"His car here? The shooter?"

"We're thinking it's this Lexus, parked around the block. Stolen out of New Jersey, illegal New York plates. Had 'em bring the drug dog, sniff around. Dog lit up."

"Drugs in the car?" Brandon said.

"No, but lots of residue."

"So he's a runner?"

"Musta already made the drop," O'Farrell said. "This Winston guy dealing, you think? Out of the restaurant or something?"

"No sign of it that I've seen. But I can say he's no wimp. Guy tried to pick a fight with me here at their house, this dinner party we were at. Had a thing about cops. Winston slapped him down, hustled him out the door, nice wrist lock."

"Well, Mr. Tough Guy oughta be glad his lady friend is quick on the draw."

They stood for a few minutes, O'Farrell on the phone to New York, Brandon watching the scene. He turned to watch as the ME's people bumped down the steps with a stretcher, a green plastic sheet over the dead guy, the legs of the stretcher scissoring out. The guy's feet were sticking out, Nike logo on the soles of his shoes. The stretcher rattled by, and Brandon got a closer look. Air Jordans. O'Farrell turned to go, turned back. "Blake. You know the *Tribune* is asking about you."

"Estusa?"

"It's been a year, hasn't it?" O'Farrell said.

"And three weeks."

"They're cooking up something."

"What'd you tell him?" Brandon said.

"That you had the makings of a very good cop," O'Farrell said.

"Thanks."

"I got you hired, Blake," O'Farrell said, with the barest hint of a smile. "Just protecting my ass."

Lily and Mia were still in the back of the cruiser, Mia's arm around Lily, Lily's face pressed against Mia's shoulder. Brandon walked by the car, heard Lily's sobs through the glass, saw Mia patting Lily's arm. He read her lips: "It's going to be okay."

It hadn't been okay for Brandon and Mia, not for a long time. Mia had wanted to go to counseling, so Brandon had gone with her, but the counselor, a bald guy with a beard and little round glasses, kept asking Brandon how he felt.

"Relieved," Brandon had said.

"That's good, but aren't you also troubled, having taken a life?"

"Not really," Brandon had said. "I'm just glad he was the only one."

"It's really okay to let it out," the counselor said, smiling in a way Brandon supposed was meant to get him to spill his guts. "What are you feeling deep down?"

"Deep down?" Brandon said. "I'm really, really glad I didn't miss."

But everybody was different. That's what the shrink at the Academy—another guy with a beard and glasses—had said. After a fatal shooting some cops were fit for duty the next week. Others were never the same.

So Brandon could try to talk to Lily, tell her not to focus on her shooting the guy, but on the alternative. This dirtbag kills her. He kills Winston. He goes and spends their money on a week of hookers and a couple of cases of Cristal.

Be glad you didn't miss.

Brandon walked up toward the side door of the house, saw curtains move in the windows of the big Victorian next door. When he turned the corner he saw Winston, head in his hands, sitting at a patio table with Pelletier and a detective from homicide named Amy Smythe, worked day shift. Brandon had seen her picture in the paper, nodded to her in the hall. She was a stud; he was a newbie.

"Officer Blake," Smythe said.

He walked over as they all got up. Smythe put a recorder in her jacket pocket. Winston looked at her and she nodded, and he walked toward Brandon. He looked weary, like he might fall. He extended his hand and Brandon took it and Winston drew him close, clasped his arm, then pulled him into a hug. Brandon felt the other cops watching, the rookie all tight with some guy mixed up in a drug shooting. He stiffened, tried not to recoil.

"Brandon," Winston said. "It's crazy, man. I can't believe it. It's like a movie."

"I know. But it turned out all right. It'll be okay."

"Coming from you, I believe that, man. Keep telling me. Lily—"

"Mia's with her."

"The detectives, they'll talk to her now?"

"Nothing to worry about. She just tells exactly what happened. It'll sort itself out."

"Right. But man, this guy, he was gonna kill us, I know. He wanted us to go in the car, go to the bank."

"That's never good."

"Lily had no choice."

"I'm sure."

"Brandon, they said you could take me for a coffee. We can't go back in the house."

Brandon said okay, and they turned. Smythe had gotten in the cruiser, on the other side of Lily, Mia still sitting there, Lily with her head raised, wiping her eyes.

"Oh, baby," Winston said, and he started for the car.

Brandon grabbed his arm, said, "You can't talk to her yet. Let's go."

"She's gonna have trouble with this. I mean, man, she's, like, sensitive."

Brandon led Winston away, toward the truck. "She'll get over it," he said. "Believe me."

They were crossing the lawn when someone called, "Officer Blake."

Brandon turned back, saw Smythe, beckoning him with a forefinger, like a schoolteacher pulling him aside on the playground. He walked over as Pelletier led Lily back to the patio table, Mia standing by the cruiser.

"Your buddy there," Smythe said.

"Not really my buddy."

"Whatever. Pay attention to what he says."

"Why?"

"Easy to tell the truth twice," Smythe said. "If you're fudging it, then each time it gets harder. You lose track."

"You think something's not right?"

"I don't think anything, Blake, not until I've got all the data."

Data, Brandon thought. It was like she was a teacher. Blonde hair pulled back, square serious jaw. Mrs. Smythe, cute but tough.

"Kinda awkward, like I'm wearing a wire or something. I mean, these are my girlfriend's friends."

"You're a cop, Blake," Smythe said, as she turned away. "Get used to it."

TWENTY-FOUR

They went to Starbucks, the triangle building at Monument Square, took a table in the far corner. Winston sat on one side, Mia and Brandon on the other. Mia had tea, Brandon a black Colombian, Winston a mocha latte. They sat with their hands wrapped around the hot cups. Nobody spoke, and finally they sipped.

"She saved my life," Winston said.

"Thank God," Mia said.

"And now she pays a price," Winston said.

"There's counseling," Brandon said.

"You tell me who's good," Winston said. "We'll get her right in. Fix this before it burrows into her, you know? Before these guilty thoughts, they find a home inside her."

Odd the way he used the language, Brandon thought. A different culture.

"She had no choice," Mia said. "We just have to keep telling her that. This was a situation that was put in front of her. She didn't cause it."

"Right," Winston said.

They were quiet again. Sipped. A woman came and sat at the next table, opened a book.

"She didn't want to have a gun in the house," Winston said.

The woman looked up, just her eyes.

"I said it was insurance, you know? I leave the restaurant last. People, they watch you."

"Were you carrying it?" Brandon said.

"No. Lily said it scared her. She said I'd shoot myself."

"But you kept it?"

"Put it in the drawer in the table by the bed. Kind of forgot about it."

"But Lily remembered," Mia said.

"Yes."

"How did she get to it?" Brandon said.

"He said to get out of the bed. Lily, she had on underpants only. She didn't want to get out of the bed without a top. He pointed the gun at her. She said, 'Let me get my shirt.' I get out, take my jeans, my shirt off the chair. He says, 'Get the effing money.' I say okay, he puts the gun on the back of my neck, and we start to walk out of the bedroom. Lily opens a drawer in the bureau. He spins around with the gun."

"Oh, my God," Mia said.

"I thought he was going to shoot her, right in the back. He says, 'Put up your hands, you—.' He used some bad words. She did, and he said, 'Turn around.' I think he wanted to see her. See her from the front. He says, 'Very nice.' I say, 'Do you want the money or what?' I didn't want him to, you know, get other ideas. So I start out of the room and he turns to follow me, and she must've turned around again, taken the gun from the drawer."

Winston paused. The woman with the book pretended not to listen.

"The gun was loaded?" Brandon said.

"Yes."

"You'd showed her how to use it?" he asked.

"No. She wouldn't touch it. She said it scared her."

"Where did you get it?" Brandon said.

He felt Mia's glance.

"From a guy who used to work in the restaurant. Washing dishes. He saw me with the money bag, he say, 'Winston, man, you need protection.' I say, 'This is Portland, Maine. Not New York or LA or even Atlanta.' He says, 'You think there aren't bad guys out there? You're kidding yourself, man.' "

"Did you?" Brandon said. "Buy the gun?"

"No. I mean, I kinda forgot about it. Then this dishwasher

guy, his name was Jake—he worked under the table. He brings the gun in. We go out to his car. He says he'll sell it cheap. He's selling stuff to pay child support. I pay him three hundred dollars. The gun and a box of bullets."

"Where's Jake now?" Brandon said.

"He quit. Said he was leaving the state, going to Florida or someplace. Something about the ex-wife hounding him."

"Well, thank God you had it there," Mia said. "Who knows what would have—"

"He had to kill us," Winston said. "I mean, we could identify him. His face."

"Probably right," Brandon said.

"He said, 'We're going to take a ride.' I'm thinking, we're not coming back from this. What do I do? Drive the car into a tree? Tell Lily to jump out? I'm thinking this, and he has the gun back on my neck, pressing it hard."

Winston turned, showed a pinkish circle on the back of his neck. "It made a mark?" he said.

"Yes," Mia said.

"So then what happened?" Brandon said.

"I'm thinking, what are we going to do? And then Lily, she just—"

"Shot him," Brandon said.

"Yes. He falls down. Looks up at me for a second, like he couldn't believe it. And then he sort of breathed really hard. Three or four breaths, and then nothing."

He exhaled, like he was reenacting the guy's last breath.

"Winston, I'm so sorry," Mia said.

"I'm not," Brandon said. "What kind of gun is it?" They both looked at him. Winston thought for a moment.

"A Smith and Wesson. I don't know much about guns. I remember Jake said they use the same gun on *CSI Miami.*"

"So you had the safety on?"

"In the drawer? Yes. I mean, you can't just leave a gun around with the safety off, right?"

"Good thing Lily knew to take the safety off."

"If it had just clicked or something?" Winston said. "Good Lord, I don't want to think about it."

"Oh, don't even say it," Mia said.

"She said she slid the thing forward, figured I wouldn't have left it with the safety off," Winston said.

"Smart," Brandon said. "Some people, they would have just panicked. Pointed it and tried to pull the trigger.

"I mean, to think of it, to get the gun out, with this guy standing there with his gun on my neck." Winston shook his head.

"And she didn't miss," Brandon said.

"Lily," Winston said. "She's just unbelievable. I love her so much."

The woman with the book looked up at the last part and smiled.

TWENTY-FIVE

They were in the galley, Mia making chicken caesar salad for lunch She hacked some cooked chicken breast into pieces with a butcher knife.

"It was like you were interrogating him," she said. "What difference does it make, what kind of gun it was? Was the safety thing on or off?"

"I was just curious," Brandon said. "It was pretty amazing, what she did."

"So just say that."

"Winston didn't mind talking about it. Maybe it was good for him."

Mia chopped, put down the knife. She opened the refrigerator and took out a bunch of lettuce, started to tear it apart.

"I think we should just let them talk about it when they want to. It doesn't have to be this kind of grilling."

"It wasn't a grilling," Brandon said. "You want to see a grilling, wait until O'Farrell gets ahold of him the second time around. Every little detail."

"Let him do it, then. These are our friends."

"More yours than mine."

Mia took out two tomatoes, slammed the refrigerator door shut.

"Why is everything so separate, Brandon? My friends, your friends. My life, your life. We're supposed to be together. It's supposed to be one life."

"It is, but you just know her better. I'm not in your book club."

"You can at least be nice to her."

"I am nice to her."

"So just try to think about what she's been through."

"I know what she's been through, Mia," Brandon said. "Have you forgotten?"

"I haven't forgotten," Mia said. "You're the one who's forgetting."

She let go of a tomato. It rolled off the counter, across the deck. Mia stood with her eyes closed and started to cry. Brandon went to her, took her in his arms.

"It's okay," he whispered.

"I'm sorry. All of this—it just came flooding back."

"I know."

"I was all right. I've been all right."

"Yes, you have."

"I want it to stay away."

"I know."

"But Lily, sitting in the police car with her, it was like she was me. I was holding her but I was watching myself, all over again."

"I know. The guy on the stretcher, that's when I felt it."

"We've got to stay together, Brandon. We're in this together, right?"

"Yes," Brandon said. "We're—"

"Ahoy," a voice called from outside the boat.

They turned and saw Winston and Lily on the dock. Mia hurried aft and out onto the stern deck. Brandon picked up the tomato, put it in the bowl, and followed.

They were hugging on the dock when he emerged. Lily, in khaki shorts and a sweater, looked frail and somber. Her eyes were hidden by big sunglasses, but her face was red and puffy. They came up the steps and Mia helped her aboard. Brandon leaned to her and gave her a kiss on the cheek.

"How you doing?" he said.

"Okay," Lily said. "Just kinda worn out."

Winston said sorry, he had to run, he was late for the restaurant, Saturday lunch; his line chef had called in sick.

"We'll take good care of her," Mia said, smiling. "We'll see you tonight."

Winston jumped aboard, gave Lily a hug and a kiss, said, "I love you, baby," and stepped down to the dock, hurrying off with a wave.

Mia said, "Let's eat, I'm starved," and led Lily into the aft salon, up to the galley. Brandon followed, pulled a chair out for Lily, said, "After lunch, how 'bout a cruise?"

"Oh, you guys don't have to do that," Lily said, her voice weak and small. "I'm sure you have a million things to—"

"No, it's a beautiful day," Mia said. "Why should we sit here on the dock. Right, Brand?"

"Right," Brandon said. "We'll just go out to Great Diamond, anchor, soak up some sun."

"Did you bring shorts?" Mia said.

"No, I was cold," Lily said. "I've been cold ever since . . ."

Mia walked over to her, leaned down and put her hands on Lily's shoulders. "We've been there. We'll get you through this."

While they ate their salads, Brandon took a chicken sandwich up to the helm. *Bay Witch* was fueled and ready. He ran the blowers, started the engines. They rumbled and skipped, then settled into their slow rhythmic blubbing. He switched on the electronics, heard the radio traffic: lobstermen chatting, a pilot calling a tanker, tanker calling back. He climbed down the ladder, went over the stern, and slipped off the dock line. Trotting forward, he did the same at the bow, then went back aboard and up to the helm. The boat had started to drift off of the dock and he put the engines in gear and eased it out of the berth, past the floats and into the channel.

It was a busy day on the harbor: lobster boats returning to port, sailboats running with the northwest wind toward the bay, tugs pushing an oil barge toward the bridge, cruisers headed into the Portland wharves, two Marine Patrol officers on an inflatable making rounds like cops on the beat.

Mia and Lily sat on chairs on the foredeck, Brandon seeing the tops of their heads from the helm. He couldn't hear them but he could tell by the motion that they were talking, which was good for both of them, Brandon thought. "Talk it out," he said to himself, his voice lost in the rumble of the engines. "Don't internalize," he said, quoting the first shrink he'd seen after the shooting. "Get it all out in the fresh air to dry out."

He thought of that as he headed for the north side of the harbor entrance, past the Iron Works crane, the big dry dock. And then they were in more open water, the wind picking up. Mia and Lily came back along the deck on the port side, then in the aft deck, and up the ladder to the helm.

"We got cold," Mia said, and she sat down on the settee, Lily sitting beside her. She looked out through the plastic windows as Brandon pointed out Little Diamond, Great Diamond, Peaks Island beyond them. He glanced at her, saw wind-flushed cheeks, but less of the remnant of sobbing fits. When he handed her a pair of binoculars, told her to follow the red buoys up the east side of Great Diamond, Lily almost smiled. And then her expression slipped back to somber.

Mia caught it, looked at Brandon, then said to Lily: "Hey, we're almost there."

They motored along the shore, then swung east, making the narrow cut below Cow Island. Brandon told Lily about the island being a sort of getaway for famous writers like Longfellow and Harriet Beecher Stowe, then about the military buying the island and building a fort during the Spanish American War.

"Brandon, how do you know all this stuff?" Lily said.

"His head is chock full," Mia said. "I try not to respond because it encourages him."

Lily smiled but dolefully, the eyes still sad. Brandon eased back on the throttles and they turned in their seats as the cove came into view. There were three cruisers anchored by the restaurant, a Whaler on the float. Brandon swung *Bay Witch* around into the wind, then gave the throttles a nudge and eased off again. Mia took the helm while Brandon went forward and released the anchor, the chain rattling through the chock. The boat fell back and then there was a tug as the anchor caught. Back at the helm, Mia cut the motors. Water slapped the hull.

"I think it's time for a glass of wine," Mia said.

—

They sat at the stern, sheltered from the sea breeze. Mia and Lily had Chardonnay in sturdy tumblers. Brandon sipped Poland Spring from the bottle. He talked more about the island, the army barracks turned into condos. That got him onto the British shelling Portland in 1775, lighting the city on fire. He looked at Lily, gazing back out at the bay, not listening.

Brandon shot a look at Mia. She said to Lily, "You okay?"

"Sure," Lily said. "I'm fine," and she pulled the scrunchie out of her hair, yanked her hair tight, and tied it back up. She looked away, as though she didn't want them to see, but they saw her shoulders shake and then heave, and then she turned back and started to sob.

Mia moved to her, put her arm around her shoulders.

"It's okay," she said. "It's okay."

"He's dead and I did it," Lily said, between sobs. "What if he wasn't going to kill us? What if he was just going to let us go?"

"That wasn't going to happen, Lily," Brandon said. "No way."

"But what if it could have?" she said.

"It's all right," Mia said.

"He would have worn a mask if he was going to let you go," Brandon said. "He let you see him because he knew you weren't going to be able to tell anyone. You weren't going to the police."

"But—"

"There was very little chance of you getting out of that alive," Brandon said. "Almost none."

"We could have run away or something," Lily said, wiping her eyes, her nose.

Mia reached under the cabinet, found a box of tissues, and pulled one out and handed it to her.

"We could have given him the money and then—"

"And then he would have shot both of you," Brandon said. "Winston first."

"Brandon's right," Mia said. "People like that, they don't even think twice about it."

"When it happened to you," Lily said. "When that guy had you—"

"He was going to kill me probably anyway," Mia said. "And then when everything fell apart, he definitely was going to take me with him."

"But Brandon—"

She searched for the words.

"—got him first?"

Mia nodded.

"But how did you deal with that, Brandon?" Lily said. "Killing someone."

"I didn't choose the situation," Brandon said. "You didn't, either. Given all of the possible outcomes, this was the best one."

"But that sounds so, I don't know, cold or something. I mean, this was a human being. He had a family, maybe. I don't know. Maybe kids someplace. Probably had some awful childhood, a father who—"

"Not your problem, Lily," Brandon said.

"I know, but—"

"No buts," Brandon said.

"What you did took a lot of courage, it really did," Mia said.

"What does Winston think?" Brandon said.

"He says I saved his life," Lily said softly.

"Yours and his," Mia said.

She gave Lily a hug and held out her glass. Lily reluctantly clinked.

"I'm proud of you," Mia said.

"Thank you, guys," Lily said. "For being here."

They were quiet for a minute. Gulls cried overhead, squabbled over something on the float. One emerged with the morsel and flew off, chased by the others. One of us has something, the others try to take it away, Brandon thought.

"I still wonder why he picked Winston," he said. "Of all people."

Lily shook her head and shrugged.

"I wish to hell he hadn't," she said.

TWENTY-SIX

After lunch on the stern, Mia took the boat out of the cove and turned southeast, running through the passage between Long and Peaks islands. Brandon sat with Lily on the settee on the starboard side, pointed out seals popping up and watching the boat pass. "Oh, they're so cute," Lily said. "They're like little puppies."

Boats were motoring through the passage, a pretty Hinckley sloop, a couple of teenage boys on a Grady-White. They waved and Lily waved back, seemed to be regaining her strength. Mia looked at Brandon and nodded toward Lily, looking at the Victorian cottages on the north side of Peaks. "Winston would so love this," she said.

Brandon nodded to Mia, said, "Lily, want to take the helm?"

"Drive the boat?" she said. "If you're sure I won't crash into a rock or something."

They ran out to the buoy east of Peaks and swung southwest. Lily went to the helm and took the wheel, peering seriously out at the sea. It was rougher here, out on the bay, and *Bay Witch* rode the swells, the motor rumbling, louder as the bow fell and the stern rose. Mia showed Lily the compass, told her to keep it at about 210 southwest. Lily stared at the compass intently, jiggling the wheel.

"You can still look out," Mia said, and she looked to Brandon and winked.

They had Lily throttle back south of the island, turn west to thread their way through Peaks and Cushings, north of House, and then west toward Portland Harbor. Mia told Lily about the buoys, "red right returning, green right going." Lily repeated it over and over, then clutched the wheel tightly as they navigated the passage. When a ferry appeared, crossing their bow, headed into Peaks, Lily said, "Oh my gosh, you take it," and Mia did. Lily sat with Brandon and smiled.

"How did I do?" she said.

"Just fine," Brandon said.

Lily looked at him, smiled, and said, "Thank you for this," and gave his arm a pat that ended with a squeeze.

Mia brought the boat into the marina, feathering the engines to back into the slip. Brandon hopped off and tied up, gave her a thumbs-up. Every time was smoother, and now Brandon trusted her to take *Bay Witch* most places he would. During the day, not at night. Nighttime on the water, like on land, could be dangerous.

Lily came to the stern while Mia was still up on the helm. She stepped off onto the dock and stood.

"So how are things with you, Brandon?" Lily said. "I feel like we spent the whole day talking about me."

"Understandable," Brandon said.

"Thanks for being there for us."

"Anytime. Except I hope there isn't another one."

"God forbid," Lily said. "To go through this twice. But you could, couldn't you, with what you do."

"Occupational hazard—even though some cops go a whole career without even firing their gun."

They stood for a moment, could see Mia up top, putting things away.

"What's happening with the baby?" Lily said.

"Nothing good. The mom's dead, no sign of the kid. Stopped at the building last night, and the Sudanese family is thinking of moving out. Say the place is haunted. The baby's ghost."

"Africans are superstitious," Lily said. "Even Winston. He takes all that stuff very seriously. *Duppies,* they call them."

"I've heard of that."

"Yeah, they're afraid of them. A dead person's shadow or something. If a *duppy* touches you, or even breathes on you, you get sick."

"But I thought *duppies* were Jamaican," Brandon said.

"It must be in Barbados, too," Lily said. "Winston talks about them, and he's never even been to Jamaica."

"Really?"

"No. I guess they don't even like each other. Jamaicans think Barbadians are uppity. Or maybe it's the other way around."

"So he won't go there?"

"I don't know about that. But I think when he decided to leave Barbados, he didn't want to just go to another island."

"Where did he go?"

"Canada. A lot of Barbadians in Canada."

"Jamaicans, too," Brandon said. "Big posses. You know, criminal gangs. In Toronto they run the drug trade."

"You do know a lot of random stuff, Brandon Blake," Lily said.

They stood, heard Mia coming down the ladder.

"So, this *duppy* thing," Lily said. "If that's true, would that mean the baby is dead, too?"

"I suppose so," Brandon said. "Can't be a shadow of someone if they're still alive."

Brandon had to be at the PD at 5 p.m. to start his shift. Lily was asleep in the forward cabin, finally able to wind down. Mia had gone to unlock the gas dock for the Aldens in their motorsailer and now she was on the foredeck, a legal pad on her lap, laptop beside her.

"I'm going," he said, coming around the side deck, leaning over to kiss her forehead.

"She's better, don't you think?" Mia whispered.

"Seems okay. Is she staying tonight?"

"Winston, too, I think. Is that okay?"

"Sure. But they're going to have to go home sometime."

"I think there's still blood."

"Crime-scene people are done by now," Brandon said. "So they should have it cleaned up and get on with their lives."

"Getting back on the horse?" Mia said.

"Something like that."

"It took us a while, remember?"

"I do," Brandon said.

Mia's nightmares. Whimpering beside him until he'd finally reach over to wake her, save her once again. For Brandon, the dreams lasted a couple of weeks. Mia still had them, but only once or twice a month. Her fear of small, closed spaces lingered.

He kissed her again. She squeezed his hand, held it a little longer than usual.

"You stopping to see Nessa?"

"Yes."

"Give her my love," Mia said.

"I will."

"Are we okay?" Mia said.

"I am. Are you?"

"Yeah."

"You don't sound sure," Brandon said.

"It just brings it all back," Mia said.

"Yeah, it does."

"That, plus everything else."

"I know," Brandon said.

"Well, be careful, baby."

"Always." Brandon said.

TWENTY-SEVEN

Nessa was at Maple Grove, a rehab center in South Portland. It was out by the mall, at the end of a drive that cut through woods that were mostly scrub oak. There was no grove; no maples either.

Brandon parked and walked in, waved to the nursing station on the way by. "Good day?" he said.

"Not so good," said the nurse's aide, a young woman named Shardi, big and cheerful and chatty, with a tattoo of barbed wire around her upper right bicep. Brandon nodded, kept walking.

Nessa was in the chair by the window, dressed in black slacks, a red sweater, matching red driving moccasins. It was outfit number four, put together by Mia. There were seven others hanging in the closet.

The television was on, a cooking show. A jovial woman cracking eggs and jokes. She plopped some stuff into a food processor, hit the button, said of the pale green goop, "Now doesn't that look yummy?"

Nessa was staring out the window, which faced a garden with concrete frogs and turtles, like a witch had turned them to stone.

"Nessa," Brandon said. "How are you doing?"

She turned to him, surprised. Her hair was pulled back, her makeup done. Shardi was good that way.

She took his hand, held it to her face, the sagging side, from the stroke that took her ability to speak.

"I love you, too," Brandon said.

He pulled the other chair over and sat, arranging his gear.

"On the way to work," Brandon said. "Just wanted to see how you're doing."

Nessa shrugged, her thin shoulders jabbing at the sweater like sticks.

"Shardi said you're a little sad today. How come?"

Another shrug, a half-smile, with the side of her mouth that worked.

"Can't waste time being sad," Brandon said. "Every day's precious, right? You always said that."

A halfhearted nod, Brandon remembering that Nessa said it in the morning, by lunch was drunk, by suppertime passed out. Her precious days were short.

"Mia's good. She's writing, and still working at the library. She says hi."

Nessa tried to say something but it came out as gibberish, always the same sound since the stroke.

Brandon looked for her keypad, a little clipboard thing with a keyboard and screen. It was under a stack of books on the bedside table.

"You're supposed to keep this with you," he said, retrieving the keypad and handing it to her. Nessa held it on her lap, typed with her good hand, the left. Brandon waited as she hunted and pecked, then held the screen up.

SHE'S A SWEET GIRL. DON'T LOSE HER.

"I won't. Don't worry."

More typing, Nessa concentrating, eyes screwed up tight. It was an expression he hadn't seen much growing up with her, Nessa floating along for years in a Chardonnay haze. She held up the screen.

POLICEMEN GET DIVORCED A LOT.

"I'm not married, Nessa."

More typing.

SHE'LL BE A GOOD MOTHER.

"Maybe someday."

I WASN'T A GOOD MOTHER. OR A GOOD GRANDMOTHER.

"You were fine. Is that what you're sad about?"

I LET YOU ALL DOWN.

"You did the best you could, Nessa. But it was a long time ago. Let's not get all bogged down in the past."

YOUR MOTHER WAS A LOVELY GIRL.

"Yes, she was. Pretty like you."

YOU HAVE HER EYES.

"So you've told me. I'm glad."

I LOOK AT YOU AND SEE HER.

"I know you do."

He patted her arm, the sweater draped over the hard bone. "I've got to go. Can't be late for roll call."

A last message on the board.

YOU WOULD HAVE ARRESTED ME.

"Enough of this crazy talk," Brandon said, getting up, grinning. "Gimme that thing."

He took the tablet, put it back on the table. Leaned over her and kissed her forehead. "I love you. Take care. I'll see you in a day or two."

She reached for his hand, gave it a weak, trembling squeeze. Brandon peeled her fingers away and walked out of the room.

He passed Shardi at the desk. He said, "You were right. Not a good day."

"I know," and then she was up, coming around the counter to waylay him. She got close to him, looked around as though checking to see if someone was listening.

"What's going on with that baby?" Shardi said. "The one they can't find. I saw your name in the paper."

"We're still looking for him."

"Well, I know I'm not a cop, but I think somebody stole him."

"Really."

"Oh yeah. I know these people—I used to take care of the granddad—they're from the West End. They're, like, wicked rich, even though they're practically my age. They paid, like, forty thousand dollars to adopt this little girl from South America. Is Guatemala in South America?"

"Central America, but close."

"Right. So I'm thinking, there must be people out there desperate for a kid who don't have forty grand. What do *they* do?"

"I don't know," Brandon said. "What?"

"Maybe they just take one."

"Could be."

"I'm surprised it doesn't happen more often," Shardi said, "the way babies are left lying around."

"You're probably right."

"'Cause people who are desperate to have a kid, they're not necessarily in their right minds."

"I'm sure."

"I been thinking about this. All you gotta do is grab the baby and take off. Who knows who anybody is anymore? This guy moved in next door to me and my fiancé. He says he's from Tennessee or Arkansas or one of those states. Divorced and his kids are grown. But who knows?"

"I guess you don't."

"I mean, it's not like you can ask for an ID," Shardi said. "He could've escaped from a penitentiary, you know what I'm saying?"

"Could be."

"So with this little baby here, I'd look for somebody who just picked up and moved out of state."

"Not a bad thought."

"Not to tell you how to do your business."

"No, that's fine. We're looking for suggestions."

"But how many people around there are leaving? In that neighborhood, I mean. You could investigate that."

"Right."

"All they gotta do is take the kid someplace where nobody knows them."

"You've thought about this," Brandon said.

"My fiancé and me, we've been trying to have a baby."

"Really."

"We don't have forty thousand dollars lying around, so we're doing it the old-fashioned way."

"You're not thinking of stealing one, are you?" Brandon said. He smiled.

"No, but I gotta say, sometimes it pisses us off, these other people, pumping out kids like rabbits."

"I'm sure."

"And then they don't even keep track of them. I mean, how do you lose a baby? I'm sorry, but jeez—"

"I know."

"Unless he was stolen."

"By someone who doesn't have forty grand," Brandon said.

"Doesn't really narrow it down, does it?" Shardi said. "I mean, in terms of, what do you call them—suspects?"

And then Shardi's phone rang and he was outside, fighting off the urge to call Mia and say, "Nessa's doing it again."

"The guilt thing," Mia would say, as she had a dozen times.

"Yup."

"It's understandable."

"Yes, it is. She's responsible for the death of her own daughter, her only child. If it hadn't been for Nessa putting in the drug money, the boat wouldn't have sailed, my mom wouldn't have died, I wouldn't have been raised by a drunk."

"You turned out okay, Brandon."

"Dumb luck. Well, anyway. I've vented. Now I think I'll go to work, nail somebody's ass."

"Take a deep breath."

"Right."

"Did you do it?"

"Yes," Brandon always said. He lied.

TWENTY-EIGHT

Kat met Brandon in the parking lot before they started their five to midnight shift. The lot was crowded, people shifted from the overnight because of the missing baby.

"You okay?" Kat said, her eyes searching Brandon's for clues.

"Fine."

"I mean, you know these people on the Eastern Prom, right?"

"Yeah. Mia's a little shook."

"Understandable."

"Yeah."

"But you're holding it together?"

"Not a problem."

They started walking, both carrying their gear, leather creaking. "I hear the deceased was a hard-core dirtbag," Kat said.

"Professional. From New York."

"Musta thought Portland, Maine, was full of a bunch of hicks, there for the taking."

"Instead he gets popped by a woman who's into yoga and sushi," Brandon said.

"Ha," Kat said. "How's the sushi shooter doing?"

"What you'd expect. Second-guessing the hell out of herself."

"Could I have just fired a warning shot? Could I have just run for it?"

"Right."

"World's a better place without that scumbag," Kat said.

"You and I can see that. Hard for Lily."

They buzzed themselves inside, started down the corridor. Kat said, "There's a story up online in the *Tribune*."

"Didn't see it."

"There's pictures. Lily something-or-other consoled by her friend Mia. You conferring with detectives at the scene."

"Great."

"How's the boyfriend?"

"Winston seems to be handling it better than Lily."

" 'Cause he's alive," Kat said. "Not in the trunk of his car out by the interstate, bullet in his head."

"If that doesn't make your day," Brandon said.

They were upstairs, hit the squad room. Other cops were getting ready. Dever looked up from the bench, said, "Hey, Blake. Came in off duty just to get your picture in the paper?"

Brandon didn't answer.

"You giving autographs?" Dever called after him as Brandon went out the door, headed for the briefing room, Kat beside him.

"What is it?" she said.

"I know I'm not supposed to work alone," Brandon said. He paused.

"Spit it out, Blake," Kat said.

He did: the stop at Granite Street, the Ottos thinking about moving out, Fatima and the *shabah,* her hearing the baby's ghost.

"Gonna come back to bite you, sketching around off duty," Kat said.

"Yeah, well . . . kind of hard to just turn it off and on."

"It's a job, Blake."

"Right. But aside from that?"

"These people," Kat said. "They're from a completely different culture. It's like dogs, you know. Dogs can hear frequencies people can't hear at all. These Africans, the traditional ones, they're, like, spiritually tuned in to a whole different world."

"So you believe in ghosts?"

"Sure," Kat said. "Do you?"

"No, I don't."

"What *do* you believe in?"

"Nothing I can't see," Brandon said.

Perry gave them the latest on the shooting. They wanted to know who Gayle had seen in Portland, where he'd made the delivery. Perry said to put the word out on the street.

He paused, the cops fidgeting, picking at radios, pepper spray, Taser guns. They looked up as Chief Garcia walked in, O'Farrell behind him. The cops were still. Garcia, in suit and tie, stood erect, his face stern. He let the silence hang. Someone coughed. A chair creaked.

"Bottom line, folks: Babies do not just disappear," Garcia said. "Not in this city. Not on my watch."

He paused, looked from face to face. "So he is somewhere. Dead or alive—I want Lincoln Anthony. His smiling face or his remains. I want to know how he left the apartment that night. I want to know who is responsible. And we will put that person or persons in jail."

Another pause.

"I want your A-game, gentlemen and ladies. I want you to put it in a gear you never thought you had."

Garcia moved back as O'Farrell stepped forward. He said a detective division task force had been established. He pointed to a stack of paper on the desk, a ream of flyers with a photo of Lincoln. They were to grab some on the way out, distribute them around the city.

"Blake and Malone, see me before you leave."

O'Farrell stood back and the cops got up, chairs scraping. Brandon made his way through to the front, saw O'Farrell leave the room, followed him. Kat followed Brandon. In O'Farrell's office, they watched as the chief detective flung a clipboard onto his desk. He turned.

"Blake," he said. "Tell me about the Eastern Prom shooter."

Brandon did: Lily's regrets, the weight of the whole thing hitting her.

"No surprise there, though I gotta tell you, lady oughta get a medal. World is a better place without that dog turd in it. She shouldn't lose a minute of sleep over him."

"Sometimes it's not that easy," Brandon said.

"So any indication it didn't go down the way they said it did?" O'Farrell said, head down as he shuffled papers on his desk.

"Not really. Not that I can tell."

"Fine. We got enough problems."

From behind Brandon, Kat nudged him.

"The baby, sir," Brandon said, and O'Farrell looked up. Brandon launched in, told him about the Ottos, Fatima, the ghost.

"They got all kinds of superstitions, these people," O'Farrell said. "Back in their country, somebody feels some bad juju, they pick up and move the whole goddamn village, goats and all. You hear about the albinos? They kidnap 'em, cut out their organs to make magic potions."

"That's mostly in Tanzania," Brandon said.

"We're not talking about that kind of stuff," Kat said. "We're just talking about traditional-belief sort of thing, the spirit world."

"Hard enough dealing with liars," O'Farrell said. "Now we're supposed to listen to people who hear ghosts."

He picked up the phone—their dismissal. Kat turned to leave. Brandon started to follow her, then turned back.

"I talked to someone today who had a theory," he said.

O'Farrell was still holding the phone, ready to dial.

"Who doesn't?" he said.

Brandon told them what the woman at the nursing home had said.

"So the Sudanese people," O'Farrell said. "We see if they have Lincoln, trying to pass him off as an African."

"Or we see if the biker dude has a sudden influx of cash," Kat said.

"Like what? He put an ad on Craigslist?" O'Farrell said. "One kid, slightly used. Raised by a crackhead."

"The child has value," Brandon said. "This woman was right about that."

"The dad," O'Farrell said. "He hired somebody to grab him. Only thing that makes sense."

"He seemed pretty truthful when we had him in the car," Kat said.

"Operative word, *seemed,*" O'Farrell said. "Detectives are gonna hammer the players a few more times. Pass out the flyers, guys. Keep your eyes and ears open."

They did, all over Parkside: Granite, Sherman, Cumberland.

They handed out flyers with Lincoln's photo to everyone they saw, people staring at it, saying, "So that's the baby, the one that's gone."

They stapled the flyers to poles, a few trees, the wall outside the Granite Street community center. They talked to old people, college kids, junkies, prostitutes, a guy in a Yankees hat who asked if there was a reward.

"Yeah," Brandon said. "You get to be a decent person."

And then they were back on Granite Street, in front of 317, sitting in the cruiser, drawn like moths to a light.

"What now?" Kat said.

Brandon shut off the motor and they got out. "I want to hear the ghost," he said.

He led the way. There were lights on in the first-floor apartment, TV glowing in the first-floor flat, lights on at Ottos'. Chantelle's windows were cold and dark.

Kat went first up the stairs, thinking it would be better for a woman to knock at the door. They stopped at the Ottos' apartment, stood in the hallway. Listened.

They heard hip-hop music. Soft voices. A motorcycle passed and then it was quiet. Kat knocked.

After a minute there were footsteps. They waited. The footsteps stopped on the other side of the door. Kat said, "Mr. and Mrs. Otto? Fatima? Samir?"

But it was Edgard who opened the door three inches, said, "Yo, my father's working. Come back in the morning."

"Is Fatima here, Edgard?" Brandon said. "We just need to talk to her for a minute."

Edgard turned his head and Kat pushed the door open.

"Hey, you can't just walk in here, not without no warrant," Edgard said.

"Just here to talk," Kat said, and stepped in, Brandon behind her. To their left was a couch. Fatima was curled up on it, feet tucked under a blanket, sweatshirt hood pulled up.

"Fatima," Kat said. "We need to hear the spirit. The *shabah*."

Fatima turned to the wall, shook her head.

"She's kinda freaked out," Edgard said.

"Did you hear the spirit tonight?" Brandon said.

She nodded.

"Where, honey?" Kat said.

A motion of the head, toward her bedroom.

"Please, can we just check it?" Kat said.

No answer, taken for a yes. They crossed the room, Edgard behind them. Kat opened the door and they stepped into the dim light. There were futon mattresses on the floor. Brandon closed the door, Edgard on the other side.

"You ever hear it?" Brandon said.

"Shit, no," Edgard said.

They waited.

"Maybe it'll come if it knows we're here," Kat said.

They stood. On the other side of the door, Edgard coughed. They heard another voice, Samir, saying "Whassup?"

"Five-Oh," Edgard said. "Looking for Fatima's *shabah*."

"You kidding me?" Samir said.

And then it was quiet again. They listened. The room smelled of musky perfume. Brandon was thinking of the trade routes through North Africa, from the Red Sea into Sudan, Egypt, Tunisia, Morocco, across to Spain. It was spices and perfume, and—

They heard it. So faint they thought they might have imagined it. Then again.

A baby crying.

TWENTY-NINE

"Holy crap," Kat said.

"It's downstairs," Brandon said.

They turned, yanked the door open, strode past Edgard and Samir, Fatima, still on the couch.

"We heard it," Kat said, and then they were out the door, down the stairs, outside into the driveway. They turned, looked at the house.

"I'll take the biker," Kat said.

"I'll take the ladies," Brandon said.

They rapped on both doors. There were lights on in the Youngs' apartment, a dim glow in Cawley's. They rapped again. Brandon said, "Police." Kat said, "Portland PD."

The Youngs' door opened a crack and Annie Young peered out. Brandon saw the neckline of a bright blue bathrobe, a flowered flannel nightgown.

"Miss Young," Brandon said. "Brandon Blake, Portland PD. May I come in and talk to you and your mother?"

"But it's late," Annie Young said. "We're not dressed."

Dressed enough, Brandon thought. He said, "It will only take a few minutes."

The door closed. Brandon heard her shuffling away, then talking. Getting her mother's permission?

He'd raised his hand to knock again when the shuffling came back his way. He stopped and the door swung open. Annie Young stood there in matching slippers. "Mother's in her chair," she said, and she turned and walked into the apartment.

Brandon followed. And heard it again.

A baby crying.

He strode after her, saw Mrs. Young from the hallway, sitting in her chair, her bathrobe and nightgown a rosy pink.

"Mama, it's Officer Blake. You remember him. From the problem upstairs?"

The baby cried. Brandon turned. Saw the baby—on the television.

It was sitting on the lap of a tired-looking mother dressed in ragged clothes. The mother was sitting on the steps of a shack.

"*Grapes of Wrath,*" Annie said. "It's one of Mama's favorites."

Mrs. Young turned to Brandon.

"They find the child?"

"No," Brandon said. "Not yet."

"Probably better off, if they're going to give him back to that drug addict."

Brandon looked at Annie. She put a finger to her lips, shook her head.

"Mrs. Young," Brandon said. "Have you watched this movie before?"

"I got it on Netflix," Annie said. "We can keep it as long as we want."

"So you've watched it more than once?"

"Better than the smut they have on television now," Mrs. Young said. "Don't dare to turn the thing on after eight o'clock. Except the Red Sox. My husband and I used to watch the Sox. For him it was the Sox and his ham radio. Didn't see the fun in that, buncha strangers jabbering away about the weather in Iceland or some dreary place."

"The movie," Brandon said.

"Yes."

"You watch it late at night?" Brandon said.

The baby cried. The weathered mother turned away from the camera and held it to her breast.

"Most nights, lately," Annie said. "Mama's been congested. Makes it hard for her to sleep."

"The baby cries a lot on there?" Brandon said.

"He's hungry," Mrs. Young said. "They were poor."

Brandon took a last glance at the room, the television against the wall directly under Fatima's bedroom. The *shabah* had been part of the cast, along with Henry Fonda.

Annie followed Brandon out, her slippers shuffling.

"I haven't told her about Chantelle," she said. "She seemed almost cheerful today. I didn't want to spoil it."

"She doesn't watch the news?"

"Not lately. She says it's depressing."

"Ignorance is bliss," Brandon said.

"She's eighty-three years old. I think she's entitled."

"Most old people read the obituaries first. See who they've outlasted."

"I figure, if she wants to watch old movies, so what?" Annie said. "After everything she's been through in her life."

"Your dad's accident, you mean," Brandon said.

"It left her very fragile."

"Must've been hard on you, too. Losing your dad."

"You can't imagine," Annie said.

"Oh, I think maybe I can," Brandon said.

"I was fourteen. I look back now, I can see it cost me a big chunk of my life. I retreated, you know?"

"I do know. You grow a pretty thick shell."

"You lost a parent, Officer Blake?" Annie said.

"Something like that," Brandon said.

He paused, hand on the door.

"You watched Chantelle and her friends. What do you think happened to the baby?"

"If I had to guess?"

"Yeah."

"I think they killed him. Could have been an accident. Dropped him or stepped on him or he suffocated in his bed or something equally awful."

"Huh."

"And then they got rid of him so they wouldn't get in trouble. Afterwards the guilt was too much for her to bear, so—"

"So she killed herself."

"Wouldn't you?" Annie said.

"Yes," Brandon said. "I would."

"You're shitting me," Kat said as they got in the car.

"Nope."

"Could be a coincidence."

"A ghost crying *and* a kid crying on the TV?"

"Why not? Let's bring Fatima there, have her listen, see if it's the same baby. Maybe it's two entirely different cries."

Brandon looked at her, put the cruiser in gear and pulled away. "Or we could tell Fatima it's the twenty-first century and this is America. Drop the ghost crap."

"It's not—"

The radio spat: Dever calling in, two large groups squaring off outside the Circus Club on Exchange. "Probably watching through binoculars," Kat said.

Brandon looked at her, his FTO, for the go-ahead.

"Okay, Blake," Kat said. "Let's rock and roll."

Brandon hit the siren and the lights and they swung onto State Street, the cruiser roaring. He eased through the intersection at Congress, horn sounding, hit the gas again.

"Go a little easy," Kat said. "Run somebody over, we'll be filling out forms all night."

Brandon took Spring Street, a right at Center past Brian Boru's. Two more cruisers were ahead of them, blue lights already at the scene. Brandon drove down the center line, cars squeezing over on both sides. There was a mass of people on the brick sidewalk outside the club, punches being thrown. Kat put on her latex gloves.

As they got out, Brandon and Kat could see cops grappling, pepper spray out. "Fundamentals, Blake," Kat called, running beside him. "Subdue and control."

As they waded in, Kat delivered the last bit of advice, hollering,

"Stay on your feet, Blake!"

A street fight was like an onion, Brandon thought, taking the first guy from behind, putting him on the ground, arm bent behind his back. You peeled enough layers away, you got to the core.

"Get your fucking hands off me," the guy was screaming, and then he was kicking back, until Brandon pinned his legs, too.

A girl came out of the crowd of bystanders, snarling, "Leave him alone, you bastard," and landed on Brandon's back. She rode him as he snapped cuffs on the guy, wrist and ankle, then stood and spun, flashing back to another brawl, a woman clawing at his eyes. But then the girl was off of him, Kat picking her up from under the arms, whirling her around, and easing her to the ground, too. Cuffs went on, the girl, trussed up on the sidewalk, one high-heeled shoe gone, screaming, "You dyke bitch," over and over.

A kid—skinny, flannel shirt, bandanna headband—had fallen, and two guys were kicking him, grunting. Brandon ran one kicker back, shouting, "Enough. Stop now!"

The guy smelled of alcohol and cigarettes and sweat, and he writhed loose, took a roundhouse swing. Brandon stepped inside the punch, got the other arm and yanked it back, and the guy bellowed, tried to punch with the free hand. Brandon tripped him, put him on the cobblestones, hard.

He felt teeth brush his arm, yanked harder, and the guy bellowed, "You motherfucker!" Someone was shouting *Kill the cops!*, and then Brandon, crouched beside the guy, pressing him down, felt someone grabbing for his belt, his gun.

Twisting away, he saw a young woman, small and lithe, blonde hair in her face, reaching in for his gun.

Brandon fumbled, got his pepper spray out, gave her a blast, the guy under him, too. The girl screamed, stumbled back with her hands over her face. Brandon got up, turned as another kid, big and thick, face screwed up in a grimace, launched at him, took him down. Brandon was pinned, got his arm loose and sprayed the guy, but the guy's hands clamped down on Brandon's throat.

"Get him off me!" Brandon shouted through clenched teeth.

He saw blue trousers, black shoes, but they ran past. He looked up, saw Dever going to the edge of the crowd, telling them, "Get back."

"Kill him!" someone screamed.

"Get him off!" Brandon shouted.

He saw Dever turn and look at him, hesitate, then lunge away, into the crowd. Brandon was losing his grip on the guy's wrist, the big hands clamping harder, slipping under Brandon's chin. He jerked his legs up, got a knee into the guy's groin, and the grip loosened. He felt hot breath and spittle as the guy grunted.

Then an arm wrapped around the guy's neck and Brandon sprayed him again, point blank, eyes and the open mouth. The weight lifted and Kat rolled the guy off, landed on his chest, and got one wrist cuffed. The guy swung with his free arm, and Kat raked the cuff chain across his face. Brandon grabbed the free arm and they rolled the guy over.

Kat cuffed the other wrist, said in the cacophony of screams and shouts, "Pick a bigger one next time, Blake."

The layers had fallen away, cops at the core now, three guys on their faces, hands cuffed on their backs, cops—including Kat— hovering over them. A fourth guy was on his back, arms splayed up and out, head lolled back, face a mass of blood. Perry crouched beside him, turned to his shoulder mic.

"We'll need EMS, ASAP," he said.

The guy with Kat suddenly started to kick, rolled onto his side, screaming, "He stole my baby. He stole my fucking baby."

Kat dropped down, put a hand on his shoulder and pressed him still.

"Easy there, Toby," she said. "We'll find him. I promise."

THIRTY

It was Lance on the ground. Brandon almost didn't recognize him with both eyes swollen shut, lips puffed out, one eyebrow split wide open, blood smeared like ketchup over the whole mess.

The EMTs looked him over, Lance muttering all the while, "Didn't take no kid."

Brandon and Kat stepped away.

"If he didn't take him, he got a wicked beating for nothing," Kat said. "Toby had the whole crew from the boat, looks like."

"If Lance didn't take the kid, he didn't help him out, either," Brandon said.

Kat glanced at him, as they followed the arrest wagon out of the Old Port. "Hard beyond your years, Blake. Hard beyond your freakin' years."

They did the arrest reports back at the PD. Brandon had the guy with the flannel shirt and the girl who went for his gun. Kat wrote up the fat guy on Brandon's back, a couple of others. Everybody was charged with failure to submit to arrest, assault on a police officer, disorderly conduct. The girl who grabbed for Brandon's Glock got interfering with government administration, attempted possession of a firearm, possession of a scheduled drug—methamphetamine.

"Maine," Kat said, typing on her laptop. "The way life should be."

Toby, on Perry's orders, got one count of disorderly conduct. Lance was treated at the ER at Maine Med and charged with a probation violation—no alcohol or drugs—and taken back to Cumberland County Jail.

The reports took an hour. In the mirror in the locker room, Brandon inspected his face: a long scrape across his cheekbone, an eye starting to swell a bit, his right ear tender to the touch. He dabbed at the scrape with a towel, saw Dever come through the door. He saw Brandon and turned to go back out but Brandon whirled, kicked the door shut.

They were alone. Dever turned.

"Calm down there, Blake," he said. "Little street brawl, you're all wound up."

Brandon moved to him, backed him to the wall, got in his face.

"Now you know and I know," he said. "You're a chickenshit."

"Strong words there, rookie," Dever said.

"He had me by the throat."

"I saw someone in the crowd with a knife. You looked like you had it under control."

"Bullshit. You're a coward."

"Fuck off, Blake," Dever said. "Get out of my face."

He started to shove Brandon away but Brandon caught his wrist, slowly pushed it back. "What goes around comes around," he said.

"Is that a threat, Blake?"

"Fact of life," Brandon said.

Brandon still had Dever's wrist, clenched in front of him like a bouquet. Dever yanked his arm away.

"Tough guy, shoot somebody about to drop his gun," Dever said.

"What?"

"What I heard, Mr. Hero. The guy says, 'I'm dropping it,' gun pointed at the floor, and you put a whole clip into him."

"Bullshit. Read the report."

"Just telling you what I heard," Dever said, his smirk back, flexing his wrist.

"A coward *and* a liar," Brandon said.

Dever smiled. "Just so we understand each other," he said, and he turned and left the room. The door banged shut.

Brandon was sitting in the truck on Granite Street, the end of the block. It was 12:45 and people were on the streets, the sidewalks, the stoops. He watched them pass: teenagers dressed as gangbangers, college kids lurching along on their way back from the bars. An old man with a cat on a leash. He was considering that, why you'd walk a cat—when she appeared.

Fatima. Alone. She had come around the corner from Park Street, was hurrying in the direction of home. A car slowed and kids leaned out and said something and Fatima kept walking. The car rolled along beside her and then a girl inside said, "Stuck-up bitch," and the others laughed and the car sped up, down the street.

Up the block, under some trees, Fatima had stopped. She was loitering—waiting for them to pass out of sight?—like she was waiting for someone. Brandon watched the way she held her head high and proud. She didn't need them. They were jerks anyway. He felt a tingle of déjà vu, fought the memory back but it slipped through.

He was eight, maybe nine, the first year he'd started slipping off to the marina, rowing along the shore, leaving Nessa drunk, asleep in her chair.

Two boat owners' kids, he could picture them. About his age, the girl a little older than her brother. Blond, tanned, big smiles. The parents were rigging a sailboat in the yard; the kids approached him like butt-sniffing dogs. The girl asked which boat his parents owned. He said his parents didn't have a boat there. He came in his own boat. They walked down to the floats, saw Brandon's wooden pram tied up. Cracked oars held together with duct tape; water pooling in the stern from the leaks in the bottom, the bailing bucket floating.

There was some click of recognition, that Brandon wasn't like them, that he was somehow loose, that whoever his parents were, they weren't like theirs.

Brandon still remembered the sly look from the girl as she said, "Let's play hide-and-seek. You count."

So he did, face in his hands against the cool, damp, muck-smelling piling. And then he turned and they were gone.

Brandon searched the yard, peering under the boats and tarps. He searched the boat sheds, scary dark places filled with ropes and chains and faded hulls. He ran up and down the floats, looking behind the boat steps, into the boats.

Then, coming back up the floats toward shore, he heard a motor start, saw a glimpse of a car leaving beyond the gate, the two kids in the backseat. And it came to him, like a pail of sea water slowly poured over his head, leaving him sopped in humiliation.

They weren't coming out. They were gone. They hadn't wanted to play at all. It was a joke, and it was on him.

So, like Fatima, Brandon grew another layer of calloused skin, stowed his smile away, pulling it out only for very special occasions.

He watched as she approached, walking quickly in small, graceful steps, her mouth a thin dark line. Brandon got out of the truck, waited. Fatima didn't acknowledge him until he stepped out, held up his hand.

"Hi, there," Brandon said.

Fatima nodded, kept walking. He fell in beside her.

"People in the car give you a hard time?" he said.

"They're from school," Fatima said. "I don't need them."

Her voice was low, the accent faintly musical.

"I know the feeling," Brandon said.

They walked the last half-block in silence, Brandon aware of the swish of her *jilbab,* the smell of her shampoo, her pink-painted toenails, a gold toe ring on each foot. When they reached the house, Fatima looked up and down the block, then up at the windows of the apartment. No one showed, and she moved close to the building and stopped, back to the wall. Brandon followed and stood beside her, both of them facing out.

"Do you like it here?" Brandon said.

"Where?"

"In Portland."

Fatima shrugged. "It's where I am. It doesn't matter if I like it."

"Better than before?"

"The camp? Yeah. Before that, before the war, I barely remember that."

"Nothing?"

Fatima paused, deciding whether to share more.

"I remember our goats," she said. "I gave them all names. And I remember that my parents smiled a lot."

"They don't smile much now?"

"No. They wear their brave faces. For us."

They stood. Brandon was about to ask her about school when she spoke first.

"Are you working now?" Fatima said.

"No," Brandon said. "I go on at six."

"Why are you here?"

He hesitated. "I was thinking about things, and this seemed like a good place to do it."

"You have a girlfriend?"

Brandon nodded. "Yes."

"Why don't you go home to her?"

"I will."

"You're fighting?"

"I'd call it a rough patch," Brandon said.

"You talk like a book sometimes."

They stood some more, Brandon trying not to look at her feet.

"Do you have a lot of friends?" Fatima said.

"Not really. Not many."

"Why not? Because you're a cop?"

Brandon shrugged. "Maybe that. But I guess I just don't."

They stood. A little boy rode by on a bicycle, circled, called out something in Arabic to kids at the end of the block. A guy in leather and chains and a hot-pink mohawk hurried by carrying a bag of groceries.

"Did you grow up here?" Fatima said.

"Yeah."

"Who are your parents?"

"They're gone. My mother died when I was three. My dad took off before I was born."

"So the State took you?"

"My grandmother."

"Where's she?"

"Nursing home," Brandon said. "Had a stroke."

"Where's your grandfather?"

"He's dead. I never knew him."

Another long pause, but they were comfortable with it now. Fatima leaned against the wall, her hands clasped behind her. The kid on the bike rode by again, glanced at them.

"So we're kind of the same."

She glanced at him for the first time since they'd begun talking. Brandon took in the lovely shade of her skin, the elegant shape of her face. She looked out from under the pale blue *hijab* like a dark flower.

"How's that?" Brandon said.

"We don't really fit in anywhere," Fatima said.

Brandon smiled. "I suppose we don't," he said.

"I knew it the first time you came to the house."

"You did?"

"Yeah. I have a way of knowing these things."

"Is that why you don't fit in? Hearing ghosts and all that?"

"It's all kinds of reasons," Fatima said. "It's being part of my old life and part of this life and not really part of either of them, you know? It's my parents—like, they aren't really here in the U.S., they just have to be. So it's like we're visiting but we're staying, too. Because we've got no other place to go."

"Your brothers seem to fit in fine."

"Oh, them, they don't care. Samir has his schoolwork. Edgard, he's all into LeBron and rappers and rims and stuff."

"They found a home."

"Yeah."

"But you didn't."

Fatima shrugged. They moved away from the wall. She looked down at her feet and Brandon did, too. The pink nail polish and gold rings.

"The baby crying. Could it just be a baby on television?"

She shook her head."

"No way."

"It might sound realistic, through the floor."

"It was a baby. It was crying. It was real."

"As real as a ghost, you mean,"Brandon said.

Fatima didn't answer, looked away from him. "If you had to guess," he said, "where would you say the baby is?"

She looked up the street. Reached up and, under the cloth, fiddled with her hair, pulling out a long dark shock and twisting it.

He waited.

"I think—"

A long pause.

"You think what?"

She twisted her hair, kept her gaze away, then suddenly turned to him.

"I think the baby's with somebody who really wanted one," Fatima said. "I think they wanted one and they saw this one that nobody really wanted. So they took it. Like a kitten you find on the street."

"So you don't think he's dead?"

"I think they're trying to put him in a new life and he's still partly in the old one, with his mom."

"Who's a ghost, too?" Brandon said.

"Yes. It would just be her spirit that's left. But I think it stays close to the baby. Like a memory, you know?"

A pause, the two of them standing close. In the quiet a new awkwardness coming over them.

"If you're through with your questions, you can go," Fatima said.

"No," Brandon said. "I like talking to you."

Fatima looked at him.

"You shouldn't say things like that if you don't mean them."

"I mean everything I say," Brandon said.

Fatima looked away, her expression hardening. "Sometimes things mean more than you know," she said, and with a swish of her *hijab,* was in the door and gone.

The marina was dark at 1:30, lights showing on a few boats like campfires by a caravan stopped on a desert trail. The image popped into his head because of the spices at the Ottos, Brandon knew. The highlight video played in his head: Fatima. The ghost that turned out to be a DVD. Maybe. Crazy old lady and her weirdo daughter. The girl on his back, knees in his ribs. Dever, the son of a bitch.

He looked out as he walked through the boatyard, saw the lights glowing on *Bay Witch.*

"Shit," Brandon said.

He went aboard quietly, slipped below and stowed his gun and gear. Stripping off his uniform, he stepped into the tiny shower, ran water on his back, got washed, shampoo rinsed before the water began to run cold. He stood in the cool water, too, stayed until it was icy, cleared his head.

Stepping out, he heard their voices above him, Winston's bass, Mia answering, Lily louder.

"Shit," Brandon said again.

He put on shorts and a T-shirt, slipped into flip-flops, and climbed to the lounge by the helm. They were on the settee, candles burning, a table of food set up, wine and beer bottles all around, mostly empty.

"Hey, baby," Mia said, sliding off the couch, coming to give him a kiss. "Oh, my God. What happened?"

"Oh, just another Saturday night in the Old Port," Brandon said.

"Brandon, your poor face," Lily said, a little loud, a little drunk.

"I think you need a cold beer, my friend," Winston said.

"So are you okay?" Mia said, touching his cheek.

"Just a flesh wound," Brandon said, smiling. Mia led him to a place on the settee. Winston got up, handed him a bottle of Red Stripe from the cooler.

"Winston brought all this great food from the restaurant," Mia said.

"My friend, you worked up an appetite, looks like," Winston said.

He was up, fixing a plate from the dishes on the side table. He brought it to Brandon. "We've got red snapper, Cajun sauce. Some Vietnamese couscous. It's bigger than the regular couscous, much better. Fresh green beans sprinkled with feta. These scallops, we sauté them in white wine and garlic. Then chill them."

Brandon sipped the beer.

"Thanks, Winston," he said. "Would have come home early if I knew about all this delicious stuff."

"We were just sitting, talking," Mia said, slipping between Brandon and Lily.

"While you were out wrestling drunks," Lily said. "I don't know how you can do that awful job."

"Well, thank the good Lord that he does," Winston said.

"Oh, I know," Lily said, pouring Mia another glass of wine. "I just can't imagine it. Coming home from work all cut up."

"It's not every night," Brandon said.

"And I'm sure Mia takes good care of you," Winston said.

"Do you have a little nurse outfit, Mia?" Lily said. "Some of those white fishnets?"

They laughed. Brandon smiled, sipped the beer, thinking he'd come in way too late for this party.

"So tell us, Brand," Lily said, tucking her legs underneath her, her feet bare. "Any news on the baby?"

Brandon took another swallow, a deep breath. Told them about Lance and Toby, Fatima and her brothers, Annie and her mother. When he came to the part about the DVD, Lily sputtered. "It was a freakin' movie?" she said.

"Fatima says no," Brandon said. "But that's what we found."

"A *duppy*," Winston said, "he could will those people to watch that movie, throw you off the track."

"Oh, Winston, you've got to be kidding," Lily said.

"It's true," Winston said, a trace of irritation creeping in.

"I think the supernatural is very real," Mia said.

"Oh my God, I'm living with a witch doctor," Lily said.

She guffawed. Quite a recovery after shooting a man dead, Brandon thought.

Lily, as though reading his mind, sagged and said, "I don't want there to be ghosts. I don't want him coming back."

Mia put her hand on Lily's shoulder, bare in her tank top, patted. "It's okay," Mia said. "He's not coming back."

"Not everyone who dies turns into a *duppy*," Winston said.

"Probably professional criminals don't get to be ghosts," Brandon said.

"Is that what he was?" Lily said.

"I don't know. I haven't heard. But he wasn't some local junkie, scoring cash for the day. He was delivering drugs from New York."

"Oh, then most def he don't get to be a *duppy*," Winston said.

"You're just saying that," Lily said, and she wiped away tears. She looked to Brandon, said, "When will they know?"

"Soon," he said. "Maybe they know now. I didn't see Smythe tonight."

"I just need to know. It will give me some—"

"Closure," Mia said. "You need to finish this chapter and move on to the next one."

"You think I should write about this?" Lily said.

"It may help you, not let it stay bottled up," Mia said.

"Good to air things out," Winston said.

"What do you think, Brandon?" Lily said. "Is it better to talk about something like this?"

She looked at him, a hint of flirtation in her plaintive voice, her wide eyes. The wine, Brandon thought.

"You're asking the wrong person," Mia said. "Brandon carries everything around inside him. Thinks therapy is for sissies."

"That's not true," Brandon said. "It helps a lot of people, I'm sure."

"My mom went every week for years," Lily said. "I think it just didn't let her forget she was screwed up."

"What was her issue?" Mia said.

"Oh, do you have a few hours?" Lily said, and she reached for her glass, drank.

The short version of the story took twenty minutes: growing up in Greenwich, Connecticut, her mom's brothers running the family company, an outfit that made valves for heating systems. "Kajillions of them," Lily said. Lily's uncles not letting her mom into the business, even her dad ending up with a job there, her mom tracing it all back to her father, Lily's grandfather, who never empowered his daughter to stand alone, kept her subordinate to men who supplied the money and left her dependent.

"Even now," Lily said, still drinking. "The company supports me, but I have no real say. My little brother, who was a total fuckup, got kicked out of, like, five prep schools, he's the heir apparent. In my family it's like women don't have brains."

Brandon was quiet, his bruised back stiffening in the cool salt air. When it seemed the conversation was winding down, he got up, said he was going to check the docklines, take a walk around the marina. He put on a fleece, grabbed a flashlight, and made his rounds. The gate was locked. The yard was still except for the storm of bugs swarming the lights. The ice machine was running. The freshwater hoses turned off. Even the city across the harbor was quiet.

He came back to *Bay Witch* to find the lights dimmed, everyone gone to bed. Winston and Lily had the forward stateroom, the cabin door closed. Brandon got out of his clothes, slipped into the berth beside Mia. She turned her back to him and he snuggled close to her.

"You okay?" she said.

"Yeah. Just tired."

"Me, too," Mia said.

"Nice of you to help her," Brandon said.

"She has some issues. The family."

"Shooting somebody isn't going to help," he said.

"I know. But I think she'll work her way through it."

"She seems pretty well adjusted to it," Brandon said. "Considering."

"And I can talk to her," Mia said. "Her therapist, I'm sure will—"

She paused. They listened. There was a faint rhythmic thumping. A muffled cry, a pause, and the thumping resumed.

"Oh, my God," Mia whispered. "Are they having sex?"

"Sounds like it."

"Huh."

"Yeah."

"Maybe they're feeling better," Mia said.

"I'd say so, at least for the minute," Brandon said.

They lay there, tried not to listen. Lily cried out, the words garbled like she was covering her mouth.

"Maybe it's a way for them to stay close, after everything that's happened," Mia said.

"Could have gone for a walk," Brandon said. "Held hands."

They lay there, didn't move. Winston grunted and Lily moaned.

"Is this bad boat etiquette?" Mia said.

"To have wild sex ten feet away from your hosts, separated by a quarter-inch sheet of plywood?"

"So the answer's yes?"

"Unless you're on the *Love Boat*."

They lay on their backs. The thumping continued, then turned to creaking, and then the creaking stopped.

"Was it good for you?" Brandon said.

"Ssshhh," Mia said.

"And that's with a vee berth. If they'd been in here—I don't even want to think about it."

They were quiet, heard Lily or Winston get up and go to the head. Brandon decided it was Winston.

"I don't get them," he said softly.

"They've been through a lot," Mia said.

"I don't mean right now. I mean in general."

"You don't like them?"

"They're fine."

"You don't like anybody."

"That's not true. You like them?"

"Sure. She's fun and smart and funny and he's a nice guy."

"Just seems like they don't belong together," Brandon said.

"People probably say that about us," Mia said.

"That's just your parents."

Brandon smiled in the dark, squeezed her hand.

"So this company, she just gets a fat check in the mail every month?"

"I guess."

"Must be nice."

"I don't know. Sometimes I think it just lets her drift. Money is a big enabler."

"What's the name of the company? Acme Valve or something?"

"I have no idea. That's the most I've ever heard her talk about it."

"Sounded pretty bitter."

"Wouldn't you be?"

"If I had a paycheck coming in, never had to work?"

"You'd hate it," Mia said.

"A lot of boat time."

They lay still, listened to the water lap the side of the hull.

"He works his butt off," Brandon said, "and she doesn't work at all."

"Suits them, I guess."

"Weird about the New York guy."

"Awful."

"I would think he'd want to make the drop, get the hell out of Dodge," Brandon said.

Mia didn't reply.

"Instead he does a home invasion robbery thing. All by himself. No mask. Pretty much has to kill two people to pull it off. For the night's take at a restaurant with what, ten tables?"

"Must've been a pretty horrible person."

"Pretty stupid, too," Brandon said.

"Aren't there stupid criminals?"

"They don't live long."

"Well," Mia said, "he didn't."

THIRTY-ONE

The baby liked the toys well enough. He squeezed the rubber duck, smiled when she said *duckie* over and over. He threw the plastic rings, though it wasn't really throwing. It was more like he held them and then waved his arms and the rings flew off. Collect them, give them back, he'd do it again. Red was his favorite. He always picked red first.

But it was paper he most loved to play with. Crumple up the tissue paper from the toy boxes and hold it out to him and he'd grab the paper ball and tear at it like a puppy, grinning his toothless grin. He'd fling the paper, tear at it, fling it again, chuckling to himself.

It was the sound he liked, that was clear, so he must have very good hearing. The idea was to sit with him, talking for as long as he'd listen, as long as he was awake. The mom probably hadn't been much of a talker, on drugs the way she was. But maybe that was good because the books talked about imprinting, and maybe that hadn't happened yet.

It was a wonder he was as healthy as he was, growing up with druggies and drunks. But he was active and happy and seemed to enjoy the company, all the attention. Playing catch with the ball (though he didn't catch it as much as push it), hitting the floor with the rubber hammer (he was a typical boy, wasn't he?), ripping his paper.

He didn't even mind when they changed him, grinning up at them, sometimes peeing straight up into the air, like one of those cherubs in a fountain. And the whole time, his name was repeated to him, over and over.

"Sam. Your name is Sam. My name is . . ."

THIRTY-TWO

A text at 5:10 a.m. Brandon rolled off the berth, checked the message. It was from Kat: LOOK AT THE PAPER BUT DON'T WORRY ABOUT IT. He opened the cabin door, heard Mia say, "Oh, my God."

She was on the stern deck, sitting in a canvas chair with her laptop and coffee, a blanket wrapped around her, writing pads on the deck. Brandon came out in his boxers, carrying his jeans, T-shirt.

"You'd better see this," Mia said.

He pulled a chair up beside her. Mia held the laptop up and Brandon shaded the screen, read the headline:

DEATH FOLLOWS ROOKIE COP
A year after hotel shooting, Portland police officer Brandon Blake has brush with two more fatalities
By Matthew Estusa
Staff Writer

"I'm a cop," Brandon said. "Of course I'm gonna have brushes with death."

"I know," Mia said.

"Who do you call when somebody gets killed? The police."

"You don't have to tell me."

"What is this crap?"

"Brandon."

"That son of a bitch."

The story was a sidebar to a bigger article about the home invasion, Lily and Winston and Renford Gayle, the dead guy. There was a photo of Lily being consoled by Mia. The caption said,

---

Empathy: Lily Lawrence, 28, of Portland, is comforted by Mia Erickson, 24, of South Portland, after Lawrence reportedly shot and killed a man during a foiled robbery at Lawrence's Eastern Promenade home early Sunday morning. Erickson was the victim of a kidnapping-extortion plot last year that also ended with a fatal shooting, by her partner, Brandon Blake, 24, now a Portland police officer.

"Did he call you?" Brandon said.

"He left a message. I never called him back."

"You didn't tell me that."

"You weren't around."

Brandon read quickly: the Gayle shooting, Chantelle's death, him being first on the scene, no mention of Kat. . . .

Portland PD hiring him eleven months after he'd killed Joel Fuller, twenty-nine, of Portland, who had murdered another Portland police officer, Sergeant David Griffin. Some "expert" from the UMaine psychology department saying someone who had killed as a civilian would have the potential to carry that trauma into his work as a police officer.

"Bullshit," Brandon said.

"Honey," Mia said.

The chief was asked if Brandon had gotten preferred status because he'd killed a cop killer. Garcia said that a candidate who had shown coolness in high-stress situations would be looked upon favorably. "That's why police departments often hire from the military," Garcia said.

O'Farrell said Brandon was a hardworking young cop who took his job seriously. The fact that he was connected to investigations of the deaths of Ms. Anthony and Mr. Gayle was purely coincidental.

Did O'Farrell feel indebted to Blake after Blake had killed the man who killed O'Farrell's colleague and one-time partner, Griffin?

"In the sense that I'm glad Mr. Fuller is not able to kill another police officer?" O'Farrell said. "Yes."

No charges were filed against Blake in that shooting.

But Estusa went on to quote one unnamed officer who said Blake was "more gung-ho than most young cops," and that, "he'd have to learn to tone it down."

"We're here to do community policing," the officer said. "The days of busting heads are long over."

That officer was asked about Blake's off-duty arrest in the Old Port domestic violence case. Was it common for officers to make arrests while off duty? "Not really." In this case, the incident prompted a complaint of excessive force.

"We were having a disagreement, a private conversation," Louis T. Duguay, 31, of Westbrook told the Tribune. *"This guy, no uniform, comes out of nowhere and knocks me down, sprays me with Mace, slams my head on the pavement. My fiancée was screaming at him to stop."*

"He was slapping her in the face, punched her in the head," Brandon said. "And he came after me."

"I know," Mia said.

Duguay said he had contacted an attorney and was considering legal action against both Blake and the police department. "The guy is out of control," Duguay said.

Chief Garcia said complaints of excessive force are taken seriously and are investigated internally.

"Taken seriously?" Brandon said. "Every dirtbag says they're gonna sue. Don't give me this bureaucratic bullshit."

"Brandon," Mia said. "Easy."

The story ended with Sergeant Perry saying Blake was performing his duties satisfactorily.

"It's like baseball," he said. "Some players always want the extra base, dive for the ground ball. Same in law enforcement. Some officers just tend to be in the action, to want to be in the thick of things," Perry said. "Officer Blake appears to have that quality."

Calls to Blake's field training officer, Katherine Malone, were not returned. Blake declined comment. "Go to hell," he said.

Brandon shook his head.

"That son of a bitch. That wasn't on the record. And Dever, he's gotta be the one. Well, what goes around, comes around. My turn will come, and—"

"Brandon, don't," Mia said. "Let it go."

"And you're on the front page of the paper," Brandon said. "For helping your friend? That piece of—"

"Brandon," Mia said. "Stop. It's okay."

"No it isn't. It's—"

"It is what it is. It was a very public thing."

"But why drag it all back up? That's news?"

"It's still there. It'll always be there. It's just part of us. Part of who we are."

"And every time I come anywhere near a fatality somebody'll trot this out again? This is bullshit."

"Brandon."

"What?"

Mia took his hand in hers, stroked it gently.

"Remember what they told us. Put it in boxes. Don't seal them up, but close the lid."

"That was bullshit, too," Brandon said.

Mia waited. Clasped his hand in both of hers. "No, it wasn't. And deep down you know that."

"I don't need any goddamn therapy. I just don't need for it to be in here all over again. When I'm on the street, 'Oh, you're the cop who killed the guy.' And this asshole we arrested for domestic violence. Like he's a victim, his girlfriend there, scared shitless of the son of a bitch. I should have—"

"Brandon, let it roll off. For me."

He looked at her.

"I'm just trying to protect you," he said.

"But you're not. You're all angry and swearing. And we just had Lily and Winston and that guy dead. It's all so horrible, I could just—"

"It's okay."

"No, it's not. And it's because you're not thinking of me. You're not thinking of us. You're only thinking of yourself."

Brandon didn't answer.

"We've got to be together, baby," she said. "It's the only way."

"We are," Brandon said.

"I used to think so," Mia said. "Now I'm not so sure."

"Sorry," Brandon said.

She looked away, took a deep breath.

"I'm thinking of going home to see my mom, just so you know . . ." Mia said.

She got up from her chair and, with the blanket still wrapped around her, went back inside and below. Brandon stared out at the boats, the harbor, the gulls. Saw none of it.

A few minutes after eight o'clock, pans rattling in the galley, Winston and Lily's cheery voices, chipper and refreshed. Brandon had already eaten a bowl of cereal. He said he had to check on the marina, stepped off the boat, walked up the float to the yard. It was overcast and still, headed for afternoon rain. He passed white-haired Mrs. Forsythe from *Windrunner,* walking back to her boat with her little terrier on a leash, plastic bag in her hand.

"Morning, Mrs. Forsythe," Brandon said.

"Morning," Mrs. Forsythe said, but looked away and hurried past.

What to say to your local rogue cop?

At the office, he unlocked the door, went in and checked the answering machine. Three calls: two selling marine parts. The third, at 7:58, from Matt Estusa at the *Tribune*. "Hi, Brandon. Sorry to have to do the story without you. Love to talk, today or anytime. Left a message at the PD, too."

He'd left his cell number. Brandon wrote it down, left the office, locking the door behind him, and went out to the truck.

Twenty minutes later he was sitting in the parking lot of the South Portland Dunkin' Donuts, sipping a coffee, listening to the news on public radio. Oil well leaking in the Gulf of Mexico. Marine from Kansas killed in Afghanistan. Task force set up to bring jobs to northern Maine. New York man killed in a Portland home invasion, identified as Renford Gayle.

Lily Lawrence and Winston Clarke, the alleged victims. Lawrence the shooter, the incident still under investigation. Nothing about Mia or him. Too hard to explain in thirty seconds.

The door opened. Kat climbed in. Her hair was tucked under a white baseball cap. She was dressed in running shoes, spandex tights over muscular calves, a shell that said SUGARLOAF MARATHON, 2007.

"Did you run here?"

"Over the bridge. Could see your boat."

"Still floating?"

"High and dry."

"Good to know. When I left they were making breakfast. Might've burned it to the waterline."

"Who?"

Brandon told her: the food, the talk, the sex in the vee berth.

"I guess that's how some people react to stress," Kat said. "Sex as medication."

"I suppose."

"Of course, most people are the opposite," she said.

She leaned down, took a coffee out of the tray on the floor, a muffin out of the bag. She opened the coffee and steam rose. Kat smelled it and smiled.

"The way to a woman's heart, Blake," she said.

"Good to know," Brandon said. "May need it."

She sipped, looked at him.

"Trouble in paradise?"

"Ah, it's tough being with me."

"But tougher being without you?"

"Not necessarily."

"It may not be you, Blake," Kat said. "It's tough being with any cop."

"The combination—being with me and a cop—I don't know. It may be too much for her."

Kat sipped again, looked out the window the other way. "I'd hate to see that," she said.

"Me, too."

"So what are you doing about it?"

"At the moment? Sitting here with you."

"That's a start," Kat said. "I'm gay. Better than sitting here with somebody's gonna jump your bones."

Brandon smiled.

"Like they're lined up."

"Hey, if I was bi—"

"Are you?"

"Not in the least."

"So we're both safe," Brandon said.

"Yes," Kat said. "We are."

Brandon sipped his coffee, rolled the window down to let out some of the moist air.

"You read the story," he said.

"Yeah."

"You think I'm doing a bad job?"

Kat hesitated. "Not bad."

"But not good."

"You're doing fine. Just the one thing."

"What?"

"Not seeing the gray," Kat said. "You see everything so black and white."

"It's how I raised myself," Brandon said. "There's right and there's wrong."

"Not the way the world works—not all the time. Not in our business."

"But if not in this business, then where? There are laws. If you break them, we arrest you. That's why I got into this. It was the only place I could think of where the rules totally mattered. It's what we do."

"And we talk to mentally ill people. And drug addicts. And prostitutes. And idiots. And people who need their cars unlocked. And tourists and lost kids."

"I'm not a social worker," Brandon said. "I got into this to put bad guys away."

"Oughta be in homicide, Blake," Kat said.

"Maybe I will."

"Not if you can't deal with people. Get 'em to talk to you. Figure out what makes them tick."

"I can do that."

"Not with your mind locked up tight."

Brandon thought for a moment, relived getting in Chantelle's face. *What the hell's the matter with you?*

"What did you think of the brass's comments?" he said.

"I think they circled the wagons."

"Is that why you didn't call Estusa back? Didn't want to lie and say I was a good cop?"

"I'll lie anytime," Kat said. "I just don't like talking to the press."

They both sat, sipped, stared. The day had started low, was sinking. He steeled himself, the way he always had, growing up alone, watching other kids from a distance. Friggin' reporter, he thought. Some wife-beating dirtbag and he takes the guy's side. The cop is always guilty until proven innocent.

"I want you to do something for me, Blake," Kat said.

"Try to understand the socioeconomic causes of criminal behavior?" Brandon said.

"That, and stop being such a hard-ass. And try to work this out with Mia. Try real hard."

"She says I don't like her friends," Brandon said.

"Do you?"

"Not really."

"Why not?"

"They're okay. I mean, they're nice enough. Just sort of presumptuous. Patronizing. They all grew up with money, families. It's like I'm a novelty or something. Lily, the shooter, she asks all these questions, but it's because she's never seen a cop up close before. She's rich, gets some check from the family company, doesn't have to work."

"They can't help what they were born into," Kat said.

"They can help how they treat people."

He stopped.

"Exactly, Blake," Kat said.

Another pause. They were quiet but comfortable like that, all those hours in the cruiser. Cups moved up and down. Kat finished her muffin, wiped her fingers. People walked into Dunkin' Donuts in pairs like animals marching onto the Ark.

"The baby," Kat said.

"Winston says the *duppy*—that's the Caribbean version of the ghost—the *duppy* could make the Youngs watch that movie."

"Just to mess with Fatima's head?"

Blake nodded.

"So we need a *duppy* detector?"

"I guess," Brandon said.

"Is that all we've got?" Kat said. "I mean, seriously. Three days the kid's been gone, and we're talking about ghosts."

"The boat is back tonight."

"What? The fishing boat?"

"*Marie G.* And Booker."

"You're thinking—"

"We should meet it at the dock. Talk to Booker again."

"How 'bout we tell O'Farrell and he can send a detective."

"He knows us. Tell him we just want to catch him up."

"What are you thinking, Blake?"

"He grabs the kid while Toby is at sea. He stashes him with a friend or something, and then they trade places. Now Booker's gone. Toby's back, but you don't suspect a guy who was fifty miles offshore when it happened."

"And the goal was?"

"Get the kid away from Chantelle. Wait a month or two, then split. Say there are too many bad associations in Portland. You're gonna try fishing in Alaska or Florida, whatever. You move around a couple of times, and then Booker, or whoever has Lincoln, that person delivers him to you."

"Big risk to take," Kat said. "Kidnapping? Class A felony. They could get twenty years."

"It's his kid," Brandon said. "People'll do anything for their kid."

Kat glanced at him. "Present company excepted," she said.

"Right," Brandon said. "You and me, we were raised by wolves."

Kat smiled, reached for the door handle.

"How's Miss Shooter doing, by the way?" she said.

"Lily? She's okay. Pretty jolly, actually."

"She oughta be," Kat said. "Heard this morning, the guy she shot was a serious badass. Long sheet. Drug smuggling, armed robbery, extortion, aggravated assault. Just got out of a medium-security lockup, Altona, a few months ago."

"Huh. Who told you that?"

"Chooch. I stopped at my locker this morning."

"So our friends really dodged a bullet."

"Or two, probably to the back of the head," Kat said.

"And Mr. Gayle, he has bad luck. He gets out of prison in New York, gets sent on a drug delivery to Maine, then decides to rob a random restaurant owner. Gets popped by a trust-funder."

"Lesson here, Blake: Even if you're a badass, don't turn your back on the girl in the J. Crew." And Kat was out the door, trotting away.

THIRTY-THREE

Brandon sat for another twenty minutes. Mulled over most of it: the baby, Renford Gayle and his unlikely demise. Mia, his future with her, with the Portland PD. He felt like he was circling, not finding a way to break through. Finally he tossed his coffee trash in the garbage can, got in the truck, and drove back to the marina. He was going through the gate as Lily and Winston were coming up the float.

He braced himself, put on a smile.

"There he is," Lily said. "We thought you'd gone undercover."

"Brandon can't sit around and chitchat," Winston said to her. "Gotta get ready to hit the streets."

"First there's things to do here," Brandon said.

"Well, you might want to stop back at the boat," Lily said. "Your darling girlfriend has some news."

She dangled it, gave Brandon a hug, a peck on the cheek. Brandon waited until the gate clanged behind them, then walked down the float to *Bay Witch*.

Mia was in the galley, squirting the counter with cleaner, swiping with a cloth.

"What's up?" Brandon said.

"My dad's coming," Mia said.

"What? When?"

"In forty-five minutes. He called from New Hampshire."

"Not much notice."

"He flew into Boston this morning."

"To come here?" Brandon said.

"He has business in Boston. He said he grabbed an early flight."

"It's a spot check. Coming to see how you really are."

"If it was that, he wouldn't have called at all," Mia said.

"How long's he staying?"

"I don't know. The day? He has meetings early in the morning."

Brandon sighed.

"I'll do the helm," he said.

He picked up wine bottles, plates. Wiped the table and settee down. He brought the dishes to the galley and Mia washed them. Brandon took the trash off, threw it in the dumpster. Back on board, he washed down the foredeck, the windscreen, coiled lines. He was wiping down the brass when Mia shouted up, "He's here. I'll meet him at the gate."

"Pipe the admiral aboard," Brandon muttered.

He took a deep breath, headed for the stern.

They came down the float, father and daughter. Brandon met them on the dock, took Carl Erickson in. He was tall, tanned, handsome, with Mia's green eyes. His hair was thick, silver at the temples. He was wearing a black polo shirt with the name of a country club on the left breast in gold. His khakis were creased and his loafers looked soft and expensive. He wasn't wearing socks.

His jaw was set hard, and when he leaned forward to shake Brandon's hand, he looked him in the eye, held his gaze. Brandon stared back, his jaw clenched, too.

"Brandon," Mr. Erickson said.

"Mr. Erickson," Brandon said.

"I've heard a lot about you."

"Don't believe everything Mia says."

"Read your local paper, too," Mr. Erickson said. "They had it at the rest stop on the turnpike."

He paused, let it sink in.

"Don't believe all of that, either," Brandon said.

They released their grips like sumo wrestlers backing off.

"Come aboard, Daddy," Mia said, and he did, stepping over the transom and pausing, hands on his hips.

"Wood, huh?" Mr. Erickson said.

"Yes," Brandon said. "Built in the sixties."

"A lot of maintenance?"

"Some. More if you let it go."

Mr. Erickson didn't answer. Mia said, "Let me show you below."

She led the tour: the salon and galley, the stateroom and forward berth. Brandon led the way up to the helm and Mr. Erickson went up the ladder quickly, stood and scanned the controls.

"Looks appropriately equipped," he said, like this was a Coast Guard inspection.

"Everything you need," Brandon said. "We keep mostly to the bay."

"Must get rough here sometimes."

"It can."

"You spent a lot of time on boats?"

"Kind of grew up here, right in this marina."

"Family have boats?"

"Daddy," Mia said. "You remember—I told you. Brandon's mom died when he was little."

"Oh, yeah," Mr. Erickson said. "Sorry. Some sort of boating accident?"

"Yeah," Brandon said. "Some sort."

"And your dad? Wasn't there something about—"

"I never knew my father," Brandon said, a hard edge creeping in.

"Well," Mr. Erickson said. "That'll toughen you up."

He said it like it was going to wilderness camp, having no parents.

"Brandon's very tough," Mia said. "He has to be."

"Oh, you mean the police work," Mr. Erickson said. "Read about that in the article, the fellow getting an attorney."

"They all say that," Brandon said.

"Well, you still need to protect yourself. I know you've only got this old boat here, but you still don't want to end up on the losing end of a civil judgment. I don't know the law in Maine, but in most states, police officers can be held personally liable for damages."

He paused as he looked around the helm. "Of course, you probably know that," he said.

"I didn't do anything wrong," Brandon said.

"That's a hell of a defense," Erickson said, chuckling. "Hope your lawyer comes up with something a little more effective. Like the plaintiff's history of violent behavior. A credible witness to say you gave him adequate warning, that he threw the first punch, that you had to subdue him to protect yourself and others."

"I had to subdue him because he was hitting his fiancée."

"And you weren't working?"

"Off-duty police officers are still responsible for upholding the law," Brandon said.

"Daddy, if you'd seen—"

Mr. Erickson held up his hand to silence his daughter.

"Complicates things, the off-duty part. He can argue that he didn't know you were a police officer, that you didn't identify yourself, that he was defending himself from what he thought was an attack by another civilian."

"Daddy—"

"That's why—I mean, I'm not an expert, but I would think taking action while off duty would be something you'd only do in unusual circumstances, just because of the increased liability."

Brandon didn't answer.

"Just a little advice," Mr. Erickson said. "I don't know who you have for your personal attorney, but if you're looking for somebody, I can have somebody at the firm make some phone calls."

He reached for the throttle controls, tapped at them.

"Problem is, the fees are still considerable, even if you successfully defend yourself. I mean, it's not like you have deep pockets."

"My pockets are fine," Brandon said.

Mr. Erickson turned away.

"Well, what do you say, Mia?" he said. "Can I take you two kids to lunch?"

"Sure," Mia said.

"You guys go," Brandon said. "I have to be in early. Mandatory OT."

"What, this missing baby thing?" Mr. Erickson said.

"Yeah," Brandon said. "It's a priority."

"Don't know why police bother with these custody battles," Mr. Erickson said. "Isn't there enough real crime to keep you busy?"

THIRTY-FOUR

A kiss on the cheek from Mia as he left the boat, a whispered, "He doesn't mean anything by it." A firm handshake from her dad, Brandon squeezing back like the hand was Mr. Erickson's throat.

"Doesn't Brandon look good in his uniform?" Mia said.

Mr. Erickson ignored his daughter, said, "E-mail me if you need that lawyer."

An hour later Brandon was idling down Exchange Street in uniform, in the truck, slowing as he passed Rendezvous. There were three older couples at a table in the window, tourists sipping wine, resting their feet. Brandon took a left, glanced into the service alley that ran behind the block. When he looked up, the silver Mercedes was coming toward him. Winston was driving, waiting to turn. Lily was beside him, big sunglasses on for a cloudy day. The Mercedes pulled in and parked. Brandon slid into a space, adjusted the mirrors, and watched.

Winston and Lily stayed in the SUV. Brandon watched and waited.

Ten minutes went by. Were they talking? Why didn't they go inside?

Cars passed. A traffic cop doing tickets. A white delivery van pulled in and parked behind the Mercedes.

The driver of the van—white, clean-shaven, shock of red hair, black T-shirt and black jeans—got out and approached the SUV. He spoke to Winston for a moment, walked back to the van, opened the side door, and came out with a cardboard shoebox.

Walking to the back door of the restaurant, he put the box

down on the step, turned, and strode back to the van. He had a jaunty stride, up on the balls of his feet. He climbed in and started to back the van out, the backup thing beeping.

The van edged toward the street, the guy in the passenger seat looking back to check traffic. Brandon turned.

Bruises. Cuts.

Lance. Chantelle's Lance.

He turned in his seat as the truck pulled away, got the plate number, and scrawled it quickly on his notepad. "Small world, Portland," Brandon said.

Winston got out of the Mercedes and Lily slid into the driver's seat. He walked to the door, opened it with a key, picked up the box, and, pushing the door open with his shoulder, went inside. Lily jockeyed the SUV around and drove back out. Brandon turned away as she passed. He pulled out and followed.

She went to Whole Foods, came out with two bags. Drove to Home Depot in South Portland and came out with two more. Stopped back in the Old Port at a wine shop, returned to the car with a cloth sack, full. The next stop was the gym on Forest Avenue. Carrying a backpack, she went inside.

Lily was keeping herself busy, take her mind off it?

Brandon headed for the PD, feeling a little guilty, staking them out, following Lily. It was something he couldn't tell Mia, another wedge driven between them.

He still was an hour early for his shift, went up to Dispatch, the big room dark, lighted by computer screens. Chooch, a tiny woman with an outsized voice, was in her chair, saying, "Yes, ma'am, an ambulance is on its way. Can he talk to you? So he's conscious, that's good . . ."

Brandon tapped her on the shoulder. She looked up.

"New York?" he mouthed.

Chooch nodded, sorted through the papers in a wire basket. Found a sheet of paper, handed it to him.

He mouthed, "Thanks." She said, into the phone. "So he's talking now. That's a good thing."

Brandon read the sheet in Starbucks, tucking himself in a corner booth with his laptop. It was all Brooklyn, all the time, mostly drugs: possession of a scheduled substance (crack cocaine) with intent to distribute, illegal possession of firearms, aggravated assault (four charges, three dropped), criminal threatening.

The home address was Flatbush Avenue. Brandon googled NYPD Brooklyn gangs, searched around, got a number for the Brooklyn North Gang Unit. He called it, waited. A woman answered, barking her name: "Mastro."

Brandon identified himself as Portland, Maine, PD, said he had questions about a guy killed in a shooting: Renford Gayle. "Hey," Mastro said. "We were just talking about that." And then, away from the phone, "Hey, Luis. We got Portland, Maine, PD on the phone, wants to know about Swinger."

A rattle, the phone handed off.

"Gang Unit, this is Detective Martinez."

"Brandon Blake, Portland PD. In Maine."

"Hey, Mr. Maine. What can I do for you?"

Brandon could hear typing. A pause. More typing. Martinez googling him. Brandon heard him say, "Huh." The shooting story.

"We have a dead guy up here, one of yours."

"And we got a few busloads more, gonna send 'em north."

"What'd you call him—Swinger?"

"Baseball bat," Martinez said. "One of his weapons of choice. Aluminum. Softball, 'cause they got the skinny handle, good bat speed."

"Nice."

"Also known to shoot people in the legs."

"Nicer. This is all drug-related?"

"What else is there?"

"So Gayle was—?"

"Low-level. Deliveries. Message boy. Enforcer. They'd point Swinger at somebody, he'd deliver the message; hence, the name."

"Why Portland, do you think?"

"Don't know. Yet. Somebody probably knew somebody who knew somebody who wanted to buy a quantity of crack. My guess is he was doing a little freelance on the side."

"Would Swinger be likely to do a robbery while he was up here?"

"Well, it's like I was telling somebody else in your department yesterday, Detective—"

A rustling sound.

"—O'Farrell. Like I was telling your Detective O'Farrell, Mr. Gayle wasn't the sharpest tool in the shed, you know what I'm saying? He may have gotten way up there in Maine, figured it was ripe for the picking. Sees some chump with a wad of cash, figures he'll supplement his income."

"No mask."

"I guess he wasn't planning on leaving witnesses."

"Instead, a young woman shoots him dead."

"Hooray for her," Martinez said. "I got a few more I'd like her to dispose of. Freakin' Garden Posse."

"Was Gayle one of them?"

"Yeah. I told O'Farrell that. Support staff, but still a posse member in good standing, with all the associated rights and privileges."

"It's all Jamaicans, right?"

"Oh, yeah. Why we let them into this country, I don't know. I mean, don't get me wrong. Some hardworking people. But these guys, like inviting termites into your house. You know where the name comes from? They get into a place, they blossom. Like that stuff in Florida. What is it, that jungle weed you can't get rid of?"

"Kudzu," Brandon said.

"Right."

"You know one of the victims—not the shooter—is from Barbados."

"Huh," Martinez said.

"Not a whole lot of West Indians in Portland."

"Hey, so Brandon—it's Brandon, right?"

"Yeah."

"That's the one explanation, Brandon. Swinger is up there, makes the drop, has some time to kill. Maybe goes to this guy's place—they serve that kinda cuisine?"

"Yeah. Plantains and fish and stuff."

"Okay. So Swinger goes in, has a drink, some Jamaican soul food, whatever. Scopes the place out, too. Picks out this guy as his mark. Gonna grab some spending money. He follows 'em home. Sticks 'em up. Plan is to drive 'em out to some deserted place, pop the two of 'em, head back to New York. I mean, it's Portland freakin' Maine. How hard could it be?"

"Kill two people? Doesn't happen too often around here."

"Lucky you, up there in the country," Martinez said. "Down here, Brandon? Had four yesterday. One fourteen years old. A baby. Three the day before. More coming tonight. They leave 'em on the sidewalk, we sweep up after 'em. Life is cheap, you know what I'm saying?"

"I guess so," Brandon said.

"But, like I said, that's one theory. Not the most likely one."

"Why not?"

"Because these posse guys, I mean, random crime? Bad for business."

"Yeah?"

"Whack another gangbanger, well, it's not like we don't care, but we don't care as much. Hey, they know what they signed up for."

"Sure."

"But some regular guy, kid caught in the crossfire. That's a motivator."

"Right."

"So this restaurateur. Good guy?"

"Appears to be."

"Not a known criminal?"

"Not that I know of."

"What about the shooter?"

"Young woman, mid-twenties. Pretty. Rich family. Kind of a preppie."

Martinez guffawed. "Renford Gayle popped by a preppie," he said. "Well, stranger things have happened, I suppose."

"What about the posse guys? They gonna miss Mr. Gayle?"

"Probably not terribly. But this is a gang, remember. You hurt one of their own, that demands a response. This preppie lady?"

"Yeah?"

"I was her and her boyfriend, I'd watch my freakin' back. And front and sideways, too."

THIRTY-FIVE

Brandon texted Mia, asked her to call him. She texted back, said her dad was still there. It was 5:15. A serious lecture.

Brandon and Kat were walking down the hallway to the stairs.

"Blake," the voice barked.

They turned. Perry was at the top of the stairs. He jerked his chin, a summons.

"You, too, Malone."

They did an about-face, headed back to the detectives' offices, found Perry behind his desk, looking at a notepad.

"NYPD just called. Looking for Detective Blake."

"They got that mixed up," Brandon said.

"Quickest promotion in the history of law enforcement," Perry said. "You talk to them?"

"I wanted to know more about Renford Gayle. What he was into."

"They tell you they'd already talked to O'Farrell?"

"Yeah. This was sorta personal. Lily Lawrence and her boyfriend there, Winston—they're friends of Mia's. I wanted to know if this was likely to be over."

"Could've asked me," Perry said.

"Yeah. I'm sorry."

"Next time, clear it. I don't like to look stupid."

"Right."

"So?"

"So what?"

"What'd they say?"

"It's a gang. They always get even."

"But they don't usually have somebody taken out by a law-abiding woman from Maine," Kat said.

"Maybe they'll think of it like an accident," Perry said. "Like Gayle got hit by a truck."

"Sounds like wishful thinking," Brandon said.

The phone buzzed. Perry looked at the ID, picked it up.

"No, not really. Working it hard, of course. Something will break. . . . Right. Okay."

He put the phone down, said, "This goddamn baby."

Perry took a deep breath, reached for his coffee mug, looked into it, put it back down. "How you doing?" he said to Brandon.

"Fine," Brandon said.

"The newspaper?"

Brandon shrugged. "Is what it is."

"I'll find out who talked to them from here."

"I'm not worried about it," Brandon said.

"I am," Perry said. "The coach calls the plays. I didn't call this one."

"Fatima Otto," Brandon said. "She says she's hearing the baby's ghost."

Perry looked over the desk at him. "What?"

Brandon explained. The *shabah.* The Youngs. The movie.

"When was this?" O'Farrell said.

"Yesterday."

"Were you gonna tell me?"

"I sent you and Perry an e-mail."

"Fucking e-mail. I'm buried."

"I didn't think it was really founded," Brandon said.

"Why not?"

"Well, the movie with the baby crying. The old lady watching it over and over."

"Go get Miss Otto and bring her in here. We want to talk to her."

"Really? About the ghost?" Kat said.

"This freakin' baby. The mom, the hub of the whole investigation jumps off a bridge. Everybody else is drugged out. Her family is totally dysfunctional, no surprise. And the dad was fifty miles out at sea on a fucking fishing boat. So yeah, we want to talk to this girl."

He flung his pen onto the desk. It rolled in a semicircle and fell to the floor.

"She can imagine the baby's ghost, I can imagine we're making some progress," Perry said.

They were out back in the cruiser, unpacking, settling in, when they heard the radio traffic—Bannon asking for some help with crowd control on Granite Street.

"Go," Kat said.

They cut around past the Oaks, down Park and up State. By the time they got to Granite Street, other units had arrived. Cruisers were sideways on both ends of the block, blue lights flashing. Beyond the cruisers was a mob in the street. Beyond the mob were two TV satellite trucks, booms extended.

"Whoa, live feed," Kat said.

Brandon eased past one cruiser, pulled in just short of the house. He and Kat got out, walked closer. A camera was set up on a tripod. A handsome guy reporter, mic to his mouth, was ushering a blonde woman closer, his arm clamped around her shoulders, bare and tattooed under her sleeveless tank top.

Chantelle's mother, Stacy. Her sister, standing in the wings. A crowd encircling the whole scene. Milling teenagers, the kids on bicycles, a very young mom jiggling a toddler in her arms, a kid on a skateboard, doing tricks in place. Another tank-topped woman was in front of the crowd, holding up a sign for the TV camera. *portland pd: find lincoln anthony.* A heavy guy beside her had a sign, too, this one on a stick: *we're poor but we count.* He started a chant: "Portland PD, you don't care. Portland PD, you don't care."

The crowd joined in, turning to the nearest cop and pointing. Kat stood with her hands on her hips, expression hard and neutral. "Stay cool, Blake," she murmured.

"You see her?" Brandon said.

"Not out here," Kat said.

"I'll check the house," Brandon said.

He skirted the cameras and the crowd, made his way to the side door. Cawley was leaning on his Harley in the driveway, watching the festivities. Snuggled against him was a woman with a mane of red hair, a t-shirt stuffed with breasts, denim short-shorts. Cawley had his arms around her waist. He grinned at Brandon, said, "Sucks to be you, huh?" Brandon didn't answer, walked past. He could see the Youngs in their parlor window, glaring out. Looking up, he saw Mr. Otto in a window on the second floor.

Brandon went inside, bounded up. At the Ottos' door, he knocked. Waited. Knocked again. Waited and turned the knob. The door opened.

"Mr. Otto," he called. "Brandon Blake, Portland Police Department."

He walked into the living room, started toward the front of the house. He called again, no answer. When he got to the front room—a double mattress on the floor, a dyed-red mat-like thing on the wall—he saw Otto still standing in the window. Mrs. Otto, in a black *jilbab,* was sitting on a folding chair, arms folded. Samir and Edgard—shorts, NBA jerseys, Samir in Timberlands and Edgard in Jordans—leaned against the wall, staring grimly. Mrs. Otto got up and walked out of the room. The crowd still was chanting. Nobody looked at Brandon. The cop in the room.

"Mr. Otto," Brandon said.

Otto, in his blue work clothes, finally turned. His eyes were big and dark and moist.

"Officer Blake," he said.

"Mr. Otto, is Fatima here? We'd like to talk to her. At the police station."

"No," Otto said.

"You can come with her, sir. I'm sure it won't take long. My partner and I can drive you both over, bring you back."

"No," Otto said. "My daughter, she's not here."

"Is she outside?"

"No. She's gone."

"Gone where?"

Otto turned away.

"Just gone," he said.

Brandon looked at him, glanced at the brothers.

"The *shabah* didn't take her, Baba," Edgard said. "That's bullshit."

Otto snapped at his son in Arabic. Edgard scowled but kept silent.

"They lead you away, Officer Blake," Otto said. "They lead you out of this world."

THIRTY-SIX

The room filled up with cops. Brandon and Kat, O'Farrell and Sergeant Perry. Detective Smythe. They stood. Otto, looking weary, sat on a folding chair. The brothers leaned.

"So, one more time, Mr. Otto. At three-twenty in the morning Fatima gets up," O'Farrell said.

Otto nodded.

"You think she's going to the bathroom."

Another nod.

"And you go back to sleep."

"Yes."

"You don't hear the door open. The outside door, I mean."

"Right."

"And when you wake up, she's gone."

"I think she's gone out."

"Fatima gets up and goes out without leaving you a note or anything? Telling her mom?"

"My daughter, she's been acting strange. Since the *shabah*."

"The baby's ghost," O'Farrell said.

"Right."

"She gets up and wanders off?"

"She gets up. Can't sleep with hearing the crying."

"But she doesn't usually just take off."

Otto shook his head.

"But I saw her out walking after midnight," Brandon said. "And then she went into the house."

"She's outside middle of the night," Otto said. "They lead her away. Little by little."

Another cop came in, shook his head.

"Dog lost her in the driveway," he said.

"Like she got in a car?"

"Maybe," the cop said.

"Where do *you* think she's gone?" O'Farrell asked Samir.

Samir, startled, looked at his father, hesitated. "She's been hanging out with this guy," he said.

"Hanging out?" Otto said. "What do you mean, hanging out?"

"You know. Talking. Chillin'," Edgard said.

"Who's the guy?" O'Farrell said.

"Some art-school dude," Samir said.

"This guy have a name and address?"

"Kids call him Lil Messy," Edgard said.

"Has paint all over his clothes," Samir said.

"Where's he live?"

"Other side of State Street, the corner. Top floor. Across from the community center."

Perry nodded at Kat and Brandon.

"Description?" Kat said.

"Skinny," Edgard said. "Kind of a beard, long hair."

"Like hanging down on his face," Samir said.

"This Messy, he violated my daughter, it's all over for him," Otto said.

"Easy," O'Farrell said. "Easy."

"We escaped. We had very many difficulties. This cannot happen."

The demonstration had folded as soon as the TV trucks left. A few kids lingered, the heavy guy leaning on his sign, smoking a cigarette. Kat and Brandon scanned the street to the corner. No one in sight who fit the description of Lil Messy.

They pulled up across from the community center first, Perry behind them. Brandon and Kat got out and Kat walked across the street to a group of children on bikes, some of the same from the demonstration. They pointed to the top floor of a triple-decker at the corner.

Kat came back and they started for the door as O'Farrell and Smythe arrived. The detectives started up the alleyway to the back of the house. Brandon and Kat took the front stairs.

There were toys in the entryway, a plastic tricycle. On the second-floor landing a mountain bike was chained to the wooden railing and there were running shoes lined up. Third floor there were white trash bags, two of them, stuffed full. Brandon stepped over and lifted them. They were light, too light. He looked at Kat and shook his head.

She knocked with her flashlight, the rapping filling the hallway.

"Portland PD," Kat said.

She rapped again, harder. Perry came up behind them. They looked back at him and he nodded.

Kat tried the knob, pushed. The door was locked. She took two steps back and squared her shoulder. The door swung open.

A sleepy-looking guy stared out. He was wearing gym shorts, no shirt. He was skinny, a tuft of hair that looked like it had been glued to his sunken chest. Another tuft under his lip. His dark straight hair fell over his eyes and his forearms were spattered with paint. Tattoos showed between the spatters.

"Lil Messy?" Brandon said.

"What? Yeah—I mean, what's with all the cops?"

"We're looking for Fatima Otto," Kat said. "Got a minute?"

THIRTY-SEVEN

It was one big room, a kitchen in an alcove. The furniture was a couch covered with a once-white sheet, a sleeping bag open on top of it. There were paintings strewn on the spattered floor: on paper, a piece of plywood, sketches of all sizes. Jars of thinner. Coffee cans holding brushes. Squashed tubes of paint. Spatula-looking things.

The paintings were of disjointed, fractured faces. One, on the easel, was of a young black woman, eyes disproportionately large. Fatima stared from the canvas.

He knew the kids on the street called him Lil Messy, but he said his real name was Paul Boekamp. "It's Dutch," he said.

"You and Van Gogh," Brandon said.

"Yeah," Boekamp said.

"So she hasn't been here?" O'Farrell said.

"She's never been in here. I asked her up once. She said her brothers would kill me. Some Sudanese thing. Whatever."

"But you painted her?"

"Yeah."

"Where did you meet?"

He shrugged his hair out of his face. It fell back. He shrugged again.

"On the sidewalk. What, you're thinking something happened to her?"

"Just want to find her," O'Farrell said.

"Who else does she hang out with?" Brandon said.

"The brothers," Boekamp said. "Some other Sudanese girls, I guess. She walked by with them sometimes."

"Any reason you can think of why she'd take off?" O'Farrell said.

Boekamp hesitated, flipped his hair. "I don't know. It's kind of crazy."

"The ghost," Kat said.

"You know about that?"

"Yeah," she said.

"Then you know it was inside her head. I mean, sometimes she heard it. Sometimes she thought she imagined it."

"It was bothering her a lot?"

"Oh, yeah. I mean, dude, wouldn't it bother you? She said that house was freakin' cursed. Like somebody put some sort of hex on the place. Africans believe all that shit. But I think she was right. The kid disappears. The mom jumps off the bridge. Now Fatima. Oughta burn the place down."

He looked at them. "Without the people in it, of course," Boekamp said.

"Of course," said O'Farrell.

They all waited. Boekamp messed with his hair, crossed his bare legs, fingered his soul patch. "You don't know what's going on inside people," he said.

"No?" Brandon said.

"I mean, these North Africans. The women all covered up, don't talk to men. I mean, not white dudes like me."

"It's not proper," Kat said.

"No, but Fatima, she had a lot going on. Her interior self, you know what I'm saying? She was thinking, watching, all the time."

"She observe her neighbors?" Brandon said.

"Oh, yeah. She had her thoughts. Her opinions. Like I said, a lot going on inside there."

"Like what?" O'Farrell said. "What were her opinions?"

"I don't know if she—"

"If I were you, I'd keep sharing," Kat said.

Boekamp, startled by her serious tone, looked at Kat. Swallowed. Started in.

"She thought the mother with the kid, she was very sad. Very damaged. Only thing she had, the baby, and she, the mom, I mean, like, totally messed it up."

"Was she surprised Chantelle killed herself?" Kat said.

"No," Boekamp said. "Were you?"

"The others?" Brandon said.

"Okay, let's see. She talked about this biker dude," he said. "Said he was a creeper. Like he was looking through her clothes. No easy thing, either, all the crap she wore. One time he told her she was too good-looking to be all covered up, that he'd like to see her in a halter top and shorts. You know, sketchy stuff. She said Chantelle, the druggie, even she told her to stay away from him."

"And Mrs. Young and her daughter?"

"The lady and her mom, she said they were sour people. Really pissed off at the world, you know? Like they never smiled. Never laughed. Just sat in the apartment, peeking out the windows and grousing about the neighbors. Peeking out the windows, hiding behind the curtains."

"About right," Brandon said. He thought of the movie, the baby crying in the otherwise-silent apartment.

"And she also told me stuff about Sudan, you know, the camp they were in? Except it was in Chad, which is the next country over, I guess."

"To the east," Brandon said.

"Yeah, well, she said babies died, kids died, people half starved walking across this shithole of a country to get to the place. Well, she didn't say it was a shithole. That's my word, freakin' a hundred degrees and desert and no government, just a total friggin' free-for-all."

"It's more an ethnic thing, fighting over land," Brandon said. "But keep going."

"Right, well, they make it, the lucky ones, they find there's guards beating the crap out of people, trading food for sex. I mean, these girls having to put out to feed their mom and dad, brothers and sisters."

He looked at them, relaxing now, maybe enjoying it. Brandon had a flash of Jesus as a kid, preaching in the temple.

"You know the Darfur thing. Janjaweed and all that. People getting raped and murdered and shit, and this country, the good old US of A, won't do anything to stop it because there's no oil there."

He paused, started to say something, stopped.

"What?" O'Farrell said.

"You can tell us, Paul," Kat said.

"You're not protecting her now," Brandon said. "It's time to help her out."

Boekamp scratched his nose, fidgeted with his feet. Then, without looking at any of them, he said, "She said she thought the ghost was trying to lead her to something—that's why it wouldn't leave her alone. She was gonna go check it out. But she had to sketch around, 'cause of her father. He was, like, way protective."

"When?" O'Farrell said.

"Last night. Like, two-thirty. She texted me."

"Go where?" Kat said.

"She didn't say. But, I mean, she didn't drive or anything. How far could it be?"

THIRTY-EIGHT

It was seven-ten, the kids back in the middle of Granite Street, bikes swerving, skateboards clattering. Brandon parked in the driveway of 317 and he and Kat got out, started for the side door. Outside Cawley's window they heard the bedspring squeak, a woman say, "Oh, baby."

"Gonna be glad to see us," Kat said.

Brandon knocked, first his fist, then the flashlight. After a minute they heard a door open inside, footsteps. The door cracked. Cawley peered through.

"Yeah."

"Need to talk to you," Brandon said.

"Kinda tied up."

"Important."

"Yeah, well."

"This or a warrant," Brandon said.

Cawley stared. Waited a three-count.

"With a warrant we search every inch of the place," Brandon said. "Without it, we just talk."

Cawley looked at Kat, back to Brandon. "Learning fast, ain'tcha, kid?" he said.

"Your call," Brandon said.

A long stare, and then Cawley turned away. "I'll tell her to get dressed," he said.

They leaned in the kitchen, the blonde woman, Tiffany, back in her shorts and tank top, hair disheveled, smelling of sweat and sex. She sipped Diet Coke out of a can. Cawley, bare-chested and muscled, in gym shorts, took a long pull on a Budweiser longneck. On his big shoulder was the grinning-skull tattoo, Brandon getting a better look now, seeing the knife through the eye socket.

"Muslim chick never talked to me. Acted like I'd rip her robe thing off. I mean, you say hello and they freak out, these Somalians."

"Sudanese," Brandons said.

"What?"

"The Ottos are from Sudan."

"What is this? Fucking geography class?" Cawley said.

"Okay," Kat said. "Let's stay on track. You saw her early this morning?"

"Yeah. Out in the driveway, her outfit on, the head thing. Looked like some kinda witch, standing there."

"Just standing there?" Brandon said.

"Yeah."

"Like she was waiting for someone?" Kat said.

"No," Cawley said. "More like a dog, sniffing the air."

"Sniffing?" Tiffany said. "What was she sniffing for?"

"I don't know," Cawley said. "She was just standing there, like listening."

"To what?" Tiffany said.

"Jesus, babe, how the hell should I know?"

"This was around three o'clock?" Brandon said.

"About that. I don't know. I got up to take a leak."

"And then what?" Kat said.

"I went back to bed," Cawley said.

"You hear a car pull up?" Brandon said.

"No."

"You awake long?" Kat said.

"A while."

He and Tiffany exchanged glances.

"You hear Fatima go back inside?"

"No."

"You hear anything?" Brandon said.

"Her talking."

"To who?" Kat said.

"I don't know. Nobody talked back. Maybe just herself. These people, they're different, you know?"

"What was she saying?" Kat said.

"I have no idea. It wasn't in English."

"And then what? Anything?" Brandon said.

"I heard her walking. She was just kinda shuffling. That's what it sounded like."

"Like walking away? Like—down the street?" Kat said.

"Down the driveway, past the window."

"Toward the street," Kat said.

"Yeah."

"Did you hear her, Tiffany?" Brandon said.

"No. I was, uh, distracted."

The glance again.

"And then?" Kat said.

"Then I didn't hear her no more," Cawley said.

They stood, the four of them, didn't speak. Tiffany raised the Diet Coke and drank, then held it in two hands in front of her, like a goblet of wine.

"I bet I know who saw where she went," she said.

They all looked at her.

"That old lady and her daughter. They don't miss a thing. I came here the other day, she's in the window, giving me the evil eye."

"Which one?" Brandon said.

"Which eye?"

"No, which of the Youngs."

"Oh," Tiffany said. "The old one."

"You think they'd be up at three in the morning?" Kat said.

"The old lady, she never sleeps," Cawley said. "I get off the bike, look over, there she is."

"Nosy old bag," Tiffany said. "Always watching. Probably listening, too, the perv."

"I thought she watched movies all the time," Kat said.

"That's the thing," Tiffany said. She looked around, like Mrs. Young might be listening. "Sometimes you can hear the TV, see the light on. But she isn't in there watching it. She's in the other room, in the window, standing there in the dark, looking out."

"Ever hear a movie with a baby crying?" Brandon said.

"No, I hear mostly talk shows. You know, like *Judge Judy, Dr. Phil*," Tiffany said.

"But she's in the window," Kat said.

"Right," Tiffany said. "Like the TV is a . . ." She searched for the word.

"A diversion?" Brandon said.

"Right," she said. "You read my mind."

Tiffany recrossed her legs. Jiggled her foot. She smiled, like the conversation was a game show and she'd just scored.

Kat looked at Cawley. "Fatima, in the driveway," she said. "Ever seen her out there at that time before?"

Cawley shook his head. "Nope."

"I been telling him, 'You gotta move. This place has got the voodoo hex on it,' " Tiffany said.

Kat looked at Brandon.

Tiffany continued. "The missing baby. The dead junkie. Now this African girl. It's like it's working its way down, you know what I'm saying? Knocking us off, one by one."

THIRTY-NINE

"Mama's resting," Annie Young said. "Can you come back tomorrow?"

"No," Kat said. "It won't take long."

Annie Young scowled from behind the cracked door. Closed it. They heard footsteps receding. After a minute, she was back. The chain rattled and she opened the door and turned away. They followed her into the apartment, smelled a strong waft of air freshener. Marguerite Young was in her chair, crumpled-up tissues arranged on the upholstered arm. She was in her pink bathrobe, blue-veined feet in white terrycloth slippers. The TV was on, cowboys heading off a stampede. Lightning and thunder.

Mrs. Young glared.

"Isn't there any crime going on in this godforsaken city?" she said.

"Yes, Mrs. Young," Kat said. "That's why we're here."

"Suppose you caught the circus outside. I'm sick, too. No consideration, these people."

"No," Kat said. "But we want to talk to you about Fatima."

"Who?"

"Fatima Otto. From upstairs."

"Talk to Catholic Charities. They bring these foreigners here."

"She's missing," Brandon said.

"The girl? Says who?"

"Her father."

"Probably ran off with one of her brothers' hoodlum friends," Mrs. Young said. "Those two are headed for trouble, mark my words."

"Maybe," Kat said, "but we heard she may have been out in the driveway. Early this morning, around three."

"So?"

"So we thought you may have been up, noticed her outside."

"I'm sick. I'm not up at three in the morning, babysitting the neighborhood."

"So you haven't seen Fatima? You, Miss Young?"

The two heads shook in unison. Then Annie Young looked away and back. "I don't want to start rumors," she said.

"About what?" Brandon said.

"I have seen her. I mean, not today or yesterday, but lately. Down the street, with a boy."

"Across State Street?" Brandon said.

"Yes. Around there, on that corner."

She paused, added, "A white boy."

"Well, there's your answer," Mrs. Young said. "Somebody got to her. Matter of time."

"We've talked to that young man. He says he hasn't seen her in a couple of days."

"Lucky if he sees her ever again," the old woman said. "These people, one of their young women starts fooling around—doesn't have to be a white boy. Could be someone from the wrong tribe or clan, or someone who didn't pay enough goats." She blew her nose. Folded the tissue and dabbed.

"It was on TV. One of these Moslem girls, she starts dating this boy. Not some hoodlum, either. Did something with computers."

"Mama," Annie Young said. "I don't think the officers—"

"Pretty girl, too, what you could see of her."

"Mama, they're here about—"

"Well, her family, they got wind of it. But you see, they hadn't approved of it or arranged the marriage, whatever it is they do."

"Mama, I think that was in Pakistan," Annie Young said.

"All the same, these places—hot and dusty. Can see why they want to get the hell out. But anyway, this girl's male relatives, her uncles and brothers and her father, too, they locked her in a room and they beat the daylights out of her. Whips and tree branches and all sorts of things. Horrible. And the poor defenseless girl, she died."

"So you think—" Kat said.

"And when they caught them? Didn't even deny it. Said she disgraced her family and had to be punished."

"I don't think—" Brandon began.

"Only difference may be that this Mr. Otto, the father, he's been here long enough to try to get away with it. Isn't going to prison for twenty years."

"Have you seen him punishing Fatima?" Kat said.

"They don't do it in the middle of the street," Mrs. Young said.

"Heard anything?" Brandon said.

"No, but they might've put a pillow over her face or something. They're crafty, these people. Guess they have to be, to survive in that horrible desert. But they don't belong here. It's like putting a camel in the Maine woods. Nothing wrong with a camel—if you keep it where it belongs."

"Mama, please," Annie Young said, putting a hand on her mother's shoulder.

"Women do all the work, too," Mrs. Young said. "And they're treated like second-class citizens."

"Mama," Annie Young said.

"Don't shush me, dear," Mrs. Young said, and then, to the cops, she said, "I'd go ask the Somalis, if I was you."

"They're Sudanese," Brandon said.

"Same difference," Mrs. Young said. "Wouldn't surprise me one bit, you find out they have her locked up someplace, beating her with sticks."

Kat and Brandon exchanged glances. Annie Young rubbed her mother's shoulder. Mrs. Young blew her nose again, crumpled the tissue, and lined it up with the others on the arm of the chair, like cookies on a baking sheet.

"So, neither of you has seen Fatima in the last day or so?" Brandon said.

The heads shook, stopped.

Outside, Kat and Brandon gave the house a last look. Brandon was thinking of Tiffany's notion that bad karma was working itself down from the top. Kat was picturing Fatima Otto getting a whipping for talking to an art student from down the block.

They got in the cruiser and Brandon backed out, headed up the block toward State Street.

"I know how she feels," Kat said.

"Who?" Brandon said.

"Fatima. I mean, if she got in trouble at home for hanging out with Lil Messy there."

"You hang out with art students?"

"No," Kat said. "I hung out with a girl who was a very out lesbian."

"Your family beat you with sticks?"

"Different culture," Kat said, half smiling as she remembered. "We weren't Amish, but my family had the shunning thing down pretty good."

"Lay the guilt on you?"

"Disappointed them. Hurt them. Disgraced them. Humiliated them."

"So they stopped talking to you?" Brandon said.

"More or less. Shut me right out."

"For how long?"

"It's been almost eleven years."

"That's shunning, all right," Brandon said.

"I don't see Otto hurting his daughter."

"If she was having sex with a white American art student?"

"Well, maybe the art student part," Kat said.

He looked at her.

"Just kidding. But I think he might send her away," Kat said.

"But why would he report her missing, then?" Brandon said.

Kat thought for a second. "Maybe because the punishment got out of hand and she died?" she said.

They rode in silence, both contemplating that sad prospect. Brandon turned onto State Street and started up the hill. Coming down the sidewalk toward them were three women in head scarves, colorful long skirts. Not Fatima.

The cruiser passed them. They looked at the cops, then quickly looked away.

"No," Kat said. "Mr. Otto wouldn't want to get involved with us."

"Then we're left with the *shabah,*" Brandon said.

They cruised Parkside up to Longfellow Square. Students, a few homeless guys, blending in with their backpacks. A drunk with a coffee cup, panhandling. Out Congress toward Maine Med, three African guys walking, in no hurry. Brandon slowed, pulled over. He and Kat got out, walked back. The African guys put on their masks, no expressions, like tigers going still in the grass.

Brandon remembered Sergeant Perry's instruction: *Remember—where these people come from, men in uniforms rob and rape you.*

"These are Somalis," Kat said.

"Can't hurt to ask," Brandon said.

They stopped and gave their spiel. The three Somali guys shook their heads, a runaway Sudanese girl not their problem, white cops holding nothing but trouble.

Back in the cruiser, circling down the hill toward the Expo. Two guys on a stoop, both sex offenders. "Maybe somebody grabbed her off the street," Brandon said.

"There's one I haven't seen yet," Kat said, "somebody picking off Sudanese girls."

Driving past the Oaks, the park quiet, a bald white guy sitting alone in a parked Jeep under the trees. "Always a first time," Brandon said. He was writing the guy's plate number down when his phone buzzed.

Mia.

"Hey," Brandon said.

"Something's going on."

She was breathless, tense.

"What? Where are you?"

"Lily's. She didn't want to come back all alone."

"Where's Winston?"

"The restaurant."

"So—"

"There were two guys. Sitting in a car out front, up a little."

"Yeah."

"I saw them. A white guy and a black guy. . . I don't know. They just didn't look like they belonged here. Looked, I don't know. Big city. I said to Lily, 'Probably it's nothing but—' "

FORTY

Brandon ran a yellow light, headed east. Kat watched him, listened.

"They still there?"

"I don't know. I'm in the bedroom."

"Where's Lily?"

"She took off. When I told her, it was like she'd seen a ghost."

Another one, Brandon thought.

"Took off where?"

"I don't know. The restaurant? She said to stay, lock the door."

"Did you?"

He hit the gas, the blue lights, crossed the intersection at Forest.

"Yeah."

"What kind of car are they in?"

"A blue one. A Toyota or something. But not a little one. Maybe a Camry? But maybe I was imagining things, but they seemed to be watching the house. I mean, I looked at them and they looked right at me."

"Stay there."

"Brandon," Mia said. "Please get here fast."

Kat and Brandon came in from Washington Avenue, down the Eastern Prom. Perry came in from the east, Bannon and Dever down Congress.

The blue car wasn't in front of the house.

Brandon and Kat pulled up in front and got out, trotted up the drive, the stairs. Brandon called again.

"We're here."

The security chain rattled and there was Mia, pale, wired. Brandon took her hand, squeezed it. He looked back and they stepped out, then up to the deck.

"Hi, Kat," Mia said.

"Hey, Mia," Kat said. "How you doing?"

"Show us," Brandon said.

Mia pointed down at the empty street.

"They were there."

"Maybe they followed her," Brandon said.

"Or they were just two guys minding their own business and I'm being paranoid," Mia said.

"Maine plates?"

"I don't know. I just saw the men."

"And they saw you?"

"Must have. I mean, when I pulled in I looked right at them."

"Old? Young?"

"Thirties. One, the driver, was sort of good-looking. Kind of like Winston."

"Jamaican?"

"I don't know. Does 'Jamaican' have a look? They didn't have dreads, if that's what you mean."

"And the other one?"

"Really short hair. A goatee thing."

"It was a Toyota?"

"Or something like that. They kind of all look the same."

"Would you know the car if you saw it again? The guys?"

"Probably. Maybe."

They got back in the cruiser, Mia in the backseat. Brandon swung down the hill to the boat ramp and they did a sweep. A pickup, a couple necking, wide-eyed in the spotlight, the woman clutching at her shirt. A minivan, kids hiding beers. An old guy in a white Nissan, doing who knows what.

No blue Toyota.

Bannon and Dever were back up Congress, swinging off onto

the side streets. Perry was on the east side of Congress, working his way north.

"Nothing yet," Perry said.

"Negatory," Bannon said. "Girlfriend sure it was blue?"

They took the Prom down to Commercial Street, shot over to the restaurant. It was closed. Monday.

Brandon swung around the block, up the alley. Lily's Land Rover was parked there. They got out, checked the car. Locked, empty. Brandon banged with his flashlight on the back door of the restaurant. He called out, "Winston. Lily."

A door rattled next door and a kid—long hair, blue bandanna—popped his head out.

"They split," he said.

"When?"

"Five minutes. Lily came and they left."

"Say where they were going?"

"No. Just waved and backed out."

"See a blue car in here at all?"

Bandanna shook his head.

They walked back to the cruiser, Mia out now, leaning against the car.

"Can you call her?" Brandon said to Mia.

She did. No answer. She left a voice-mail message: "I'm fine, but call me. Brandon, I mean, the police, are looking for you."

They swung through the Old Port, coursing the blocks, waiting for tourists, eyeing the couples headed for dinner, the college kids hurrying to the bars. There were three blue sedans. A BMW. A Nissan. A Ford.

Mia shook her head.

There were a few black men, some white. No pairs.

Mia shook her head again.

And her phone buzzed.

"Yeah. . . . Where are you?"

She put the phone down.

"She's back at the house. With Winston."

"They're okay?" Kat said.

"Fine. They were looking for me."

The cruisers pulled off the Prom, into the driveway. Neighbors watched from porches. Winston and Lily came down the stairs, approached holding hands, apologetic smiles in place.

"Oh, I'm so sorry to get everyone all worried," Lily said. "But with everything that's happened—"

"It's okay," Perry said. "What we're here for."

"You ladies can call anytime," Bannon said.

"You didn't see them?" Brandon said.

"No," Winston said. "Nobody."

"Check the whole house?" Perry said.

"Yes," Lily said. "It's fine. I'm sorry. I guess I just panicked."

"For good reason," the sergeant said.

"Nobody came to the restaurant?" Brandon said.

Winston shook his head.

"No, I was cleaning up, doing some ordering, planning for the week. I don't hear from nobody. Lily, she came, we come back to check on Mia. When she's not there, oh, boy." He grinned.

"I'm sorry to worry you," Mia said. "You were worried about me. I was worried about you."

"And all's well that ends well," Perry said. He looked at Mia. "But next time, get a plate number, if you can."

She nodded, looked to Brandon. "Sorry."

"It's okay," he said, the other cops moving toward the cruisers, the radios rasping new calls. Winston and Lily started for the house and Brandon took Mia's hand. Kat waited until the others had pulled away, then said, "You ride home with her, I'll follow you over."

She smiled.

"Some quality time," Kat said.

They were quiet in the car, Mia at the wheel, Brandon and his equipment belt squeezed into the Saab.

"I texted you," he said.

"I got it. I was with my dad, and then I was going to call you, and then I decided to wait."

"What'd he say?"

They were on Congress, headed toward downtown. Brandon looked out, waited for Mia to answer. He recognized a junkie he'd warned for panhandling, another guy brought in for car burglaries, a kid who'd stolen women's underwear off a clothesline, a woman who thought she was Howard Hughes's granddaughter and the CIA was hunting for her. Right up there with Big Liz.

"Oh, the usual," Mia said.

"Like what?"

A longer pause this time, until they were at the light on Franklin Street, a skateboarder crossing in front of them, board clacking.

"He's worried about me."

"What about you?"

"My life. My job at the library. He calls it desk duty. My writing, which he sees as a total dead end. He says I'm veering too far off course."

"With your cop boyfriend."

"No, from the usual college-graduate route."

"What'd you say?" Brandon asked as the light changed. Two young guys, slouched under hoodies, saw the green and sauntered in front of the car anyway. Mia waited. Brandon, too.

"I didn't say anything."

"Nothing about love will find a way?"

She didn't answer.

"He's only looking out for me."

"I am, too."

"Meaning?"

"You were right to call me about those guys. Even if it was nothing—this time."

"You think somebody else will come?"

"The guy Lily shot? He's a member of a Jamaican posse. They may want payback."

"But it wasn't her fault. He came after them."

"I'm not sure they'd look at it that way?"

Mia was quiet, turning and driving toward the harbor.

"He also said it's pretty unlikely this guy Gayle would just pick somebody out on the street and rob them."

"Then why did he?" Mia said.

"Where did they meet?" Brandon said. "Winston and Lily?"

Mia thought. "When he came to look at property in Portland. Some real estate broker friend of hers met him, they had dinner with a group. Lily was there, they hit it off."

"They usually keep it in the gang world."

Mia turned.

"Brandon, what are you saying? That Winston is in a gang? That's absurd."

"No, I'm just saying it's unusual for somebody like Renford Gayle to get involved with people like Winston and Lily."

"They weren't involved. He tried to rob them."

"Still. How long has Winston been in the United States?"

They were on Commercial Street, cars moving slowly, people crossing in clumps.

"Because when you think about it, what do you really know about the guy? Hard to make a go of a restaurant. Maybe he's got a side business. Maybe he owed Gayle money? How much does Lily really know about—"

A car had pulled out on their right. Mia swerved the Saab into the parking space, slammed to a halt.

"Stop it."

"Stop what?"

"They're my friends. You can't just go around investigating my friends."

"She shot a guy dead, Mia."

"In self-defense, for God's sake," Mia snapped. "She's a freaking hero, Brandon. You, of all people, should know that. And Winston loves her completely. He's a good person. Don't turn my friends into criminals just because you want to play your little cops-and-robbers game."

Mia caught herself. For a moment they were both quiet.

"Is that what you think I do?" Brandon said.

Mia didn't answer.

"Or is that what your father calls it?"

"My father's got nothing to do with this."

"It's not a game."

"I know that. I just think you can stick to reality. Plenty of stuff around here to deal with without making things up."

"The Garden Posse isn't made up," Brandon said.

"You know I'm not saying that. Don't twist my words."

"I'm not. I'm just telling you, I don't think you should be around them if somebody from New York comes calling."

"So I drop my friends?"

"I'd just give them a wide berth, I guess. Until we figure out whether this really was some random thing."

"And you'll tell me when it's safe for me to go outside?"

"I'll tell you what I find out."

"Goddamn it, Brandon. So I'm supposed to pretend to be friends with these people while you're playing detective?"

A couple, sweaters tied around their necks, a baby in a stroller, turned and looked at the couple arguing.

"I'm not playing anything. I'm trying to keep something bad from happening to you."

"Well, I don't need protection. I just need a normal life. I just need us to be us, and not you be a cop all the time and have me standing there on the sidelines, waiting for you to come home. And I want to be able to go out. And I want to have friends. I want us to have friends, together. I want things to be the way they were before."

Mia paused.

"Before I joined?"

"Right."

Another long pause, both of them staring straight ahead.

"I can't go back," Brandon said.

"I'm beginning to see that."

They sat. Brandon heard a radio squawk, turned to see Kat waiting in the cruiser. Mia saw Brandon look over, said, "Go ahead, go with her."

"I'll get you home," he said.

"I can get myself home."

She put the car in gear, turned away from him.

"Mia, this is—"

"Go, Brandon. It's what you want, so just fucking go."

He put his hand on her arm but she shrugged him off.

Brandon got out and walked to the waiting cruiser. Kat waited as Mia backed out and pulled away.

"Follow her across the bridge?" Kat said.

"Yeah," Brandon said. "But hang way back."

FORTY-ONE

They followed the Saab, saw Mia punch in at the marina and slam the gate behind her. A silent ride back over the bridge, Brandon grim as the night began.

A DWI stop on Park Street, habitual offender from Westbrook, floor covered with empty Bud cans. Woman on Munjoy Hill, somebody covering her car with poop. Guy reported saying lewd things to girls from a car in the Eastern Prom Park. They located him, Brandon telling him to go back to Lewiston; if he saw him in Portland again, he'd arrest him so fast his pervert head would spin.

Kat gave Brandon the look.

Dinner was takeout from Whole Foods, eaten in the car. Brandon was quiet and Kat waited until they were done before she asked.

"So what is it?"

"What?"

"The trouble on the home front."

He told her: Mia's dad, Mia wanting him to turn it off and on, being a cop.

"Isn't that easy. Kind of like being a minister—you're never totally off duty."

"That's what she's afraid of."

"You care about each other, you'll work it out," Kat said. "We did. When I first met Roberta, I mean, she's teaching at USM. I'm out on the streets, wrestling drunks. Then turns out she's really afraid of guns."

They tossed the trash in the bin, headed back out. Chooch called, said a subject on Mellen Street was reporting his Nissan

SUV stolen. Kat said they'd head over. Brandon drove.

"So she's afraid of guns?" he said.

"Can't even look at them."

"So what'd you do?"

"We found a way. Guns in the gun locker. I go easy with the stories from work."

"But do you go to faculty cocktail parties?"

"Sacrifices, Blake," Kat said. "The things you do for love."

They were headed in town on Forest, took a left onto Park. Chooch again, saying the guy had called back, his girlfriend had the car. Never mind. Brandon took the left on Mellen anyway, a right on Granite.

"How'd I know you were gonna do that?" Kat said.

Brandon didn't answer, drove down the block. Approaching 317 he slowed. There were two Harleys in the driveway, black and stripped down, both with Massachusetts plates.

"Cawley's got company?" Kat said.

"Mi biker casa es su biker casa," Brandon said.

"When Cawley's away?" Kat said.

They parked across the street, Brandon typing in the registrations of the bikes on the laptop. They came up with owners in Revere and Chelsea. Brandon ran the names, came back with nicknames (Chico and Hammer) and gang affiliations: Blades Motorcycle Club.

Chico and Hammer had not unsubstantial criminal records—assault, criminal threatening, drug trafficking—but nothing recent, no active warrants.

"We'll just see if they can direct us to Mr. Cawley," Kat said.

They went in the side door, heard heavy metal playing, Brandon stepping up to knock. Both of them freezing. Listening.

A girl's voice saying, "Stop it, stop it. No, don't."

Kat and Brandon looked at each other, heard the girl again, "Let me out of here. Stop it!"

Brandon lifted his boot, kicked the door open.

The girl was sitting on the couch—skinny, hair dyed clown

red—a big bearded guy on each side. Her top was hiked up above her breasts, her shorts pulled down. A Jack Daniel's bottle on the floor.

"Friggin' A," the guy on the left said, the other guy coming off the couch, the girl bolting for the door, little steps as she pulled her shorts up. Kat reached for her but the girl ducked and dodged, was out into the hall, the outside door banging.

"I'll get her," Kat said, and ran out. The other guy stood, too, said, "You ain't got no warrant."

"Girl was in distress."

"Says who?"

It was the guy on the right—way over six feet, jacked, tattoos covering both arms, the skull with the knife in the eye socket.

"Says me."

"Why don't you go find your mama," the other guy said, "and get the fuck out of here."

They started toward him.

"I wouldn't advise you to do that," Brandon said.

They stopped. Grinned. The smaller guy—six feet, shoulders like a wrestler, shaved head and goatee—said, "What are you gonna do? Shoot us?"

"Only as a last resort," Brandon said.

The radio spat. "She's fourteen," Kat said. "Hold 'em."

"Said she was eighteen," the big guy said.

"Wanted it bad," the smaller guy said.

"Sit back down," Brandon said.

"You don't know who you're fucking with," the wrestler said.

"Chico and Hammer," Brandon said.

They stared. "You better hope you got help coming," the wrestler said.

Brandon reached for his belt.

"Gonna spray me, kid?" Hammer said.

"Gonna arrest you," Brandon said.

Hammer leapt, grabbed for Brandon's shoulders. They spun together, Chico watching, waiting for an opening. They slammed against the wall and Brandon got the pepper spray out, gave Hammer a blast. He hung on and Brandon sprayed him again, Hammer letting go with one hand, reaching for his eyes, Brandon putting a leg in, slamming him to the floor.

The house shook. Brandon was on Hammer's back, yanking the arms up, the guy pulling one arm underneath him.

"Stop resisting!" Brandon shouted, reaching for the yellow Taser gun, turning and aiming it at Chico, coming toward him.

"You first," Brandon said, the gun's ready-light on, and Chico stopped. Kat blew into the room, leapt over Brandon and Hammer, and drove Chico back onto the couch, kicked his legs out, rolled him over, locked his legs up with hers, and cuffed him.

"You're under arrest," she said, "on a charge of unlawful sexual contact, criminal restraint, supplying alcohol to a minor. You have the right to remain silent," Kat said.

"Kiss my ass—," Chico said.

"Wouldn't kiss your shadow," Kat said. "And I promise that every filthy word that comes out of your filthy mouth will be held against you."

Hammer let his other arm go slack and Brandon yanked it up, got the cuff on the wrist.

"Where's Cawley?" Brandon said.

"You're a dead man," Hammer said.

The arrest wagon, Hammer and Chico with fists full of cash for bail, the girl turned over to a state child protective worker. More reports, typed out in the cruiser, e-mailed in.

"They can say what they want about you, Blake," Kat said. "You're no pussy."

Brandon pulled away, headed toward the ballpark, quiet with the Sea Dogs away. He took a right and Kat cleared her throat, said, "This thing with Mia."

"Yeah," Brandon said. "I guess she just feels like—"

Kat held up her hand. The radio had garbled something and they'd missed it, but other units were coming back.

"Black or white?" someone said. Perry.

The dispatcher, Mary Vee, not Chooch, said, "Young black female."

"Shit," Kat said.

"What?" Brandon said.

"Another floater, Blake," she said.

FORTY-TWO

Cruisers on the wharf, a police launch easing up to the float below, a lump under a green tarp on the stern deck, water puddled around it. Cops peering down.

Déjà vu.

It had started to rain, a shower that came in bursts with the wind. A rescue truck rolled in, no siren, lights flashing, wipers keeping time. The crew yanked a stretcher from the back, dropped the wheels down, rolled it to the edge of the ramp, carried it down to the float, lowered it again. The EMTs stepped over the gunwales of the launch, reached back and eased the stretcher onto the deck. For a moment they stood, looking down, and then they squatted. Lifted. Water ran onto the deck, then onto the stretcher as they laid the body on it. The rescue crew, a man and woman, hopped onto the float. The launch officers lifted the stretcher back onto the float and the rescue crew raised the stretcher and pushed it up the ramp to the wharf.

Gulls circled and cried, waiting for scraps from the catch. A bare foot dropped from the edge of the tarp, the sole the color of cooked salmon.

"Oh, no," Brandon murmured. Kat, standing beside him, touched his arm.

O'Farrell and Smythe, grim-faced, stepped closer. It was O'Farrell who nodded to the woman from Rescue. She reached for the edge of the tarp, peeled it back. Fatima Otto stared up at them like a patient from a hospital bed. Rain fell on her skin. One drop. Another. Another.

"God damn it, " Brandon said.

O'Farrell looked at him.

"The Otto girl?"

Brandon nodded. O'Farrell crouched over Fatima, her open lips pinkish like her feet. The rose-colored *hijab* had slipped down and was gathered in a sodden lump under her neck. Her hair was black and thick, clinging to her head like seaweed. Crabs had already started on her nose and ears, the picks showing white.

"Going over the rail here like freaking lemmings," Perry said.

"That's a myth," Brandon said.

"What?" Perry said.

"That lemmings commit mass suicide."

Perry looked at Kat.

"It's like riding with a Trivial Pursuit game," she said.

"Yeah, well, these girls, no myth about that," O'Farrell said.

O'Farrell nodded to the Rescue tech and she covered Fatima gently, as if not to wake her. The detective stood.

"I can see Chantelle, blaming herself for losing her child," Brandon said. "But not Fatima."

"You don't always know what's going on in a person's head," Kat said.

"We'll look for a note," O'Farrell said. "Maybe she told somebody."

"We can round up the Ottos," Perry said.

"The painter kid," Kat said.

"Cawley, the biker," Brandon said. "He hit on her. At least, that's what she told Lil Messy."

"Who else did she talk to?" O'Farrell said. "Who were her confidants?"

"I talked to her once," Brandon said.

"What'd she say?"

"Said she didn't really fit in here. Felt like she didn't fit in anywhere."

"And she had this ghost thing going on," O'Farrell said.

"So the ghost, it's one more thing that isolates Fatima, makes her feel even more alienated," Kat said.

"It's never just one thing," O'Farrell said. "It's a lot of straws, and one just happens to break the camel's back."

He looked over as the rescue techs slid Fatima into the back of the truck.

"So to speak," O'Farrell said.

The three cruisers rolled down Granite Street, Kat and Brandon, O'Farrell and Smythe, Perry alone. Well past midnight, and kids were on the sidewalks, looking up, calling out, "Hey, Five-Oh." The cars pulled up like they were delivering an important person, not just grim news.

O'Farrell led the way up the driveway, motioned to Brandon and Kat, saying, "Start on the building but give me five. I want to tell the dad first, out of respect."

He went inside with Smythe. Brandon checked his watch. Kids had gathered at the end of the driveway, wondering what the cops wanted, sensing that this wasn't the usual noise complaint, someone serving a warrant. The crowd started to grow, bicycles coursing back and forth, one kid dribbling a basketball. And then, four minutes gone, there was a shriek from inside. Then a wail.

The kid held the basketball. Mrs. Otto had gotten the news. They waited and O'Farrell got on the radio. They were going to have tea with the parents. Everybody else could move.

"Let's go," Perry said.

Kat and Brandon hit the first floor, no answer at Cawley's, no bike in the driveway. The Youngs were home, the television cackling. They rang the bell, waited. After five minutes they heard shuffling inside, the TV still playing loudly. Brandon hit the bell again and they stood close, out of the rain. Another five minutes passed and then the chains rattled and the door shuddered open.

Annie Young appeared, bathrobe snugly in place.

"Now what?" she said.

"Sorry to bother you," Kat said.

"I'd like to say it's no bother, but it is, getting someone out of the shower at one in the morning."

"Sorry," Kat said. "But it's important."

Kat told her why they were there. Annie Young said, "I'm very sorry. She seemed like a nice girl. Isn't that always the way, though? The good suffer all sorts of calamities while the hooligans and criminals go their merry way."

"Had you seen Fatima recently?"

"Just walking down the street."

"Not to talk to?"

"No. We wouldn't have much to talk about."

"The weather? Things in the neighborhood?" Brandon said.

"Africans don't make small talk with white people," Annie Young said.

"So you wouldn't know if she'd been despondent?" Kat said.

"The black thing on their heads, they always look like they're going to a funeral," Annie Young said. "But no. She was very quiet. Kept in her place by her father, I would say. That's how those families work."

"Really."

"You should know that, working with these people. Cultural differences are very important."

"Thanks for the advice," Kat said.

"How is your mother?" Brandon said.

"In general, fine. This moment, sleeping."

"I hear her TV," Brandon said.

"She sleeps right through it. And it drowns out the scum on the street and the fornicators next door."

"Fornicators?" Kat said.

"The biker and his porn star."

"Oh."

"I tell you, this street has gone completely to hell."

"In general, or in the past few days?" Brandon said.

"In general."

"It does seem like one thing after another," Kat said. "Especially since Chantelle's baby went missing."

She looked away, then back at Annie Young.

"What do you think happened there—if you had to come up with a theory?"

"Well, none of my business, but Mom and I figure she probably gave it away. Traded it for pot or something."

"Is that right?" Brandon said.

"Too addled in the head to know what she had."

"What she had?" Kat said.

"You know what white families will pay for a healthy white American baby?"

"It's illegal to sell a child," Brandon said.

"Oh, there are ways a mother can be compensated. Look at the way these women rent out their wombs."

"Surrogates," Kat said.

"Right. It's like these lesbians and gays, they can't make their own so they need to adopt from someone normal. Sometimes they even take the egg from the lesbian and the, well, you know, from some man, and they do the implant thing and the lesbian actually has a baby."

"No kidding," Kat said.

"Any aberration you can think of, it's out there."

"Really," Brandon said.

"I think one of her crew, the druggie crowd, they looked at that little baby and they saw a gold mine. Stole him and sold him on the black market. You'll never find him."

"We're working on it," Kat said.

"Might be a good thing in the end. He had no future there. Fifteen years, he'd have been drinking and drugging himself."

"You sound like your mother," Brandon said.

"Like my mother says, apple doesn't fall far from the tree," Annie Young said.

They paused. Brandon thought Annie Young seemed remarkably chipper for someone who had just learned that one of her neighbors had been fished out of the harbor.

"So, Fatima, she would have been imagining the ghost, if Lincoln had been sold to some couple somewhere."

"Those people conjure up all sorts of hoodoo and voodoo. It's part of their nature."

"And they're good dancers," Brandon said.

She looked at him.

"You think we should be concentrating on Chantelle's friends and acquaintances?" Kat said.

"No," Annie Young said. "You find him, her dysfunctional drug-addicted family will just drag him back down. I think wherever he is, most likely he's better off."

The conversation paused, the rain falling steadily and dripping from the overhang onto the steps. Annie Young said, "Well, I guess—"

"Your neighbor, Mr. Cawley," Brandon said.

"The fornicator."

"Yeah. Have you ever heard him or seen him behave inappropriately toward Fatima Otto?"

"The man wouldn't know appropriate if it hit him in the head. I've felt him looking me over."

Now that's inappropriate, Brandon thought.

"Did he say something?" he said.

"No, but women can sense these things."

Annie Young looked at Kat for confirmation.

Kat smiled. "Men," she said. "They're animals."

"Anything else about Fatima that you can think of?" Brandon said.

Annie Young hesitated, looked up and down the street, as though someone might be listening out there in the dark and the rain.

"I've seen her talking with the white boy," she said. "Down the street. And you know how these people are about their daughters. If they're not virgins—"

"Was she talking with him or having sex with him?" Kat said.

"One leads to the other," Annie Young said, tightening the belt on her robe. "Maybe he tried to force himself on her and she was so ashamed that—"

"Small guy, artsy-looking?" Brandon said.

"I don't know about artsy. I just remember he looked dirty. Clothes all raggedy, hair hanging down on his face. I said to myself, 'Oh, dear. They come all the way from Somalia—' "

"Sudan," Brandon said.

"Whatever. They come all this way and think they're going to get a piece of the American dream, and this is what this poor girl ends up with? This raggedy mongrel? It was really kind of sad."

"Oh, it is sad all right," Brandon said. "It's sad all around."

FORTY-THREE

If it had been TV, they would have pounded on Lil Messy's door, told him paint from his apartment had been found on Fatima, interrogated him until he confessed, Lil Messy in tears, saying he didn't mean to kill her. But if he couldn't have her, nobody could.

As it was, Brandon and Mia sat in the cruiser in the 7-Eleven parking lot, wrote up their interview with Annie Young, e-mailed it to Perry and O'Farrell, and spent the rest of the night answering calls.

They arrested a guy at Longfellow Square for public drinking, added an assault charge after he spat beer in Brandon's face.

A traffic stop on Sherman Street brought in a guy wanted for failure to appear in court in Bangor, his girlfriend for being a fugitive from justice in Massachusetts, where she'd jumped bail on a heroin possession charge. At 2 a.m., they stopped a pickup on State Street for a taillight out, found a two-year-old without a car seat, the driver drunk but not as drunk as her boyfriend, who was sitting in the passenger seat covered with vomit. At 3:45, a domestic on Sherman Street ended with the guy arrested for possession of a firearm, a loaded shotgun, by a felon.

Writing the stuff up took until just before six, when Brandon and Kat stepped out into the gray rain and headed for the parking lot. Kat said she was going for a training swim off Scarborough Beach. Brandon said, "You know Lance, Chantelle's boyfriend."

"Yeah," Kat said.

"I saw him with another guy, delivering something to a restaurant in the Old Port."

"Lance got a job?"

"Would he?"

"It'd be a first. What's the restaurant?"

He told her.

"But that's your friend there, on the Eastern Prom. The girlfriend—"

"Right."

"Who was Lance with?"

"Didn't recognize him. I have a plate number."

"Strange, but there's no shortage of dirtbags working in restaurants."

"But there was something weird about it. They brought in this little package, size of a shoe box."

"Organic foie gras."

"I was thinking more like an ounce of coke."

"Be right up Lance's alley," Kat said. "Your friend a cokehead?"

"I don't think so."

"Dealing out of the place?"

"I don't know. Doubt it."

"Don't need track marks to be in the drug business," Kat said.

They paused.

"This isn't going to help you at home," Kat said.

"No."

"You going to tell her?"

"I don't know."

"Discretion, Brandon," Kat said. "It's the better part of valor."

"That was Falstaff, in *Henry the Fourth*. He was a coward."

"No getting anything past you, Blake," Kat said, and she slapped him on the shoulder and started for her car. Brandon walked toward his truck, turned around as Kat's SUV pulled away, and walked back to the building. He tapped in the code, strode down the corridor, stepped into the dim dispatch center. Two dispatchers on, and one was Chooch. She smiled when she saw him, took a pull on her Diet Coke.

"Only come to see me when you want something, Blake," she said, in her smoker's rasp.

"Not true, Chooch. I come by to enjoy your company."

Chooch said the van was registered to Wyatt Gross, twenty-six, Washington Street address. Record showed a few misdemeanors. Pot. Civil possession. DWI, but only one. Criminal threatening reduced to disorderly conduct. And way back, illegal transportation of a firearm. A loaded rifle in a moving vehicle.

"Date on that one?" Brandon said.

"November twelfth," Chooch said.

"Deer season."

"Nothing for almost a year," Chooch said. "Been a good boy."

"Regular Eagle Scout," Brandon said. "Or he hasn't been caught."

"Those are the choices, Blake," Chooch said. She handed his pad back, Gross's address scribbled in. Sipped her soda. Put it down with a thump. The phone light flashed and she hit the button, winked at Brandon and said, "Call me when you're single, Blake. I could use a boy toy." Then, "Portland Police Department. How can I help you?"

A cold summer rain, the boats in the harbor faded into the mist. This was the real ocean, Brandon thought. Like a gun: gray and cold and deadly in the wrong hands. The sunny days, blue skies, white sails pasted on the glittering bay—that was the illusion, the bait to suck you in.

He drove slowly, lost in thought as he crossed the bridge. Lance with a guy who knew Winston. The two of them delivering something. But what? Food? Drugs? A gun? Maybe that was where Winston had picked up the handgun Lily used. But why not buy one at Cabela's or someplace? Because he's from Barbados? Can you buy a firearm if you're here with a green card?

He was still mulling everything over as he came off the bridge.

Winston and Fatima, Annie Young and Renford Gayle, Fatima's ghetto-fabulous brothers, Mr. Otto, inviting the cops to come in and have tea. When your life is pockmarked with tragedy, you come up with rituals to maintain your dignity. Tea. Funerals.

Out of the truck, across the lot. Another code punched in. Brandon thinking he was going to have to filter his day for Mia—tell her about Fatima, nothing about the gun guy. He scowled at the prospect: half-truths, lies of omission. What sort of relationship was that? Or he could just tell her everything, let the chips fall—

He saw the dock cart at the stern of the boat. It was loaded up, duffels, backpacks, garbage bags. He stepped around the cart, onto the stern. Mia was at the desk in the salon, writing. She turned. Her eyes were puffy and pink.

"Hey," Brandon said.

"I was writing you a note."

She looked down at the paper.

"I'm moving back to the apartment, Brandon."

"You're leaving?"

Mia turned and looked at him.

"I need a break. I need to think, and I can't do it here. With you."

"Are you coming back?"

Mia balled up the paper, held it in her fist, stood up from the stool.

"I'm going home to see my mother. I'm flying out tonight."

"Okay."

"I need some Mom time. I haven't seen her in, like, three months."

"How long are you going to be out there?"

"A week."

"And then what?"

Mia crumpled up the note, moved from the desk, picked up her bag from the counter, put the note in.

"I don't know. I mean, I'm coming back to Portland."

"But not to me?"

She stood in front of him, far away even in the small space.

"I don't know. Like I said, I have to think."

"Fine."

She took a step toward him. "I do love you, you know."

"Right."

"I just need to figure out whether this is right. For both of us."

"Do I get a vote?" Brandon said.

Mia took his hand, just one.

"Please understand."

Brandon let her hand fall away, felt himself coiling back into his shell. Everyone left, eventually. And then you were alone. Alone was natural. The rest was like the sunny days on the bay—an illusion. A big con.

"So why the note?" he said, not looking at her.

"I didn't know when you were coming home," Mia said. "I never know."

"I always come back," Brandon said.

Mia slung her bag over her shoulder. "What was it this time?"

Fatima, her nose nibbled by the crabs. Mr. Otto, the weight of his daughter's death settling over him. Annie Young, cold and callous, like Fatima was a cat run over by a car. The guy spitting in his face, the kid in the car with the drunks. Winston consorting with criminals.

"The usual," Brandon said.

FORTY-FOUR

He helped her wheel the cart up the ramp, loaded the bags in the Saab. Good-bye was a peck on his cheek. Mia was wiping her eyes as she drove off.

Brandon dropped his gear on the counter, peeled off his uniform, fell back on the berth. He lay there and stared, listened to the rain on the deck above him. The tide was out and the damp cabin smelled of mud and fish and diesel and decay. Something big passed out on the harbor, the thump of the engine carrying over the water, and minutes later *Bay Witch* began to rock. It heaved against the float, fenders grinding, and Brandon thought of Winston and Lily having a romp in the next cabin.

Violence followed by sex. Were they aroused by the shooting, the killing? Or was Brandon really imagining the worst, playing cops and robbers? Was Mia right? What had he done to drive her away? And why?

Two hours later, he jerked awake. Footsteps on the float, a knock on the transom.

"Anybody aboard?"

A woman's voice. He staggered to his feet, said, "Wait a sec," and pulled on a pair of paint-spattered khaki shorts. He stepped out of the cabin, saw a fiftyish woman standing at the stern. Jeans and a red fleece vest. Small, short dark hair, pretty. She turned to him and smiled.

"Sorry to bother you, but the man out at the fuel dock said you were the person to see about a guest mooring."

Brandon said he was, hopped over the transom, and led the

way up the dock to the office. She said her name was Murphy, Mary-Ellen Murphy, and she and her husband had motored up from Marblehead. She turned and pointed at the sleek blue-hulled cruiser at the far end of the float. A Hinckley Talaria, million dollars plus. Her husband was puttering on the foredeck.

Brandon opened the office door and she followed him in.

"First time in Portland?" he said.

"Yes, on the boat. Other time we were here was on a cruise."

"Really. How was that?"

Brandon took the clipboard from the hook on the wall.

"We really liked it. Portland, I mean. Great little city. Good restaurants."

"Yes, it's becoming known for that."

"The cruise, well, my husband's office crew gave it to us. Our twenty-fifth. We were between boats, and they thought we'd like to be on the water. We would have rather stayed home but we didn't want to hurt their feelings."

"I'm sure."

He put the clipboard on the desk, began to fill in the date, time.

"So where'd you cruise to?"

"It was New York, Portland, Bar Harbor, and St. John, New Brunswick. We flew home after that."

"Had enough?"

"Yeah. But Portland was really our favorite. Bar Harbor was wall-to-wall tourists. St. John was okay, but a little rough around the edges. Some pretty tough sections."

"Really."

Brandon set the clipboard in front of her. She had her wallet out, was fishing for a credit card.

"Oh, yeah. Some rough customers, if you got off the beaten track. Robert, my husband, he's a walker when he gets off the boat. We'll walk all over Portland."

"Lots to see," Brandon said.

"The steward warned us about St. John. You couldn't go to certain parts of the city after dark."

She bent over the clipboard, filled in her name, phone, the boat's name: *Flying Fish*. There was a big diamond on her left hand, a bigger sapphire on her right.

"They said a crewman on another cruise ship, he'd gotten killed there. A month earlier, I think. Some drug thing."

"Too bad," Brandon said.

She handed him the credit card. He put it in the machine, ran it through. He gave her the card back. She stood like she was in no hurry to go back aboard. Brandon figured Mr. Murphy wasn't much of a talker.

"You think of Canada, all peaceful and friendly."

"I suppose you do," he said.

"Well, turns out there's a lot of pretty unsavory characters there."

"Really."

"They have biker gangs, drug dealers. I was amazed. The guy who sort of took care of us, he was from Puerto Rico. Sent money home to his family and all that."

"Uh-huh."

Brandon handed her the receipt, $150 for three nights, the form that spelled out the rules for guests, a mooring map.

"Your cruise ship," he said. "What was the name of it?"

"*Sea Star*," Mary-Ellen Murphy said. "It really was amazing. A floating hotel."

Brandon hesitated, then said, "Ever hear of the *Ocean Princess*?"

"Yes. I think *Ocean Princess* was there when we were in St. John. In fact, the crewman who died came from that ship."

Mrs. Murphy folded her receipt, put it in her wallet, the wallet in the pocket of her fleece. "Our fellow, his name was Ramon, he said the crew on *Ocean Princess* was made up of a lot of Jamaicans. I think there was some sort of resentment there. You know, Puerto Ricans not liking the Jamaicans, and vice versa."

"Isn't that always the way?" Brandon said. "We have Somalis in Portland, other refugees. Some locals don't like them. Some of them don't like each other."

Mrs. Murphy smiled. "I don't know why people can't just get along," she said.

"Everybody scrambling for a piece of the pie," Brandon said.

She looked at him and smiled. Yup, Brandon thought. Mr. Murphy was a man of few words and it was a big ocean.

"When was this, that you were up in St. John?" Brandon said.

"Let's see. Two years ago in September. I mean, don't get me wrong. It was a nice city. But Canadian drug dealers—who knew?"

FORTY-FIVE

Munjoy Hill was quiet in the rain: a guy walking a couple of terriers, a woman on a bike, groceries in baskets on the back. Brandon drove slowly up Vesper Street from the Eastern Prom, slowed at the corner of Moody and looked right. Mia's car was in her driveway. He rolled through the intersection, circling the block. Maybe get some coffees, bring them up to the apartment, have a talk. Mia could still go home to her mom, but maybe they'd be one step closer to resolving this thing.

He passed a guy walking, an OxyContin junkie he and Kat had arrested for burglaries, nasty little bastard, a commando knife inside his jeans.

The guy spotted him, looked worried. Brandon glanced in the mirror, saw the guy was wearing a backpack and the pack looked full. He reached for his radio, wondered who he could call to roust the bastard. Second arrest in a month—no bail this time, chump.

Brandon caught himself. He put the radio down on the seat. At Congress, he took a left, headed over the hill to the Starbucks at Back Bay. He bought two large lattes, regular for himself, mocha for Mia, with her sweet tooth. He sipped his on the way back to Munjoy Hill, felt the jolt of caffeine start to override his two hours of sleep.

She'd be happy to see him. They'd talk. Maybe cry. Hug. Get this sorted out. He took a right off Congress, coasted down the street, the truck rattling over the potholes. As he approached Mia's building, a Land Rover crossed the intersection. Pulled in behind Mia's Saab. Lily got out, hood of her red Gore-Tex jacket up, coffees in hand. She closed the door with a flip of her hip.

Brandon drove on.

Had Mia called her? Is that who she was turning to, the shoulder she'd cry on while she unloaded about him? *Brandon is never home. Brandon puts his job before me. He thinks everybody is a criminal. He even thinks Winston . . .*

Brandon drove on, back downtown. Parked on Congress by Monument Square, eyed the soggy panhandlers and winos, the eccentrics and mentally ill, sitting on benches in the détente of daylight. He saw two street kids approach a third and sit, saw money change hands, an envelope slipped across.

Maybe I think everybody's a criminal because most people are, he thought. He made a mental note of the seller, got out of the truck and walked up the block to the public library. A guy asked him for spare change, saw Brandon's hard look, turned away.

Jeanine at the circulation desk waved to Brandon, a library regular. Kenneth behind the reference desk saluted, his joke since Brandon had started asking for war books a decade before. No books today.

The computers were on the first floor, lines of them, most of them taken, a place for street people to get out of the rain. Brandon sat between a man on genealogy.com and a giggling girl on G-Chat. He googled *Ocean Princess* and Portland, Maine, and saw the schedules pop up.

The coming fall. Last year. He put in the year before and waited and a port schedule came up, two years old.

Ocean Princess had stopped in Portland twice that September, once on the way north, and a week later, on the way back south. Northbound, it had stopped in Bar Harbor for two days before sailing to St. John, docking at the Marco Polo Cruise Terminal on 15 September, 0800 hours. The ship had left that night at 2000 hours, 8 p.m.

The newspaper was the *St. John Telegram,* a weird mix of local and national news, car accidents and Parliament. Brandon searched the newspaper archives for *Ocean Princess,* got the schedules, a story about a new terminal facility, which was then "state of the art" and expected to attract more ships and money to the city. And a fourth story, from the police news.

Cruise Ship Crewman Killed in Prince Street Fire

*Authorities have identified the third body found in the rubble
of a Prince Street fire as Alston Kelley, 31, of Kingston, Jamaica.
Kelley was a crewman on the visiting cruise ship* Ocean Princess
*and did not return to the ship after taking a day's leave Sept. 8,
said spokesman Margaret Leighton of the St. John Police Force.*

*Five people were killed in the fast-moving blaze. Previously
indentified were Cargill McDonald, 28, of Toronto, and Delton
Luton, 40, of St. John. Two others were burned beyond recognition and remain unidentified.*

*Authorities continue to investigate the cause of the fire,
which destroyed the wood-frame house on Prince Street West.
Sources say the home, rented by Luton, was in an area frequented
by drug users. McDonald and Luton, both recently moved to
Canada from Jamaica, had criminal records with convictions for
drug possession and trafficking.*

*Leighton said the cause of death had not been positively
established for the three men because of the intensity of the blaze.
Fire investigators believe the fire started in a room where McDonald and Luton were using a gas stove for drug processing, turning
cocaine into its crystalline or "crack" form. Kelley, police said,
was found in an adjoining room. The crewman "may have been
incapacitated by drugs" and was unable to flee the blaze.*

Brandon said softly, "Looking for some blow for the cruise
home."

The girl on G-Chat looked over at him. Brandon glanced at
her and smiled. She looked away quickly and he hit PRINT, walked
down the row of cubicles to the printer, took the piece of paper,
folded it, and put it in his pocket.

He waved to the librarians on the way out, had just turned
down the sidewalk when he heard someone call, "Hey, Blake."

Brandon turned. It was Big Liz, pushing her grocery cart, which was bulging like an overloaded pack mule. He walked over to her and she grinned, put her hand on his arm. Her fingernails were blackened with crud, and there were notes scrawled on the hand, running up her wrist, under the tattered and stained sleeve of her sodden sweatshirt.

"Been doing some serious writing there, Liz," Brandon said.

Big Liz looked at her hand like it belonged to someone else. She looked back at him. "You gotta keep track," she said.

"Of what?" Brandon said.

"Them. Because they're down there."

"Who's that, Liz?"

"The undergrounders."

"They're down there? Down where?"

"Under us," Big Liz snapped, tightening her grip on his arm. "You gotta be on your toes, Blake. They'll grab you."

She shuffled her feet in their unlaced basketball shoes. Yanked on his arm, still held on.

"So what are you writing down, Lizzie?"

"Their secret holes, Blake. They don't know I'm keepin' track."

"Good for you, Lizzie."

"I can hear 'em. Most people can't. Too bad for them. 'Cause they get hold of you, they pull you down the sewers. They get you down there, you ain't never gettin' out. Not once they start torturin' you. Learned from the Iraqis. Put needles in your eyes, Blake. Stick 'em in slow."

Brandon started to pull away but Big Liz hung on, shuffled after him, pulling the cart, the wheels squeaking.

"I don't want them to get you, Blake." She held out her arm with the writing.

"What's that?"

Brandon looked at the scrawl on her wrinkled skin. Lizzie took a Sharpie from her other pocket and thrust it at him.

"The list."

"You're running out of room there," Brandon said, smiling.

"Want me to write it on you?" Lizzie said. She looked up at him, eyes wide, odor rising from her like steam. Brandon looked at the wizened arm, speckled and striped with scars and scrapes and bug bites. She'd scrawled streets and numbers: 770 State, 138 Bramhall, 87 Charles, up by the hospital, 223 Mellen.

Then, 317 Granite.

Brandon took hold of her arm, the flesh hanging loose like cloth draped on a stick. He held it closer.

"What's with Granite Street, Liz? That's where the Ottos live. The baby."

Lizzie's eyes narrowed as she looked at her own arm, put a finger on the address. "Yeah. Yeah. They got the baby, all right."

"These underground people."

"Uh-huh."

She looked up at him. He could see the grit in the corner of her eyes, flakes of dried mucus on her cheekbone. "They like babies. They like 'em cause they're so innocent." Her eyes widened.

"I've heard it, Blake. I've heard 'em screamin'. The head one, he tells 'em what to do. Stick the knife in here. Hold the candle there."

She dug her filthy nails into his arm. "Peel the blister back," she hissed.

"So you've heard this, Lizzie?"

"Oh, yeah. Heard it like I hear you talkin' right now. People sayin', 'No, please, no.' Little baby screamin'. Babies can't talk, but they're thinkin' it. Nothin' I can do, Blake. I try to save him, they pull me down, too."

Brandon felt a chill rattle his spine.

"Hear 'em all the time, Blake. And they know I can hear. That's why I gotta keep movin'. They know I'm onto 'em. They're lookin' for me. If I stop too long, they can reach up and"—she lunged at him, grabbed his arm—"get me," she snarled.

He stepped back. Lizzie turned to her cart, shoved and prodded the bags and blankets and empty bottles. "Stayed here too long, Elizabeth," she muttered. "Can't screw up. You know better than that."

"Lizzie," Brandon said. "Lizzie."

She looked up at him like they'd never met.

"Where'd you hear the baby? The baby crying? I mean, where at 317 Granite was it?"

Lizzie smiled slyly. "If I told you that I'd have to kill you," she said.

"I won't tell anyone." He smiled back. "Our secret."

Lizzie looked up and down the block. A bus passed and splashed a puddle up, a near miss. Lizzie looked up at the passengers in the windows. She muttered, not looking at him: "The gutter, Blake. You only hear the cellar people when you're in the gutter."

FORTY-SIX

The Land Rover was gone. Brandon parked behind Mia's Saab, took the cold coffees upstairs, let himself in.

"Hey, Mia," he called.

He walked through the apartment, the air stale and close, and into the kitchen. He heard a rattle out on the deck. He stepped outside. She was sitting in a plastic lawn chair, Starbucks cup in her hand.

"Hi, Brandon," Lily said, a sad face like someone had died.

"Oh. I thought you'd left."

"Mia went to the store to get something for her trip. I was blocking her in so she took my car."

"Oh."

He stood. She patted the chair beside hers.

"Sit."

Brandon did. Sipped the cold coffee. Lily crossed her legs. She was wearing yoga pants, flip-flops, a loose camisole over a sports bra. Leaning forward, she put a hand on his knee. Her expression was somber, but her eyes glittered.

"You're losing a good one," Lily said.

"I don't think I'm losing anyone. She's going to see her mother."

"Brandon."

"What?"

"You're losing her, bro. You're making a big mistake."

Mind your own goddamn business, he thought. He sipped the coffee, looked over the rooftops toward the bay, a pale hazy blue. A lighter was leaving the harbor, smoke trailing from its stack.

"We'll work it out," he said.

"You have to work *at* it," Lily said, taking her hand away, reaching for her coffee.

"Yes," Brandon said. "Sometimes you do."

"Before Winston I was with Geoff, G-E-O-F-F."

Of course, Brandon thought.

"Geoff was a fund manager. Worked, like, eighty hours a week. Up in the middle of the night checking the Asian markets, always on his BlackBerry."

"Good for him."

"One night we're in bed—we're, you know . . . I mean, we're not sleeping." She smiled. "And the damn BlackBerry buzzes and he reaches for it. I say, 'Geoff, what are you doing?' "

"What'd he say?"

" 'Market's tanking in Tokyo,' or something like that. Didn't even look up. Starts texting. It was the job, twenty-four seven. We didn't talk. Our sex life sucked."

Brandon smiled sympathetically. Lily said, "I'm not saying you're like Geoff, but you've got to give the other person priority. Not all the time, but at least some of the time."

"Uh-huh."

"A relationship is an investment, two ways. Winston and I, we work hard, but we take time to step back, remember what's important."

Brandon, wondering what Lily worked hard at, said, "And what's important is—"

"Our relationship. When Winston is with me, he's *with* me."

"Uh-huh."

"You guys should go away. Just the two of you. Go to New York. Or Paris. Or maybe Tuscany. I love Tuscany. One time we rented this farmhouse outside of Volterra. It was fantastic. That's what you need. Someplace romantic where the relationship is your *raison d'être*."

She said it with a heavy French accent.

"Or we could go on a cruise," Brandon said.

Lily looked at him, mouth open. Recovered.

"Ick," she said.

"What?"

"My God, Brandon. Cruises are for old people. You see the cruise ship people here. Guidebooks and fanny packs."

"I don't know. They look happy. And maybe it would be fun— put your feet up and watch the ocean go by."

"Like watching paint dry," Lily said.

"And then you go to the floor show. Magicians and karaoke."

"Brandon, you aren't serious."

"Maybe not. But I was just looking into it. The route they go. New York, Portland, Bar Harbor, St. John."

"Oh, boy. All the hot spots."

"It's a work thing."

"What did I just tell you, Brandon? Life is more than a job. It's—"

"But I did find out one thing. You know the woman in the restaurant. The one who thought Winston was the Jamaican guy from the cruise ship?"

"He gets that, being big and black," Lily said. "One time somebody thought he was some NBA basketball player, asked for his autograph. So Winston, he's so funny, he just goes along. Signs the name on a napkin—"

"The guy, Alston Kelley. I googled him. He worked on a cruise ship, but he died. In Canada. In a fire."

"Ohhh, the poor man."

"It was some drug thing. So you know, this Gayle guy from New York, he was into drugs, too. Maybe Winston really does resemble this Alston Kelley, and that's why Gayle picked him out. Thought he was a drug trafficker, or whatever Kelley was."

Lily frowned, thinking. "Gayle didn't say anything about drugs. He just said he wanted the money."

"From drugs," Brandon said. "Makes more sense than money from a restaurant."

"I suppose."

"And the ship Kelley was on stopped in New York. Gayle was from New York, and he's Jamaican."

"But this guy is dead. The one in Canada."

"Maybe Gayle didn't know that. Drug people probably come and go."

Lily was looking away. She lifted her Starbucks cup and sipped. "So," she said, dribbling coffee, wiping her chin with her hand, "is this part of your investigation? Of our shooting thing?"

"It has to be, don't you think? It would answer the question, Why does a New York drug runner pick out some random guy in Portland, Maine, to rob?"

Lily considered it. "Because the Portland guy looks just like a drug dealer he knew?" she said.

"Right. Could have been a rival gang. Whatever. I'll check out that end of it. Shouldn't be too hard to find out. I'll call the Brooklyn detective back tomorrow."

"And we almost got killed for it?"

"You know how close you came."

"My God, Brandon. It's so random."

"Life is mostly random," he said. "We just convince ourselves it makes sense."

"And it's all because Winston maybe looks like some dead guy? It's kind of unbelievable."

Lily's gaze fell away. "So, have you talked to them yet? The New York police?"

"No, I just found out about Kelley this morning."

They were quiet for a moment, Lily thinking. "I suppose it doesn't really matter. The reason, I mean. He's gone. We go on with our lives."

"Not if they send somebody to take you out," Brandon said.

"Oh, Brandon," Lily said. "I think you watch too much TV."

Brandon looked at her. "But I don't even have one," he said.

FORTY-SEVEN

He'd been crying for almost two hours, a frantic wail broken up by gasps when he ran out of breath. It had to be a stomachache, the way he was pulling up his legs and writhing. Maybe something he ate. The pureed peas and carrots. Maybe he had gas.

Holding him helped for a few minutes, but then he'd start to scream again, his knees yanked up against his little belly. Probably addicted to drugs, poor little thing, going through some sort of withdrawal. What was it they called them—crack babies? Except that was newborns, wasn't it? Getting the drugs in the womb, in the mother's blood. Unless she'd been giving him drugs . . . Wouldn't put it past her, the weak, selfish thing she was. Probably did it to shut him up when he fussed.

He screamed, thrashed. Yes, maybe it was stomach cramps, but burping him didn't help, nothing coming up. Maybe some bicarbonate of soda, mix some in his bottle, see if he would take it, even a little. Was that okay for babies?

Now he was gasping like he was hyperventilating, then seemed to relax, crying still but more like a whimper. When he was put in the bed, he seemed to relax a little, poor exhausted thing. It was a chance to go get the bicarb, while he was sort of quiet. The door slid across, and he chose that moment to let out a wail.

FORTY-EIGHT

They heard Mia on the stairs, coming up. Brandon thought Lily might offer to leave them alone but she didn't. The key turned in the door and Mia came into the kitchen, put a bag on the table, looked at Brandon.

"Hey."

"Just came to wish you a good trip."

"Thanks."

"I was telling Lily about the cruise ship guy."

He ran through it again.

"So it was mistaken identity?" Mia said. "That's all?"

"Looks like it."

"Isn't that just insane?" Lily said.

"Huh," Mia said. "So you just tell these criminals that they've got the wrong guy, that their guy's dead."

"Hope they don't still want revenge," Brandon said.

"But it wasn't our fault," Lily said. "They started it."

"When it comes to things like revenge, people aren't always rational," Brandon said.

"Huh," Mia said again. She turned away, started pulling stuff from the refrigerator, emptied milk into the sink.

"Well, you don't think about this. Just have some good quality time with your mum," Lily said, sliding off the stool. She touched Brandon on the arm, came around the counter and gave Mia a peck on the cheek. "Take good care of yourself," Lily said. "Call when you get back."

She grabbed her bag, swung it over her shoulder, walked down the hallway and out. After the door clicked shut, there was a moment of silence.

Mia took stuff from the bag: a jar of Maine blueberry jam, a bottle of Maine maple syrup.

"For your mom?" Brandon said.

Mia didn't look at him, didn't reply.

"We're not talking?" Brandon said.

"I told you I wanted to think," Mia said. "I can't think while I'm talking to you."

"It's been hard lately. The job."

Mia took juice from the refrigerator, dumped it out.

"Like it will ever be easy?" she said.

"Fatima. The Sudanese girl. They found her in the harbor. Drowned."

"I'm sorry," Mia said.

"It just threw me. First Chantelle, then Fatima."

"You liked the Sudanese girl."

"I did. There was something about her. Like she was lost. I felt like I knew where she was coming from, not fitting in. Now this New York guy, the guy on the ship, dead in a fire. It's like it's all sort of out of control, like—"

"Brandon," Mia said.

"What?"

"I meant what I said. I need to think."

"Okay, but what I wanted to tell you is, I think you should stay in Minnesota for a while," Brandon said.

"What?"

"Until we figure this out. Because they will be back, Mia. They won't just let it go."

"I didn't shoot that man," Mia said.

"You saw them outside the house. Maybe they'll wait until you're with Lily. Two birds."

"I have a job here. My writing. A life."

"I don't want anything to happen to you."

"Yeah, well, right now I have to pack."

"Keep the door locked. Your car, too. You have your Mace? Check the backseat before you get in, because—"

"Jesus," Mia snapped. "Don't you get it? I don't want to deal with it right now, all of your police crap. Check it at the door, Brandon. Leave me out of it."

She turned, slammed the refrigerator door shut, stormed out of the room. Brandon heard the bedroom door shut, drawers opening and closing. He let himself out.

He made sure the door locked behind him.

The TV cameras were back at Granite Street. A missing baby; two young women leap to their deaths. One of the news crews was from Boston. The reporter—an unnaturally handsome young guy—had cornered a couple of passing Somali kids and was interviewing them, the camera rolling.

"Their fifteen minutes," Kat said.

"The American dream," Brandon said.

The radio chirped.

"O'Farrell," Kat said. "The Oaks."

The brown Crown Vic was parked east of the duck pond. Brandon pulled up alongside, buzzed the windows down. O'Farrell was on the phone. They waited.

"Yeah. New ball game. Oh, yeah. Full crew. We're ready to rock and roll."

O'Farrell put the phone down. He looked somber, serious, even more so than usual.

"How's it going, Kat?" he said. "Blake."

"Got something for you," Kat said.

"Likewise," O'Farrell said. He reached over, tapped at his laptop. Said, without looking back, "Shoot."

Kat looked at Brandon and nodded. Brandon told the cruise ship story: Alston Kelley on the ship, then dead in St. John, New Brunswick. More Jamaicans and drugs.

O'Farrell looked up from the laptop, across at them. "Makes more sense than what we've got." He thought for a moment. "Need a photo of this Kelley character. Cruise line can supply it."

"You want me to—" Brandon began.

"What, you doing this on your own time, Blake?" O'Farrell said.

Brandon shrugged. "Kinda hard to get anything done, chasing drunks all night in the Old Port," he said.

"Short on experience, long on ambition," Kat said.

"How 'bout you, Kat," O'Farrell said.

"Supplying sage guidance, when I can," she said. "For my headstrong assistant."

"Speaking of which, keep it zipped on what I'm about to tell you. Won't be released to the press for a couple of days."

The cops waited.

"Fatima Otto," O'Farrell said. "Prelim on cause of death. Drowning."

Something in the way he said it. They listened.

"Water in the lungs."

"No other way to drown, right?" Kat said.

"But it wasn't water from the harbor."

They waited.

"Freshwater," O'Farrell said.

"What?" Kat said. "Like she drowned in a stream and washed down?"

"Freshwater with chlorine in it. Like she drowned in a bath-tub, or a swimming pool."

"Fucking A," Kat said.

"Killed her," Brandon said, "and then threw her off the bridge."

"She was pregnant," O'Farrell said. "Four, five weeks."

"Oh, jeez," Kat said.

"Talk about dishonor," Brandon said.

"Tell me about it," O'Farrell said. "We got shame coming every which way but Sunday."

FORTY-NINE

The plan was to hit the house, twenty-one hundred hours. "After the news crews are gone," O'Farrell said. "Check the bathtubs, the toilets, the sinks. Want you there, 'cause you know these people."

"Drown somebody in a sink?" Kat said.

"You can drown somebody with a garden hose," O'Farrell said, "if you can hold 'em down."

They assembled with the command unit at the Oaks, went to the apartments simultaneously, patrol cops and detectives, evidence techs heading for the bathrooms, bags in hand.

The Ottos sat on the couch, all lined up like they were waiting for an audition. The boys kept checking their phones, looked sullen when Kat said, "No texting, please." Mr. and Mrs. Otto looked defeated, murmuring a couple of words in Arabic but mostly staring straight ahead, like life as they knew it was over—again.

Other cops had Cawley and the Youngs. The techs lighted the bathrooms for blood traces, found some in the Youngs' bathtub, Cawley's bathroom sink. The Ottos' place was scoured.

Everybody gave blood samples, Mrs. Otto clutching her husband as the process was explained to her by the interpreter, a pretty Iraqi woman with gold hoop earrings. Mrs. Otto kept shaking her head until Edgard rattled off something in Arabic, the only English words, *TV* and *Law & Order*. Once the techs had packed up and left, O'Farrell and Smythe took the Ottos out to the kitchen, one by one.

Brandon and Kat stood in the living room. The boys had put earbuds in, sat on the couch, flicking through their iPhones. Mrs. Otto sat on the other end of the couch, legs pressed together, feet in turquoise-blue slippers. She jerked when she heard her husband's anguished cry, "No."

O'Farrell and Smythe came back to the living room, Mr. Otto was wobbly, ashen-faced, like he'd just been tortured. Smythe smiled at Mrs. Otto and she looked to her husband. He murmured in Arabic and Mrs. Otto got up and walked to the kitchen, Smythe behind her.

This time the cry had no words, just a soft wail. On the couch, the brothers were oblivious. When their time came, O'Farrell, leading the way to the kitchen, had to tell them to take the earbuds out.

Brandon and Kat waited, standing by the television, Fatima's framed photograph on the table beside it. A high school picture, the dark-skinned girl leaning against a white birch tree. Another weird American custom. Brandon kept glancing at the picture, Fatima barely smiling, but still a presence, something in the eyes.

The Ottos sat side by side, upright and stiff, stared straight ahead. And then the brothers came out, sobered, the detectives behind them. "Mr. Otto," O'Farrell said. "I'm sorry for your loss, and I thank you for your time."

Otto nodded, got up from the couch. His wife remained seated. The cops headed for the door, Brandon bringing up the rear. He felt a tug on his arm and turned back.

Otto stood there, his wife watching from the couch. The boys stood side by side and listened.

"Officer Blake," Otto said. "When you know who killed my daughter, I only ask you this one favor."

Brandon waited.

"Give us the name first. That's all I ask."

"I really can't do that, Mr. Otto," Brandon said.

"I will pay you," Otto said. "You tell me how much. Whatever it is, I will find the money."

"I don't want your money, sir," Brandon said.

Edgard looked at him. "Get lost, Five-Oh," he said.

"We take care of this ourselves," Samir said.

They clasped hands, twisted them, tapped them together. The

good son. The gangbanger son. Their father leaned over, put his hand over theirs, like he was giving his blessing.

Brandon was about to say, "Let the police handle it," but he caught himself. He was the police. He turned and let himself out.

"If you lie about an honor killing, does it diminish it somehow?" Brandon said.

"Like, where's the honor if you have to lie about it?" Kat said.

"Something like that."

. "If they're really gonna handle it themselves, why tell us?" she said.

Brandon thought. The motor idled. The strobes flashed and clicked. "Because they already handled it?" he said.

"Just part of it, unless they got their own sister pregnant," Kat said.

They were on Preble Street, just down from Congress, backing up Dever and Bannon on a DWI stop. Dever was giving a kid a field sobriety test, a young woman sitting on the curb watching, talking on the phone. The kid, a skinny white guy in gigantic shorts, staggered. Dever shook his head wearily, turned the kid and put on the cuffs. The girl, in short-shorts and heels, got up, started walking wobbily down the block, still on the phone.

Dever, stuffing the guy into the back of the cruiser, looked up to give her backside a long look.

"What a slime," Kat said.

"And then there's Fatima, all those clothes on. The artist, you think?"

"I think Lil Messy might be gay."

"No, he's just a hipster," Brandon said.

"So who's that leave? Cawley the Creeper?"

"Could have been a relative stranger. Think Fatima would have told anybody if she were assaulted, or even coerced?"

Brandon thought. "Maybe not right away," he said.

"Not if the guy used that as leverage," Kat said.

"More sex or he tells her father?"

"And the woman is maybe even more responsible."

"For dishonoring the family," Brandon said.

"Right."

"But she says she's going to tell. Can't live like this."

"Guy knows the brothers will be coming after him, the gang maybe," Kat said. "So he has to kill her before she rats him out."

"Make it look like suicide."

"But clumsily, it turns out," Brandon said. "Who would know they could test the water in her lungs?"

"Cops," Kat said. "Anybody who reads Patricia Cornwell."

"Or watches *CSI*."

"So we find somebody who doesn't read and doesn't watch TV," Kat said.

"Narrows it down," Brandon said.

"Tell O'Farrell we broke the case," Kat said, as Dever's cruiser pulled away. Brandon switched off the lights and pulled away. At the corner of Congress they looked right, saw the girlfriend. She'd stopped and was leaning against a storefront, taking off her shoes. Barefoot, she continued on.

"Give her a lift?" Brandon said.

"Sure," Kat said. "I don't feel like pulling another one out of the harbor."

They dropped the girlfriend at an apartment house on Brackett Street, across from the school. There was a group hanging out on the basketball court, Cambodian gangbangers, their girls. Brandon and Kat sat in the cruiser while the woman, shoes in hand, fiddled with the key in the lock, then went inside.

"This car stinks now," Kat said. "Cigarettes."

"One of the brothers' friends?" Brandon said. "Some gang thing?"

"Hook up with the homie's sister, keep it in the family?" Kat said. "I suppose. We still got that air freshener?"

"In the trunk. Could've been some sort of offering."

"Their little sister?"

"What's mine is yours," Brandon said. "To prove their allegiance."

"Jesus, Brandon," Kat said, getting out to find the Lysol, the Cambodian guys watching. "Couldn't they just shoot somebody?"

FIFTY

A fight on Free Street, a kitchen knife on the ground but nobody stabbed. Two guys who ran from a convenience store on Munjoy Hill, picked up as they climbed a fire escape with the stolen thirty-pack of Bud. A three-year-old wandering down Congress, mom all apologies when they located her, said she fell asleep watching Comedy Central. "The kid musta got away. Oh, my God. Thank you. Thank you so much."

Brandon said she was welcome. Next time they'd call Human Services, so she'd better start watching her son a little more closely, unless she wanted the social worker knocking on her door. Parenting, he said, is a full-time job.

The mom looked hurt and flounced away. Kat said, "That's better."

It was almost 1:30 a.m. when Brandon pulled into the marina lot, shut off the motor. It ticked. Brandon reached for the door handle. There was a footstep to his left.

Brandon turned, his hand to his gun.

"Don't shoot," Winston said, flashing his big grin. "I'm just the delivery boy." He was by the driver's door, a white takeout tray in one hand, a plastic cup in the other.

"Sorry," Brandon said. "Didn't see you coming."

"That's because the night and me, we're both very dark."

Another grin, Brandon opening the door, sliding out. Winston put the cup on the roof of the truck, held out his hand. Brandon clasped it, squeezed.

"Good to see you. They got you on deliveries now?"

"Oh, no, we just closed up. Lily, she tells me you having a bad day, my friend. So I'm thinking you need a good meal and a drink. Cheer you right up."

He held out the tray and Brandon took it.

"Some curried lamb, macaroni pie," Winston said. "Bajan comfort food."

"Thanks. That's nice of you."

"Oh, and that's not the nicest part." He reached for the cup, covered with a lid. "This is the nicest part. A nice rum punch, my secret recipe, with the Foursquare rum. Everybody knows the Mount Gay. It's very good, but the Foursquare—that to me is Barbados rum."

Brandon took the cup, ice rattling inside. "You didn't bring two?"

"Oh, gotta be up early, time to get home. Next time you have a day off, I'll bring the bottle. To thank you."

"For what?"

"For the explanation. The guy on the ship who musta looked like me. Without that, none of it made sense, you know? Why me? I mean, I run a little restaurant. What's that got to do with these posse guys?"

"It could be the answer," Brandon said. "Just a weird coincidence."

"Dodged the bullet, man," Winston said.

"You're very lucky."

"I got a good woman, I'll tell you that. I'm lucky to have her."

"Yes," Brandon said. "And that you had a gun. And that she knew how to shoot."

"Oh, yes," Winston said, smiling. "You don't want to miss, not with these bad boys."

He patted Brandon's arm.

"Hey, but this is work for you. You go eat, have your drink. We'll sit another time and solve all our problems," Winston said.

"It's a deal."

"Things will work out. Mia, she loves you, man. I mean, you can tell."

"Not lately."

"Oh, women, they gotta process things, you know?" Winston said. "She'll be back."

"If you say so."

"Been there, done that, my friend. I know a good lady when I see one. Learn that the hard way. Come to this country, get settled in. Bring my lady friend up from the island. Man, I thought it was true love, you know. Gonna have babies, get old and gray together."

"Didn't work out?"

"Oh, Regina, she's a beautiful woman. Oh, yeah. She's here with me for three months. We're in Atlanta. Then she trades up. A real estate man. Millionaire. Many millions. Regina, she kicked me to the curb."

He grinned.

"Hey, I don't blame her. We all trying to get ahead. Last time I see her she's getting out of a new Lexus, a convertible. Gorgeous black woman in this fancy car. People turn and look. Who's that? Some supermodel? They don't know it's just Regina from Bridgetown, little two-room house with her brothers and sisters, Papa works on a golf course, keeping it green and smooth for the tourists. Now his little girl, she's uptown, baby. Hey, all the power to her."

Brandon smiled. "I don't think Mia's moving up. I think she's just moving out."

"Well, you don't know. Absence, it makes the heart grow fonder. Sometimes people just need a little break."

"You and Lily?"

"Hey, we got a good thing going. But that girl, she needs her space—you know what I'm saying?"

"Mia says I'm not around enough. And when I am—"

"Oh, time, it's the great healer. You guys, you'll work it out."

Brandon didn't answer. Winston leaned forward and they clasped hands again.

"You take care now, man. Tomorrow, it's always another day, right?"

Brandon nodded. Winston walked back to his Mercedes, parked in the darkness at the back of the lot. He must have been sitting there waiting for me to pull in, Brandon thought. It gave him a tingle of nervousness, that anyone could wait for him in this lot, nobody around at 2 a.m. A shot in the dark.

He balanced the cup on top of the box, carried his bag in the other hand. The gate hadn't closed and he was thankful for a second, pulling it open, no need to put his stuff down to punch in the code. He pulled the gate hard behind him, and it rattled, didn't latch. He tried again.

"Damn thing," Brandon muttered, added it to his list for the morning.

He crossed the yard, a cloud of bugs fluttering around the light on top of the main shed. A rat scurried under a rotting skiff, reminding Brandon it was time to put out more poison. His footsteps were muffled on the gravel and then he was on the ramp, walking quietly down. There were lights showing here and there on the boats, and he didn't want to wake the live-aboards, anyone who had decided to stay over. The float creaked, rattling softly. When he came to *Bay Witch*, he put the food on the transom and stepped aboard. He slid the door open, carried the food into the salon, put it down on the table. Then he went below, got out of his gear, kicked off his boots, peeled out of his uniform. He put on shorts and a T-shirt, found his flip-flops in the locker, and went back up to collect the food.

Nice of them. Maybe he was wrong, always thinking the worst.

Grabbing a fork from the galley, he went out the sliding door, circled along the rail and up to the foredeck. There were two chairs there, only one needed now, and he pulled one to him, facing the water. Brandon sat.

Fog was draped over the harbor, blurring the lights of the city skyline. The red strobes on the towers flashed like fireflies. A truck rattled across the bridge. A gull cried in the darkness.

Brandon opened the box and the aroma billowed out. Curry and onion. He took a bite of the macaroni pie and it was good and rich. He tried the curry and the spices were hot, a slow burn. Brandon reached for the rum punch, popped the lid off the cup and sipped.

Rum. He tasted lime, too, and sugar. Maybe nutmeg? He sipped again. Turned to the meal, ate it mechanically. If Mia had been there, they'd have talked about it, the spices, the curry. It was Mia who'd told him there were hundreds of different curries, that chefs blended them. Interesting, but mostly he enjoyed listening to her, the sound of her voice, her expressions. For all the years he'd lived alone—alone on the boat, alone growing up, with Nessa passed out in her chair—this new "alone" was different. Mia had filled a void in his life that he hadn't admitted existed. And with her gone, the hole in his life seemed bigger. It made him ache all over. It pressed down on him like a crushing weight.

He drank more of the punch, felt like it was growing on him. He went over the events of the day: a sad story with a bad ending. He felt emotionally drained. Suddenly exhausted.

Brandon got to his feet. Carried the tray and cup along the side deck. Halfway to the stern, he lost his balance in the dark and had to grab for the rail. The half-empty cup slid, hit the deck and rolled under the rail, into the water. "Damn," Brandon said, easing his way along, jumping down to the stern deck, staggering slightly.

The rum. He felt it. He wasn't much of a drinker, another thing that kept him from fitting in with Mia's crowd. For him two beers was plenty. Too many years spent watching Nessa drink herself into a stupor.

He slid the hatch shut behind him, left the tray by the galley sink, stepped down into the berth. Kicking off his flip-flops, Brandon fell to the mattress, took a deep breath, and felt sleep sweep over him like he was drowning.

Brandon slept as fog settled over the harbor. Someone coughed on one of the boats. A car horn sounded on the Portland side, the sound drifting over the water. Gulls cried and squawked on their roost on the shed roof. A bilge pump kicked in, followed by the gurgle of running water. A lobster boat got under way at one of the Portland piers and chugged out into the channel, running lights quickly fading into the haze. Its wake rolled silently across the harbor and swept under the floats. Fenders creaked. Hardware rattled.

Outside the fence, there were slow footsteps. Then a pause. A barely audible squeak as the gate swung open.

FIFTY-ONE

You could swear he was getting bigger, but could that be? In just a few days?

Maybe the mom hadn't fed him much, and now he was finally getting enough calories. The magazines talked about how babies didn't grow steadily but in spurts.

And it wasn't just the growing—his legs getting fatter, his little belly hanging over the top of his diaper like a beer gut. He was also getting stronger, lifting himself up on the sides of the playpen, standing there and rocking like a gorilla in a cage. When he was out of the playpen, he'd push himself up on his arms, and now he was starting to crawl. He'd move forward, a few inches at a time. He'd look surprised when he realized he'd traveled across the floor, and he'd grin if you said, "You're crawling! Good boy, Sam!"

He did know his name—well, not his full name, not yet, but Sam—that was certain. And that meant the rest of it was fading from his memory bank. One of the websites had said that year-old babies only retained information for a month. That meant that in a few weeks, everything in the first year of Sam's life would be erased. It would be like none of it had ever happened.

FIFTY-TWO

Mary-Ellen Murphy was a light sleeper. She said it was because Robert snored; he said it was because she had a guilty conscience. In the sprawling house in Marblehead it wasn't an issue, with lots of room to spread out. In warm weather, she liked to go out onto the big screened porch and sit with a cup of coffee, classical music on NPR. She'd put her feet up and watch the dawn unfold, the pink glow seeping up past the horizon. On the Hinckley she had to go up on deck, which was okay if they were anchored, or even on their mooring. But in a marina like this one, she didn't want to turn lights on, or music, the boats all lined up. But the snoring . . .

He was going great guns and she was awake at three. She lay there for a few minutes, listening to the snorting and snoggering, and then reached for a sweatshirt and shorts and got up.

On the aft deck she got dressed, slipped on her sandals and stepped off. They were at the harbor end of the float, the nice marina guy setting them up with a big slip with easy access. Mary-Ellen had this idea that she could walk up to the bridge that over-looked the harbor, look out on the city and the harbor lights. She'd be back before Robert awoke, and maybe she wouldn't even tell him where she'd gone, not have to listen to him say she was out of her mind, walking around a strange city at that hour.

She stepped off the boat lightly, paused to look out at the harbor, the skyline fuzzy in the fog, like an Impressionist painting. Yes, like Monet had painted it, she thought, everything fuzzy and the light playing on the fog.

Mary-Ellen Murphy smiled and turned away and started down the dock. And then she saw more light, an odd sort of flickering, up near the ramp. For some reason it reminded her of a screensaver on a computer, and she even wondered for a moment whether someone had left a laptop on deck and those psychedelic swirly patterns were playing over and over . . . But didn't the screens go blank after a while? Otherwise—

And then she smelled it. The smoke. Ran toward the boat and saw the flames, in the stern of the old cruiser. The marina guy's boat. "Fire!" she shouted, but it barely came out, and she tried again, this time as loud as she could.

Brandon could hear them, the Somali pirates. They were boarding the boat, had their AK-47s, rocket launchers. He was below, trapped in the engine compartment, trying to get out. Could hear them shouting, "Where is he? Where is he?" Except it was in Arabic. Somehow he understood, knew they were looking for him.

He tried again to get up, got his legs loose, but they were heavy, weighted down. He struggled to get the weights off, but his arms wouldn't move, and they were coming in. He had to get to his radio, put in a call, 911, officer needs help. Where was Kat? What if Kat wasn't working? He had to get out, get his gun, before they started shooting, shoot first—but what if it wasn't justified? They were going to kill him . . . pirates don't care if you die.

And then he felt himself falling, twisting, the pirates yelling. They'd thrown him overboard and he fell for such a long time, trying to scream but nothing coming out, and then he landed—

Got to his knees. Smelled smoke. Had he landed in Hell? Thought of Big Liz and her devil people. And then he saw the flames, the flickering light and shadows. The aft deck. The fuel tanks.

Brandon lurched to his feet, went up the three steps, saw the flames tonguing the hatch door. He fell back, stumbled on his leaden legs, grabbed the side of the berth to steady himself, stepped up. Grabbed for the hatch handle, missed, and fell off the berth. He caught himself on the starboard berth, climbed back up, reached again.

He caught it this time, half hung from it, then pulled it down and over and pushed.

The hatch didn't open.

He repeated the steps: pull, yank, push. It didn't budge.

"In here," Brandon shouted. "I'm in here. In the cabin. The bow."

He dropped to the floor, crawled to the bow locker, flung the door open. His rifle was there and he pulled it out, stood in the center of the cabin and, holding it by the barrel, rammed it upwards.

The hatch held. He slammed it again, glancing off the aluminum hinge. Again. Again.

He could hear sounds, voices through the crack. He squatted, rifle in hand, and exploded upwards—and the hatch blew open, something rattling on the deck above his head.

Brandon jumped, got his arms through the hatch, swung in the air as he pulled himself up. Arms. Shoulders, his bare torso against the cool deck, his legs squirming through.

He got to his feet, moved to the side deck, climbed the rail, and jumped. He hit the float, stumbled and rolled. Lay still.

"Over here," a woman shouted, and she ran to him, the lady from the Hinckley.

"Anyone else on board?" the woman said.

"No," Brandon said. "I'm alone."

He sat up, watched as barefoot men pounded by them, in boxer shorts, shirtless, all carrying fire extinguishers. There was a swish, a hiss, another, someone shouting, "Just empty it, for God's sake."

And then it was quiet. The woman stood by him, awkwardly patted his bare shoulder.

South Portland cops were there, four patrolmen, a sergeant, the shift commander, a big guy with a barrel chest, looked like he'd played football. A fire truck came, and Rescue, but the fire was out and Brandon wasn't hurt, so they left. A state fire investigator was called, but she was coming from Pownal so it would be a while.

They were waiting, standing on the dock by *Bay Witch*, when Kat showed up, hurrying down the ramp, looking skinny in her track suit without her body armor. She nodded at the South

Portland cops, and she and Brandon bumped fists and she looked at him, in borrowed jeans and sweatshirt, the boat, the crime-scene tape across the stern.

"Never a dull moment, Blake," Kat said.

"What else would you be doing, three a.m.," Brandon said.

"You're right. I was up anyway, sitting around waiting for something to happen," Kat said.

"Somebody got it in for your boy here," the big sergeant said.

"Coulda told you that," Kat said.

"Jammed a chair in the trapdoor thing up front, poured some gas on the door back here."

"A woman from another boat couldn't sleep," Brandon said. "Saw the fire."

"Husband snores," the sergeant said.

They stared at *Bay Witch,* the black stain on the deck.

"Somebody up there likes you, Blake," Kat said.

"And somebody down here doesn't," the sergeant said. "Me and Officer Blake were just talking about who that might be."

"The Anthonys," Kat said. "Family of the girl who went off the bridge. The first one, with the baby."

"The brother," Brandon said. "His name is Jason. Blames me for her jumping. Said I should pay for it. I figured he was just running his mouth."

"And remember the guy from Commercial Street, the domestic assault?" Kat said. "He was pretty pissed, too."

"I don't know," " Brandon said. "He seemed like he was all talk."

"And what about the Otto brothers?" Kat said. "The Sudanese Warriors."

"Maybe," Brandon said.

"And there's Mia," Kat said.

"Yes."

She told the sergeant about Mia seeing the guys parked outside on the Eastern Prom. The sergeant nodded.

"They see her?" the sergeant said.

"Yeah."

"Where is she now?" the sergeant said.

"Minnesota," Brandon said. "Went to see her mother."

"Smart move," the sergeant said.

Brandon hesitated.

"For all kinds of reasons," he said.

The fire investigator's name was Lucci. She had graying hair cropped short, wore a blue jumpsuit and baseball hat. They watched as she took lots of photos, scraped some ashes into a bag. She sealed the bag, dropped it into a backpack with the camera. Climbed back over the transom onto the dock.

Lucci stood with them and they all stared at the boat.

"Where are the fuel tanks on this thing?" she said finally.

"Below that deck," Brandon said.

"Lucky you," Lucci said.

"That right?" Brandon said.

"Well, maybe not. They poured the accelerant—gasoline—onto the floor there and lit it. But it's the vapor that burns first and almost all of the heat goes straight up into the air. They'd been smart, they would have poured it on the walls, get it trapped under the roof."

"Nothing like a dumb arsonist," Kat said.

"Isn't like television," Lucci said. "Splash some gas, one match, poof, the whole thing goes up. Fire is a complicated thing, all those laws of thermodynamics at play. I've seen people pour a gallon of gas in their living room, light it up, in ten minutes they've got no fire, just a bunch of melted carpeting and a load of trouble. Your boat here, you got some scorched wood is all. Of course, another few minutes, if it'd had more time to burn down, gathering some momentum in the floor itself—"

"Kaboom?" the sergeant said.

"Maybe. Or maybe just a big old fire."

She turned to Brandon.

"Boat all wood?"

"Yeah. Plywood. Oak framing. Built in the sixties."

Lucci shook her head. "You're living in a box made of kindling, my friend."

They shifted on their feet. Lucci reached in her breast pocket for a card, handed it to Brandon. "But hey," the fire investigator said. "Probably they've shot their wad on the fire thing. Next time they'll try something else."

"Thanks," Brandon said. "Good to know."

FIFTY-THREE

The motion detector cost twenty bucks and change. Brandon set it up along the gunwale at the stern, on the port side. Anybody coming aboard at the stern would set off the alarm in the cabin.

"What if they climb on the front?" Kat said.

Brandon, kneeling to connect the wires to the electrical panel under the helm, said, "The bow."

"Whatever."

"I'd hear them. It's pretty high to climb up there, and it's right over my head."

"You didn't hear them last night."

"No."

"Go down in the bedroom," Kat said, and she turned and left the salon. Brandon snapped the last wire in place, got up and went below. He heard Kat shuffle along the side deck, her legs moving past the porthole. He closed his eyes, heard her move to the center of the foredeck. When she knelt, he heard her knees thump against the plywood.

She came back down, sat on the berth across from him. She was in shorts and a bicycle jersey, muscles defined.

"Well?"

"I could hear everything."

"Last night?"

"I was really out," Brandon said.

"Were you drunk? Upset about Mia or something?"

"Nah. Half a drink. I was just really tired."

"And emotionally spent?"

"Maybe. Had something to eat and just crashed."

"That can happen when you've been all keyed up and—" The motion detector alarm went off. It was O'Farrell and Perry, the big sergeant in uniform. They were on the stern deck, staring at the black patch.

"Who'd want to burn you up?" the sergeant said.

"Let's make a list," O'Farrell said.

Brandon looked at him, saw he wasn't joking.

Kat said, "I'll start."

She rattled them off, the ones already mentioned.

O'Farrell took it up: whoever killed Fatima, thinking Brandon was a threat. Cawley's biker buddy, for the sex charge.

"Seems extreme," O'Farrell said. "Hasn't even gone to trial."

Brandon said, "So what do I—"

"You take a few days off, Blake," Perry said. "Clean up your boat. Try to stay out of trouble. Go stay with friends or family."

He and O'Farrell turned toward the stern, then turned back. "Listen, Brandon," O'Farrell said, his voice low. "You're not a detective."

"You're not even a full patrolman," Perry said.

"And when you're not working, Brandon, you're not working," O'Farrell said.

"There's a reason you aren't in a patrol car alone," Perry said. "You're like a pitcher, just up from the minors. You start in the bullpen. Work your way up to the rotation. If you're lucky."

"We have a whole bunch of cops working on all of this," O'Farrell said, "and they're very experienced, and their investigation will get to the bottom of it. We don't need—"

"May be a bad day to say this, but Blake, you gotta take it a little slower," Perry said. "You're stirring shit up everywhere you go."

"You don't have to save the world," O'Farrell said.

"Go easy," Kat said.

"I didn't take this job to go easy," Brandon said. "Did you?"

He sanded the burnt wood off, taking it down an eighth of an inch. While he worked, the other boat owners came by, watched and asked questions: Who would do this? Was it because he was a cop? Or was there some nutcase arsonist running around marinas? Was he going to fix the gate so it closed right? Wasn't he lucky? What if Mrs. Murphy hadn't been awake? What were the chances? Is that a motion detector? Should we all have them?

Brandon answered their questions, the ones he could. Yes, to the gate. He did know there was an arsonist. He didn't know if he was running around. Or she.

It was 4 p.m. before he finished, the burnt area repainted gray. There was a blemish and the paint didn't quite match, the old gray faded by the sun. Looks like hell, he thought. The good news? He wasn't dead.

Going below, he took a shower, his loaded gun on the tiny counter outside the stall. In the cabin, he dressed in jeans and a black T-shirt, dark blue running shoes, a black baseball cap, too. He came above deck, stepped out onto the dock. Turned to walk out to the Hinckley and thank his savior.

And the boat was gone.

He turned around, headed for the gate. He felt a little regret, more relief. As Mia had said, he didn't like to owe anyone.

The gate had sagged and he bent it back into place with a steel bar. He swung it open and shut, punching in the code each time, the gate swinging. Then he returned to *Bay Witch*, set the alarm, and went inside. He took a beer and a block of cheddar cheese from the refrigerator in the galley, a box of stoned wheat crackers from the cupboard. Parking himself in the salon, he sat with his back to the harbor, facing the yard. On the table beside him was a knife, for the cheese, and his loaded Glock 26, for all sorts of reasons.

The morning air was still and humid on Granite Street, the pavement heating up under a hazy sun. Brandon sat in the truck a half block from 317, hunched back in the seat, watching the house.

Perry had said to take a couple of days off, and Brandon was. He was off, sitting. Watching. The police radio was on the seat, turned down low.

Three Somali kids wheeled up and down on bikes. A guy with a gray ponytail and a red bandanna headband was walking a three-legged dog, a black-and-white shepherd mutt. By 317 the dog paused to sniff, pee, and maybe poop in the gutter. A car, an older Chevy sedan, pulled up, turned into the driveway, and stopped. Annie Young got out, said something to the guy with the dog. He said something back. The driver's door still open, she walked toward him, pointing her finger.

"What did you say?" Annie Young shouted.

The guy turned, raised a fist. The dog turned, too, barked at Annie Young, who was shouting, "Go ahead. Go ahead." The kids on bikes had passed but they were circling back. Brandon got out of the truck, hurried across the street, came up behind the guy.

"Calm it down," he said, flashing his badge. "Portland PD. Just cool it."

The guy turned. "This woman threatened me. I want to press charges."

"No charges. Hey, it's a nice day. You and your dog, go enjoy it."

"There's a dog ordinance in this city," Annie Young said. "And you, Officer Blake, have a responsibility to enforce it."

"Miss Young."

"You guys know each other?" the guy said. "What is this? A sting?"

"One more minute and you're going in for failure to disperse," Brandon said.

"I ain't done nothin'. My dog ain't done nothin'. This lady's whacked. I have a right to walk down the street."

"Not if your filthy mutt defecates all over my property."

"He ain't defecated yet. He's still sniffing. He's got a right to sniff."

"He's smelling other dogs' shit," one of the kids said, sitting on his bike. "Dogs is always smelling shit."

"I'm gonna count to ten," Brandon said. "One, two, three—"

"Okay," the guy said. "I'm leaving. You can have your property, lady, you crazy bitch."

"Don't you ever—" Annie Young said.

Brandon held up his hand.

"Enough," he said.

The guy turned, yanked the leash. The dog hopped after him. The kids on the bikes followed, one of them saying, "Hey, Dog Man. Where's his other leg?"

"Filth," Annie Young said. She turned and walked back to the car.

Brandon followed. He saw grocery bags in the backseat, said, "You need any help?"

"No," Annie Young said. She turned back to him, said, "Why are you out of uniform?"

"It's a long story," Brandon said.

"Hmmph," she said.

"You sure I can't help you bring those in?"

"No, thank you. I'm fine."

Annie Young stood by the back door of the car, facing him. Brandon stood, too.

"I'd like to talk to you more about Fatima," he said.

"Poor girl. But that's what happens with these Africans. Mama's right; the women are treated like livestock."

"And you think that had something to do with her death?"

She stood in place, arms folded under her bust. "That girl was between a rock and a hard place. Try to be totally American and they'd beat her. Stay African, they treat her like a servant. You know they don't let the girls go to school?"

"Fatima went to school."

"For now," Annie Young said. "They don't last."

"You seem to know a lot about Sudanese culture." Brandon moved closer.

She stepped toward him, took him by the shoulder, turned him away. Whispered, "I was going to call you."

"Yeah?"

"Early this morning, around two. The African hoodlums from upstairs—"

"Edgard and Samir?"

"Whatever their names are. They came outside, and three or four of their gang, or whatever they call it, they stood out here and talked, and then they started off down the block."

"So?"

"I heard them say something. They said, 'Messy, going to mess him up.' And then they said some things about what they were going to do. Things I won't repeat."

"Lil Messy. He's an art student, lives down the street. Mess him up?"

"That's what they said."

"Was it Samir or Edgard saying that?"

"I don't know. They all sound the same to me."

Brandon started back toward his truck. Annie Young stood by the car, like she was waiting for someone to come out. Brandon got back in the truck, picked up the radio, put it back down.

He looked at the house, Annie Young standing there. He looked to the front apartment, seeing if her mother was in the window. She wasn't. He looked upstairs, saw the curtain move in the front room of the Ottos' apartment on the second floor. The third floor was still. He glanced up at the roof, the rusty ham radio antenna, Mr. Young talking to people around the world to keep from having to talk to the two of them.

He started off. Annie Young, still by the car, watched him pass.

Could have been just talk, Brandon thought. He was at the front door of Messy's building, pressed the broken button for apartment 4, waited a minute, then pressed the buttons for 1, 2, and 3. He rapped on the door with his flashlight, heard rattling inside.

The door fell open and a guy peered out: fiftyish, unshaven, a stain on the swollen belly of his white T-shirt. TV noise could be heard in the background. Someone shouting, "Police! Put down your weapon!" Then shots.

Brandon showed his badge.

"The kid upstairs. Seen him lately?"

The guy shook his head. "Nah."

"Heard anything up there?"

"Nope."

"Seen anybody coming or going?"

"Mind my own business. Got enough problems."

"Sure," Brandon said, and he pushed the door open wider, the guy pushed backward with it.

"Hey," the guy said.

"Sorry," Brandon said.

"What's your name, anyway?"

"Blake."

"Young for a detective, ain'tcha?"

"Very," Brandon said, and he squeezed by, bounded up the stairs.

Second floor: auto parts laid out on greasy rags, a baby stroller at the door. Third floor: boxes of clothes, CDs scattered on the floor, stuff left behind when a tenant skipped. Fourth floor: the door closed but the jamb splintered. Brandon pushed with the flashlight and the door opened. He slipped his gun out, stepped in.

Paint everywhere, smeared, spattered, tubes flattened on the floor. Paintings ripped, smashed, stomped. Graffiti on the walls, gang signs. TSW. True Sudanese Warriors. Brandon called, "Police. Anyone here?"

Nothing.

He crossed the room, feet sticking on the paint. The bathroom door was closed. Brandon listened, looked down. Blood had seeped from underneath, the edges of the puddle dried dark.

He pushed the door open with the flashlight, gun low and

ready. Saw a bare foot, the ankle purple and swollen. The rest of Lil Messy, curled up on the floor between the tub and the toilet.

FIFTY-FOUR

Messy was alive. Barely. A weak pulse in the carotid artery. His face was covered in crusted blood, eyes swollen shut, nose torn, lips ballooned. The blood seemed to have come from his scalp, where it was split, and skull showed through the hair.

One arm broken, still raised in a defensive position. The ankle broken, too.

"Stomped," Perry said.

Lil Messy was wearing green gym shorts and a white T-shirt, now black with dried blood. They'd dumped a bottle of shampoo on him, shaken out a can of Ajax.

"Ran in here to get away," Detective Smythe said.

"Think they thought he was dead?" Brandon said, as the paramedics poked in the needle for the IV, eased Lil Messy onto his back.

"Could be, soon," the sergeant said.

The evidence tech was taking pictures of the footprints.

"I think it's art," Dever said. "Who's the guy who just threw all the paint on the floor, mushed it around? The one who was in the movie."

"Jackson Pollock," the tech said.

"Right. Monkey could do it, and they sell the pictures for a million bucks."

"We've got an Air Jordan. A couple of different Reeboks," the tech said.

"Better check Blake's shoes," Dever said. "Hey, Blake. Didn't they teach you not to walk through the crime scene?"

The EMTs wheeled the stretcher out of the bathroom, Lil

Messy strapped down, IV bag beside him. He looked small and battered, like a child pulled from a plane crash.

"What'd the lady at the house say again?" Perry said.

Brandon repeated it. "An honor thing. They avenged what he did to dishonor their sister. Or at least what they think he did."

"What, you the expert on Sudanese now?" Dever said.

Perry nodded to Smythe. "We'll hit the kids' apartment first. They're not there, we'll just keep looking."

"Let's go," Perry said.

"Could work out for you, Blake," Dever said, as they headed for the door. "Get off the street, just go around being a consultant. Explain all this African shit to us dumb street cops."

Outside, the usual gawkers had gathered, kids maneuvering to get a look at Lil Messy on the way to the ambulance. "It's all about the drugs," the guy from the first floor was saying, to no one in particular.

"The first-floor neighbor," Brandon said to Perry.

"Dever," Perry said. "Talk to that guy."

"You sure you don't want the ace detective to do it?" Dever said, but he turned back, headed into the crowd.

O'Farrell was waiting outside 317 Granite. He nodded to Brandon as he got out of his truck, then went in the side door of the building with two of the day-shift patrolmen. Smythe parked behind Brandon, walked up, all business, said, "Fill me in on the mother-daughter thing."

Brandon did. Annie Young and her mom hunkered down, resenting the Africans, druggies, most everyone else. "Annie's pretty sour, mom's a total curmudgeon. Like life is a crime and she's the victim. Dad died in an accident and—"

"That's enough," Smythe said, and strode away. She went to the Youngs' door and knocked. It opened. Smythe stepped inside.

Brandon waited.

O'Farrell and the patrolmen emerged first. They climbed in the black-and-white, the kids from the street just arriving from Lil Messy's building. Then Smythe came out of the Youngs' apartment, tucking a notebook in her pocket. She nodded to Brandon, walked over to O'Farrell and talked briefly. Smythe got in her car and pulled away. O'Farrell walked back to Brandon, stood by the truck.

"We'll find them. Nowhere to go but Portland," O'Farrell said.

"Maybe they don't think they did anything wrong," Brandon said. "An honor killing."

"Except he lived."

"Pays to double-check your work," Brandon said.

"Think the painter knocked up this African girl?"

"Kat says Lil Messy is probably gay."

"Yeah, well, some people, it isn't either-or."

"I suppose," Brandon said. "But I don't know."

O'Farrell looked at the apartment house. Cleared his throat. "I thought Perry told you to take a day off," O'Farrell said.

"I am off," Brandon said.

"Interesting hobby you have, Blake."

"Yeah, well—"

"Go fix your boat."

"I did that."

"Then take it out for a sail."

"It's a powerboat," Brandon said.

"Watch the Red Sox."

"No TV."

"Then just hang out with your friends."

Brandon didn't answer.

"There's an order to this," O'Farrell said. "It's like the military. I need to know who's running around the battlefield."

"I know."

"No room for freelance."

"Right."

They stood for a minute.

"I was talking to this homeless lady, Big Liz," Brandon said.

"Oh, yeah?"

"She says she hears people from underground. The undergrounders, she calls them. Or the cellar people."

"I'm sure she hears people in the fucking trees, too," O'Farrell said.

"She says they have Chantelle's baby. She's heard him crying."

"Uh-huh."

"Maybe she's right. Walks all the time, out all night. Maybe she heard the kid."

"Any particular place?"

"I don't know. But she has a list of addresses where she hears these voices. Writes them on her arm. Wouldn't take long to—"

"Brandon."

"Yeah?"

"No."

"What if somebody has him—"

"In the sewer? She makes the whack jobs who've been calling in baby sightings seem credible."

Brandon didn't answer.

"Go home," O'Farrell said. "Stay there."

Again, no answer.

"Word to the wise," O'Farrell said. "If you want to keep this job."

He turned and walked to his car, got on the radio. Brandon heard O'Farrell talking to Smythe, Smythe saying Dever had spotted two gangbangers on the basketball court in Kennedy Park. Perry got on, telling Dever to wait—like he'd roust a Boy Scout without backup. The sergeant was calling the team in, putting people in place for a felony arrest, without the warrants.

Damn, Brandon thought. O'Farrell looked back at Brandon, sitting in the truck, listening. On the radio, Brandon heard him say to somebody, "Call my cell."

Brandon started the truck. O'Farrell pulled away. Brandon glanced up at 317. Annie Young was in the window, watching him. He waved. The curtains pulled shut.

FIFTY-FIVE

The sun had been overtaken by clouds, the wind shifting from the southwest to the southeast. By noon it was raining, dark clouds rolling over from the west, showers spattering the deck, flattening the little bit of chop on the harbor. Brandon was at the table in the salon, laptop open, police radio beside it. They'd picked up the two guys at Kennedy Park, found one in possession of a handgun. Good thing to have a weapons charge, leverage if they were going to try to turn the guy. Brandon listened but the radio went quiet.

He'd searched for the *Ocean Princess,* found the cruise line headquarters in San Diego, a contact-us 800 number. He called, got a woman with a purring telephone voice, better to soothe somebody who'd left a diamond ring in the bathroom on level six.

Brandon said he was from the Portland, Maine, police department. He was looking for information in relation to a shooting; who could he talk to? The woman said, "Oh, my goodness," said he'd have to call a different number. He did, and another woman answered, this one all business. He repeated his question, got silence, then a third number. A man picked up, southern American accent, said "Ms. Alvarez's office. This is Jamie."

Brandon repeated his request. Jamie said Ms. Alvarez wasn't in.

"I'll talk to her supervisor," Brandon said.

"That's assistant vice president level," Jamie said.

"Good," Brandon said.

"I don't think they'll be able to help you right away."

"This involves a shooting that resulted in a homicide—an official police investigation."

"I'm sorry, sir, but—"

"What's above assistant vice president?" Brandon said.

"I don't think it will be necessary to—"

"How 'bout if I just start at the top and work my way back down to you." He tapped at the keyboard. "The CEO. Let's see. Here's her name right here. There's even a phone number. Nice website, by the way."

There was a click, a silence.

"Ms. Alvarez just came back."

"Lucky me," Brandon said.

Another click.

"Lucille Alvarez."

Brandon made his pitch: attempted homicide, an actual death resulting. Police searching for a motive, an indication that the shooting could have stemmed from a case of mistaken identity involving a crewman on the *Ocean Princess*.

"How unfortunate," Ms. Alvarez said.

"Yes."

"And you want the crew list?"

"Yes."

"That information really is confidential."

"This is a police matter. Do we need a subpoena?"

"It's just that we pledge to our passengers that—"

"We could query on all the cruise ship travel websites, making sure we name the ship and your company. And the fact that there was a shooting."

"To which our ship is only tangentially connected, if that," Ms. Alvarez said.

"Most homicide investigations are filled with tangential connections," Brandon said.

"Who is the crewman?"

"Alston Kelley. Jamaican. But he died in a fire in Canada, while your ship was in port there."

"Oh, dear."

"Yes. Very sad."

A long pause.

"I'll have to run this by Legal," she said.

"Okay."

"And if they approve it, we'll need the request in writing. And a copy of your ID. It's Brandon Blake?"

"Yes."

"And you are?"

"Assisting with this investigation," Brandon said. "If you'll give me your fax number, I'll get that right out—so when you hear back from your people, you're ready to go."

"They might say no," Ms. Alvarez said.

"Aren't they there to protect your interests?"

"Of course."

"Then they'll say yes," Brandon said.

Brandon had letterhead from the department, atop a letter outlining his benefits. He put it in an envelope, put on a windbreaker, slipping the envelope underneath. Closing the hatch door, he switched on the motion alarm, stepped off the stern, and headed for the truck, radio in hand, the Glock snug to his waist.

The squalls had turned to a steady rain, keeping boaters home or snug inside their cabins, no one on the docks or in the yard. Brandon made sure the security gate was closed behind him, walked to the truck, unlocked it, got in. He sat—motor running, no wipers—and texted Mia.

THINKING OF YOU. ALL QUIET HERE. MISS THE SOUND OF YOUR VOICE. LOVE, BRANDON

He added another:

WORKING ON THE NY QUESTION. SEE YOU SOON, I HOPE.

He sent it. All the way into Portland he watched the phone. It lay there on the seat beside him. Silent.

There was a fax machine at the library by the computers. He copied the letterhead onto a blank piece of paper, typed his request to Alvarez, asking for a reply via e-mail. He walked across the room to the printer, took the blank paper out, slipped his letterhead in. Hurried back and hit PRINT, waited a moment, and trashed the document, emptied the trash. One of the genealogists, an old guy with a pencil behind his ear, stepped in front of him and pulled the paper out as it slipped from the printer.

"Whoa, that's not mine," he said, as Brandon took the letter from him.

"No," Brandon said, smiling.

"Budget cuts? No printer at the department?"

"On the blink," Brandon said, as the guy looked him over.

"Don't want to leave that paper around."

"No."

"Somebody might use it for the wrong reasons."

"Yes."

"How long have you been with the police?"

"A year or so."

"I was gonna say."

"Say what?"

"That you look young."

"I suppose," Brandon said.

"Probably look older in uniform," the guy said.

"Oh, yeah."

"Not to pry or anything, but I've always thought you fellas should be looking at these cruise ships."

Brandon turned the letter away.

"That right?"

"Sure. I told my wife, two thousand people get off that boat, they march around downtown. We have no idea who they are."

"I suppose not," Brandon said.

"Nobody checks them. Could be a terrorist in there someplace. This one of those terrorist things? Homeland Security involved?"

"Confidential. Police business."

Brandon winked. The man adjusted his pencil, smiled.

"Gotcha."

"Keep it between us," Brandon said.

"No problem. I was in the MPs. Vietnam, but I never got out of California. I can keep a secret. Good to know."

"What's that?"

"That you boys are working on it. Undercover, too. You can tell your bosses I said so. Name's John Q. Public."

He winked back.

Brandon bought coffee at Starbucks on Congress, drove slowly back down the hill and up onto the bridge. The moored boats in the harbor were all turned to the southeast, like gulls facing the wind. He got a glimpse of *Bay Witch* from the peak of the bridge, looked back again and saw two tiny figures on the ramp.

One had hands raised. Taking pictures.

Crime-scene techs long gone, no reason to come back. He sped up, swung left, made the light on the yellow. One of the detectives? The fire marshal's office?

He made the second light on green, drove the three blocks, took the left. The pickup banged over the speed bumps, swung into the lot. Brandon slid out, trotted to the gate, punched in the code. He crossed the yard, started down the ramp. On the dock beyond *Bay Witch* two people were sauntering out, a man and a woman.

Brandon hurried down the ramp, passed his boat. The man turned. Grinned.

"Officer Blake."

Brandon slowed. Matt Estusa tapped the woman, who turned, a camera slung over her shoulder. They started toward him. The woman, in a red rain jacket, black baseball cap, hung back, took a step to the right, framing Brandon with *Bay Witch* behind him. The shutter clicked. Brandon waited.

"Officer Blake," Estusa said.

"The marina is private property," Brandon said.

"Oh, we didn't know. The gate was open."

"That right?"

"Listen, sorry about your boat. But man, sounds like you were lucky to get out alive." Estusa smiled, feigning relief that Brandon wasn't dead.

"Who says?"

"Oh, I just heard around that somebody torched the boat. Stuck a chair in the trapdoor thing. Somebody happened to come by, or you would've been toast."

"No comment."

"Because it's under investigation?"

"No comment because I have no comment."

"Oh, sure. Well, between us, I'm glad that you're okay."

Brandon nodded.

"So, I'll have to talk to somebody else at the department?"

"Talk to whomever you'd like."

The photographer fired off a few more frames. Brandon looked at her. "I don't want photos of my boat in the paper," he said. "I prefer that the general public not know where I live."

The photographer shrugged, looked to Estusa.

"This is Jane," Estusa said. "I'll have to take that up with my editors."

"Photos taken without permission on private property?"

"I could shoot with a telephoto, get the same shot from the road," Jane said.

"I could take your camera, toss it in the water," Brandon said.

"And we'd write about that in the paper," Estusa said.

"Might be worth it."

"Brandon, come on. What's with all the negativity?" Estusa said.

"I don't like you. I don't like this invasion of privacy."

"Just doing my job."

"Likewise—or trying to."

Estusa shifted on his feet, looked up as a gull swooped low. "Another reason I came by, Brandon," Estusa said.

Brandon waited.

"I'm working on a story. It's about PTSD in police officers. We had cops in fatal shootings, a couple of them didn't come back. So I'm interested in the psychological trauma that something like that can cause."

Brandon stared. Estusa paused, cleared his throat.

"So I know you haven't had a fatal shooting on duty," Estusa said. "But you had one before you came on the force."

Brandon waited, teeth clenched.

"And I'm interested in how you've coped with that. I mean, I know you had to shoot Joel Fuller to save your girlfriend's life. Mia, I mean. But still, it has to be something you carry around. And I'm interested in how that affects a police officer's ability to do his job."

Brandon took a step toward the boat.

"Just because you don't talk doesn't mean I can't include you in the story, Brandon. You're a public person. It was a public event, the Fuller shooting. The investigation, the whole thing. Losing your mother at a young age. The circumstances of her death."

Brandon turned away.

"And I have to tell you—sources are telling me there's some concern about your performance on the job."

Brandon turned back. "Who's your source?"

"I can't disclose that."

"You're both chickenshits," Brandon said.

"I've been told there's concern about your ability to put your work aside. I was told you were warned not to fraternize with people involved in ongoing cases, while you're off duty. Are you too emotionally involved? Does that stem from your recent trauma? And is that something that could affect your ability to protect the public? Can a police officer really go on and do the job effectively after one of these incidents? How does it affect the judgment you need to be a good officer?"

He paused.

"You and the others. I mean, you'd just be one example."

Brandon faced him, the rain coming down, puddling on the dock. Estusa stood with his hands in the pockets of his anorak, water dripping from the bill of his Sea Dogs cap. Jane stood off to the side, stone-faced, watching.

"Gonna come back to bite you," Brandon said.

"Is that a threat?" Estusa said.

"Just what I said."

"Can I quote you on that, Officer Blake?"

"I don't care what you do," Brandon said, stepping up onto the boat.

"Anything else you'd care to say?" Estusa said, edging closer.

"Yeah," Brandon said, stepping down from the transom and turning back. "Fuck off."

"Sorry you feel that way," Estusa said, with a half-smile.

They were halfway across the boatyard when Estusa took the recorder from his pocket. He switched it off.

"Not once did he say any of that was off the record," Estusa said.

"Nope," Jane said. "Boss cops ain't gonna like that. Six-thousand-dollar camera? I don't think so, pal."

She wiped the viewfinder of the camera, held it up for Estusa to see. In the photo Brandon was scowling in front of his boat, BAY WITCH, PORTLAND, MAINE showing plainly behind him.

"That captures it nicely," Estusa said. "Officer Brandon Blake, walking time bomb."

FIFTY-SIX

The shore power and water lines were disconnected, the engine idling. Brandon had undone the bowline, was walking to the stern, ready to shove off. He bent to slip the line off the cleat on the dock, turned and looked up.

Kat was standing there, rain dripping off her jacket, her hair shiny wet.

"Nice day for a boat ride," she said.

"I like it out on the bay in the rain," Brandon said. "Nobody around. Gives you a chance to think."

"Want a passenger?"

He looked at her.

"Sure."

Kat stepped aboard. She was wearing a yellow anorak, black yoga pants, and running shoes. Her cap said TEAM GLOCK.

"Hat must intimidate the other triathloners," Brandon said.

"I intimidate the other triathloners," Kat said.

Brandon trotted up the ladder and moved to the helm. Kat stood beside him as he eased on the throttles, cut the wheel hard to port, cleared the pilings, and idled past the slips, into the harbor.

"Where we headed?" Kat said. "Portugal? 'Cause I'm on at five."

"Miss me?"

"Yeah, if you want to know."

"I'm not sure when I'll be back."

"Yeah, you kinda pissed Perry off."

"O'Farrell, too," Brandon said.

"Yup."

"So, you heard anything on Lil Messy?"

"Out of the woods, but he'll be in the hospital a while. Lots of stuff to fix."

"They pick up the Ottos?"

"Last I heard, still looking."

"Somebody's hiding them."

"Yeah. Now they're talking a Sudanese safehouse in another state."

"Protect their own," Brandon said. "To be expected."

"Like us."

"Except we don't," Brandon said.

Standing there at the helm, he told her the Estusa story. Somebody saying he was too gung-ho, couldn't let the job go, Estusa making the jump to say it was due to Brandon's history.

"Who told him all that?"

"His buddy Dever, be my bet."

"Gonna catch up with him, yapping to the press," Kat said.

"Yup."

They were in the channel, moored sailboats on both sides. To starboard, a lighter was unloading, the oil smell heavy on the water. To port an offshore lobster boat was approaching, loaded, low in the water. Brandon reached for binoculars, checked to see if it was the *Marie G.* It wasn't.

"Well, I think we've got to talk to Booker," he said. "And Toby."

"Right."

"And Cawley. Bikers are into drug dealing, extortion, prostitution. Why not sell stolen babies? Couples spend tens of thousands of dollars for a baby. Sell the stolen one cheap. Say twenty grand."

"I'm sure it's been done," Kat said.

"Blades have other chapters. They could whisk the kid away, sell him in California or someplace. Who the hell's gonna know? New couple moves in, has a kid. You gonna ask them if their baby was abducted?"

"Probably not," Kat said. "They got four, five years to come up with a fake birth certificate for school registration."

"Bikers just change a few diapers."

"Easy money."

Brandon eased the throttles forward and *Bay Witch* gathered herself up, then pitched into the chop, building from the southeast. Spray spattered the windscreen as the wiper waved and Kat grabbed Brandon's arm to steady herself.

"Brandon," she said, over the rumble of the engine.

"Yeah?"

"What is it?"

"What's what?"

"What's bothering you?"

"Nothing."

Kat looked at him.

"Okay, maybe it's not nothing."

"Spill it."

"Or you'll get out the rubber hose?"

"Or I won't be able to help you."

Brandon looked out at the gray water, the gulls lifting off in front of them. "Wanted this for a long time," he said. "Trying to do the job right, and now I'm getting slapped for it."

"That's the surface," Kat said. "I want to know what's underneath."

A longer pause. Brandon adjusted course, bore for the buoy west of Great Diamond Island.

"It's because of me, at least partly, that Chantelle's dead."

"You can't say that. She was a total wreck, physically, emotionally. Who knows what went through her head?"

"I pushed her too hard, made her blame herself."

Kat looked out at the bay, said, "Who knows how that affected her? If at all."

"Can I tell you something?"

"Sure."

"I'm still pissed about my mother."

"I know."

"I mean, who goes off marijuana smuggling, leaves a three-year-old at home?"

"Yup."

"That shrink they sent me to at the Academy, he said I had unresolved issues relating to my feelings of abandonment."

"Don't we all."

They were quiet. They were moving beyond the point on the South Portland side and the chop was bigger, the spray coming across the bow.

"And?" Kat said.

"And what?"

"And what else?"

Brandon moved the wheel back and forth, throttled down slightly.

"I don't know if I can do this Mia thing."

"You don't love her?"

"I do. But I don't know how we're gonna work together. I don't fit in with her friends, her whole world."

"The trust-fund woman, the guy from Barbados?"

Brandon hesitated. The boat rose and fell. The wiper slapped.

"I just don't buy it. His act."

"They ran him after the shooting. Nothing showed up."

"I know," Brandon said. "Emigrated to Canada from Barbados. Moved to New York, then to Maine. No criminal record in any of those places. Successful in the restaurant business. And he's a nice guy. Even brought me dinner from the restaurant. After Mia left. But still, something odd."

"Like what?," Kat said.

"He has a handgun."

"So do a lot of law-abiding people."

"And he gets home-invaded by a guy from a Jamaican gang."

"And then somebody tries to burn you up in your boat."

"Or Mia."

"Uh-huh."

"Who saw the New York guys outside the house. We think."

They paused. The Eastern Prom was passing to port. Somewhere up there in the gray rain was the house where Renford Gayle had died.

"So what are you going to do?" Kat said.

He told her—checking out the link to the dead guy.

"And the baby?" Kat said.

"I want to talk to Cawley. Love to know where he's traveled since Lincoln disappeared. Maybe spend some more time with Big Liz. She said she's heard a baby crying."

"Brandon," Kat said.

"Yeah?"

"You're not getting it."

"What?"

"Listen to me now, and you're not gonna like this, but I'm saying it to help you. You didn't go to the cops when Fuller and Kelvin took Mia. No, you handled it alone, and . . ." She paused. "And it almost got her killed. That's a hard fact."

Brandon didn't answer.

"Now it's the same thing. Let the detective division handle it."

"They're not doing it. I told O'Farrell about Big Liz, he acted like I was as nuts as she is."

"Brandon, listen to me, as your field training officer and your friend. None of that is your job."

"But that's just it," Brandon said, staring out at the rainswept bay. "This is more than a job to me."

"So what is it? Your mother was killed, and you spend the rest of your life getting revenge?"

Brandon didn't answer.

"Keep it up, I won't be able to protect you," Kat said. "You'll be on your own."

"Always have been," Brandon said.

She looked away at the gray sea, the splintering chop.

"I gotta head back," Kat said, nothing more.

He spun the wheel, put the bow into the wind.

FIFTY-SEVEN

There was a single text from Mia, two words: STILL THINKING. He tried calling but her phone went directly to voice mail, and he left another message, said he hoped all was well. And then he sat at the helm seat and listened to the rain.

It continued to fall, steady and patient, the weather radar showing a swath all the way to Massachusetts. The rain kept the boaters inside or ashore and the marina was quiet. It was after six. Roll call was done, the team would be headed out. Perry and O'Farrell, their two-hour overlap. Kat and Dever and Smythe. The K-9 unit and the drug guys popping up here and there around the city.

And Brandon on the bench because—how had Kat put it?— his mother killed, Brandon spending the rest of his life getting revenge. But that wasn't true, was it? He'd taken care of Nessa; he still did. He stood from his vantage point at the helm, went below and changed his shirt.

Nessa had finished her dinner, was sitting in the chair in her room. The television was on: Julie Andrews in *The Sound of Music*. Brandon stood in the doorway, watched as Nessa tried to mouth the words.

Brandon stepped in.

"Hey, there," he said, and he moved to the edge of the bed and leaned, gave her forehead a peck. She looked up at him and smiled her lopsided smile.

"Good movie," Brandon said. "I remember watching it at home, on the VCR."

On the TV Julie and the kids were a show, the boys in

lederhosen. Julie and the dad had some kind of moment, their eyes meeting. Nessa reached for the remote, turned down the sound.

Brandon handed her the keypad.

"How are you doing? I'm sorry I haven't been around. Work's been busy."

She typed.

I KNOW. IT'S OKAY.

"You know? You've been watching the news?"

AND READING THE PAPER. ON THE COMPUTER IN THE LOBBY.

"Aren't you getting high-tech."

YES.

"So did you read about the thing on the Eastern Prom?"

HORRIBLE.

"The woman who shot the man, that's Mia's friend. From her book club."

SHE WAS IN THE PICTURE.

"Right. She and Mia. Mia went to help her out, give her some support."

MIA IS VERY KIND.

"Yes, she is. Kinder than me."

YES.

Brandon looked at her, wondering if that was a joke. No sign of it. Then Nessa was typing again.

WORRIED ABOUT YOU.

"I'm fine. Really."

I HATE TO SEE YOU IN TROUBLE.

"Oh, I'm not in trouble. Just been a lot happening and I think I need a little time off. Get away from it."

YOU'RE NOT GOING TO BE FIRED, ARE YOU? BECAUSE THE PAPER SAID—

Brandon stopped her, mid-sentence.

"The paper said what?"

Nessa looked up, her lopsided face full of sympathy. Brandon said, "Excuse me, Nessa," and left the room, went to the station, where Shardi was bent over, rummaging for something under the counter. She stood, saw Brandon, said, "Oh, my goodness. You scared me." She patted her chest.

"Can I use a computer? I need to look at—"

"The story? Yeah, it wasn't there this morning. You know the stories just show up all day long, with the Internet. I saw that, your picture, I said, 'Well, he's not having a good day.' "

Brandon was already at the desk.

"Log-in is 'maple,' " Shardi said. "The password is 'syrup.' "

Brandon logged on, went to the *Tribune* site. Saw himself staring back from the screen.

It was the photo from the dock, *Bay Witch* plainly shown. The caption said:

> Patrolman Brandon Blake, Portland Police Department, put on paid administrative leave this week after his superiors reportedly questioned his off-duty investigations. Blake, then a civilian, was defending his girlfriend when he shot and killed Joel Fuller, 29, in a Portland hotel in 2008. Some experts are questioning whether current policies for psychological assessment of police involved in fatal shootings are adequate.

"Those bastards," Brandon said. "Those fucking bastards."

Shardi said, "You okay?"

The story went back ten years, discussing five fatal shootings by Portland police officers—six, if you counted Brandon. Estusa had interviewed psychologists in Maine and elsewhere, including two who worked with lawyers who had sued Portland PD on behalf of the families of shooting victims. The critics said the cops were put back on duty way too soon. A cop who had left the force declined to comment. A cop who had stayed said, "I'm fine."

Estusa then rehashed the Joel Fuller fatal shooting—Fuller kidnapping Mia, holding her at gunpoint, Brandon shooting him five times in the chest as police closed in. "Blake," it said, "emptied his weapon."

And then there was the stuff attributed to "sources within the police department." Some rehash. O'Farrell going to bat for Blake because, some said, Fuller had killed O'Farrell's longtime partner and Blake had killed Fuller.

The complaints from Chantelle Anthony's family. The guy in the domestic in the Old Port and his lawyer. The most recent situation on State Street, Brandon finding Paul Boekamp, twenty-one, badly beaten in his apartment. An unnamed source saying, "We can't have cops running all over the city, doing independent investigations on their own time. It would be anarchy."

The same source said he couldn't tie Blake's recent actions to the 2008 fatal shooting. "But it raises red flags," the source said. "If a guy shoots someone, even with justification, as a civilian, what judgment will he have as a police officer?"

Blake, approached by a reporter and photographer Wednesday at the South Portland marina where he lives aboard a cabin cruiser, said he had no comment. "F—— off," he said.

A police spokesman, public information officer Sandra Wooley, said she could not comment on Blake's reported leave, saying all actions involving discipline are personnel matters and are confidential.

"Discipline," Brandon exploded. "Who the hell is talking about discipline?" He pounded his fist once on the table, looked up to see Shardi watching him, wide-eyed.

"Sorry," he said.

"It's okay," she said.

"Tell Nessa I had to go. Police business," he said.

He got up from the table, walked to the doors, and banged them hard. They rattled but didn't open, Shardi calling, "After eight I have to let you out." The door buzzed, and Brandon pushed through. He strode out into the night, where the rain had dwindled to a drizzle. His truck sat alone under the pines, and he walked to it, climbed in, slammed the door shut. "That son of a bitch," he said.

He started the truck, backed up, stomped the gas. The tires spun on the wet pavement and Brandon caught himself, slowed as he left the lot. He forced himself to stay under the 15 mph limit on the winding drive through the woods.

All he needed was to get stopped the same day he was on the front page as a wacko. But what was he supposed to do? Not care about a missing baby? Not want to find the kid? Ignore the lady when she says a bunch of guys went off to beat the crap out of somebody, a guy who was a witness in a suspicious death?"

Mia would see the story. Her father would see it. Everyone in the marina would see it—those people read the paper, every page. Everyone in the city would see it. Anyone who googled "Portland PD and Brandon Blake" would see him standing there, looking like he'd killed once, he'd like to it again. Maybe kill the reporter, the photographer, too.

F—— off.

He hadn't been disciplined, not like they were implying. Perry just told him to take a break. Go relax, hang out. There was no hearing, no human resources person, no union rep taking his—

He slowed for a speed bump.

The windshield shattered.

FIFTY-EIGHT

The bullet hole was in front of his face, to the right. The truck hit the curb and bounced. Another crack, another hole in front of him, this one a foot to the left and down. The windshield was opaque, the truck half off the pavement, straddling the curb, exhaust scraping underneath.

A third shot, the passenger window, all of the glass spidered now, Brandon wrenching the wheel to the left, bouncing back onto the pavement, flooring the truck into a U-turn, the back end sliding around. He hit the gas, the curb. The motor stalled. Brandon had the door open, his radio up, gun out, safety off.

"This is three-twenty-three, three-twenty-three. I'm taking fire. South Portland, access road to Maple Grove rehab center. Repeat, I'm taking fire."

Brandon slid off the seat as the truck rolled to a stop. Crouched behind the truck bed, listened. He heard Chooch's voice, calm but tense, "All available units." South Portland was on, a woman officer's voice—he'd met her. Jennifer? Jessica?—saying, "I'm there, ETA five minutes." Everybody from Portland, state troopers from the turnpike, the South Portland deputy chief, a game warden from somewhere—all of the radio traffic coming with the background roar of engines, cruisers running flat out.

Smack, another shot, hearing it now, a deer-rifle sound echoing in the trees. The slug tore through the truck bed just to his right. He moved left, got behind the cab, the motor between him and the shooter. He eased up, peeked over, saw the muzzle flash in the trees, the *whoof-clang* of the slug hitting something heavy under the hood. He rose, aimed where the flash had been, got off three shots, shooting in a close spread.

He ducked back as another slug tore into the cab, this time high, just above his head. He moved to the bed, rose and fired twice, ducked back and scooched toward the front again. Another shot, the windshield shattering more, glass showering his head. He felt the sting, the warm ooze of blood on his forehead. He shot through the cab windows, fell back down, counted his shots. Six fired, four left. He heard distant sirens, then the cracking of someone running through the woods, the sound fading. Brandon radioed, "He's running, he's moving west. A deer rifle or assault rifle."

He ran to the edge of the woods, crouched and listened. The crashing was faint now, the guy coming out on the far side. He called that in, and in minutes cops were everywhere, like a movie. Cruisers and SUVs were on the drive, fore and aft of his battered truck. Blue lights showed through the trees; a tracking dog barked in one of the cruisers. The other side of the woods was a road that bordered the Maine Mall, a steady stream of traffic. Brandon could hear them closing it off, asking whether the command post thought the shooter could have gotten past them.

"What do you think?" a voice behind Brandon said.

It was Perry, one hand on his weapon, the other on his mic.

"I don't know. He really booked it. If a car was waiting, took right off, maybe . . ."

"I want this fucker," another voice said.

It was Kat. She touched his shoulder, then started across the drive, following Christiansen, the jump-booted handler running behind the dog, SWAT cops following with night-vision goggles, assault rifles.

"And there's no indication you hit him?" Perry said.

"Why they call it a shot in the dark," Brandon said.

The dogs tracked the shooter to the road along the mall, the turnpike access-road side. The track ended on the pavement fifty yards from the Hampton Inn.

"Car waiting," said Christiansen, on the radio. "Track stopped like he stepped off a cliff."

"Any mall surveillance cameras out that far?" a South Portland SWAT officer said.

The patrol commander, the woman Brandon had heard on the radio, shook her head. "Negative," she said.

The driveway was cordoned as evidence techs swept the area. Brandon's pickup was hoisted onto a ramp truck, to be hauled back to the crime lab. After Brandon had told the story three times, he told it twice more. And then Kat was back, led him back to the cruiser, parked where the road was cordoned off and the press waited, baying like the dog.

"Did you get a look at him?"

"Who has it in for you, Officer Blake?"

"Was there more than one shooter?"

Brandon waited as Kat unlocked the door from inside. And then Estusa, the group parting for him as he pushed his way to the front, pressed the crime-scene tape back to lean close to Brandon, holding out his recorder. The lock thunked, Brandon yanked the door open, Kat still shoving her stuff out of the way, unlocking the laptop swivel arm to make room for him.

Estusa again. "Do you feel you're a liability to your fellow officers? What do you know, Officer Blake, that someone would kill for?"

Brandon slammed the front door shut, opened the back door and heaved himself in. Strobes flashed. The police tape broke and the reporters moved closer, getting his picture as he sat in the back of the cruiser, stone-faced, facing forward, like he'd just been arrested. Kat eased through the scrum, and then they were away, moving along the road in the dark. Brandon looked out at the black shadows that were the trees.

"What do you know, Brandon?" Kat said, glancing at him. "I mean, are you keeping something from me or what?"

FIFTY-NINE

"I've told you everything," Brandon said.

"South Portland will watch the nursing home."

"I know, they told me."

"Who knew where you were going?" Kat said.

"Nobody. But all they had to do was follow me, set up in the woods, and wait for me to come back out."

"Why you?"

"I don't know."

"Fuller's friends?" Kat said.

"After more than a year? And anyway, I don't know that he had any—not any who would kill for him."

They were crossing the bridge into the West End, the yellow glow of the oil docks on their right, a lighter at the terminal, spotlights glaring.

Brandon was quiet as the cruiser turned onto Commercial Street, the dark and lonely end. He had a moment of deja vu, riding this same stretch of road with Griffin, a week before he was killed, Griffin asking him what it was like to live on a boat. Brandon shook it off, the injustice of it all, a death for a death coming up horribly short.

"I made some inquiries," he said.

"Like what?" Kat said.

"Called the cruise line, requested the crew list."

"Saying you were—"

"An investigator. Same with Brooklyn detective division."

"Playing detective?"

"Not playing," Brandon said. "I'm serious."

"I know you are," Kat said.

"I can't stand for them to get away with it."

"With what?"

"Any of it. The baby. Killing Fatima. Coming from New York to kill Lily. Maybe Mia."

They slipped under the bridge, saw the glow of a campfire down by the harbor's edge, not far from where Fatima's body had been found. Brandon saw her eyes, the light gone out, dead as glass. He looked up at Kat, her face illuminated by the laptop's icy glow.

"Lil Messy. That little girl in Cawley's apartment."

"We'll get them."

"But what if we don't?" Brandon said.

"You're not the only cop in Portland," Kat said.

"I know. Besides, they just took my gun."

"But you really don't know it, do you. You don't trust anybody. You won't let yourself depend on anyone. Not good, Brandon, if you're supposed to be part of a team."

Brandon watched the harbor lights, his boat out there, across the black water. Where he lived alone. Where he'd grown up alone. Maybe this team thing just wasn't going to work. Not the PD, not Mia.

"We could do bonding exercises," he said. "I fall backwards, you catch me."

"That's what I'm trying to do," Kat said. "Catch you before you hit the ground."

Kat said Brandon could stay with her. Roberta would be locked away, working on her dissertation—all Milton, all the time. Brandon said he'd be fine; better to have some quiet, clear his head. He asked Kat to drive him to Atlantic Street to Mia's apartment. Brandon needed transportation and had a key to her Saab.

"When's Mia coming back to Portland?" Kat said.

"I don't know," Brandon said.

"I'd tell her to wait. Until things settle down."

"I'll call her."

"We'll talk in the a.m.," Kat said.

"Yes," Brandon said, standing by the cruiser.

"You be careful."

"You, too."

"And let us do our work," Kat said. "You're not alone."

Brandon turned toward the dark driveway. "Right," he said.

Kat hit the side spot, flooded the driveway with light. She waited until Brandon had pulled away, heading for the Prom. Kat took a right, headed downtown to meet up with Perry, the rest of the team, talk this thing over.

"Brandon Blake," she said, as she swung back toward Congress. "What are we gonna do with you?"

Brandon took a right at the Prom, back down Commercial through the Old Port. Couples and kids were crossing, hitting the bars, the restaurants. Cars inched along, looking for parking spaces. BMWs, Volvos, new SUVs with college stickers. In the Saab with the Colby sticker, Brandon blended.

His radio squawked. Reflexively, he reached for his missing gun. Felt naked without it, vulnerable. He was out of the Old Port traffic, hit the gas, ran a light and swung up onto the bridge. Crossing, he looked out on the harbor, saw a few lights flickering on boats, but mostly a deep, enveloping darkness. All the way off the bridge, out to the marina, he felt an urge to disappear, take *Bay Witch* out into the bay right now, past the harbor markers, find a cove on Peaks, even out to Chebeague, anchor and hide.

It had been his refuge in the past, when things had gotten bad—with Nessa, with the shooting. He and Mia had gone out to the back side of Chebeague, on a southwest wind. Anchored and sat on deck in the sun, until the wind swung around to the southeast and brought rain and a stiff chop, and they'd pulled anchor and headed back in, Mia close beside him at the helm.

Back when she needed him, when she thought he could do no wrong.

No more.

It was after ten, breeze out of the southeast again. The yard lights reflected off the fog, welling up off the water. Brandon parked in the back of the lot in the shadows, watched and waited. It was quiet, muffled voices, someone calling from boat to boat. He looked the cars and trucks over in the lot, nobody showing. Then he reached up, turned the dome light off, popped the door open. Got out and closed it, locked the car. Waited and watched, listened hard.

The traffic rumble on the bridge. A foghorn out on the harbor. Quiet.

Brandon let himself in, shut the gate firmly behind him. He walked through the boatyard, full of places to hide, watching the shadows. Down the ramp, a few lights showing. He stood near *Bay Witch*, watched and listened, then stepped to the stern, reached over the gunwale, and disabled the motion alarm. Hopping aboard, he walked up the side deck, checked the bow. Back to the stern, he went below, moving slowly in the darkness. Up the steps to the salon, lights glowing at the helm. Back down the steps, he listened, then slipped below.

Dark. Silent. A faint whiff of Mia's shampoo, her clothes. Brandon went to the storage cupboard in the bow cabin, unlocked it, took out his Glock. He pulled the magazine, snapped it back in. Put the gun in the waistband of his jeans and went back out and up to the helm. Slipped the key in and started the engine, the rumble sweeping over the sleeping marina.

The motor lapsed into a smooth idle and Brandon slipped out and unhooked the shore power. He went to the dinghy, overturned on the float, flipped it over and slipped it into the water, fastened the painter to a stern cleat. Then he jumped aboard, undid the stern line, slipped along to the bow and threw that dockline clear.

As *Bay Witch* started to drift, he hurried to the helm, put the boat in gear and, hitting the nav lights, eased out. The boat idled past the slips, nightlights glowing at helms, cabin lights below. In front of him the Portland skyline glowed in the fog, like the city was on fire again, just like in 1775. *Bay Witch* moved through the passage between the moored boats, bows pointed into the breeze. The tide was incoming, swinging the boat to port, and he adjusted, moved out into the dark harbor, red channel markers showing under the bridge. Brandon made a quick loop and turned back.

There were three guest moorings, empty on a weeknight. Brandon turned the bow spotlight on, picked up the white buoy, eased back on the throttle, kept the buoy just to the port side. He pulled his gun out, laid it on the console, then slipped the boat into neutral, felt it start to drift back on the current as he hurried to the bow. He was down the side deck and out, grabbing a boat hook on the way. Kneeling at the bow, he leaned over, snagged the mooring line, lifted it on board, cold and dripping. He made it fast to the cleat, slipped the line through the chock. Then he moved quickly back to the helm, shut off the lights and the motor, felt *Bay Witch* pull against the mooring, the bow swinging, the boat creaking.

Brandon looked out from the darkened helm at the black moat of water between the boat and the marina. A shot from a dock? From the bridge, above and to his right? From the abandoned pier that abutted the boatyard?

Better here. Not perfect.

Brandon picked up his gun, tucked it back in his jeans, moved to the stern, where the dinghy was swinging. He reached back and armed the alarm, then pulled the dinghy close, eased aboard, and, in the darkness, rowed in to the docks. He tied the dinghy up in an empty slip, not his own. No need to advertise that he'd moved *Bay Witch* only rowing distance away, that he was still here.

The floats creaked and rattled as he made his way to the ramp and up to the yard. But nobody showed, and he paused as he crossed the yard. He listened, crossed to the office, pulled a couple of notes from the bulletin board by the door. Let them think he was on the job, when really he was—

He was what?

On the hunt.

SIXTY

The gate clanged shut behind him. He walked along the edge of the lot, staying in the shadows, then crossed behind the Saab and got in. He laid his gun and radio on the passenger seat, sat in the dark. He watched the lot. Listened. Bugs. Traffic. Scurrying in the brush behind the car.

He picked up the gun, heavy and cold. Slipped the safety off. Watched the mirrors. A cat slipped out, a rat hanging from its mouth, rattail swinging.

The safety back on. The gun on the seat. The lot quiet.

Eleven-forty. A South Portland cruiser swung in, pulled up to the gate. The cop got out, rattled it. Stood for a moment and looked across the boatyard, then got back in. Brandon heard him on the radio, reporting in, all secure. The cruiser turned around, Brandon sliding down in the seat just before the headlights swept past. He heard the sound of gravel spraying, the motor revving, the cruiser speeding away.

Quiet again. The sound of bugs. A diesel idling somewhere out on the water. Brandon picked up the phone, texted Mia again. THINKING OF YOU. Put it back down, waited. This time a response. One word.

THANKS.

Then headlights on the road, swinging in, raking the lot, short of the Saab. A Honda, primer black, exhaust throbbing. The driver rolled along the vine-covered fence. Killed the lights. In the yellow wash of the streetlight, three heads showed, one in back, leaning forward to talk. The driver killed the motor.

They were looking at the yard, the gate, that direction. Brandon reached up, flicked the interior light switch to off. Picked up the Glock and popped the door open. He eased out, moved behind the car. Stayed low, on the edge of the brush, and moved slowly across to the fence. He waited, motionless, watching. The three heads were moving back and forth, muffled voices carrying. Brandon took a step, then another, the gun down. Two more steps, laying his feet down. Forty feet back now.

Music, Jay-Z, a cell phone.

"I told you to shut that fucking thing off."

"Thought I did," the guy in the back said, the rapper getting louder with each ring, *I will never tell, even if it means sittin' in a cell . . . I ain't never ran, never will.*

"Fuckin' A, Mario," the guy said.

Mario? Mario, the guy in the car with Lance the day after Lincoln Anthony had gone missing. Mario, the guy who had bought the diapers?

And then Jay-Z was gone, the phone glow illuminating the side of a face. A white guy. Chantelle's brother, Jason.

"Let's just get outta here," the driver said, and the motor revved, lights glared on, the car kicking gravel as it spun around, swung around as Brandon stepped out into the lot. He held up his police ID.

"Police," he shouted.

Mario braked, the car slid to a stop. He floored it and the car leapt forward, Brandon leaping aside like a bullfighter. The car brushed him on the way by, the guys hunched inside. The Honda spun around, motor revving, started back. Brandon trotted backwards, the car staying with him. He pulled his gun, pointed it at the windshield.

The car slid to a halt.

Mario was trying to get the car into reverse when Brandon put the gun through the window, shoved him over onto Lance, in the passenger seat, reached in and shut the car off. Brandon yanked the door open, shouted, "Hands on the dash, hands on the dash!"

In the back seat, Jason was moving and Brandon shouted, "Show your hands!" Mario had his hands by his side. Brandon reached in, dragged him out. Mario staggered, said, "What the fuck?" He started to slip one hand into the waistband of his shorts.

"Hands up, hands up!," Brandon shouted. "Get 'em out now."

Mario took his hand from his shorts, said, "Guy can't scratch his balls?" But the hands were still at his sides and Brandon took three steps, pushed him back into the side of the car, spun him, and jerked his arm up, pushed his face down onto the car roof.

"Fuckin' A, dude. Calm the fuck down."

Brandon had the gun trained on Jason in the back, Lance still in the front seat. "Hands on the dash, Lance," Brandon shouted. "Hands on the dash." Lance slapped them down, and Brandon told Jason, "Hands where I can see 'em. Get out, on the ground, face down. Hands behind your neck."

Jason heaved himself out of the car, started to stand, and Brandon moved over, put a foot to his ankle, yanked him to the ground, jammed his arm up to his neck. "I said on the ground."

"Killed my sister—gonna kill me, too, Blake?"

"Shut up," Brandon said, and he trained the gun on Lance, said, "Now you—out of the car!" Lance swung out, his feet on the ground, faced bruised, Brandon running to the front of the car, motioning him over with the others, saying, "On the fucking ground." Lance dropped to his knees in his basketball shorts, knelt there until Brandon put him down.

Then he leapt to Mario, still against the car, searched him, too, the gun in one hand. Mario had a clasp knife in his left Air Jordan, and Brandon pulled it out and slid it into the back pocket of his jeans. Lance lifted himself to his elbows and Brandon said, "On your face," and pushed him flat, patting him down, one side, then the other.

He reached for his radio, nothing there, the portable left on the seat of the Saab. He said, "Stay right there—don't be stupid," and sprinted to the car, yanked the door open, grabbed the radio, and trotted back.

"I ain't done nothin'," Mario was saying, lifting up again. Brandon had the radio to his mouth, lowered it as he slammed Mario back down, said, "Shut the hell up," and called in.

"Blake, he's fucking nuts," Lance was saying as they cuffed him, marched him to a South Portland cruiser. "He's gonna fucking kill somebody else, I'm telling you."

More cops, some of the same faces. They searched the car and found a nugget of crack stuffed into the back seat, four papers of heroin in the passenger-side vent. Trunk smelled like gasoline but Mario said it was because the gas tank leaked if you filled it more than halfway, and sometimes he forgot. All three were asked where they were earlier that night, and all three gave the same answer: "Just chillin'."

"Where?"

"Here and there."

The three of them saying they wanted their lawyers, Mario saying his neck was hurt, his left arm was numb, Jason pointing to a gash on his cheekbone, a rock under his face when Brandon had put him down on the gravel. "Your officer pistol-whipped me," he said. "I am gonna sue his ass—yours, too. And I want medical attention."

They had Lance in the back of the cruiser, South Portland and Portland both questioning him, first one, then the other. Perry did the initial round, the sergeant in this one because it was a cop who was targeted, his cop. They pulled Lance out, leaned him against the side of the car. Perry leaned beside him.

"You in South Portland all night?"

"Nah. Just came over a little while ago. To see if Blake was around."

"What for?"

"To talk things out."

"What things?"

"Chantelle dying."

"Why Officer Blake?"

"He made her feel like shit, so then she goes off the bridge."

"Her baby was missing. Was she supposed to feel good?"

" 'Course she was gonna feel bad about Lincoln, but he made her blame herself. He wasn't supportive."

"Supportive?"

"Right. I mean, Chantelle—she didn't kidnap her own baby."

"Who do you think did?"

"I have no fucking idea. Wasn't my kid."

"You think he's dead? The baby, I mean."

"I don't know."

"Then it's present tense. *Isn't* your kid."

"What?"

"Never mind. Were you going to kill Officer Blake? Beat him up?"

"No, just gonna talk to him."

"Don't bullshit me, Lance."

"I'm not."

"What's your probation hold for?"

"Two years."

"There was crack in the car."

"Wasn't mine. Wasn't my car."

"I gotta assign it to somebody."

"Yeah, well—"

"So you were going to assault Officer Blake?"

"No. No way."

"What were you going to do."

"Talk to him, like I said."

"In his boat."

"I guess."

"Which you tried to burn up, with him in it."

"No friggin' way."

"You said you were getting even. Buddy there, Jason, saying what goes around, comes around. Your girlfriend's dead, but you were just going to talk to Officer Blake? What's even about that?"

"I don't know."

"You bring a gun along tonight, Lance?"

"Nope, don't own one."

"None of you did?"

"No way, Sergeant. You know we can't have guns." Lance smiled. "We're all convicted felons."

Brandon saw Lance's smile from Kat's cruiser as he sat in the driver's seat, typing his report onto the computer.

I recognized the subjects in the vehicle as Jason Anthony, Lance McCabe, and a third subject, the driver, a subject named Mario. Anthony and McCabe have been heard to have threatened me, are known to carry weapons, and therefore, their presence in the private parking lot of the marina was seen as threatening. I showed my police ID, identified myself as a police officer, and ordered the driver to stop the car. Upon being ordered to stop the car, driver Mario accelerated toward me in what I believed was an attempt to run me over. I evaded the car but he turned around and came back, driving straight at me. I drew my weapon and he stopped and I disabled the vehicle by taking the keys out. Anthony and McCabe were moving within the vehicle, in what could have been an attempt to secure weapons. I ordered all three subjects to exit the vehicle. Upon being ordered to show their hands, they did not do so, continuing with movements in the car that appeared threatening and caused me to continue to train my weapon. They then exited the vehicle and were ordered to the ground. Jason Anthony refused to comply with the order and was placed in that position. This resulted in a scrape to his cheekbone, apparently from a stone in the gravel of the parking lot. The same circumstances resulted in abrasions to the forehead of Lance McCabe.

A search of their persons resulted in seizure of two knives, which they had concealed. Subsequent search of the vehicle resulted in discovery and seizure of a quantity of crack cocaine and heroin, approximately five grams.

He stopped typing, reread it.

"Let me see that," Kat said, "make sure you have all the bases covered."

Brandon swiveled the laptop toward the driver's seat. Kat peered at the screen.

"The vehicle was coming at you in the lot and that's why you drew your weapon?"

"Right. They were trying to leave and I jumped out in front of them."

"With your badge out."

"Right."

"They're gonna say that in the dark, they didn't know you were a cop, thought you were just some robber."

"They know me. They were there to beat me up, or worse."

"Is there a light there?"

"Yeah."

"Let's say you were under the streetlight and clearly recognizable."

Kat typed, concentrating.

"Did you identify yourself as a police officer?"

"Yes."

"Good thing we found the crack. Some leverage," Kat said. She read the report again, swung the computer back.

"You know they're claiming excessive force," Kat said.

"Uh-huh."

"They also say they came over to talk," she said.

"Equally preposterous," Brandon said.

"I gotta say it again, Brandon—"

"Say what?"

"Never a dull moment around you."

"Actually, I'm pretty boring. Ask Mia."

"Not lately."

"No."

"This is getting to be problematic," Kat said.

Brandon didn't answer. Kat looked out her window.

"You're getting a rep as a cowboy."

"What was I supposed to do? Let 'em go?"

"Call it in. Let patrol take it, control the stop, not one on three in a dark parking lot. And you off duty, no radio on you—"

"Somebody just took a shot at me. I'm not gonna sit here like a big fat target. Let 'em go so they can try again."

"You think these guys are the shooters?" Kat said.

"I don't know."

"Why not bring a gun for the second try?"

"Maybe this was reconnaissance."

Kat shrugged. They sat for a minute, then another, not talking, the radio murmuring. People from the boats were standing in clusters at the edge of the yard, watching. Perry was talking to Lance, then to Jason. Jason kept pointing to the cut on his face. An ambulance rolled in, lights flashing.

"Where can you go?"

Brandon thought.

"I've got responsibilities here in the marina."

"Nobody here who can do it? No friends you can ask?"

Brandon felt his expression harden, his jaw clench. "I'll figure it out," he said.

"Don't want to lose you, Brandon," Kat said.

"If I get canned?"

"That, too," Kat said.

SIXTY-ONE

Kat called it. This time Perry flat out ordered Brandon to take a week off, find a place to hole up. "Don't want you on the field, don't want you in the clubhouse." Brandon said okay. Perry said to let Kat know his whereabouts. Brandon said he would. And then the last of the cruisers pulled out. Kat was the last cop to leave.

Brandon stood in the empty lot, the boat owners trickling back down the docks two by two. He walked to Mia's car, got in and smelled her smell—chai tea and organic shampoo and a hint of the perfume she'd worn for only two types of occasions: when they went to a fancy restaurant, and when they made love.

Brandon started the motor, checked his phone. There was one new text, not from Minnesota.

OMG. SAW THE NEWS. U OK? CALL ASAP. WRRIED ABT U. DOES MIA KNOW? U STAYING ON BOAT? WE'RE @RENDEZVU TIL LATE. STP BY. L & W.

Nice of Lily, Brandon thought. Maybe. He typed THANKS. I'M FINE. He paused, looked up and out at the darkened lot, moths circling the floodlight, bats swooping through the moths. Big fish after smaller fish. Everything preying on something else.

He looked back to the phone, texted SEE YOU SOON.

At Rendezvous, the wait staff, prep cooks, and dishwashers— everyone was around the bar, the last diner gone, the doors locked. At the afternoon meeting, Winston had said he wanted to do something special for his mother's birthday. She was buried in Barbados, had never seen her son and his restaurant in America.

"To my mama, America was somewhere just this side of Heaven," Winston said. "And she was right. I thank you all for your hard work and your friendship. So tonight, after close, we have a little party for my mama, let her know we're thinking of her up in Heaven, that we're right close by."

By midnight, the waiters were into the single malt, a bottle of Cragganmore open on the bar. The dishwashers were doing shots of Chinaco tequila, and the waitresses were opening bottles of Cristal. Winston, in tan linen slacks and a white silk shirt, towered over the party, his booming laugh echoing like cannon shots. Lily, in a short, pink, sleeveless slip dress, sipped champagne and looked on like a loyal first lady, admiring Winston and the admiration he engendered. They all talked, laughed, drank, and every little while Winston offered a toast, a snifter of special-occasion Cockspur rum in his big hand.

To his mama, who worked so hard for her children. To his papa, who worked so hard and loved his mama so much. To his brothers and sisters, scattered around the world. To his lovely Lily, "who was named just right for her, because she truly is a beautiful flower." Lily beamed.

And late in the night, the dishwashers just back from smoking a joint in the alley, two waitresses in the restroom snorting coke off the side of the washbasin, Winston held his glass up again. "Another toast," he said. "To our friend Brandon Blake, young officer of the Portland Police Department. Brandon had a very close call tonight. It was on the news. But the Lord was watching over him and saved him from harm. So here is to the good Lord, and to Officer Brandon Blake."

"To Brandon," Lily called.

Everyone cheered. The stoned dishwashers drank to the Portland cop. After a moment, Lily and Winston raised their glasses for a private toast. And smiled.

In the Saab, Brandon felt invisible. He drove up Commercial Street, the drizzle keeping the Old Port crowds down, guys still standing in bunches outside the pizza shop at the corner of Silver. Two groups were jawing at each other, one guy gesturing, "Come here and say that." Brandon reached for his radio, thinking to tell the team somebody might want to slide that way. He caught himself. Put the radio down beside the Glock.

It was eleven-forty on the Time and Temperature Building. Brandon swung up to Congress, letting couples cross, clumps of drunk college guys. He took a right on Congress, drove slowly away from the downtown, a group of homeless people settled down in the park by the courthouse. Driving up Munjoy Hill, he saw some young Somali guys leaning into a black SUV, one guy on the sidewalk watching out. Outside a tavern two women were kissing.

He passed the firehouse, driving slowly, letting people cross. A guy on a bike slipped up beside the car on the right and Brandon reached for his gun. The guy—hard, gaunt face, looked familiar—glanced at him and their eyes locked, the guy looking like he was trying to place Brandon, too.

Brandon continued on, took a right down Morning Street, drove the two blocks to Mia's, recycling bins out on the sidewalks on a Tuesday night. Her windows on the third floor glowed yellow from the nightlights she kept on in every room—ever since Joel Fuller. There was a light on in the apartment on the first floor, the second floor empty and dark. Brandon drove by slowly, watching the mirrors. Headlights showed a block back and he watched them, then took a left toward the Prom. The car followed and he took a right, drove a half-block down, and swung onto the darkened access road to the park, the shore.

There were cars parked here—people looking for drugs, sex?—and he slowed, watched the mirror. Headlights appeared. The same car? He continued down to the parking lot by the boat ramp, pulled between two trucks, and killed the lights. The car—a white Lexus SUV, New York tags—passed him and continued to the end of the lot, backed into a space, and parked.

Brandon waited, then took the gun, got out of the car, and walked down the ramp road, then back. He walked in the shadows, approaching the Lexus from behind, thinking Brooklyn and Garden Posse. He heard a woman giggle, then the sound of kissing, whispering.

The woman sighed. Brandon turned and walked slowly back to the car.

An eye on the mirror out of the park, down the Prom. A right back onto Morning Street, another look at Mia's, the yellow glow, the driveway empty. He parked down the block. Picked up his phone and called. A woman answered, a strong accent. Russian?

"This is Brandon Blake, Nessa's grandson. I'm just checking on her."

"Oh, yeah, Mr. Brandon. The police, he came by. I tell him, 'Everything quiet here. All the old people, they sleeping like little babies.'"

Brandon thanked her and rang off. Sat and looked out at the dark street, the wind ruffling the shade trees. He could go up, lock himself in, sit there with a beer and the Glock. He stayed in the car, checked the time, and texted Mia again. THINKING OF YOU. MAYBE TALK TOMORROW? He waited. No reply. He put the phone down. The police radio chirped, a traffic stop on Washington Avenue, the drug guys calling for the dog. The K-9 guy called back, the dog barking in the background.

The phone buzzed.

YEAH, TOMORROW.

Brandon nearly smiled.

He pulled away, took a left, a right, snaking his way through the Hill, the streets quiet. He continued down Congress, a few people walking toward him, making their way home from the bars. A girl walking alone, carrying her shoes, weaving down the sidewalk. Brandon slowed, thought of following to make sure she made it home safe. Then he saw another girl trotting after the barefoot one, saying, "Hey, wait up."

He drove on, the downtown quiet in the rain. A stocky black woman with a satchel, plodding along in green hospital scrubs. A kid wheeling a bike past the art school, the locked back wheel lifted off the ground. Brandon reached for his radio, put it back down.

Skaters in the park at Congress Square, boards clattering. Brandon smelled weed, saw a kid lift a forty-sized paper bag to his mouth. A Mercedes stopped at the red light in front of him, Brandon seeing two heads, a couple arguing. The guy driving shouted something, then ran the light. Brandon waited for the green, continued on past the welfare hotels, the old guys standing out front like they were waiting for the bus, anything but going up to the room. He took a right by the American Legion, swung down to Deering Street, and cut across.

A right, a left, and he was there. Drawn to the place like a stray dog making its way home.

The building was quiet. Third floor dark. The Youngs' place, too. Lights on at Cawley's and the Ottos', the living room but not the bedrooms. The Ottos sitting up, worrying, Samir and Edgard on the run, Fatima dead. How many times can your world come apart before it doesn't go back together again?

Brandon rolled slowly past, buzzed the window down. He looked up, his gaze falling just in time to lock eyes with a guy standing at the side of the building. Young, black. He spun around, a cell phone in his hand, sprinted down the alley into the darkness.

Somebody sitting on the building, a True Sudanese Warrior? Brandon hit the gas, took a right at the corner, another right at Park. Pulled in and killed the lights and sat. Waited. People were coming down the block, a couple with bags, a couple pushing carts. Street pretty active for midnight They paused over the recycling bins, heads bobbing up and down like sandpipers on a beach. Cans clanked. A bottle fell to the bricks and smashed. A guy came out a driveway, talking on his phone.

The kid from the house.

Brandon got out, slipped the gun in his waistband, pulled his shirt over it. Started down the sidewalk. Saw a woman come around the corner at State, her cart rattling.

Big Liz.

Brandon stopped, stepped to the side in front of a big brick tenement. Big Liz approached, the wheels on the shopping cart squeaking, the cans and bottles rattling. She was muttering to herself, ". . . not going there . . . not me . . . no way, motherfucker."

Brandon stepped out. "Big Liz," he said. "How you doing?"

The old woman shrieked and pulled back, cans spilling to the sidewalk. "I'm not goin' there, Blake. You can't make me. You can't make me."

She was backing up, the cart in front of her. Brandon started after her, saying, "It's okay, Liz. It's okay." He grabbed the front of the cart and Liz stumbled, pulled herself back.

"I don't know nothin', Blake," she said.

"Didn't say you did, Big Liz," Brandon said.

"Not goin' there, not anymore. You want to go, you go by yourself."

"Go where?"

She pushed the cart toward him, tried to wrestle it around. "It isn't my fault he's burnin', Blake," Big Liz said. "The cellar people, they're mean bastards."

Brandon held the cart. "Who's burning? Who is it, Big Liz?"

"The baby. He's burnin', but I can't do nothin'. I ain't goin' back there. Sorry. I shouldn'ta looked. Shouldn'ta listened. They know you know, they drag you down, Blake."

"You aren't going back where, Big Liz?"

"What?" she said.

"Where? Where are you not going back to?"

Big Liz yanked the cart back, moved it to the right to pass. "To the hell hole," she said. "To the hell hole where the baby's burnin'."

"I'll go, Big Liz," Brandon said. "Where is it?"

"You know, Blake," Big Liz said. "You don't need me to tell you."

"What do I know?"

"They sucked the baby down. They can do that, with their big suckin' hell machines."

"They sucked it right out of the apartment?" Brandon said.

"And under the ground, Blake."

"Where is it now?"

"Burnin', Blake."

"Burning where, Big Liz? Can you show me?"

Big Liz yanked the cart away, her eyes narrowed. "It's bottle night. You know I don't have time for this talkin' shit."

Brandon fell away. Turned back up toward the car, the kid from 317, now long gone. He looked at his phone. It was 12:15. Ten-fifteen in Minneapolis. He walked back to the car, slung himself into the seat. Started a text and then stopped. Called. The phone rang. Again. Again. He was about to put it aside when there was a rattle, a bump. Mia's voice. Scratchy. A bad connection.

"Hey."

"Hi," Brandon said. "How are you?"

"I'm okay."

He read her tone. No anger, maybe some sadness.

"You sure?"

"Yeah. I'm doing fine."

"I'm sorry," Brandon said.

"It's okay. Me, too."

"You don't have anything to be sorry about."

"Sure, I do," Mia said. "I've been thinking. I think I've been trying to make you into something you're not."

"Well, maybe the something I am wasn't so good. I don't blame you."

"But I do love you, Brandon," Mia said. "I just had to figure that out, I guess. That I do want to be with you."

She'd started to cry.

"But not now. They haven't caught the guy—and I think maybe it could be somebody from New York, those posse guys down there, after you saw the guys they sent up."

"What, Brandon?" Mia said. "I couldn't hear all of that."

"It's still not good here."

"I want to come back," Mia said.

"When?'

"Soon."

"I don't know," Brandon said, the words eaten up by the static.

"We'll figure things out," Mia said. "We'll find a way."

"How?"

"We just will," Mia said, the phone crackling. "We just have to."

"I love you, you know,' Brandon said.

"I do—." More static. "—you. That'll be enough, right?"

"What?"

The call broke off. Mia was gone. Brandon sat for a moment, then put the phone down and looked out at the dark street, the darker park, and picked up his gun.

TWENTY-SEVEN

Chooch got up from her chair because she felt like her butt was going to sleep. That and phlebitis. She'd read that people who sit for more than two hours straight have a 40 percent higher chance of developing phlebitis—blood clots. The blood clots can move to the brain and cause all sorts of trouble. Like death. She'd told Johnny, the other dispatcher who worked ten to six, but Johnny said he didn't believe all that crap on television, said they just wanted to sell you drugs.

But Chooch got up anyway, walked out of the darkened dispatch room, down the hall. Did some knee bends. Looked at the bulletin board. Guns for sale. Lieutenant's kid wanting to mow your lawn. One of the secretaries starting a cycling club. A clerk from City Hall advertising "a business opportunity" that everyone knew was Amway.

Nothing new.

Chooch had a liter of Diet Coke in the fridge, way cheaper than the Big Gulp from 7-Eleven. She got the soda, some ice from the freezer, refilled her big plastic jug with the straw sticking out.

She headed back, hoping for a quiet rest of the night. So far, it had been one thing after another. A schizophrenic guy who said there was a burglar in his apartment with a gun, only they didn't know he was ill until they got there, six units, Christiansen and his dog, SWAT getting ready. All that firepower and they find the guy sitting in bed with his fingers in his ears, telling the cops to stop making so much noise.

Trouble with people coming and going in the city so much, you didn't know who was who, who was wacked out and who was just a criminal. But that was the population out there, the reality you had to deal with.

"There but for the grace of God," Chooch said, arranging her soda, her pad, a plastic bag of green grapes. Antioxidants. Johnny got up to go to the restroom, and Chooch was about to sit when she heard the fax machine start to spew.

Lately it had been like spam: ads for uniform supply companies, law enforcement conferences, the pages filling the tray, spilling onto the floor.

"What a waste of trees," Chooch said, and walked over, took the sheaf of paper from the machine.

It was from a cruise line—so they had this number now? What? Send a boatload of cops down to Montego Bay, blow all that OT money, come back broke and hungover?

Chooch crumpled the papers, started to fling them into the trash can. Glanced down. Saw the name, INVESTIGATOR BRANDON BLAKE, PORTLAND POLICE DEPARTMENT. Investigator? These guys needed a better list. Chooch looked more closely.

It was from a public relations assistant named Alicia, Mermaid Cruise Lines, West Palm Beach, Florida.

> *Dear Investigator Blake:*
> *Here is the information you requested regarding the passen-*
> *ger and crew list for the* Ocean Princess . . .

Investigator Blake? The information he requested? "Freakin' Blake," Chooch said. "How does such a quiet guy manage to stir up so much shit?"

She took the papers down to the mailroom, started to stick them in Blake's mailbox. Stopped. Looked down at them. Lists of names. Passengers on a ship. Crew, too. Passengers from all over the country, crew from all over the world. Lots of Filipinos. One of those places people went off to work, sent money home. Good for them, busting their butts, Chooch thought, walking back down the corridor with the papers still in her hand. She thought of her father, came to America from Mexico, hardest working, most generous guy she'd ever known, put his kids through college, half his family at home, too. People they dealt with now, half of them never worked a day in their life. Reason they got in so much trouble—too much time on their hands. Devil's workshop and all that. Drugs, drinking, fighting.

She was back at her desk, the phone going before she sat down, Johnny on another call. Chooch put the papers down, made a mental note to call Blake in the morning before she left. Who knew when he'd be in. She reached for the headphones, heard Johnny beat her to it: "Portland Police Department, may I help you?"

Chooch sipped her Diet Coke. Picked up Blake's stuff again. The passenger list was on top, alphabetical. *Ocean Princess*. People from Florida, New Jersey, North Carolina. She ran a pencil down the column, saw a few Mainers. Why would you go on a cruise to Maine if you were from Maine? Chooch said to herself. Johnny was still on the call, some lady who wanted her drunken son removed from the house.

The ships went to Canada, too, but still. If she went on a cruise, she was going to the Caribbean. Or Greece. She'd seen pictures of the Greek Isles.

"What ocean is in Greece, Johnny?" Chooch said when he was off the call.

"I don't know. The Mediterranean?" Johnny said.

"I was thinking the Aegean," Chooch said.

"Maybe there's two."

Another call; Johnny picked up. Chooch was picturing clear blue water, blue as mouthwash. White sand beaches, all the buildings painted white, too. Who goes on a cruise to St. John, freakin' New Brunswick?

She picked the Mainers out. Kennebunk. Brunswick. Retired people; probably their kids gave them a cruise for their anniversary. "Go for a boat ride, eat a lot of food, go to the shows. Good times," Chooch said aloud.

Hey. Here was one from Portland. What, get off the ship down on Commercial Street, walk up to the house? Now that made no sense. Well, fools and their money. From the Eastern Prom, too. Could see her house from the ship.

Lily Lawrence. Now, why was that name so familiar?

Chooch typed it in. Up it came. Lily G. Lawrence, twenty-eight. Hey, the shooter in that Eastern Prom home invasion. There was a connection to Blake. Something with his girlfriend?

"Oh, Brandon," Chooch said, picturing it now. The friend wants to find an address for the cute guy in the next cabin. Says to Brandon, You're a cop? Can't you find that out? To which Brandon is supposed to say, Sorry, no can do. Instead . . .

Chooch turned the papers over. "Gonna have to have a talk with that boy," she said. "If it isn't too late."

SIXTY-THREE

Twelve-forty, the rain stopped, the city still dripping. Brandon was on Park Street, sitting in the car. A woman walked by—short white skirt, heels, sodden top, red hair wet and straggly—and then stopped. Fiddled in her bag and walked back. She leaned down, tapped on the passenger window.

Brandon opened it, and she leaned her head in, breasts dangling, peering at him with hollow junkie eyes. Brandon thought of Chantelle as the woman said, "Hey. Wanna party?"

And then she saw the gun, stuck between the seat and the console. She said, "Whoa," and pulled back.

"Portland PD," Brandon said.

"Fuck," the woman said.

"I'm off duty," Brandon said.

"Oh," the woman said, leaning in again, flashing a smile, brown teeth. "So you wanna—"

"No—listen. Question for you. You know Chantelle Anthony?"

The woman looked at him warily. "The one with the baby?"

"Yeah."

"The jumper."

"Yeah, that one. You have kids?"

A long pause, and then the woman said, "If we're going to talk, can I get in? I'm freezing my ass off."

Brandon hesitated, then popped the lock. He took the gun, moved it to the other side of his seat. The woman opened the door, slung herself into the seat, her bag on her lap.

"How 'bout some heat?" she said.

He started the motor, turned the dial, cranked the fan. She sniffed. Flipped the visor down, snapped the mirror out. It was lighted. She tried to fluff her hair, dug mascara from her bag.

"You mind?" she said.

"No," Brandon said. "Knock yourself out."

She did the left eye, then the right. When she was done she turned and looked at Brandon. "You're pretty cute. You sure you don't wanna—"

"So, you have kids?" he asked again.

The woman fell back, resigned. "Yeah. Two."

"How old?"

"Eric is three and Marise is one."

"Where are they now?"

"With my mom."

"Because you're working?"

"Just because."

"You ever worry about somebody stealing your kids?"

She considered it. "Yeah. I mean, my mom, she's all right, but she drinks pretty hard. Puts the old coffee brandy away."

"Who do you think would do that? Steal your kids."

The woman pulled at her skirt, rubbed a hand over her bare thighs, lifting her leg where it stuck to the leather seat. Brandon saw bruises, faint splotches in the dark.

"You asking me?"

"Yeah."

She thought, staring straight ahead. "I guess I think it would have to be somebody who didn't have any," she said.

They sat, quiet for a moment.

"And no chance of having any," Brandon said.

"Right. I mean, some seventeen-year-old, she don't need my kids. She can crank out some of her own."

Another long pause, cars passing, tires hissing on the wet pavement. A cruiser crossed at State Street, bounced over the hump.

"They never found that kid, huh?" the woman said.

"No," Brandon said.

"But you're working on it?"

"Yeah."

A pause.

"You want coffee? Warm yourself up?" Brandon said. "I'll drop you."

"Sure," the woman said.

He dug in his jeans, pulled out a twenty-dollar bill, handed it to her. She took it and tucked it deep in her bag.

"Playing it a little close, aren't you?" the woman said. "An off-duty cop, in a car with a"—she made the quotation-mark gesture with her fingers—"known prostitute? Handing her cash?"

"Way I roll," Brandon said, and he started the car and pulled away.

Brandon dropped her at the Dunkin' Donuts on Forest Avenue, gave her another $20 for a taxi before she got out. The guys sitting at the window counter eyed her, then Brandon, then the red Saab pulling away.

He headed back downtown, deciding to give Big Liz another shot. If she showed him how the baby was burning a hundred feet under Longfellow Square, he'd know she was nuts and leave her alone. But what if she wasn't totally nuts? What if there was a kernel of truth in what she was saying? Hell and burning, screaming babies.

He was driving up Preble Street, soggy stragglers camped out on the sidewalk around the shelter. Brandon was thinking of what the woman had said. You steal a baby if you don't have one. Or do you steal a baby because you know someone who doesn't have one—and will pay?

Lance, or any of the other crackheads, seeing the kid as a crawling, breathing, winning lottery ticket. But could they pull it off—not taking Lincoln, but passing him on?

Brandon swung onto Congress, listening to the radio chatter—Dever with a DWI on Riverside, Perry back in South Portland, talking to their shift commander out by the shooting scene near the mall. And then Kat, back in service after a bathroom break. Brandon reached for the phone, felt it ring in his hand. Ready to say, *Great minds think—*

"Hey," he said.

"Brandon," a woman said. The sound of a car door closing. "It's Lily."

"Hey."

"You okay?"

"Fine."

"We need to talk. Where are you?" Lily said.

"Congress. Downtown."

"Working?"

"More wandering."

"Do you have a key to Mia's? We can talk there."

"About?"

"Different things. Mia. Important things."

"I'll come to you," Brandon said.

"No, I've been cooped up with people all night. Big party at the restaurant. I'll just walk over."

"You sure?" Brandon said, but Lily didn't answer.

SIXTY-FOUR

Brandon drove down Morning Street, slowed when he could see Mia's building, big and square and plain, the lamps glowing in her apartment windows like it was a lighthouse.

He pulled over. Parked. Killed the lights. Watched and waited. A tipsy couple walked by under the shade trees, the woman leaning on the guy for support. Was this whole city drunk?

Two guys in baggy shorts, sideways hats, came toward the Saab. Slowed. He tensed, held the gun low. They looked at Brandon, he looked back.

They kept walking.

Brandon laid the Glock down, started the car. He pulled out and drove slowly past the building, nobody showing. He circled the block, down to the Prom and back around. A woman was walking a small black dog, a baggie in her hand, the dog sniffing each slat on a fence.

And then Brandon was back.

He parked in the street. Shut off the motor and waited. After a minute, he got tired of waiting and got out, stood by the car in the shadows. He was fishing in his jeans pocket for the key when Lily appeared beside him.

"Hey," she said. She smiled, snuggled into him, then fell away. "You okay?"

"Yeah."

"We were so worried."

"Thanks, but I'm fine."

"Thank goodness," Lily said, and she gave him a quick hug. They turned and she tugged his arm as she led him to the door on the driveway side. Brandon opened the outside door and they moved into the landing, the staircase dark. She reached around his waist, felt the Glock sticking out of his jeans."

"Whoa. That kind of startled me."

"Never leave home without it," Brandon said.

"Really?" Lily said.

He patted along the wall, found the switch. The light glared. They started up, Lily first. She was wearing black jeans, a black blouse, her hard back showing, buttocks snapping from side to side. She walked like a runway model, Brandon thought, something provocative about it.

The hallway was dank, stuffy. On the second floor there were two mountain bikes, seats removed. The third floor: a ski rack, a snowboard, Mia's hiking boots covered with mud. Lily turned and Brandon stepped in, opened the inside door.

"You smell like cheap perfume," Lily said.

"A hooker on Park Street," Brandon said.

"Really?"

"I talked to her. About the baby."

"I was going to say—" Lily said, and she stepped inside, flicked on a lamp. The front room was lifeless, silent, like the people who lived there had died. The windows were shut and the air was tepid and dense, made Brandon want to take a deep breath.

Lily closed the door, started toward the back of the apartment. She took Brandon's arm, said, "Stay with me."

They started for the kitchen, Lily leading the way, then turned right toward the bedrooms. The guestroom door was open, and Lily started to tow Brandon in.

He stopped, she turned.

"Don't you know how much I've wanted you?" Lily said. "Can't you tell, Brandon?"

"Whoa, wait a second," Brandon said.

"Just kiss me once. Mia will come back, I'll go home with Winston. It will be our little secret. Don't you feel anything toward me, Brandon? I feel like you do. I know it. Women can sense these things. If we'd met in different circumstances—who knows?"

"Lily, I don't think this is a good idea at all."

"One kiss. Just one and we'll know how good an idea it is."

She stretched out her arms, moved toward him, and wrapped her arms around his neck, her hands clasped. "Who cares about a kiss? It's not like—"

Brandon's phone rang in his pocket, a persistent buzzing. Lily laughed, swinging him toward the doorway. "Is that a phone in your pocket or are you just glad to see me?"

He ducked, said to Lily, "Just a sec," got the phone out. Said, "Yeah."

"Blake. Chooch."

"Hi. What's happening?"

Lily was nuzzling him, her tongue flicking across his neck. Still trying to pull him into the bedroom, the big bed.

"You got some stuff over the fax. Didn't know when you'd be in. Mr. Investigator."

"Really."

"Calling to give you a word to the wise. Perry, he'd be fried. And you're in deep enough, my friend."

Lily kissed his neck, put her tongue in his ear.

"This a bad time, Blake?"

"No. It's fine."

Another nuzzle. He pushed her away.

"Stuff is from the cruise ship people. Lists of names."

"Right."

"Didn't know when you'd be in, with everything that's happening."

"Yeah, well—"

"But I was just looking at it. For shits and giggles, you know? See who goes on these things."

"Yeah, I was curious—"

"Even a few from Maine. You live in Maine, you go on a cruise to Canada? I mean, hello. The other way is south. It's warm down there."

"It does seem sort of—"

Lily pulled harder and Brandon took two stumbling steps over the threshold to the bedroom. Sensed something, smelled something.

"You know the lady from the home-invasion thing was on that one? Yeah. Lily Lawrence. Eastern Prom. The lady who shot the guy?"

Brandon lowered the phone, flung Lily backwards onto the bed. "What the hell—"

The door crashed behind him, an arm wrapped around his neck, Brandon's phone clattering to the floor. He clutched at the arm, Lily saying, very calmly, coming off the bed, "He's got a gun. Back of his waist."

The other arm, big and strong, wrapped around Brandon's chest, pinned his right. A grunt. "Mine's in front. Get it."

Winston.

Brandon kicked back, jammed his running shoe hard onto Winton's insteps, stomped again and again, the three of them circling, Lily trying to get between them, to get the Glock.

The arm squeezing Brandon's neck like a python, Brandon forcing his chin down, sinking his teeth into Winston's forearm, taste of salt and blood, Winston grunting, Lily saying, still calmly, "Hold him still."

"No," Brandon bellowed, and the arm came up from his neck, covered his mouth. He felt Lily's hand sliding in between them, two guns there, and he threw an elbow, caught her in the neck, slammed her backwards.

Lily was up, gasping, clutching at her throat, then back to the floor, coming up with a white trashbag, a red tie showing. She opened it, started at Brandon like she was catching butterflies, the bag aimed for his head. She was muttering through clenched teeth, "You bastard—try to hit me."

Brandon and Winston spun aside, slamming the door, crashing onto the bed. Winston was underneath, legs over the edge, and Brandon punched him twice in the groin, felt the arm go slack, twisted loose.

He reached for his gun, but it was gone. Saw the phone on the floor, ducked for it as Lily lurched with the bag. Said, "Chooch, Chooch," but the call had broken off.

And then the bag was over his face, his head, Winston pulling at him, the plastic sucking into his mouth. Brandon panicked, thrashed, felt Lily's knuckles pressing into his neck as she held the bag tight. He turned and they came with him, the three of them crashing to the floor, Brandon shaking his head, tearing at the bag with his teeth.

He felt the phone underneath him, pressed it to the bag. Shouted, "Lily and Winston. Trying to kill me. Lily Lawrence."

They were on his back, crushing him down, clawing for the phone. He lost it underneath him, clawed at the bag, someone yanking the ties tight. Tried to inhale, got a mouth full of plastic. Tried again, still nothing, no breath.

He was suffocating. He felt the phone underneath his belly, got it up to his face, screamed through the bag, "Morning Street. Twenty-seven. The top." Once. Then again.

And then, "Officer needs assistance."

And then they were grabbing for the phone again, so they let go of the bag and his arms, and he tore at the plastic, ripped a hole with his fingers, gasped as the cool air rushed in.

He jammed his elbows back, caught Lily in the chest, kicked at Winston, rolled away, dove into the space between bed and wall.

A shot. He crawled, yanked the bag down to his neck, another shot. Felt under the bed, saw the Glock. He squirmed, lunged for it, it slid away. Another shot, ears ringing, the smell, but he was still moving, reaching for the gun, feeling the barrel with his fingertip, scratching it closer. Closer.

On his back, he fired through the mattress, then at the moving feet. Heard Winston gasp. Another shot through the mattress at him, hammering the floor.

Heard a siren.

"They're coming," Brandon yelled.

"We've got to get out of here," Winston said.

"Shoot him," Lily said. "Just shoot him."

"I'm out," Winston said, and Brandon heard the door rattle open, his footsteps in the hall. And then hers.

And then the siren, a MEDCU unit, loud, louder, then fading into the distance.

SIXTY-FIVE

Brandon was on his feet, found the phone, and called. He heard Chooch put the call out as he ran down the hall, clattered down the stairs and out.

He ran to the corner, looked down the street toward the Prom. Nothing. Ran back, gun low. Looked the other way, nothing, just darkness and shadow. Then movement in a car, an SUV at the curb. In a crouch, Brandon ran toward it, put the gun at the window. A white guy with a beard turned, eyes bugging out.

Brandon ran on. It was quiet, and then there was a noise in the distance, building like a storm.

Sirens, the whoosh of V8s, tires squealing. And then there were cruisers, Perry in his SUV, cars pulling up, pulling away, searching for a tall black man, slender white woman with short dark hair, in a silver Mercedes SUV or a dark green Land Rover.

Perry told Brandon to stay put. Brandon wiped the blood on his shorts, said, "I'm fine. I can help."

"Full felony stop," Perry was saying. He looked at Brandon, who said, "At least one handgun. I think they killed somebody, so nothing to lose."

Kat figured they'd go north on the interstate, get out of Portland, then get off and head west. Cumberland. Windham, Naples. Get off in the boonies and hide.

"They've got no chance," Kat said.

"That's what makes them so dangerous," Brandon said. "Everything coming apart. May want to take a few cops with them."

They had just crossed onto Washington Avenue, headed west. State and county units were converging, an off-duty Marine Patrol cop asking for somebody to read her the plate numbers again.

Chooch did, then called Kat, asked for a return on the cell. Kat called and Chooch said, "Blake with you?"

"Yes."

"We got Big Liz going bonkers, Granite Street, waking everybody up. Screaming that she has to talk to Blake. I mean, I know everybody's tied up. Just ship her?"

Kat looked at Brandon.

"Big Liz is flipping out. Wants to talk to you."

"Where?"

"Granite."

Brandon thought for a moment, said, "You can drop me."

The headlights picked up Big Liz sitting on the street in front of 317, her cart overturned, cans and bottles and books and papers spilled onto the pavement. There was a Honda racer pulled up crookedly, doors open, music thumping.

"Crazy fucking bitch," the kid with the car—hat on sideways, shorts down low—said to Brandon. "Ran right out in front of me. Coulda run her ass down, crazy old skank."

Brandon showed his badge, said, "Watch your mouth. Shut off the music. Move the car."

"Hey, I was just—"

"Now," Brandon barked.

The kid moved, the music stopped, the car started, motor revving. Brandon and Kat moved to Big Liz, splayed in the gutter. One of her high-tops was off, her foot blue-red with sores and veins, scrapes on top.

"You okay?" Brandon said.

"Why me, Blake? Why they makin' me do it?'

"Do what, Lizzie?" Kat said.

"Making me listen. I say, 'Burn me, you bastards. Leave him alone.'"

"Who?" Brandon said. "The baby? Are they burning the baby?"

"Feet to the fire, Blake. Oh, the poor little thing. The poor thing."

She started to cry, then to cough, a harsh hack.

"Where?" Brandon said.

Big Liz looked at him, her nose running, cheeks shiny with tears.

"Can't you hear it, Blake? Can't you hear it?"

Kat turned to Brandon and said, "Let's ship her. They'll sedate her."

Brandon put a hand up, one finger. "Wait."

"Can you hear it now, Liz?" he said.

She closed her eyes. The bystanders had moved closer and a kid said, "She's nuts."

Kat turned, shooed them back. "Nothing here for you. Show's over."

Brandon crouched by Big Liz, close to the smell of her. Her eyes were closed, her mouth hung open. Suddenly her eyes snapped open.

"There," she said.

"What?"

"Can't you hear him, Blake? Can't you hear him crying?"

Brandon listened. Nothing. Lizzie twisted herself onto her hands and knees and began to crawl, out of the gutter, onto the sidewalk.

"Where you going?" Brandon said.

Across the sidewalk, the patch of lawn in front of 317, right up to the building. Brandon and Kat followed, like Christiansen the handler following his dog.

"Hear it?" Lizzie said. "You gotta hear it now. Oh, my dear sweet Jesus."

They squatted beside her, were still.

"My God," Brandon said.

Big Liz said, "See? They're here. They're all around us."

"What?" Kat said, then, "I hear it."

Brandon raised himself up, stayed in a crouch. He looked over to see Mr. Otto standing at the corner of the house, saying, "You okay?"

Then up to see Mrs. Young in her window. The curtain fell shut. "He's here," Brandon said.

Kat moved beside him, froze. Listened. Brandon crouched by the foundation. Listened again. Kat followed. "I can hear it," she said.

It was a baby. A frantic, gasping cry.

"Oh, my God," Kat said.

"I told you," Big Liz whispered. "They're burnin' him slow."

Brandon stopped in front of a cellar window, boarded over, the plywood painted black. He pulled at it, then stood. Kicked it once, twice. The wood splintered and he and Kat bent, pried the pieces loose. It was louder now—a baby crying. There was pink insulation behind the plywood and they pulled it out by the fistful until they came to an inner board. Brandon squatted and kicked again—once, twice, three times—and the inner board flew off.

He spun around, stuck his head down and in. Annie Young was looking up at him. She was holding a baby, jiggling it in her arms. The baby looked up at Brandon, too.

Lincoln Anthony stopped crying.

SIXTY-SIX

Annie Young told O'Farrell that she was just doing her moral duty—they ought to be thanking her, saving the baby from that place, from that horrible excuse for a mother.

This was in the interview room on the second floor, a digital recorder ticking off the seconds, Annie waiving her right to remain silent, instead talking for seventy-four straight minutes about Chantelle Anthony, her family, her druggie friends. About the State, how they wouldn't do anything to help the child, who Annie Young found that night, "wallowing in his own excrement."

The room was there in the basement. It was Mr. Young's old ham-radio studio, soundproofed so Mrs. Young didn't have to listen to his "infernal chatter about nothing with a bunch of nobodies." Annie Young brought Lincoln down that night and, in the days that followed, picked up baby stuff, little by little.

When O'Farrell said this was kidnapping, a Class-A felony, Annie bristled.

"What would you have done, Detective?" she said. "I mean, put yourself in my place."

"I think I would have called the police, and the police would have called Child Protective," O'Farrell said.

"And they would have handed that poor child right back," Annie Young said.

"We wouldn't have had a young woman jumping off a bridge," O'Farrell said.

"She was killing herself slowly anyway," Annie Young said. "One life sacrificed to save another."

While Annie Young was telling her story, Brandon and Perry were in another interview room down the corridor. Another recorder was running. Brandon started with Mia, her friend Lily, her partner Winston.

The woman in the restaurant from the *Ocean Princess,* the guy from New York in the home invasion, Lily armed and ready to shoot. Brandon explained that he had found out about the guy dying in St John.

"What are the chances?" he said. "A crewman dies in a crack-house, a guy breaks into their house and he turns out to be from a Jamaican posse that deals drugs. And some lady is sure that Winston was on that ship."

"So you called the cruise line, identified yourself as an investigator."

"Which I am," Brandon said.

"We'll talk about that later. Go on with the story," Perry said.

Brandon said he figured it this way: Lily had hooked up with Winston on the ship, except he wasn't Winston from Barbados. He was Alston Kelley from Jamaica, and he was delivering drugs to St. John. Except instead of making the drop, he—or they—ripped off the buyer, kept the money, and burned the other guy up.

"Who was Winston Clarke," Perry said.

"And Kelley takes his identity, too."

"But the Garden Posse didn't track him down?"

"I think they just did, by accident."

"And he's too dug in here to just pack up and go," Perry said.

"Probably began to believe his own story. Restaurant was making money. Nice life in Portland, Maine. Pretty girlfriend."

"Who's loaded."

"I think that had dried up. Why she needed this, to keep up appearances."

"Either kill and rob or get a job," Perry said.

"It's a no-brainer," Brandon said.

Perry had to smile.

"And then you started asking questions."

"About the cruise ship," Brandon said. "Lily panicked, thinking things were unraveling."

"But stopping you was the last chance to tie things back up."

"I'm glad they weren't better at that."

"Peter Principle," Perry said. "We rise to the level of mediocrity."

"A drug runner and a trust-funder," Brandon said. "I guess in Canada they just got lucky."

SIXTY-SEVEN

Mia's flight was early, the pilot saying something about strong westerly winds. She figured that was an omen, the winds blowing her back to the man she loved.

Sitting in her window seat, watching the sky turn from black to deep blue to a gorgeous salmon, she told herself they could work it out. She'd decided when she was talking to her parents, the two of them ganging up on Brandon, Mia knowing she had to come to his defense. Had to be with him.

She'd be more accommodating, go with the flow. One rule: When they did have time, they'd spend it together. Take the boat out and anchor in a secluded cove. Shut the world away.

And then she was asleep and the attendant was tapping her shoulder. She shook herself awake, got up, edged her way into the line of passengers, trotted across the tarmac, up the stairs, out into the lounge.

Mia looked for Lily, but she wasn't there, as she'd promised. Mia checked her phone. Lily hadn't sent a text. Hadn't called.

Waiting for her suitcase, she looked back toward the doors, the sidewalk. No Lily. The bag came around and she edged her way in, grabbed it, wheeled it to the door and outside, expectant.

Nobody.

She checked her phone, started to send Lily a text. And then the Saab came down the access road, her Saab. With Brandon at the wheel.

So the two of them had planned this, Mia thought. Probably Lily said, "I'm supposed to pick her up, but why don't you go. Surprise her. It'll be so romantic."

Brandon agreeing, maybe picking up some flowers.

The car rolled up and she ran to it. Brandon was smiling, happy, but something wasn't right. It was his sad smile, Mia thought, and they hugged on the sidewalk, but then she pushed his face back and said, "What?"

"We have to talk," Brandon said.

"Are we okay?" Mia said. "Please don't tell me we're not okay."

"No," Brandon said. "We're good. The two of us, we're going to do just fine. We have to."

SIXTY-EIGHT

It was Thursday, twenty-six hours later, a little before 4 a.m. In a little town called North Fryeburg, Maine, an Oxford County deputy named Beliveau was backed into the brush along a back road, just a hundred yards from the New Hampshire line. He had the plate number of the Mercedes on a sticky on his dash. When the silver SUV actually went by, Beliveau said, "Holy shit."

And then he floored it, not wanting to lose the biggest arrest of his four-month career.

He got up on the Mercedes bumper, lights and siren on, then swerved left and pulled alongside. Screamed "Pull over!" into the PA, and the Mercedes did, the cruiser cutting it off.

The driver bailed, but he wasn't running for the woods. He was coming toward the cruiser, big black guy, looked like a movie star, smiling, walking with a limp. Beliveau was out of the car, crouched behind the door, gun leveled.

"Stop right there. Put your hands up and turn around."

The guy was saying, "What's the problem, sir?" Still walking, he said, "Do you want my ID?" He reached behind him, Beliveau shouting, "Hands out, hands out."

"But I have my license right here," the guy said, still reaching—as a woman popped out of the Mercedes and screamed, "Officer, he's got a gun."

"Lily, what are you doing?" the guy screamed, turning back toward her, but when he whirled around, his gun was out and showing in the headlights, not pointed at the deputy, not yet, not ever. Beliveau fired, once, then again, the first time other than at the range. The guy stumbled backwards, dropped the gun, turned toward the woman, her head showing behind the car.

"Lily," he said as he fell.

Beliveau stepped out from behind he door. And he almost shot Lily, too, as she came running at him, crying, saying over and over, "He was holding me hostage. He was holding me hostage."

Those were the stories that played out in the *Portland Tribune*.

Portland Woman: Lover Threatened Her With Death

> *Lily Lawrence says restaurateur had secret past; if she revealed truth, she'd be killed*
> By Matt Estusa
> Staff Writer

> *The girlfriend of a prominent Portland restaurant owner says the Jamaican man forced her to witness the killing of a Canadian man two years ago, then said he or members of his drug "posse" would kill her if she ever told authorities.*
> *Lily Lawrence is facing multiple charges, including murder and the attempted murder of a Portland police officer. Lawrence said she was repeatedly threatened with death if she tried to leave or turn in her boyfriend, known as Winston Clarke.*
> *Clarke, who police say was really Alston Kelley, was shot and killed by an Oxford County deputy on July 18. "Eventually, I just gave up," Lawrence said, in an interview at the Cumberland County Jail. "I was exhausted from living in fear."*
> *Said Lawrence's attorney, Bradley Hornsby, of Portland, "It's an absolutely classic case of the Stockholm syndrome. She not only was forced to keep his secret, but she was also brainwashed into thinking this man actually loved her."*
> *Lawrence is charged with the attempted murder of Portland police officer Brandon Blake, a rookie cop who reportedly became*

suspicious of Clarke and began to investigate. In an exclusive interview, Lawrence said it was Clarke/Kelley who tried to kill Blake three times—by setting fire to his boat in a South Portland marina; shooting at his car in South Portland; and assailing him in his girlfriend's Munjoy Hill apartment.

"I couldn't stop him," Lawrence said. "He terrified me. It was like I was paralyzed."

Blake has been at the center of several police firestorms in the city, since he was hired a year after shooting a man dead in a city hotel.

Investigators concluded that Blake killed Joel Fuller, 29, of Portland, but the shooting was justified.

Art Student Pleads Guilty In Immigrant's Death

Paul Boekamp, 21, to receive 30-year sentence for drowning Sudanese teen who was carrying their unborn child
By Matt Estusa
Staff Writer

A Portland art student has pleaded guilty to the murder of a 17-year-old Sudanese immigrant, saying he was afraid of what would happen when her family learned of the relationship.

Boekamp, who lived two blocks from Fatima Otto on Granite Street in the city's Parkside neighborhood, said he drowned the young woman after she said she was pregnant, he was the father, and she was going to tell her father and brothers.

"I figured they would kill me if they found out," Boekamp wrote in a statement given to authorities.

He confessed to drowning Otto in a bathtub at his apartment, then throwing her body off the Portland bridge to make her death appear a suicide.

Otto would have been the second young woman from her tenement house on Granite Street to kill herself by jumping from the bridge. Chantelle Anthony, 23, leapt to her death from the bridge after her six-month-old son, Lincoln, went missing in July.

Police later found the boy had been taken by neighbors, who said they feared Anthony's lifestyle, which included the use of illegal drugs, was harming the child.

Portland Woman Charged In Baby's Abduction

Police say downstairs neighbor snatched Lincoln Anthony, hid him in cellar

The Portland woman charged with abducting a six-month-old baby from a neighbor in her Granite Street apartment house says she'd do the same thing again under the same circumstances. "To leave that little boy in that household—that would be a crime," Young said.

Anne J. Young, 41, is charged with kidnapping and unlawful restraint in the case. She has not yet entered a plea, but in an interview with the Tribune, *she said six-month-old Lincoln Anthony was living in deplorable conditions, and she felt she had no choice but to take him.*

Young is alleged to have kept the baby for five days in a secret basement room, before being discovered by police. In an interview at the Cumberland County Jail, where she is being held without bail, Young said she considered alerting authorities to conditions in the third-floor apartment, but felt nothing would be done.

"Drugs, drinking, smoking, neglect—you name it, that child was subjected to it," Young said. "I had no choice."

The child's mother, Chantelle Anthony, 23, leapt to her death from the Portland Bridge after the child disappeared. The woman's family charges that harsh treatment of the young mother by Portland police led to her suicide.

The child has been given to his father, Toby Koski, of Portland, a fisherman and U.S. Army veteran.

It was a Sunday, August 7, and all three stories had installments in that day's Sunday *Tribune,* including an odd follow-up to the Brandon Blake shooting. The gun was bought on craigslist. It was delivered to Winston Clarke by two men, including Lance McCabe, boyfriend of Chantelle Anthony. In a box left on a step.

Brandon didn't read it. He left the paper where it lay on the dock. Jumped off *Bay Witch*, unhooked the stern line, hopped back on. Mia throttled up, eased the boat out of the slip, past the floats and out into the harbor.

The newspaper was left behind.

They motored out of the harbor, Mia at the helm. The wind was out of the west, 10 knots. The sky was a deep, dense blue. The bay was blue-green, their wake a pale plume, like something on an exotic bird.

Bay Witch rose and fell with the slight swell, gulls rising up in front of her bow, lobster buoys swept aside. Brandon and Mia were quiet, watching the boats on the bay, the islands coming up. They passed between Great Diamond and Peaks islands, skirted the southwest tip of Long. Just south of Long Island was Vaill Island, with a sheltered cove facing the morning sun, a crescent of sandy beach.

Mia slowed as they came around the island's southeast tip. Brandon went forward and waited as she swung the boat back into the wind.

"Okay," Mia called, and Brandon released the anchor. The chain ran, then slowed as the anchor caught and the boat fell back.

Mia shut the motor off, went to the stern. Brandon was there and he pulled the dinghy in. Mia eased down the ladder and got in the stern. Brandon climbed in and rowed to the beach.

Mia carried her sandals as she waded ashore. Brandon beached the dinghy. Mia spread the blanket. They sat side by side. Brandon opened his book, about strategies used in naval battles of the War of 1812. Mia had a legal pad and she began to write.

She looked over.

"You and me, right?" she said.

"Oh, yeah," Brandon said. "Now and forever."

Mia smiled, went back to her pad, sketching out thoughts for a new story.

---

*When Margaret was twenty, she had a dozen close friends—
a big, boisterous, nosy clan that made every decision a group one,
every agreement consensus. There was one rule: Be honest. Viola-
tors were expelled.*

*By the time she was twenty-four she was left with just one
friend. The only other person on the planet she could fully trust, if
not totally understand. He was the last man standing.*